Ramses' Revenge

Text copyright 2021 Fiona Deal

All Rights Reserved

This is a work of fiction. Names, characters, places and incidents either are the product of the author's imagination or are used fictitiously.

Chapter 1

Early Autumn 2018

There's nothing quite like an Egyptian wedding for sheer joyful exuberance. As such, it reflected the groom's character down to the ground.

Ahmed, our police buddy – returned to the bosom of the Luxor tourism and antiquities police after a stint as our bodyguard – can, on occasion, be inclined to take himself the teensiest bit seriously. But there can be no doubting the vim and verve he brings to life. His wedding to Habiba – sultry and beautiful Ministry of Antiquities Inspector – was cause enough for elation. After all, they'd got off to a somewhat sticky start. He hadn't taken kindly to being assigned her 'babysitter' when she'd been posted from Cairo to Luxor a while back to investigate reports of looting in the area. Nor had he much appreciated her instinctive inclination to poke fun at him. But from such inauspicious beginnings, love had blossomed. I daresay stranger things have happened. So, here we were in the local mosque, celebrating the nuptials of Ahmed Abd el-Rassul, descended from one of Luxor's most notorious families of tomb-robbing ne'er-do-wells, and Habiba Garai, PhD graduate, one of the nation's new crop of fully emancipated young twenty-first-century women, and a Ministry of Antiquities Inspector to boot.

Quite how they would square his tomb-robbing antecedence and occasional strays from the straight and narrow with her strict ethics and modern-crusader-like tendencies would remain to be seen. That they loved each other was not in doubt. And maybe love could conquer all.

Watching them declare their commitment to making it work, I squeezed Adam's hand alongside me, suddenly dewy-eyed and nostalgic. I do so love a wedding. I'd attended quite a few in recent years. Three of them were my own.

All to the same man, I hasten to add.

The first time I married Adam we were trapped inside an undiscovered ancient Egyptian royal tomb. That it remains undiscovered to this day is a matter of immense personal satisfaction. But let me not stray into all the whys and wherefores of that particular tale.

To return to our first wedding: there was no celebrant, no exchange of rings, and no register to sign. In point of fact, it was just the two of us. We were trapped, bruised and bloodied, and fearing for our lives. Oh, and it was pitch dark. We were unable even to see each other as we spoke the vows that would bind us for life. The fact of that very life being perhaps about to ebb slowly out of us may have added piquancy to proceedings. Whatever, that ceremony will forever stand in my memory and in my heart as the first and finest of our unions.

The second time I married Adam was also inside an ancient Egyptian royal tomb. On this occasion not a real one. It had been Adam's idea to re-create the most beautifully carved chambers of the spectacular tomb of Seti I inside the British Museum for its most successful exhibition to date. As such, it seemed the most natural thing in the world for us to hold our 'official' nuptials there, and we were granted special permission to do so. If family and friends found anything macabre about witnessing our exchange of vows inside a burial chamber, they were kind enough to keep these thoughts to themselves.

Our third wedding was held the next day in a London register office for the sake of form, and to make it legal. While it may be possible to hold a marriage ceremony just about anywhere these days, it seems there are still certain niceties to observe if you want the whole thing considered binding.

So, there you have it: my trio of weddings with Adam. Three times lucky, I like to say. And I am certainly the most fortunate of women to have married my best friend, soulmate and fellow Egypt-freak.

We met here in Luxor. I'd been on a post-redundancy time-out holiday with my then boyfriend. Adam was living here following his divorce, seeking inspiration for his new life in the place he'd always loved, and picking up the threads of his long-ago abandoned Egyptological studies. So, we'd both been at a crossroads of sorts. Our shared love of this ancient magical and mystical land had drawn us together. Well, that and a rather tantalising mystery I'd stumbled across while visiting the Howard Carter Museum, once the famous excavator's home on the west bank of the Nile. It had led us on a treasure hunt of sorts, somehow resulting in a re-shuffling of relationships that had led us towards marital bliss, thankfully without breaking any hearts. Our married life since then had been a series of wonderful adventures, both in and out of Egypt. Along the way Adam had qualified as an Egyptologist and I had found favour with the head honchos at the Ministry of Antiquities and Egyptian Tourism Authorities respectively. (This was probably just as well since these two institutions were now merging to create the Ministry of Tourism and Antiquities. I couldn't help but think that maybe I had played some small part in helping the two establishments see that they were stronger together!). So, in meeting and marrying a man so well suited to me, at my side throughout numerous Egyptian escapades, I count myself well and truly blessed.

And now Ahmed and Habiba had joined the ranks of the happily wed.

Ceremony over, we left the mosque and arrived at a local hotel where the newlyweds were greeted by a parade of belly dancers and drummers. 'It's called a *Zaffa*,' Adam whispered in my ear. Although, in fairness, he could have shouted it at the top of his lungs and nobody would have heard him above the screechy discordant wail of the mini-trumpet-and-violin-type instruments being played with gusto by the small troupe of 'musicians' welcoming us to the party, decked out in brightly striped galabias with turbans wound around their heads and sandals on their stamping feet.

The heat and din, colour and tambourine bashing were about as far removed from organ music, vicars, a string quartet and confetti throwing of the clichéd English wedding as it was possible to get. To say I relished the whole experience would not be to overstate it. Yes! Even the gyrations of the belly dancers, which I noticed Adam was also eyeing, a broad grin on his face.

I laughed at his expression and gave myself up to enjoyment of this riotous, colourful, joyous din. Yes! Even the belly dancers! Although, I'd have to admit I've always found belly dancing quite hard to square in a culture that typically has women swathed from head to toe in voluminous black robes. But it's part of what makes Egypt exotic. Fascinating. Utterly captivating. I love how different it is to everything I'm more used to back home.

Take, for example, Habiba's pre-wedding party that I'd gone to a couple of evenings ago. Not a hen party, as we might know it, but a henna party: an Arabic tradition of hand painting with the bride's female friends. More fun than I'd dared imagine I could have with six Egyptian women, no alcohol, and a paintbrush! And in Ahmed's honour the celebrations today had started with a noisy car parade through Luxor's dusty streets, the cars extravagantly decked out with flowers and ribbons, accompanied by a deafening cacophony of honking horns and banging saucepans.

Now, when the belly dancing, drumming and tuneless screeching finished, we would feast on Egyptian delicacies in the hotel gardens enjoying the blanket-like warmth of evening. I took it all in with a sense of supreme contentment and wellbeing, watching the bride and groom all but consumed by their rapturous welcome party.

They made a good-looking couple, for sure. When I'd first met him, Ahmed's girth had competed with his height, which is not inconsiderable. Barrel-chested and barrel-stomached had both been apt. For, in all honesty, it had been hard to say where one ended and the other began. And good looks notwithstanding, he'd suffered the average Egyptian's woeful lack of dentistry. But, in the years since meeting Habiba, he'd slimmed-down and toned-up considerably. He'd also had his teeth fixed.

As I've always said: Ahmed is a good-looking man, if you happen to like them large. Now, with his new musculature, his pristine teeth, a seal-like cap of black hair and flashing dark-brown eyes in a deeply tanned face, he was eye-catching to say the least.

Habiba, to repeat the point, is gorgeous. With almond-shaped eyes, café latte-coloured skin, chiselled cheekbones, bronze-flecked eyes and full lips; she's an exotic, dusky, sultry beauty.

Watching them emerge from the chaos of belly dancers, drummers and musicians, bright-eyed and laughing, and in their wedding finery, I didn't dare imagine what their children might look like. Wondered if I ought perhaps to warn Hollywood.

The thought of Hollywood brought my current assignment spinning to the forefront of my mind, and, perfectly naturally, was the first question out of the groom's mouth as he and his new bride finally joined us on the grass under the spreading branches of a jacaranda tree.

'When do the movie people arrive?' Ahmed demanded excitedly, dark eyes snapping in eager anticipation.

'Not so fast!' Adam admonished with a smile. 'Before we get onto all of that... Congratulations to you both!'

But the bridegroom's impatience was obvious. He managed to contain it while our friends joined us. Shukura and Selim came first, wreathed in smiles and, in Shukura's case, eager to bestow kisses all round. Walid brought up the rear carrying a tray of glasses brimming with rose water juice. Called *sharpat*, this is the traditional drink for toasting the bride and groom at an Egyptian wedding. Ahmed shifted his weight from one foot to the other having extricated himself from Shukura's enthusiastic embrace, while we each took a glass and raised it to our lips murmuring appropriate sentiments about our hopes for their married life together. And he ran his big brown fingers along the stiff collar of his shirt as if trying to loosen it while Shukura and I oo'd and aah'd over Habiba's dress, a beautiful slim-fitting creation with long sleeves and a slashed neckline, decorated with the softest white feathers. But finally, the backslapping he was being subjected to and our wishes for their everlasting happiness became too much. He burst out,

'Please to tell to me Adam and Merry! When is it that the famous film stars are going to be arriving in Luxor?'

Now all eyes turned towards us. I felt a clutch of nervous tension in the pit of my stomach: part exhilarating thrill, part sheer terror.

Of course Hollywood had come calling.

Take Helen of Troy, Ramses the Great, Queen Nefertari, the Exodus story… oh, and huge quantities of buried treasure…gold, in fact… What right-minded movie mogul wouldn't beat a path to Egypt's door intent on bringing history to life via the medium of cinematography?

But the reality was, it wasn't just Egypt's, or even Luxor's door the Hollywood A'listers and an Oscar-winning director were beating a path to. It was ours. And that filled me with a strange sort of semi-elated panic.

'Next week,' I said weakly, wishing I could swap the *sharpat* for something very very alcoholic.

'Imagine!' Shukura said thrillingly. 'You'll be hosting the toast of Tinseltown aboard the *Queen Ahmes*!'

As if we needed telling! Adam, I think it's fair to say, was positively looking forward to it – as well he might, sharing his home with three of the world's most glamorous and beautiful female stars. Speaking for myself, I faced the prospect with decidedly mixed feelings, for quite possibly the same reasons.

But it was all settled. The Hollywood glitterati needed somewhere private to stay while filming in Luxor. Somewhere away from paparazzi and bug-eyed tourists. It seemed a luxury dahabeeyah, that is, a fully converted Victorian Nile sailboat, complete with all modern conveniences, fitted the bill perfectly. That it could be moored a little way upstream was also a distinct advantage. Oh, and the filmmakers also wanted to employ a resident Egyptologist as historical consultant to ensure every detail of the ancient tale they were bringing to the big screen was factually accurate.

Since it was the Ministry of Antiquities that granted permission for filming in and around Egypt's ancient monuments, and since the man in charge, Director Feisal Ismail, just happened to be rather well known to us – or, perhaps more to the point, *us to him* – it was perhaps unsurprising he had nominated Adam and me as both hotelier and consultant. Luckily the Hollywood contingent would be paying us handsomely. It was inducement enough, as if we needed it, for Adam to hand in his notice at the British Museum, where he'd returned after a recent sabbatical, and for us both to pack our bags and come back to Egypt after a short spell at home.

Personally, I would have preferred it if we could have returned to our anonymous little lives here, and to our original plan to operate intimate Nile cruises for discerning travellers aboard our beautifully restored dahabeeyah. But life over the last few years hadn't turned out quite the way we'd expected.

To say we'd found ourselves caught up in events beyond our wildest imaginings would be to put it mildly. Granite tablets recording the story of a fabled queen of ancient Egypt and a golden statuette linking the Trojan War to the 19th Dynasty reign of Ramses the Great were just the half of it.

Quite simply it was a moviemaker's dream.

So now, perfectly naturally, Hollywood was coming to town. Here to make a blockbuster out of revelations about how Ramses II *really* related to the Exodus story, and his hitherto unknown kinship not only to his great royal wife but also to none other than that siren of myth and legend, the face that launched a thousand ships, Helen of Troy.

'It's too thrilling for words!' Shukura rhapsodised, putting her empty glass on a nearby table and literally rubbing her hands together with glee.

It was as if she'd followed every one of my chaotic thoughts as they'd tumbled through my head. Her words snapped me back, observing her brimming excitement. Sunlight caught on the gold and precious stones of the chunky rings she wore on every one of her fingers as she rubbed her palms together. For talkativeness Shukura was unrivalled. But on this occasion the bridegroom cut her off before she could say more.

'Your wedding gift to me can be a private introduction to the film stars!' Ahmed declared. He drew himself up to his full height, puffing out his chest as if to emphasise his worthiness to meet world famous celebrities. I didn't like to remind him that Adam and I had already given him a rather lovely pair of table lamps for the apartment he and Habiba would shortly be sharing. Nor that wedding presents are intended for both parties to the marriage.

I caught the quick frowning glance Habiba sent him and knew her thoughts were running along similar lines. It was apparent there were still a few rough edges to our police buddy that his new wife would need to smooth. Although, it had to be said the new apartment was a good start. The ordinary way of things would have been for Habiba to move into the Abd el-Rassul family home with

Ahmed, his mother and two sisters. Houses in Luxor are routinely left unfinished, copper construction poles sticking up out of the top for precisely the purpose of adding a new floor to accommodate expanding families. But Habiba is a thoroughly modern young woman. And Ahmed had come under some pretty hefty Western influences in recent years. By which, of course, I mean Adam and myself. So, Ahmed had scrimped and saved until he could afford the small apartment in an up-and-coming part of Luxor with its own threshold over which he could carry his bride. I admired him for it, although I couldn't help but think he was hell bent on undoing all his manly efforts as he blithely – and obliviously – went on, 'I would like most to meet the famous actress. The one who winned the Oscar.'

I sent him a frown even fiercer than the one Habiba had bestowed, and not just because of his bombastic insensitivity. I also had to stop myself pointing out that actresses were called actors these days since it was considered sexist to distinguish them from their male counterparts. For fame it was hard to choose between them.

Shukura cut in again, rescuing me from the need to admonish Ahmed on his wedding day. She turned shining eyes on us. 'So, tell me. Has it been decided who will replace Talia Nolan as Helen of Troy? I was so disappointed to hear she'd pulled out.'

'What is this?' Ahmed demanded, still oblivious to his faux pas. 'Nobody telled to me that Talia Nolan she was not coming! Is this true?'

Adam cast him a sympathetic glance. As well he might since Talia Nolan was the pin-up of our generation. If not the face that launched a thousand ships, exactly, then certainly that of one of the most expensive brands of perfume in the world. She'd been Adam's secret crush for years. I allowed him the guilty pleasure of occasionally glancing at photographs of her when they appeared on poster boards and on magazine covers since I was happily secure in his affections. I was also willing to concede she was a superb actor. But I'll admit to the tinge of relief I'd felt when I knew she wasn't coming. Talia Nolan smiling from a poster board was one thing. Talia Nolan sitting at one's own breakfast table was quite another.

'She said she refused to work for the producer in the wake of the "#Me-Too Movement" that's been all over the Press for the last year,' I explained, putting speech marks around the words with my fingers.

'But I thought he was arrested,' Selim frowned. 'It was in all the newspapers.' Shukura's husband, a distinguished-looking man with wings of silver hair at his temples, spoke English carefully and with a pronounced accent.

Walid stood quietly in the background, listening without any apparent inclination to join in the conversation. But then, Walid had spent most of his life hunched over the precious artefacts it was his duty to conserve at the Egyptian Museum in Cairo, a role he was devoted to. It wouldn't surprise me to know he had no idea who we were talking about. Quite possibly, he had never been to see a movie in his life.

'Yes, arrested and blacklisted as a producer,' I confirmed, responding to Selim's query. 'But by then Talia Nolan had already very publicly stated she'd have nothing to do with the making of this movie since it was originally his brainchild.'

'Hmph,' Adam snorted rudely. 'Brains were hardly required! Egypt has been dramatically plastered all over the Press right across world of late. A gift to any film producer worth his salt!'

Ahmed brought us back to the essential point. 'So tell to me please... which actress will tomorrow make her arrival to replace Talia Nolan?'

'Actresses, plural' Adam corrected, unconsciously using the same old-fashioned language. 'There are three of them coming to stay.'

He said this with rather too much relish for my liking. Honestly! He and Ahmed made quite a pair! I decided it was time to get it over with. 'Natasha Redwood, Lori Scott and Skylar Harrison,' I said. I wasn't sure I had quite intended to reel off their names all at once like that. I've been known to derive a warped sort of pleasure from eking out every last drop of drama from a situation. And Ahmed loves a big build-up. It was probably unfair of me to deprive him just because I was feeling put out on Habiba's behalf by the glee with which he was anticipating their arrival. The trouble was, any of the screen sirens I'd just mentioned had dramatic impact enough on her own to fill cinemas the world over and to render me star-struck and speechless at the prospect of her coming to stay. To have all three of them about to descend on us, along with a superstar leading man and, as I may have mentioned, an Academy-Award-winning director was taking head-spinning to a whole new level. I can only think that in saying their names all together I was seeking to somehow normalise what was about to happen, make the whole thing less daunting.

Adam was grinning broadly, no doubt enjoying the way Ahmed's eyes bulged in his walnut brown face. 'So, there you have

12

it, my friend. They can boast epic space fantasies, pirate swashbucklers and comic book action adventures between them! Not to mention multi-million-dollar sales at the Box Office!'

'You are a very lucky man,' Ahmed said fervently, yet again overlooking his new wife's raised eyebrow. Or perhaps he saw it because, this time, he was quick to clarify his meaning: 'Many people would give their ears and teeth for such an honour.'

'You mean eyeteeth,' Adam corrected him automatically. Ahmed loves our idiomatic English but can usually be relied upon to mangle his own attempts to speak it.

Shukura slipped her arm through mine and winked at me. 'Now, Merry, you're being very coy not to mention it, but a little birdie told me Hollywood's latest heartthrob has been cast in the role of Ramses, fresh from his star turn alongside that chart-topping singer, and is also coming to stay.' Her faultless English was courtesy of a spell studying at the Oriental Institute in Oxford.

Now it was Habiba's turn to glance up under her lashes at her new husband and then smile meaningfully at me. 'Drew Trainer,' she murmured, managing to imbue the utterance of his name in her soft Egyptian accent with oceans of subtext. No need for her to say more. Ahmed caught the tone, and its' meaning. He had the grace to look abashed, putting a proprietorial arm around her shoulders and drawing her close.

Shukura laughed. 'Yes, Adam will not have the monopoly on things of beauty on which to feast the eyes!'

Adam grinned at her, not in the least put out. 'And that's without mentioning Hollywood's hottest film director,' he added. 'Merry's had a bit of a crush on Mackenzie King since he made a movie of her favourite fairy-tale and managed to make it believable.'

He was teasing me, so I swiped playfully at his upper arm, pretending indignation. 'Well, *The Princess and The Pea is* a perfectly ridiculous story,' I allowed. 'But, yes, it's the one I read over and over as a child. I know Mackenzie King has since made his name making blockbusters and war epics. But I thought he showed a lot of sensitivity with his screenplay. He managed to turn it into something quite charming for the Disney version.'

But Ahmed wasn't interested in Hollywood's hottest director or his deft handling of a rather absurd fairy-tale. It was those he'd seen on the big screen who'd fired his anticipation. 'Natasha Redwood, Lori Scott, Skylar Harrison *and* Drew Trainer,' he enthused, doing well, I thought, to include the male actor. 'Some of the most famous movie stars in the world! And they come here to Luxor, to live with my friends! It is a very great honour they bestow upon you,' he repeated solemnly. 'Although I remain desolate that Talia Nolan, she does not come.'

It has to be said, he didn't look it now he had Habiba locked close in against his side, adding:

'My friends, you are about to embark on a very great adventure.'

— He was probably right. But, as I said to Adam in the back of the taxi that whisked us home to our dahabeeyah later that evening, 'The trouble is, I prefer a *different* sort of adventure.'

'Hmm,' he agreed readily enough. 'I'll admit that playing host to a bunch of Hollywood superstars, it's hard to see how it might be possible to have another of *those*.'

'So much for Feisal's promise to have a little discussion about how to bring our tomb out into open,' I muttered, reminding him of the Ministry Director's words.

'The trouble is, he said we needed to let the dust settle on our discoveries first,' he pointed out.

'The dust hasn't so much settled as gone stratospheric,' I grumped.

So, all in all, the next few weeks promised another sort of adventure altogether. One I felt I could probably live quite happily without.

Chapter 2

It's difficult to describe that first afternoon and evening with what I later came to think of as 'the Hollywooders' on board.

My first concern, of course, was to make sure the *Queen Ahmes* was in tiptop shape for their arrival. A dahabeeyah is probably best described as a cross between a barge and a sailing yacht. Pioneered in Victorian times by Thomas Cook for wealthy travellers touring the ancient monuments on both banks of the mighty river, he took the basic design from ancient Egyptian prototypes carved onto tomb and temple walls in antiquity. I'd learned Cleopatra once sailed the Nile in a vessel very like ours. Except hers was covered in gold. And allegedly she instructed her servants to soak the sails in perfume so her people would get a waft of wonderful scent on the breeze as she cruised past. As Adam said, 'That's class!'

Named after a far more obscure ancient Egyptian queen, ours has a broad, shallow hull and sits long and flat in the water, mostly looking like an ordinary houseboat. Ordinary, that is, until you see her with her two sails unfurled on their long diagonal poles, the big one at the bow and the smaller at the stern.

We'd unstrung both to give the very finest of first impressions. The *Queen Ahmes* tethered against the jetty, but with both huge triangular sails billowing and snapping in the breeze was a sight to behold. I was fiercely, eye-stingingly proud of her.

We'd kitted her out as the last word in luxury Nile cabin cruising, although without such lavish touches as gold fixtures and perfumed sails! Each of our six cabins (including the one Adam and

I had claimed as our own) was an exquisite haven of quality and simple elegance, equipped with every twenty first century convenience, with decorative touches reminiscent of the heyday of Victoriana.

Even so, knowing the toast of Tinseltown was about to arrive, I joined Rabiah, our Egyptian housekeeper, in one final lightning inspection of every space. Between us we twitched the muslin drapes so they fell in perfect folds in front of the wooden shutters, ran feather dusters over the iron bedsteads and antique furniture, and placed posies of fresh flowers on every surface. By the time we were done, our already pristine cabins were softly scented and brightly gleaming, every bed made up with the purest Egyptian cotton.

Ahead of their arrival a harried-looking young man called Michael delivered five overnight bags. At my raised eyebrow at the smallness of their size he explained that each of the actors had an assistant staying locally who would bring freshly laundered and pressed clothes whenever required, along with any script revisions. The costumes needed on set would be stored in a trailer that could be moved to whichever location they happened to be filming at. It became apparent the film crew, extras and indeed the entire entourage of movie-making folk were distributed among the hotels of Luxor, ready to leap into action at the click of a finger.

Adam joined me in our wood panelled reception area just as a silver limousine with darkly tinted windows pulled up with a swish of tyres on loose scree up on the stone wharf above our landing platform. He'd been up on deck, beating dust from our oriental rugs (a daily task since Egypt is one of the dustiest places on the planet), and ensuring the cushions were plumped on our rattan armchairs and on the freshly oiled teak recliners.

Dressed in a brushed cotton shirt in the RAF blue that matched his eyes, with the cuffs turned back to reveal tanned forearms, teamed with stone-coloured chinos and brown suede deck shoes, and with a pair of sunglasses propped up on top of his glossy brown hair, he looked lean and fit and very handsome. He dropped a quick kiss on the end of my nose, hearing car doors slam outside at the top of the crumbling concrete steps leading down to the jetty. 'Ready, Merry?'

'As ready as I'll ever be.' I managed a smile, trying to ignore the nerves performing cartwheels in my stomach.

'You look lovely,' he said warmly, running an appreciative gaze over my face and allowing it to skim down the length of me.

While I would never pretend that my looks would ever elevate me beyond the moniker of "girl next door", it's fair to say I'd made an effort. What female wouldn't, knowing three of the most beautiful women in the world were coming to stay? Sure, my dress was a simple one in soft cotton as befitted the climate. But in deep apricot it suited my colouring. Especially so, now my skin had a sun-kissed glow thanks to a couple of weeks back in Egypt. I'd blow-dried my chestnut hair into a smooth bob rather than letting it dry naturally as was more typically my habit. Then slipped my feet into my favourite pair of strappy sandals with a small heel. And I'd spent some time sitting in front of a mirror earlier, dusting soft shadow onto my eyes, brushing mascara onto my lashes, a whisper of blusher to my cheekbones and a soft slick of a creamy lipstick to my lips.

I felt a more natural colour deepen the blush on my cheeks at his compliment. Adam is more used to seeing me barefaced and wearing my scruffs. It was good to know I could still draw that warmly admiring glance after a few years of marriage. In truth, this was the same outfit I'd worn to Ahmed's wedding. All I'd left off was the fringe-edged silk shawl I'd worn to dress it up a bit and to ensure my shoulders were covered inside the mosque.

Two minutes later, I found myself wishing I'd opted for something more casual and not wasted my time in front of the mirror.

Not one of the screen sirens that stepped from the back of the limousine was wearing anything more glamorous than cut down jeans, fraying at the edges, plain tee shirts and plimsolls. In fact, in the case of Lori Scott, I'd have to say it was far *less* glamorous even than that. The woollen poncho type top in dark grey she had on over a pair of black leggings looked decidedly threadbare, the leggings with gaping holes at the knees. Her feet were wedged into what my mother would call *clodhoppers:* big, black ankle boots with thick soles that made her legs look like twigs. I couldn't help but imagine how much of an effort it must be to lift each foot even as I wondered if she had perhaps not realised she was coming to Egypt: one of the hottest countries on earth.

Not one of them had a scrap of make-up on her face. All had scraped back their hair into ponytails or, in the case of Lori Scott, shoved it up underneath a baseball cap.

To say I felt over-dressed and regretted my use of cosmetics was putting it mildly. I felt a bit like a primped and painted doll by comparison.

And I could see Ahmed – for whom we'd gained special permission to provide a police escort to the arriving stars – making concerted attempts to mentally reconcile this underwhelming reality with the glowing anticipation of his imagination; failing miserably in his attempts not to look as if he was staring. Knowing him as I did, I felt I could interpret every surreptitious frowning glance and every pursed lip. While personally I might have expected something more stylish than scrubbed clean-faces and a casual-that-bordered-on-grungy look for our guests' arrival, I rather imagine Ahmed might have harboured secret fantasies of seeing them decked out in full red-carpet regalia by Versace, Valentino or maybe Vuitton.

Adam called out a greeting, took my hand and led me down the gangplank in welcome, apparently suffering none of the awkward stupefaction afflicting Ahmed and me. All easy-going charm and effortless manners, if he was at all surprised by the decidedly dressed down appearance of three of the most famous women in the world coming gingerly down the crumbling steps and along the causeway towards us, he was way too well-mannered to let it show.

'Hi there!' A shout from the stone jetty above us called my attention. 'So, this is what you guys call a dahabeeyah, huh? Wow! She's one mighty fine vessel!'

With those words Hollywood's hottest leading man endeared himself to me in a way no more personal introduction could have done. The simple fact of recognising her as 'she', as opposed to 'it' was a definite point in his favour. Drew Trainer, wearing pristine white knee-length shorts, a navy polo shirt and navy deck shoes, bounded down the crumbling steps and strode towards us, overtaking his three female co-stars, his right hand outstretched. 'You must be Adam? And, Meredith, isn't it?' He shook both of our hands in turn, shoving his sunglasses up on top of his head and smiling at us.

Now Adam is a handsome man. I've always thought his looks a bit filmstarish: lean, tanned features, dark glossy hair and deep blue eyes. But one glance at Drew Trainer's face was enough to see that he took film star looks to a whole new level. Sure, he shared the lean, tanned features, dark glossy hair and deep blue eyes of my husband. But replace tanned with bronzed, dark with jet black and deep blue with the darkest navy, then add a couple of inches in height, a slightly broader chest and muscles straining at the short sleeves of his polo shirt, and you'll get a sense of what it takes to turn a good-looking man into a drop-dead-gorgeous one. I wondered at the hours and hours he must spend in the gym, and decided he was very aptly named.

What the three women coming up behind him might lack in immediate visual impact, this man made up for in spades. He exuded a raw energy that seemed to make the airwaves crackle. His only feature to fall anywhere short of perfection was his nose. Large and prominent, it had a definite hook on the bridge. But, if anything, it served only to add a fierce masculinity to his features. Put it this way; I could see why he'd been cast as Ramses the Great. There was a sense of natural and unselfconscious power that emanated from him. And the hooked nose made him an inspired choice. Anyone glancing at the remains of possibly the most powerful pharaoh ever to rule Egypt now resting in a display case at the Cairo Museum could hardly fail to be struck by the shape of the great man's nose.

I emerged from having my hand shaken by Drew Trainer feeling decidedly weak at the knees and yes; I'll admit it, starstruck.

'Welcome on board the *Queen Ahmes*,' Adam said warmly. 'We'll do our best to make sure you have a comfortable stay.'

Drew Trainer thanked us and, at a gesture of invitation from Adam, strode along the gangplank to where Khaled and Rabiah were waiting just inside the open doorway to greet everyone. Rabiah, swathed in her usual black robes, was standing with a tray loaded with small glasses of hibiscus juice. Khaled's tray was piled with ice-chilled rolled flannels that he dispensed with a pair of silver kitchen tongs.

Khaled was Rabiah's husband and our boat manager. Though Egyptian, he was raised by his Scottish mother in that northern clime. I knew he could be relied upon to perform the welcome and introductions since Rabiah was timid in her use of English – although I'd swear she spoke and understood far more than she let on.

This allowed Adam and me to turn our attention to the three leading ladies about to step on board. Of course, they needed no introduction.

Natasha Redwood came first. Devoid of makeup she might be, but a single glance up close was sufficient to tell me this woman was beautiful. Dark-haired and brown-eyed with naturally thick lashes, perfectly shaped eyebrows, and lips with that very slight bee-stung look, she might lack obvious glamour in her cut down, ill-fitting jeans and a shapeless grey tee shirt but there was no mistaking her loveliness. She smiled, politely repeated our names back at us and stepped onto the gangplank to follow Drew Trainer.

Skylar Harrison, stepping forward to say hello, was blonde and blue-eyed. In cropped, fraying-at-the-knees jeans, plain white tee shirt and flat white plimsolls, it struck me one might overlook her entirely if one happened to pass her on the street. But I'd seen her in enough roles to know that on screen she was magnetic. The camera loved her. There was something a bit Marilyn Monroe-like about her ability to transform from something almost totally unremarkable into an out and out bombshell. With a long, swanlike neck and the most amazing bone structure, her beauty was of a more subtle variety than Natasha Redwood's, but there was no mistaking it. She, surely, must be the replacement Helen of Troy, cast into the role after Talia Nolan dramatically dropped out.

After the introductions, she took a moment to admire the *Queen Ahmes* before she stepped onto the gangplank to follow the others. 'I love that your boat has sails,' she murmured.

Whilst perhaps not quite so immediately endearing as Drew Trainer's opening remarks, this was enough to have me smiling at her with genuine warmth as she moved to join her co-stars, and I turned to greet the last of the actors.

Lori Scott, it has to be said, was not beautiful in the generally accepted sense of the word. Her mouth was too wide, her face too narrow and her eyes set too far apart. But there was something in the directness of her gaze from those hazel-almost-to-the-point-of-being-yellow-tiger-like eyes that was utterly captivating. Spellbinding might be more like it. She was so small and pale as to be almost wraithlike. Although, she looked hot. As well she might, swamped by that unbecoming woollen poncho in temperatures in the mid-thirties. Some of her hair was escaping from the baseball cap she'd shoved it up underneath and was sticking damply to her neck.

'Do you mind *very* much?' she asked before either Adam or I could get a word out. She was peering intently at me from underneath the peak of her cap.

I took a moment to register surprise at her Australian accent. I'd forgotten she'd started her acting career in a popular Ozzie soap opera. 'Mind what?' I frowned at her, genuinely confused.

She waved one tiny hand around in an expansive gesture to incorporate the *Queen Ahmes,* where Rabiah and Khaled were dispensing cold drinks and flannels, and then back to encompass the stone jetty, where Ahmed, dressed in his crisp white uniform with gold epaulets and black beret, belt and boots, was still standing stolidly alongside the silver limousine in the shade cast by the nodding palm trees, watching us. 'This whole bloody shebang,' she explained with a shrug of narrow shoulders. 'I imagine there are things you'd far rather do with your time than play host to a load of freeloaders who live in La-La Land. The land of make believe,' she added in case I might not have grasped what she meant.

'No, I – er –' I started to dissemble, wondering if she realised just how much we'd been paid to have them all to stay on board. The admitted disruption to our day-to-day lives was being very generously compensated. But she didn't let me finish.

'I used to read your blog, you know,' she said conversationally. Then turned those remarkable tiger-eyes on Adam. 'And I visited the Belzoni exhibition at the British Museum back in 2015.'

Taken aback, I was unsure how to respond.

So didn't.

Just stared.

Adam's effortless charm saved us. 'Then you'll know that the movie you're here to make has very little to do with make believe.'

'Sure,' she shrugged. 'Fact is very often far stranger than fiction, don't you think? But I've read the script. Quite why the screenwriter needed to add jealousy and rivalry to the story is beyond me. But, hey, that's movies for you! I hope you'll forgive what we're about to do to the history of this country you both evidently love so much.'

There was no opportunity to respond, even had either one of us known what to say. Drew Trainer called out to her from the doorway, 'Hey! Lori! You coming on board? I tell you, you gotta see this place!'

She shrugged those narrow shoulders again, lifted one black-booted foot and stepped onto the gangplank.

I looked at Adam a bit nonplussed. We traded glances for a moment and then he lifted his gaze towards the limousine up on the jetty, hearing the engine purr to life.

'What about Mackenzie King?' he called out to Ahmed as the car pulled away. 'The director! Isn't he here?'

Ahmed cupped his hands around his mouth and shouted down to us. 'The driver, he telled to me that the director he has a meeting with the scriptwriter. His arrival it will be in time for dinner.' Then he lowered his voice to a level I'm sure he fondly imagined couldn't be clearly heard on the far bank of the river. 'Now I am going to return home to tell to my Habiba that she is just as beautiful as the most famous actresses in the world! And she has much better way of dressing!' With that, he turned, climbed onto his scooter and zipped away.

Adam grinned at me. 'And, my lovely Merry, the same goes for you!'

I forgave him this barefaced lie since it was so well meaning. 'Well, I think it can be said I've made more of an effort to look nice today.'

25

He leaned forward to kiss my cheek, 'You don't need to make an effort.' Then took my hand. 'Well, I suppose if Mackenzie King is coming a bit later, it gives us a chance to get to know the actors. Ok; ready to give the tour?'

Actually, I thoroughly enjoyed showing them around.

Our semi-circular lounge-bar-cum-dining-room follows the curve of the stern. Furnished with deeply cushioned sofas upholstered in rich patterned silk, comfortable armchairs and occasional tables, and with a solid oak dining table stretching the length of the starboard side, this is where we would spend our evenings when it was too cool or breezy to sit comfortably up on deck.

Adam indicated the bar, inviting our guests to help themselves to whatever they may like at any time. As well he might, knowing the fee we'd been paid in advance was sufficient to keep our drinks cabinet fully stocked for years to come.

Drew Trainer made a beeline for our bookshelves groaning under the weight of our Egyptological picture and reference books, selecting one from the shelf and thumbing through it. 'You have an impressive library.'

'Just on the one subject, I'm afraid,' Adam smiled ruefully. 'Although I'm sure Merry can dig out a novel or two if ancient Egypt isn't your thing.'

'If only we were here on vacation,' Skylar Harrison said a bit wistfully. She wandered over to the picture window and looked out at the river. The sunlight streamed over her, bathing her in golden light and glossing her blonde ponytail, so her hair shone almost silver. 'I've never visited Egypt before. I should think it must be rather wonderful to spend a couple of weeks sailing the Nile with nothing to do but read, relax and maybe visit the sights.'

'Yes, if only it were possible to visit the sights without competing with them to become the main attraction,' Natasha Redwood remarked a trifle acerbically, a slight downward tilt to her full lips. 'I'm happy being paid to be in front of a camera. But it's a bit tiresome when the world-and-his-wife wants to click away at you for the family album.'

'Sadly, I think there'll be little time to relax on this trip.' Drew Trainer snapped the book closed, returned it to the shelf, then added brightly, 'So, shall we see what it's like up on deck?'

We stepped through the French doors at the back of the lounge-bar onto the little platform. Adam pointed out the steps leading down to the kitchen. 'That's Rabiah's domain,' he said. 'She and Khaled have their cabin below decks. And the engine room is down there too where Khaled spends an inordinate amount of time doing mysterious mechanical things with an oily rag.'

He turned and led us up the spiral staircase. I brought up the rear, immensely gratified to hear the reactions of our new guests as they stepped on deck.

'Wow!' Lori Scott exclaimed, tipping back her baseball cap.

'It's like stepping back in time!' Skylar Harrison added, shading her blue eyes with one hand.

'Awesome,' Natasha Redwood agreed. 'And so much better than a hotel.'

I have to admit, our upper deck is where the *Queen Ahmes* really makes a splash. Under a wide canvas awning, with rattan furniture, antique steamer-style recliners, potted palms in deep brass containers, a polished wooden handrail, and Turkish rugs scattered hither and thither across the dark wooden floorboards, this might almost have been a film set.

'Like something from a Merchant Ivory production,' Drew Trainer murmured, seeming to echo my thoughts.

'King Farouk once hosted a lavish picnic up here,' I boasted proudly. It was a titbit I loved to throw into conversation given half a chance. Right now, it was impossible to resist.

'So, it's fit for royalty, not just the Hollywood riffraff,' Lori Scott said with a tiny lift of one eyebrow and a mischievous smile.

I had a sense she might be gently poking fun at her co-stars. After all royalty – albeit of the Hollywood variety – was surely how they were used to being treated.

'We love it up here and eat on deck whenever we can,' Adam said smoothly. He indicated the large table behind us on the far side of the spiral staircase we'd just ascended. 'I thought we might do so tonight, if that works for you? How about we meet up here for pre-dinner drinks at 6pm? I know you all have an early start tomorrow.'

It was the cue to show them to their cabins. I was gratified anew by their exclamations as every door was thrown open and they each saw where they would be resting their heads at night for the next few weeks.

Now we just needed to wait for the Academy Award-winning director Mackenzie King to arrive and we would have the full contingent of Hollywooders under our roof. I don't mind admitting I was looking forward to the prospect with more than a little nervous anticipation.

Chapter 3

If I'd been asked to guess the topic of conversation for that first evening meal, I'd have said it would be all about moviemaking, a chance to hear tall tales about the Hollywood jet set. Instead, our guests chose to talk about Egypt, and even to enquire about us.

Mackenzie King arrived at the quayside just as Rabiah was serving pre-dinner drinks on deck. Adam waved me back into my seat as I jolted nervously to get up.

'I'll go,' he offered and bolted back down the spiral staircase to greet the film director and see him settled into his cabin.

He was back in what seemed like moments, but Mackenzie King was not with him. 'He's opted for a quick shower before dinner,' Adam answered my enquiring glance, and then turned his attention to lighting the hurricane lamps. These cast a soft ambient glow across the deck.

I sank back against the cushions for a second time, nursing the glass of wine Rabiah pressed into my hand.

The sun was setting behind the Theban hills, just visible along the river on the west bank beyond our landing platform. A few feluccas drifted on the Nile current, big triangular sails catching the early evening breeze. The crickets and frogs were out in force, serenading in the twilight with conversational chirruping. A flock of birds flapped silently along the shoreline, black silhouettes against the vivid orange streak where the river met the darkening sky. The palm-fringed riverbank too became a charcoal outline against the fiery glow as the sun sank low on the horizon. On the far eastern bank the line of tourist hotels softened to a smudge as evening swept in to claim the day. Another beautiful sunset, it soothed me, as it always did, and settled my nerves.

The breeze got up as the sun disappeared, sending the light from the hurricane lamps leaping into the lengthening shadows. But the evening air remained balmy. It would be at least another month before we'd need to head below deck for our evening meals.

Only two of us had changed for dinner. Lori Scott had dispensed with the threadbare poncho, leggings and clumpy black clodhoppers in exchange for white denim jeans teamed with a crop top, also in white. It exposed her taut, tanned midriff. She'd replaced the boots with a pair of flip-flops but was still wearing the baseball cap with her hair shoved up underneath it. Honestly, she looked about twelve rather than her early thirties, as I knew her to be. I'd swapped the apricot dress for cropped trousers, also white, and a simple silk shirt in coral pink. Glancing in the mirror before I left our cabin, I told myself I looked casually stylish. Within moments of being back in the company of the three screen sirens I realised my mistake.

Don't get me wrong. I don't suffer false modesty. I'm attractive enough. But I'm a normal, healthy size; not big, but not small either. I'm English too. So, although I wore a brace as a teenager, my teeth are also – well – distressingly normal.

Different though they were from each other in very many ways, these three female Hollywood stars had two things in common: they were each as slender – thin might be the word for it – as a fresh papyrus stem, and all had perfect gleaming white teeth.

Bereft of make-up though they were, a very few moments with them at close quarters was enough to have me noticing their translucent, blemish-free skin and toned, taut limbs. Ok, so make it four things.

Mackenzie King joined us just a few minutes after his arrival, with hair still damp from what must have been a very quick shower.

I sucked in a deep breath, placed my glass of wine on the occasional table alongside me and stood to greet him, inviting him to, 'please call me Merry.'

He gave my hand the briefest of shakes and grunted something unintelligible. There was no smile, but I couldn't go so far as to call him unfriendly. Distracted might be more the word for it. He seemed to be going through the motions of introduction while off somewhere else in his head. It wasn't that he'd dismissed me exactly; more that he'd barely registered me in the first place. Not rude so much as absent.

A tall, angular man with sunken cheeks below sharp cheekbones, a jutting chin, and steel grey eyes below fierce black brows, even with so perfunctory a greeting, I nevertheless saw at once who was boss on this assignment. Where Drew Trainer exuded power, the Academy Award winning director asserted absolute authority without needing to say a word.

'You're not to think me disrespectful,' he instructed in a slow drawl, accepting the gin and tonic Rabiah poured him. 'My head is full of the movie. I'll eat the food you serve me, and I'll drink whatever you pour in my glass, coca cola by preference once this is gone. But I'm not much of a one for conversation.'

And so it proved. He said not another word all through dinner. Nevertheless, he managed to be a slightly distracting and quietly brooding presence throughout.

31

I tried hard not to keep sending surreptitious glances his way. This was the director after all who had brought my favourite fairy-tale to the big screen. As Adam had said, I'd always had a bit of a crush on Mackenzie King as a result. Ok, *The Princess and the Pea* was one of his earlier films. Since then, he'd made his name in war epics and mega blockbusters. But I'd thought his screenplay revealed something softly sensitive about him; a side to his character in all honesty not much in evidence right now. Every time my gaze slipped in his direction it was to find him staring fixedly at his plate. He seemed not in the least inclined to enjoy the view. As crushes go, I was starting to consider my taste rather questionable. Up close he wasn't even particularly good looking, although I guessed I could see why he photographed well, his face all sharp contours and angles. As for personality, well, he'd yet to demonstrate he had any to speak of.

To help suffer the disappointment, I reminded myself that Ahmed had pointed out a lot of people would give their "ears and teeth" to be where I was right now: up close and personal with Hollywood's hottest property. It occurred to me I might as well enjoy it. So, I re-focused on the cast and managed to control the urge to keep stealing glances at the taciturn director.

It became apparent why each of the female actors was as slim as a papyrus reed when I saw how little they ate. All at once I found I was quite grateful for my lack of fame and fortune as I observed the way they picked at their food, almost never actually swallowing any. It meant I was at perfect liberty to enjoy the meal Rabiah had prepared and partake of a second glass of wine while they sipped on mineral water, eschewing even an aperitif of their choice. I didn't care to imagine what it must be like to live life on a permanent diet.

And my exercise of choice is a brisk walk as opposed to the weights and gym equipment Drew Trainer asked if it would be ok to have delivered and set up on deck.

I'd have to own up to remaining preoccupied by such trivial observations all through dinner and even during the conversation that ensued.

'Lori tells me you guys are experts on ancient Egypt,' Drew Trainer said, skewering a stuffed vine leaf with his fork and inspecting it before putting it in his mouth and chewing slowly, as if to make it last.

'Adam's the Egyptologist,' I corrected quickly; nervous I couldn't live up to the implicit expectation. 'I'm just an enthusiastic amateur.'

'Hardly!' Lori Scott exclaimed. 'I told you; I read almost every blog you posted on your trip recreating the Belzonis' travels in Egypt. Either you know more than you think, or else you're ridiculously modest!'

Flushing hotly, I nevertheless decided I quite liked Lori Scott. 'You're interested in Egyptian history?' I asked her, brushing aside her comment lest I got caught up in the need to dissimulate, or else bask in the unexpected praise. 'Most people have never heard of Giovanni Belzoni.'

'Oh sure, I've always been fascinated by Egypt.' She gave another of those expansive gestures, her small hand eloquently encompassing the now moonlit waters of the Nile, the enveloping warmth of the Egyptian night and the glimmering lights of Luxor across the river. 'It's so romantic, don't you think? There's all those stories about mummies and buried treasure and lots of really really ancient stuff.'

33

Drew Trainer put down his fork, propped his elbow on the table and rested his chin in the upturned palm of his hand. He regarded Adam and me, eyes pooled in the shadows cast by the hurricane lamps. As a strategy for keeping the weight off, it struck me as a good one: to take a break for conversation between each mouthful. 'Is that what got you guys hooked?' he asked. 'The logic-defying age and neck-craning scale of everything? The romance of ruined temples buried for millennia in sand, then excavated out and coaxed to give up their secrets?'

This was closer than he could know. But whether it was this, or the fact that Hollywood's hunkiest megastar was looking into my eyes and seemed genuinely interested in whatever my response may be that had me suddenly tongue-tied I wasn't sure. Put it this way: I was aware of a sudden loss of appetite for the food on my plate. Sadly, I found that, unlike our guests, I'd already eaten most of it.

'Yes, something like that,' I managed, putting down my fork.

'Was it tough to go back to England last year?' Lori Scott asked.

Somehow it was easier responding to her, and my tongue untied itself. 'Well, Adam was recalled to his job at the British Museum, so we had no choice really.' I shrugged, trying to convey professional matter-of-factness. 'We knew all along it was a time-limited assignment.' I didn't add that some time away from Egypt had seemed rather necessary after the discovery of a subterranean chamber beneath Lake Nasser at Abu Simbel, full of gold. They didn't know of the part we'd played in bringing to light the discoveries their movie was dramatising. A spell back in England to escape the media circus had suited us just fine. And of course, the Egyptian

Tourism Authority had realised it had no further need of my services to coax tourists into returning.

'We're very pleased to be back,' Adam said, reaching for my hand to make it clear he was speaking for us both. 'Egypt is where we belong.'

Drew Trainer smiled, dark eyes gleaming in the lantern light, and still didn't lift his fork from the tabletop. 'I'm looking forward to you guys giving us some history lessons. Although I've picked up one or two interesting soundbites along the way. For instance, did you know; Cleopatra was closer in time to the opening of the first Pizza Hut than to the building of the Great Pyramid? That somehow brings ancient Egypt much closer, don't you think?'

Lori Scott, not to be outdone, gave us no chance to respond. 'Yes!' she countered, very Australian in her pronunciation. She pushed her plate away to indicate she was done, although she most certainly had not eaten everything on it. 'But did *you* know that woolly mammoths still roamed the earth when the ancient Egyptian civilisation was getting started, which somehow pushes it further away, almost into pre-history, wouldn't you say?'

Despite my preoccupation with their eating habits, I'll admit it; I was impressed. 'You've done your research,' I approved, allowing myself one more mouthful after all, perhaps to compensate for the actors' small appetites. Rabiah had excelled herself this evening with a selection of traditional Egyptian *mezze*. Her homemade *baba ghanoush* dip was particularly good with freshly baked pitta bread dipped into it.

Drew Trainer smiled. 'That's our job. It helps get in character.'

Lori Scott shrugged, 'And it's a whole lot easier if you already love the subject matter. I fought hard to land a role in this movie. It's a part I was born to play.'

I caught a quick exchange of glances between Natasha Redwood and Skylar Harrison. And from the corner of my eye saw Mackenzie King frown and reach for his coca cola.

I wanted to ask Lori Scott which role she was cast in, since I didn't know. But somehow, and without knowing why, it didn't seem appropriate.

Drew Trainer seemed to me to rush unnaturally back into speech, almost as if to cover a gaffe. Although I couldn't for the life of me imagine what it might be. It was obvious of course which role he would be playing. Perhaps taking his cue from Lori Scott's words, he steered us to a discussion of his own character in the film. 'So, let's talk about Ramses the Great.' He addressed Adam. 'I am far from being the first to bring him to movie theatres across the globe. Did you know... he made his first appearance on the silver screen in 1909 in the horror tale *Mummy of the King Ramses*? Then famously in 1956 when Cecil B DeMille opened his epic *The Ten Commandments*, starring Charlton Heston as Moses and Yul Brynner as Ramses. And it's only a few years since Ridley Scott brought out the latest blockbuster *Gods and Kings* with Ramses in a starring role. Of course, all of those were before the recent revelations about the true identity of the man. I feel it is a rather different Ramses I am portraying. What do I need to know to bring him successfully to the screen?' Finally, he picked up his fork, skewered a meatball and popped it into his mouth. I cannot tell you how relieved I was to observe this; for Rabiah's sake of course.

Adam put his knife and fork together on his plate, which I was pleased to see was empty. He picked up his beer glass and swirled its contents around before taking a sip. 'A driven man,' he said at last. 'From the very beginning of his reign Ramses set out to prove that he was the greatest of all Egypt's kings: a brave warrior, mighty builder, prodigious procreator and devoted servant to the gods. He was not a man who lacked for an ego. A master of self-promotion might be one way of putting it. By the end of his reign, he'd raised enormous statues of himself in all corners of the land and stamped his cartouche on almost every monument.'

'That smacks of the actions of a self-serving man with too much power,' Skylar Harrison cut in blandly.

Lori Scott was looking at Adam intently, and nodded at her co-star's remark. 'It's got me thinking Hollywood and pharaonic Egypt have a lot in common.'

I noticed the frisson this remark sent around the table, although nobody asked her what she meant. Instead, the other actors seemed to have a renewed interest in the contents of their glasses, which, being fizzy water, was somewhat mystifying. The exception was Mackenzie King, eating while staring fixedly at his plate. Without invitation to elucidate, she nevertheless went on,

'Sounds to me as if all that unadulterated power went to his head!' She gave another of those airy gestures. 'You know that old saying about power corrupts...'

There was no mistaking it this time. Drew Trainer reached out and laid his hand on her wrist where it had come to rest on the tabletop. 'He was Pharaoh,' he reminded her. 'The most powerful man in the ancient world. Sure; he seems to have taken his self-aggrandisement a whole new level,' he smoothly steered the conversation back. 'Perhaps his need to legitimise himself was stronger because the populace believed him descended from an army general rather than royalty and he couldn't admit his true descent without linking himself to the hated Amarnan heresy.' This much, I guessed he knew from the script, if not recent world media. Removing his hand from Lori Scott's wrist, he finished, 'Ok, so, we now know Ramses wasn't the pharaoh who enslaved the Hebrews and had the ten plagues of Egypt unleashed on him. Still, I'm intrigued by the man behind the pharaonic propaganda machine.'

'You have to ask if he was the most famous man who ever lived.' This contribution to the conversation came unexpectedly from Natasha Redwood. Dressed in the same ill-fitting jeans, grey tee shirt and plimsolls as earlier, she'd added a loose black cardigan over the top, and freed her dark hair from the band so it cascaded over her shoulders. 'I mean, he was the only pharaoh to get a mention in the Bible, right? I read that most of the pharaohs who followed him onto the throne named themselves after him in the hope that some of his glory might rub off. Maybe that's why the name "Ramses" is synonymous with pharaonic Egypt.

Adam nodded, perhaps relieved to stick to a historical discussion, sensing the discomfort Lori Scott had caused. 'Yes, no fewer than nine more pharaohs named themselves Ramses when they ascended to the throne after him. But none regained anything like the power of their hero and namesake. Quite the reverse. It's probably fair to say the kings that followed Ramses the Great – with the possible exception of Ramses III, who ruled many years later – were anything but. Great, that is. The pharaohs that came after him were known more for chaos and corruption than might and majesty.'

Lori Scott nodded emphatically. 'I rest my case. Power corrupts. And absolute power corrupts absolutely.'

Guessing this to be a reference to the #Me-Too Movement that had rocked Tinseltown of late, I was aware of another prickle of unease.

'Perhaps,' Adam allowed, when nobody picked her up on this comment. He went on smoothly. 'Egypt never regained its former glory. But Ramses II became the model of kingship others aspired to. You're right in saying he was famous. By the time of his death, he had almost godlike status.'

Natasha Redwood put both elbows on the table and leaned on them. 'That might be because nobody could remember a time before he ruled the Egyptian empire. He'd been on the throne for over sixty-something years at the time of his death and was a man in his nineties – an extraordinary age for an ancient Egyptian. Twelve of his own sons were already dead before he breathed his last!'

Skylar Harrison joined in. 'Is it really true he fathered over two hundred children?'

'That's a *bit* of an exaggeration,' Adam smiled. 'Most experts today agree he had perhaps forty-five sons and maybe fifty-five daughters. Quite enough for one man! The truth is, he outlived many of them and even some of his grandchildren. Of course, infant mortality was way higher in those days.'

Lori Scott made a face. The lamplight caught on her tiger-yellow eyes as they gleamed darkly. 'So, Ramses was a man who liked to exploit women!'

'Well, he had multiple wives and a harem,' Adam said levelly, perhaps unsure where she was going with a comment like that. 'So, it seems likely there was no shortage of responsive women on whom he could father a child. But there's nothing to suggest he mistreated them.'

The Ozzie actor frowned. 'Still; how chauvinistic! But as pharaoh, I guess he had separate rules to everyone else. Seems to me, things don't change. Powerful men still think they can take what they want whenever they want it!'

This time the tension made the airwaves crackle. I wondered if I was supposed to interpret her assertion as a dig at present company. I flashed a lightning glance between the morose director and his leading man. Neither seemed inclined to rise to the bait, if indeed that's what it was.

'Whatever their progeny,' Drew Trainer laid his hand over her wrist again, effectively silencing her. 'Ramses was eventually succeeded by his thirteenth son, already an old man when he came to the throne. Isn't that right, Adam?'

'Yes,' he nodded. 'And after he died, Egypt descended into a chaotic period characterised by civil war, pretenders and anarchy.'

Even as I wondered at the interplay between the Hollywooders, I gave in to the overwhelming need to contribute to the conversation at this point, and steer away from the choppy waters Lori Scott had stirred up. 'I'm sure Ramses had high hopes of siring a long-lived dynasty. Sadly, for him, fathering such a vast number of offspring in fact guaranteed the exact opposite.'

Drew Trainer nodded. 'So, in the end, one has to wonder whether Ramses did anyone any favours, living so long.'

'It's certainly true it was all downhill from there,' Adam remarked.

'So, a complex man who did everything to the extreme.' Drew Trainer attempted to summarise the conversation, perhaps wondering how he might convey this larger-than-life character on screen. 'An egoist and possible megalomaniac, but perhaps with justification.'

Mackenzie King finally roused himself sufficiently to draw the conversation to a close. 'Ok, everyone; enough.' Clearly his head hadn't been quite so full of the movie that he'd paid no heed at all. 'We can begin to bring ancient Egypt back through cinema tomorrow. We start at dawn.'

Helping Rabiah clear away the plates after dinner, I saw the director pull Lori Scott aside as they moved to follow the others in descending the spiral staircase.

'Lori, you've made your point,' he muttered. 'Let's leave it there, shall we?'

Chapter 4

I couldn't have said at first what it was that roused me from sleep to find the pre-dawn shadows still cloaking our cabin in darkness. Adam was sleeping soundly alongside me. Thinking I must have imagined it, I rolled over ready to slide back into slumber myself but heard it again. I turned my head on the pillow to listen. Raised male voices.

It was enough to have me throwing back the covers and reaching for my robe. Shrugging it on, I crept across the room and silently opened the door just a crack, tilting my head sideways and straining my ears.

They were in the lounge-bar. Yes, definitely raised voices. But it seemed they were nearing the end of whatever altercation they were having. As I dithered, wondering if I should intervene before they woke the whole boat, I was just in time to hear Drew Trainer's voice shout,

'But you auditioned her for the role, Mac! She won it fair and square in open competition! You cast her! End of story!'

Then the lounge-bar door was flung open, and the actor stormed through it, swearing. I raised an eyebrow at his choice of words. I could only imagine these were intended as a description of the director himself. I quickly pulled back to avoid being seen. He passed within a whisker of me as he strode along the corridor, slamming his cabin door behind him.

'What was that noise?' Adam asked groggily from the bed.

'I'm not sure,' I frowned. 'An argument of some sort, I think. It's over now.'

I quietly closed the door, slipped out of my robe and got back into bed, mentally turning over what I'd heard. No sooner had I laid my head on Adam's shoulder than the alarm went off on his bedside cabinet. He grunted, reached out to silence it, and then pulled me back against him.

'I'd forgotten how much I hate early mornings and getting up in the dark,' he groaned. But he didn't ask me any more about what I'd overheard.

If I'd hoped I might see signs of discord between the director and leading man at breakfast and maybe make sense of what had gone on between them, I was disappointed. Nobody stopped for so much as a glass of orange juice.

'They'll serve coffee in our trailers,' Skylar Harrison informed me as Adam lowered the gangplank. Stupid of me, I realised. This lot almost certainly skipped breakfast in any event. You didn't get to look the way they did scoffing croissants and muffins, that was for sure.

But, as I later discovered, they had an appetising selection of fruit as well as an endless supply of coffee laid out on set.

As Egyptological consultant, Adam was a fully paid-up part of the production team, expected on hand throughout filming. Not wishing to be left out, I'd wangled an invitation too. I could be relied upon not to get in the way. And honesty compels me to admit I was excited to see for myself how the story Adam and I had unearthed would be brought to the big screen.

'There'll be lots of hanging around,' Lori Scott warned me as we carefully negotiated the steps up from our causeway mooring, still in the dark. 'Honestly, Merry; you'll be bored to death. Besides, today is just the location sequencing, testing the lighting and sound. They'll want to do some rushes, but I doubt any of what we shoot today will make it into the final film.'

There was a minibus waiting on the high bank to whisk us off. I was interested but not especially surprised to see Ahmed waiting to pull back the passenger door. He was dressed in another of his crisp white uniforms, albeit with a black leather jacket over the top against the pre-dawn chill. He grinned at me, clearly of a mind to seize the moment and enjoy himself. I grinned back, feeling the same. Now the Hollywood set was finally here, and the ice was broken, my qualms were gone. Let's be honest; there were worse ways to earn a living. I felt a small thrill of anticipation and called out a cheery good morning.

I wasn't sure how Ahmed had managed to inveigle himself onto this assignment. But then, he did have experience as our bodyguard, not just as an officer of the Tourism and Antiquities police. And, of course, filming was due to take place at some of the monuments surviving from antiquity that it was his duty to patrol. So, thinking about it, he was the perfect man for the job.

'Which reminds me,' I addressed the Hollywooders as Ahmed pulled back the door on its rollers and politely stood aside; and as if these thoughts had been aired aloud rather than inside my own head. 'I've been meaning to ask how come you're filming so much actually here in Egypt. I mean; I get that you'll want to do some sequences on the Nile and in the west bank desert. After all, the scenery along the riverbank and in the Theban hills hasn't changed much in thousands of years. But the licenses Director Ismail sent through suggest you'll set a few scenes inside the ruined temples? He mentioned Karnak, the Ramesseum and Medinet Habu.' I frowned and explained myself. 'The temples no longer look at all like they would have done in dynastic Egypt. Back then they were brightly painted and intact.'

Nobody answered me immediately as we took turns to climb on board the minibus. Drew Trainer stood back while Mackenzie King swung himself into a window seat, then sat down beside him and reached for his seatbelt. There was no residual tension left between the actor and director that I could detect. The three female actors squeezed alongside each other on the back seat, leaving Adam and me to slide into the seats at the front, immediately behind the driver. Ahmed pulled the door closed behind us, then jumped behind the wheel, turned the key in the ignition and we set off, headlights slicing through the pre-dawn darkness on the riverbank.

Adam was first to pick up the thread of conversation I'd left hanging. He levered himself sideways so he could talk over his shoulder. 'Yes, I was surprised to see Medinet Habu on the location list. That's the mortuary temple of Ramses III. He ruled around thirty years after his namesake Ramses the Great.'

It was Mackenzie King who responded. I was a bit taken aback by this willingness on the director's part to engage in conversation since it was in such marked contrast to his silence last night. 'The Medinet Habu temple has the advantage of only rarely being included in popular touring itineraries,' he said. He spoke slowly, with deliberation and a definite New York twang. 'As it's quieter we can shoot the movie with less disruption.'

He was perfectly correct in this. For reasons unbeknown to me, the impressive temple of Ramses III is largely left off the sightseeing programmes on the west bank. I guess, with limited time available, it's impossible to see everything. The Valleys of the Kings and Queens with their stunningly carved and painted tombs, the beautiful Mortuary Temple of Hatshepsut set against the curtain of cliffs rising majestically behind it, and the Colossi of Memnon sitting in splendid isolation at the roadside marking, quite literally, the line in the sand where the cultivated land meets the desert, tend to head the list of must-see west bank sites.

And, as far as temples go, it's certainly true that the magnificent ruins of Luxor and Karnak on the east bank are right at the top of the essential bucket list visits, and with good reason. Even so, I've always thought it a shame that the one-time visitor to Luxor misses out on the Medinet Habu, surely the best preserved of the truly ancient temples.

The director went on, 'And, as I understand it, Ramses III modelled his mortuary temple on the Ramesseum, just down the road, built by his more famous forebear and our movie's protagonist.'

I nodded since this also was true. 'I've often thought if you could put the ruins of the Ramesseum and the Medinet Habu together, you'd get the perfect temple.' I mused aloud, also twisted sideways so I could talk over my shoulder.

But Mackenzie King wasn't overly interested in my observations on the architecture of the temple ruins. 'The fact is, Ramses II or Ramses III is all the same thing for the vast majority of the movie-theatre-going public,' he drawled in that same deliberate manner. 'They won't notice the difference. Folks just want a couple of hours escape into another world, to forget about the cares and worries of their everyday lives, and to be told a story.'

I caught sight of Adam's raised eyebrow out of the corner of my eye. To Adam and me, saying Ramses II and III were the same was tantamount to saying a pyramid was the same as an obelisk. Sure, they both had a pointy, triangular top, but there the similarity stopped.

The director wasn't quite done. He finally answered my question and with his next words also perhaps managed to redeem himself. 'We're filming in Egypt because this is where the original action took place. Sure, we'll do some green-screen shooting, and we've got enormous sets being built at Elstree in the part of the world you guys hail from. But here in Egypt, this is where this incredible story was first told. I think something of the atmosphere here must still resonate with those long-dead personalities. Now, if a bit of that ancient aura can find its way into my camera lens –'

He trailed off and turned his head to stare out of the window where, in fact, it was still dark. Leaving me to wonder if, for the first time, I had perhaps glimpsed the instinct that had enabled him to bring my favourite fairy-tale to the screen with such sensitivity.

With the director once more lapsed into the brooding silence that had characterised his presence at dinner last night, and with the others seemingly disinclined towards conversation this early in the day, I was content to settle into my own thoughts. I faced forward again and gazed through the window as Adam's warm hand came to rest on my knee. A pale-yellow glow in the sky hailed the onset of daybreak. But for now, the passing scenery remained shadowy and indistinct.

Mackenzie King was certainly right in calling it an incredible story. I let my mind drift, wondering how the writers had gone about dramatising the fact that the great Ramses II, his principal royal wife, Queen Nefertari, and the legendary femme fatale of ancient Greek mythology, none other than Helen of Troy, were actually cousins. All three descended from the tribes of Israel after Biblical Joseph, he of the Technicolor Dreamcoat, came to Egypt to serve pharaoh. It was a re-telling of both the Exodus story and of the Trojan War. Helen, as it turned out, had sat out the entire duration of the latter here in Egypt, serving only as the excuse the Greeks needed to go into battle. And Ramses, far from being the Pharaoh of the Oppression as popular culture so often depicted him was, in fact, the son of Biblical Moses. Both Ramses and his cousin-wife Nefertari were born of the younger Amarnan princesses, daughters of the rebel pharaoh Akhenaten and his beautiful queen Nefertiti. But since they'd sworn a solemn oath to keep their ancestry secret, all this equally eye-popping ancestry had come to light only thanks to the discoveries Adam and I had been on hand to make.

It was quite a story, hardly crying out for further embellishment. So, what on earth had the scriptwriter done to further sensationalise it?

Unable to keep this thought to myself, I levered sideways once more and addressed myself over my shoulder to Lori Scott since it was she who had asked forgiveness for the liberties Hollywood was taking with history.

'Do you mind if I ask –' I started politely. She looked back at me and smiled her assent, so I went on. 'You said the real story was sensational enough, without needing to add jealousy and rivalry to the mix for the movie,' I reminded her. 'I'm intrigued to know what you meant?'

'Three warring queens,' she answered readily enough.

'Er – *three*?'

She gave another of those expansive hand gestures I was starting to recognise as one of her signature mannerisms. With this one she managed to encompass Natasha Redwood, Skylar Harrison and herself all wedged in alongside each other on the back seat of the minibus. 'Three leading female roles,' she said. 'Three warring queens.' As if it was explanation enough.

Drew Trainer cast her a frowning glance over his shoulder. Sadly, this prevented her elucidating further. She gave a small shrug – another of her trademark characteristics – and clammed up, turning her head to look out of the window, where it was starting to get light.

Frustrated, I had no choice but to let it drop. That strange undertone was back, making me wonder what might really be going on in the interplay between our guests. I pieced together some of Lori Scott's remarks of last night, and the glances I'd seen exchanged between the actors, with the altercation I'd overheard first thing; and couldn't help but wonder if the Australian actor was somehow pushing her luck. Maybe she hadn't been first choice for her role; the role she said she'd fought hard and been born for. The name Talia Nolan drifted through my head, but I quickly dismissed it. Talia Nolan had famously turned down a starring role in this movie ages ago. And I still didn't know which role Lori Scott was here to play. To distract myself, I, too, turned back to gaze out of the window at the passing scenery.

I never tire of the drive along the west bank road. From our mooring a little way north of the bridge spanning the river, it runs parallel to the Nile along an inland canal. Donkeys and cows graze among bulrushes and scrubland underneath clumps of date palms.

As the sun lifted into the vaulting sky on the east bank to our right, the golden strip of desert beyond the cultivated land on our left revealed itself: an impressionist wash of pale green, wreathed in the curling mist of early morning with the tawny expanse of desert and rock spreading beyond it lifting into the Theban hills. These seemed to me to stretch across the landscape like a recumbent lion, burnished tawny gold by the rising sun.

As we came towards the town of modern Gurna, buildings lined the kerbside on our left: mostly ramshackle dwellings of the locals behind mudbrick and plaster, some with whitewashed walls. And, across on the far side of the canal, the more substantial apartment blocks, just three or four storeys high, painted ochre, peach and dusky pink, dusty, a bit decrepit, with peeling paintwork and with carpets draped over balconies and tablecloths hung at open windows among washing lines hung with galabias and other articles of clothing.

If it were possible to wish away the rubbish that littered the canal side: plastic water bottles, carrier bags, empty food cartons, cigarette packets and all manner of other detritus, it would be quite picturesque. I'd learned to love this run down, faded, grubby, chaotic spectacle that was the west bank of Luxor waking up and getting ready to go about its business.

As I gazed out of the window, it was to see farmers already toiling in the fields before the heat of the day set in, and donkeys pulling carts even now laden with crops destined for the east bank markets of Luxor. It made me realise their owners must have been toiling long before first light.

The rising sun lit the Theban hills with a dark golden glow. I spent a moment in quiet contemplation of the treasures those terracotta hills had once contained. Still, in fact, contained. But that was not a pursuit for now.

On entering the modern town of Gurna, it's a sharp left-hand turn at a checkpoint to take the main road towards the Theban hills. The Colossi of Memnon stand at the side of the road as you pass at the demarcation line where the town gives way to an agricultural strip with rocky desert beyond. Behind them is a large excavation site where archaeologists have been at work in recent years unearthing the remains of the huge mortuary temple of Amenhotep III.

At the end of the road is a crossroads. The road ahead leads in a long sweeping curve to Deir el-Medina, the ancient village of the workers and, beyond it, to the Valley of the Queens. Turn right and the road runs parallel with the Theban hills rising from the desert basin, pockmarked Swiss-cheese-like with holes that are the tombs of the nobles. The other side of the road is lined with the ruins of the memorial temples of the great pharaohs that once stood there. Most were dismantled in antiquity, their stones re-commissioned for new building projects. Only the Ramesseum and the mortuary temple of Seti I remain relatively intact and accessible to tourists today.

On this occasion, reaching the crossroads, we turned left. There's a ticket office at the roadside where independent visitors can purchase admission to many of the west bank sights. Since the Hollywooders had commissioned exclusive access to Mackenzie King's chosen filming location, we had no need to stop. A short onward drive brought us to the ancient temple of Ramses III now known as Medinet Habu.

'This is the best preserved of all of the New Kingdom funerary temples,' Adam said as Ahmed brought the minibus to a stop in a rather dramatic spray of loose chippings in the small parking lot beyond the entranceway.

Adam had never really said as much, at least not in so many words, but I knew he was secretly thrilled to bits and as proud as punch, recruited as Egyptological consultant to the moviemakers. It was quite a feather in his cap; testament to his knowledge and proof that decades of study and a couple of years working at the British Museum had paid off.

There's a boyish enthusiasm about Adam for all things ancient Egyptian. I smiled seeing how eager he was to get started on his commission by launching into his first lecture. Even though I wasn't entirely sure lecturing was particularly what Mackenzie King had had in mind when recruiting him.

'What exactly *is* a funerary temple?' Skylar Harrison asked, apparently willing enough to play student. She unclipped her seatbelt as she went on. 'Or, perhaps I should say, what *was* it? What was it *for*?'

'The pharaohs called them their "*Mansions of Millions of Years*",' Adam supplied readily. 'They were built to serve the dead king's mortuary cult.'

'His *what*?' Natasha Redwood was looking out of the window trying for a glimpse of the temple. Seeing the slight crease between her perfectly arched eyebrows I wondered if the word "cult" had called up an image of weird sects with mysterious rituals and rather sinister customs.

It was Lori Scott who answered, proving quite knowledgeable. As she spoke, I started to wonder if Adam's services as Egyptological consultant to this movie were strictly necessary after all. She unclipped her seatbelt and swung herself out. 'Since the beginning of Egyptian history, the ideal burial was made up of two parts: a tomb and somewhere where offerings could be made to the deceased. Obviously, the ancients intended the tomb to be sealed for eternity. But the place of offerings needed to be accessible: somewhere the worlds of the living and dead could meet.'

Skylar Harrison wrinkled her nose as she moved to follow. 'Sounds a bit morbid to me.'

'No more so than laying flowers at a graveside,' Drew Trainer interjected, gesturing for her to get up ahead of him.

She swung herself out of the back seat, blonde hair falling in a curtain in front of her face and shrugged to acknowledge what he'd said. 'No, I s'pose not.'

Adam and I held back so all the actors could jump out of the minibus before us. 'Miss Scott's right,' Adam said. 'The memorial temple or "*Mansion of Millions of Years*" was where offerings could be made, and prayers intoned as part of a mortuary cult so that worship of the dead king could go on long after his death.'

'But I thought Ramses III built a royal palace on this site too,' I frowned as I too jumped down to join the others.

'Yes; although only its foundations remain,' he acknowledged. 'The palaces of the living were made of mudbrick. It was the houses of eternity that were made of stone, to honour the dead king and built to last.'

'Millions of years is right!' Drew Trainer exclaimed, catching sight of the temple façade through the scrubby thicket of hawthorn trees lining the parking lot. 'My God! It's *enormous*!'

'Medinet Habu is the best preserved of all the New Kingdom mortuary temples,' Adam repeated. 'Its' good condition is thanks to its use as the headquarters of the Theban necropolis during the latter part of the New Kingdom.'

'Which meant it avoided the dismantlement suffered by many others,' I piped up, voicing my thought of earlier. 'Apparently the late 18th Dynasty pharaohs Ay and Horemheb also had funerary temples close by, which were taken apart and used for other building projects.'

But nobody was listening to me.

'How do we get in?' Drew Trainer asked. 'Can we have a look around before we get started?' He addressed himself to Mackenzie King. 'I hear there are some cool military scenes carved on the walls here. Wasn't Ramses III the last of the great warrior pharaohs?'

'The entrance gateway is this way,' Adam pointed and took the lead. 'And yes, Ramses III fought mighty battles that kept the ancient Egyptian empire at least superficially intact while the other great powers of the late Bronze Age such as Palestine, Mesopotamia and the even the once mighty Hittite Empire were crumbling.'

Ahmed locked up the minibus and trailed behind us at what I imagine he thought an appropriately respectful distance from Hollywood royalty. Adam and I no longer suffered such hierarchical inhibitions and kept pace, while Adam continued his history lesson. I'm aware that an early morning masterclass in ancient Egyptian history is possibly not to everyone's taste. To me it is the air that I breathe; the bread and butter of my existence, the joy of shared interest that underpins my union with Adam, love of my life. I could only hope the Hollywood contingent was sufficiently motivated by the need to make a historically accurate film, to suffer at least a passing interest, or to humour us if not.

'Ramses III fought successful battles on both land and sea against the eponymous *Sea Peoples*,' Adam said. 'These marauding forces appear to have been a migrating conglomerate of people likely drawn from a geographic arc stretching from the Aegean to the Levant after the fall of so many of the Greek and Mediterranean states at around this time.'

I couldn't resist a quick glance back at Ahmed's face as Adam said this. When I first met Adam, he and Ahmed were already chums and he was teaching our policy buddy to speak English. But I doubted our friend's vocabulary stretched quite so far as to have been able to fully make sense of that particular historical soundbite. If so, it was impossible to tell. Ahmed's face was a picture of avid and intent interest. He loved hearing about his country's Imperial past.

'Ramses III's successes in battle are carved all over the temple walls here,' Adam remarked. 'In this, I am quite sure he revelled in his chance to emulate the famous war exploits of his namesake Ramses the Great, who claimed a great victory against the Hittites at the Battle of Kadesh. Once we get inside, you'll be able to see wall reliefs showing the piles of severed hands and genitalia cut from the corpses of the enemy.'

'Ugh,' Natasha Redwood exclaimed with an exaggerated shudder. 'How gruesome!'

'It was a standard means of keeping tally of the number killed in battle,' I explained, gratified she was paying attention.

'Yes, with clearly a humiliation aspect to the emasculation of the enemy corpses,' Adam added.

'These I must see!' Drew Trainer asserted, with rather too much relish for my liking, while the rest of us contemplated this rather grisly ancient practice in silence.

From the road we turned left into a short walkway flanked by black granite statues of the lion-headed goddess Sekhmet, and approached the tall Eastern High Gate, the entranceway to the huge temple complex. With features like a Syrian *"migdol"* fortress, I knew from previous visits that this had once been the site of the pharaoh's harem, where Ramses III came for leisure and to spend time with the women of his household including those whose sole purpose in life was the king's pleasure. It looks a bit like a tall garrison built of mellow golden stone. We passed through two high sentinel stone gates rising on either side and on through a third that bestrode the central entranceway, a bit like entering a medieval castle through the portcullis.

Drew Trainer might have anticipated a quick guided tour of the temple's principal points of interest before getting down to the business of moviemaking. Speaking for myself, I was quite eager to peek inside the five enormous trailers I glimpsed parked on the temple forecourt. A single glance was enough to tell me why our guests had arrived to stay on the *Queen Ahmes* so bereft of luggage. Honestly! Given the size of those trailers, I could only wonder at their need for board and lodgings in Luxor at all! I'd swear each one was as big as my flat back at home in Sevenoaks: easily possible to live in quite comfortably. I wondered how on earth the huge lorries they were attached to had gained access to the site. As far as I knew a thick mud brick perimeter wall encircled the entire temple complex. But, hey! This was Hollywood. All things were possible! I could hear sounds of industry and caught sight of what I took to be a huge camera being set up on what looked like enormous rollers, almost like a train track.

Whatever high hopes Drew Trainer and I may have been fondly nursing for how to start the day went sadly unfulfilled.

Walking just in front of me between Natasha Redwood and Lori Scott as we passed through the central *"migdol"* gateway, Skylar Harrison suddenly stopped dead in her tracks. This was so unexpected I nearly careened into the back of her.

She spun around so she was facing me, gasping as if her air supply had been abruptly severed. But it was more the look on her face that brought me skidding to a halt.

She'd gone as white as a sheet and looked frankly, well, terrified. There was no other word for it.

'I can't go in there!' she announced dramatically, eyes wide with fear, lips edged with a clear white line, smooth skin suddenly mottled and blotchy, a wild expression on her face and her voice rising in panic. 'Please! Don't make me go in!'

And then she dropped to the floor at my feet as if her legs were no longer capable of holding her upright. She sat on the dusty flagstones visibly sweating and shaking uncontrollably, eyes screwed tightly shut, knees pulled up against her chest, emitting a high-pitched keening sound.

Chapter 5

Seeing her co-star slump to the floor and hearing her making that awful wailing noise, Natasha Redwood spun back, staring down uneasily at Skylar Harrison and then back up at me in shock. 'Hey! Skylar? What's the matter? Are you ok?'

I thought it a particularly stupid question. Anyone with eyes in their head and ears to hear with could surely gather that Skylar Harrison was about as far from ok right now as it was possible to be. Although the awfulness of watching someone's demeanour change in a heartbeat from perfectly fine one moment to clearly anything *but* fine the next was decidedly unnerving. I too looked down helplessly at the actor, wondering what the hell was happening.

'Hey, what's wrong?' Lori Scott also spun around in alarm. She dropped to her knees, reaching forward to grip her co-star by her upper arms as she sat there swaying and moaning. 'Help me get her upright,' she instructed.

'No, no!' Ahmed bolted forward. 'Please do not attempt to lift her! We do not know what it is that is wrong!' Forgetting his awe of the Hollywooders, his police training took over. As I have often had cause to remark, Ahmed can seem a bit of a buffoon, until needed in a crisis. Then, he is a tower of strength; a man I'd want on my team any day of the week. 'Give her some time until we know what it is that afflicts her.'

Acting on instinct, I dropped to my knees in front of the wailing actor, joining Lori Scott on the dusty flagstones. Natasha Redwood hesitated, then crouched down too, managing to avoid the dust, squatting rather than kneeling. Skylar Harrison now had a co-star on either side, with me directly in front of her.

Lori Scott stroked her back with soothing rhythmic strokes. I laid my palm against her forehead, acting without conscious thought for the fact that I was brazenly taking the temperature of one of the world's most famous women.

'She's hot!' I informed Ahmed, joining her co-stars in murmuring soothing, incoherent sounds, trying to calm her.

It made no difference. She started to hyperventilate. Letting go of her knees, she sat rocking back and forth. Natasha Redwood and Lori Scott each grabbed one of her hands, exchanging a swift look of alarm. With no handy brown paper bag on my person to get her to blow into, I reached for her shoulders. It was an instinctive movement to keep her from pitching backwards and hurting herself. There was every chance she could crack her head open on the uneven flagstones if we let go and she kept rocking like that. Gripping her shoulders, I could feel the fight her body was putting into the simple matter of breathing. As if she couldn't quite draw the air into her lungs. She was gulping, sucking in rapid, shallow breaths, inhaling quickly as if oxygen was in short supply, and she couldn't hold it inside her. Every one of her attempts juddered through me too as I held onto her.

'See if she can hear you,' Ahmed instructed me.

'Miss Harrison – er – Skylar,' I attempted to get through to her. 'Can you tell us what's wrong?'

'Dizzy,' she rasped wildly, eyes opening and immediately closing again. 'Everything's spinning.'

Adam and Drew Trainer who'd been way out in front with Mackenzie King now turned at the commotion. Drew Trainer moved first. He was back with us in a few long strides. 'What's the matter with her?' he demanded urgently, taking in at a single glance the traumatised state of his co-star.

'She says she feels light-headed and dizzy,' Natasha Redwood filled him in. I noticed she omitted to repeat the strange and frankly unsettling bit about refusing to enter the temple.

'Oh God! Is she going to faint?' he barked as Skylar Harrison swayed where she was sitting, despite our combined efforts to hold her steady.

I looked keenly into her beautiful face. She'd opened her eyes again, hearing Drew Trainer's voice; was staring straight back at me. In truth, she could hardly do otherwise. I was kneeling right in front of her. Had hold of her by the shoulders, for God's sake! But I was sure she wasn't seeing me. She appeared to have tunnelled back inside her own head. Her blue eyes were unfocused, pupils dilated.

'I don't think so.' But my words were ill judged, or ill timed, or both. No sooner were they out of my mouth than Skylar Harrison snatched her hands back from the grasp of her female co-stars and clutched desperately at her chest. The fear on her features gave way to outright panic as she kept on struggling for breath, making awful rasping sounds, her lovely face contorted with the effort.

I realised I was now the only one holding her, so gripped her shoulders even tighter.

'Heart attack?' Natasha Redwood gasped, looking almost as frightened as her co-star.

'It's because she's asphyxiating' Lori Scott said, keeping a cool head. 'Hey! Skylar? Try to match my breathing.' And she started puffing and blowing almost as if she was a birthing partner in a maternity ward, taking hold of her co-star's hand again and motioning for Natasha Redwood to do the same.

'Oh God! I think she's going to be sick!' Rather than following Lori Scott's shining example, Natasha Redwood instead leapt to her feet and stepped hastily backwards as Skylar Harrison's shallow breathing gave way to dry retching and heaving that made her entire body convulse.

Since I was kneeling right in front of her, I rather thought I might be the one to come off worst should this prove to be the case. But I didn't pull back. There remained a very real chance of her falling backwards and whacking her head if either Lori Scott or I should let go. She was still shaking violently even while she retched, sending tremors through me too.

Drew Trainer pulled Natasha Redwood away; much, I thought, to her relief. He took her place, squatting down and putting one muscled arm around the movie star's back, joining the effort to keep her from pitching over. 'Skylar, honey; try to take a deep breath or you're gonna choke. Try to mimic Lori.'

Ahmed now dropped to one knee beside me, as Adam and Mackenzie King strode forward and stood uncertainly, taking it in. Ahmed had seen enough. 'We must get her airwaves free.'

I could see what he meant as she continued that awful combination of retching, choking and heaving, her entire body wracked by spasms. She gasped for air, her pale face now suffused with riotous colour, eyes opening and closing but still seeming not to register her surroundings.

'How do we do that?' I asked in genuine panic, wishing I'd paid more attention in the First Aid training we'd once had at work in the long-ago days before my redundancy.

'Lay her flat!' Ahmed instructed urgently, starting to push Drew Trainer aside.

Behind the Hollywood heartthrob, Adam and Mackenzie King wore matching expressions of alarm.

'You plan to give her CPR?' Drew Trainer allowed Ahmed to take his place.

I looked at him blankly.

'Mouth to mouth resuscitation,' Adam supplied, reaching into his pocket for his mobile phone. 'I'll call for an ambulance.' Moments later he was speaking a few short sentences in Arabic into the mouthpiece, language skills coming to the fore in the extremity of the moment.

Skylar Harrison pushed Ahmed away. She started clutching at her stomach with one hand, the other clamped over her mouth as nausea gripped her. She was sweating profusely, beads of perspiration breaking out all over her flushed face. At the same time, she seemed to be shivering uncontrollably. I could feel her shaking through the palms of my hands still gripping her narrow shoulders.

As Ahmed lifted her bodily out of my grip ready to lay her out flat on the ground at our feet, she finally managed to suck in a deep breath. 'Skin's burning,' she rasped.

'An allergic reaction?' Adam asked quickly. 'Anaphylaxis?'

But Skylar Harrison was shaking her head. Whatever was wrong with her, it seemed she was able finally to tune into her surroundings and had heard him. Her blonde hair stuck damply to her cheeks and neck. With my hands now free of the urgent need to steady her, I reached into my pocket for a tissue as I saw a rivulet of perspiration trickle down her neck and into the hollow at the base of her throat between her collarbones, visible beneath her tee shirt and the cardigan she was wearing.

Ahmed set her carefully on the ground, pulling her out flat so she was lying on her back. I dropped down alongside her, dabbing at her perspiring face and neck with the tissue, while our police buddy readied himself to help unblock her airwaves.

But she immediately sat up, pushing us both away. 'Please! Just get me out of here! There's something terrible...!'

'What's she talking about?' Mackenzie King broke in sharply. 'Is she hallucinating, or what?'

Seemingly coming around now, it was certainly true that she looked to me to have been in something of a trance. Sweating and shaking and with that look of abject terror on her face I couldn't shift the feeling, crazy though it may sound that she'd seen something invisible to the rest of us.

'*Please*! I can't go in there,' Skylar Harrison begged, making me think perhaps my feeling wasn't quite so crazy after all. 'Don't make me go in!'

'Go in where?' the director asked, perplexed, looking over his shoulder at the huge open forecourt behind him where movie people were milling around the five big trailers in front of the gigantic temple pylon. They looked to be setting up lighting and other movie making paraphernalia, all too busy to have registered what was going on over here at the entrance gateway.

No longer looking in imminent danger of being sick as she stopped retching; Skylar Harrison pulled her hand away from her mouth and waved it around her. 'Away from *here!*' she cried, voice rising shrilly on the last word. '*Please*! I can't *breathe!*'

'Let's get her back to the parking lot,' Lori Scott suggested. With a quick glance at Ahmed to see if he would stop her, she reached forward, tugging at Skylar Harrison's arms to pull her up from the ground. 'Something here is freaking her out. My guess is she's having a panic attack.'

Ahmed stepped back. Impossible to say if he was relieved or disappointed to be robbed of the need to perform mouth-to-mouth resuscitation on one of the world's most famous women. I got up too, swiping at the dust on my knees and thinking a panic attack did indeed seem to be the logical explanation. I'd heard of actors so traumatised by the prospect of going on set they were paralysed with fear; physically sick and crippled with anxiety.

Maybe she'd caught sight of the trailers, the camera and the lighting in the same way I had and been overcome by an extreme case of the jitters. I recalled that I'd likened her to Marilyn Monroe once already in her ability to morph from someone attractive-but-unremarkable into an out-and-out bombshell. Now I wondered if the comparison ran deeper. I'd heard that Marilyn suffered extreme and debilitating anxiety before filming; a condition that often meant she turned up hours late on set and drove her co-stars nuts.

But it was strange that Skylar Harrison had seemed perfectly fine on the way over here. But then I'm no expert on panic attacks. Perhaps it really had been the sight of all the movie equipment being set up that had freaked her out.

There was a coffee shop across the road immediately outside the temple precinct, just opening its shutters for the day. By silent mutual consent we made for it. Once we had her back on her feet, Drew Trainer scooped Skylar Harrison up into his arms as if she were no more than a child and followed Ahmed as our police pal led the way, retracing our earlier steps.

'The ambulance is on its way,' Adam announced.

The further away from the temple we all went the noticeably calmer Skylar Harrison became. Her breathing returned to normal, her skin settled back to its more natural hue and that awful expression of abject horror left her face.

'Somebody, get her some water,' Mackenzie King ordered as Ahmed strode into the coffee shop and pulled out a wooden bench covered in woven cotton throws so Drew Trainer could ease her down.

Ahmed barked out a few short sentences in Arabic to the scruffy young waiter who approached. The boy stared at us with eyes round like saucers, no doubt recognising at least one or two of his first customers of the day. He scuttled off and returned with a big bottle of water along with a basket of bread. Skylar Harrison appeared to recover herself, absent-mindedly brushing the dust off her clothes.

'Honey; what was that all about?' Drew Trainer asked her gently as she accepted the water with a brief smile of thanks at the goggle-eyed waiter.

I was interested to see how the movie star might describe what Lori Scott had called her panic attack, and what I felt sure must be the result of acute stage fright. So, I was surprised and taken aback by her response.

'That place reeks of death,' she said with an involuntary shudder. 'Something terrible happened there.'

'What the hell is she talking about?' Mackenzie King addressed himself sharply to Ahmed. 'Officer; has there been a homicide around here lately?'

Ahmed looked thoroughly bewildered, as well he might. His eyes bulged and he opened and closed his mouth a couple of times in a fair imitation of a fish. 'Er – I – er – no – I – er – I don't think so, sir. I mean; not that I know about. Although I am the tourism and antiquities police, so –'

I'm sure he would have liked to say more, but the movie director cut him off with a goaded gesture. 'Anyone who is capable of making sense, can you please tell me what the hell has got Skylar all worked up like this?'

At my elbow, Adam cleared his throat. 'Well –' he started. 'I hesitate to say this for fear of sounding ridiculous... But, strictly speaking, the answer is yes.'

All gazes swung in his direction, giving him no choice but to continue, ridiculous or not.

'A homicide, that is to say, a murder, did take place here; as far as we know at almost exactly the spot where Miss Harrison had her – er – her –' He trailed off, sending a discomfited look at the movie star, clearly not wishing to offend her by mislabelling whatever had afflicted her. I have to say; he looked very handsome with that bashful look on his face.

'I still think it was a panic attack,' Lori Scott came to his rescue. She'd plopped herself down onto the mat-topped bench alongside Skylar Harrison and was once again rubbing her co-star's back in small soothing strokes. The rest of us stood around, waiting for Adam's explanation. Although, speaking for myself, I had some inkling of what was coming.

Adam nodded gratefully and tried again. 'A murder did take place at Medinet Habu.' He paused for a moment as if gathering the courage to go on. Then added, rather thrillingly I thought. 'But it was approximately three thousand years ago.'

That got everyone's full attention. Startled and sceptical glances were exchanged. I nodded, knowing for definite now what he was about to say. Although I couldn't be at all sure how the others would react to it. They all continued to stare at him with various degrees of perplexity.

'It was the killing of the pharaoh,' he went on levelly. 'Ramses III.'

'Ramses III was murdered?' Drew Trainer cut in sharply.

'Slaughtered.' Adam stated unequivocally. 'He had his throat cut.'

But I was robbed of the chance to see how this grisly statement landed on Adam's assorted audience.

'Yes!' Skylar Harrison said in a throbbing sort of croak, pulling everyone's attention back to her face. 'I saw it!'

It was clear nobody, not even me, knew what to make of this surprising pronouncement. Glances were exchanged with varying expressions of confusion, bewilderment and concern.

But none of those quite described the look on the face of Mackenzie King. It rather reminded me of a thundercloud about to burst. 'Are you crazy?' he demanded shortly and, in my view, rudely. 'How could you possibly *see* a murder that took place three millennia ago?'

'I don't know,' she whispered in a small, frightened voice, sounding nothing at all like herself. 'I'm not sure that I *saw* it exactly –'

67

'But you just said –' he was clearly losing patience.

Drew Trainer intervened, sending the director a warning glance.

'Honey; while we're waiting for the ambulance crew to get here and check you over, why don't you tell us exactly what happened?' he suggested gently, leaning forward and squeezing her shoulder as if to put some strength into her.

She shuddered and took a long swallow of the bottled water Lori Scott had poured into a glass for her. She'd returned to something approaching her normal colour, but her skin looked mottled and her eyes, though capable now of focusing on her surroundings, still held a faraway look. She looked haunted, arrestingly lovely but somehow not quite *with* us, even now.

'It was as we went through that towering stone gateway-type structure,' she said haltingly. 'I was gripped by the most appalling terror. I felt as if I'd smacked face-first into a wall of anger and hatred. I was unable to take another step. I swear I saw the flash on an axe ripping through the air, literally right in front of me. And there was a knife! A long, ugly-looking knife, razor sharp! Then a slicing motion from behind. And blood! Blood everywhere. The choking, bubbling, hot, metallic stench of blood.'

It was quite a speech and we all stared at her.

Mackenzie King was first to gather his wits. 'For the love of Jesus!' his temper fired on all cylinders and exploded. Not so much a thundercloud as a volcano erupting. 'What in God's name is going on here?!? Am I really supposed to believe that one of my leading actors is seeing visions of a regicide that supposedly took place here a thousand years before the birth of Christ?!?' Nobody dared respond for fear of getting caught in the hail and brimstone. Looking thoroughly disgusted, he went on. 'And as if one deadly weapon wasn't enough to kill a king, it appears that both an axe *and* a knife were needed to slit the pharaoh's throat? Do you take me for a fool? What is this? Some sort of warped attempt to sabotage filming because you weren't my first choice?'

'No! But I – ' Skylar Harrison started to protest but trailed off. Perhaps there was no explanation that would make sense, even to her.

We all looked at our feet for a while. In my case I was mentally filing away the director's last remark since now was clearly not the time to pursue it. Although, I have to say, it surprised me. I'd rather thought it was Lori Scott who might be here on a wish and a prayer.

It was Adam, finally, who garnered the courage to look up, bravely meet the director's eyes and say quietly, 'It's believed the pharaoh was attacked by multiple assailants using assorted weapons. The assassins used the knife to cut his throat. Studies on Ramses III's preserved mummy show the axe most likely severed one of his big toes.'

This rather gruesome series of statements drew all gazes to his face once more.

'The pharaoh's mummy survived?' Natasha Redwood asked in some surprise.

'Yes,' Adam nodded. 'Ahmed's ancestors' – with a nod at our police buddy – 'found it in a mummy cache dating from the 18th, 19th and 20th Dynasties. These had been re-buried in the hills behind the Valley of the Kings towards the end of the New Kingdom; probably an attempt by priests to preserve the royal remains of those who ruled through Egypt's mightiest period as law and order broke down. All the A'listers were there. Nowadays they're on display in the Cairo Museum.'

'Wow!' Natasha Redwood said.

Speaking with calm and understated authority, my husband returned from this small diversion and continued, addressing himself directly to Mackenzie King. 'To give you chapter and verse: CT scans taken a few years ago on the king's mummy revealed a gash in his lower neck. It extends through the cervical vertebrae, causing a slash in the soft tissues of the neck deep enough to reach the bone. The injury was most certainly fatal. The embalmers placed a *Wadjet*-eye amulet in the wound, perhaps to magically "heal" it.' He made speech marks with his fingers around the word. Then his gaze moved from the director's face to graze each of our own before he returned it to focus on Mackenzie King's frowning and somewhat frozen countenance. 'The same study identified an additional injury inflicted around the time of death. It was the partial amputation of the left big toe by a sharp blade, consistent with an axe. At least four more *Wadjet*-eye amulets were placed within the wrappings of the feet. *Wadjet* being the cobra goddess and protector of royalty,' he finished quietly.

A profound silence greeted this speech. It's fair to say I have always found my husband's ability to retain, recall and regurgitate information quite remarkable. At first it was a source of wonder. Now it was one of pride. Adam knew his stuff. And it had the desired effect. Mackenzie King visibly deflated as if a pin had been stuck in him, popping the anger. He slumped down on the edge of the bench Skylar Harrison and Lori Scott were already sitting on and reached for the bottle of water and a glass.

'Maybe Skylar is not so crazy after all,' Lori Scott said blandly, looking sideways at the director from under her lashes.

The subject of her words sat silent and trembling on the bench alongside her. Not crazy, perhaps; but certainly in shock, and seemingly disinclined to elucidate further on what she had supposedly '*seen*'.

Possibly taking pity on her while she attempted to recover her wits, Drew Trainer shot a warning glance at the director and scratched his chin. Rather than demanding more of an explanation, he proved himself sensitive enough to give her a moment; instead opting to pursue the line of enquiry Adam had opened up. 'But the pharaohs of Egypt surely had almost godlike stature and status,' he frowned, addressing my husband. 'Weren't they seen as semi-divine by their people?' It was a rhetorical question, and he carried on without waiting for an affirmation. 'And I thought the ancient Egyptians were a load of religion freaks! All that stuff about the pantheon of animal-headed gods and goddesses, and the weighing of the heart ceremony when they died, to see if they had lived a pure and blameless life and could enter the glorious afterlife without the fear of their heart being thrown to that hideous dog-like devourer creature.' Our leading man proving once again that he'd boned up on the subject, I thought. Although it was clear the murder of Ramses III was a chapter in Egypt's long history about which he was ignorant. He frowned again and shook his head. 'It was surely a pretty big deal to set about assassinating the divinely anointed king – a man who by his position was in the full protective custody of the gods. Those guys were surely taking one hell of a risk.'

Adam sent an apologetic glance Skylar Harrison's way in case his next words should prove insensitive. 'The pharaoh was attacked within the walls of his palace harem,' he said without intonation.

This provoked no reaction from Skylar Harrison beyond her shutting her eyes. It was Lori Scott who gasped. 'His *harem*?' she repeated. 'You mean, the place he went to pleasure himself with his concubines?'

Since Skylar Harrison seemed ok for the moment and disinclined to say more, I decided it was time to join in and share a little knowledge of my own. Not in Adam's league, I nevertheless knew a bit about the grim history of the temple of Medinet Habu. 'Yes,' I confirmed. 'The Eastern Gateway through which visitors gain access to the temple forecourt today and where – er – where Miss Harrison had her unfortunate – er – panic attack,' I added haltingly, casting a quick look at her still sitting on the bench with her eyes closed, 'is believed by archaeologists to be the site of the pharaoh's harem. It seems likely we were on the very spot where the killing took place. Or certainly close to it,' I qualified. 'The walls in the upper storeys are still carved with scenes of the pharaoh at leisure and being entertained by the women who lived there.'

'Now those wall reliefs I would *really* like to see,' Drew Trainer put in lasciviously.

Adam smiled at the innuendo. 'I'm afraid there's nothing to rival the Karma Sutra,' he said dampeningly. 'It's all very tame by comparison. The meaning of the word *"harem"* has become distorted over time, despite all that it implies to us today. In ancient Egypt, as in the rest of the Middle East, what was meant by *"harem"* was most probably a designation for the site of the women's residence. It likely housed the quarters of the queen, the king's secondary and lesser wives as well as the royal daughters and younger children. But, yes, the pharaoh's concubines lived there too. And it seems very likely he went there for his sexual pleasure as well as to relax, which is perhaps how it has come down to us with all its modern connotations.'

Skylar Harrison opened her eyes but made no attempt to speak. It was Lori Scott, once again, who interjected. 'Wait a minute. Wait a minute.' The tiger-eyed actor reached out and placed her hand on Adam's sleeve. 'Are you saying what I think you're saying?'

Adam smiled at her. 'I guess that depends in what you think I'm saying.'

'That this pharaoh ... this Ramses III ... was murdered by *women*? *Women from his own household*? The women of his own *harem*?' It has to be said; she sounded quite impressed. Our clearly feminist Lori Scott cheering from the side-lines.

Adam's smile widened. I had a suspicion he was quite enjoying himself, lecturing like this to an avid audience including three of the most beautiful female actors in the world since they were all, even Skylar Harrison now, hanging on his every word. I decided I couldn't blame him and was perfectly willing to let him get on with it. Besides, I discovered I was quite enjoying myself too. There's nothing quite like an Egyptological discussion first thing in the morning to sharpen the senses and set oneself up for the day. I had no idea yet what the logical explanation for Skylar Harrison's strange behaviour would turn out to be. That there would prove to be one, I had no doubt. So, I pulled out another bench and sat down, quite content to listen as he responded. 'Well, there's abundant evidence that the women of the harem enlisted help from a bunch of male associates, whom I imagine may actually have wielded the knife and the axe,' he said. 'But essentially, yes. The women of the harem were the ones to incite the revolt. The whole saga is known historically as the "Harem Conspiracy". You can look it up on Google or Wikipedia. Entire books have been written about it.'

'But what on earth did they hope to gain?' Drew Trainer cut in again. 'Surely the ladies of the pharaoh's harem lived a life of luxury and leisure. Didn't they spend their days eating bunches of grapes while eunuchs fanned them with ostrich feathers?'

Adam smiled and shrugged. 'That sounds like a Hollywood take on it,' he said mildly. 'There's textual evidence going right back to the Old Kingdom that the pharaoh's harem was often a hotbed of treachery and intrigue. Perhaps with good reason. A good literal translation of the ancient words for pharaoh's harem is "the place of seclusion" of "the hidden ones". Interestingly, the same words were used to denote prison and prisoner. The physical separation of these women from the public and the rest of the court is supported by archaeological evidence.'

'You're saying they were forcibly segregated?' Lori Scott asked.

'Yes,' Adam nodded. 'No matter how well provided for and protected by their status within the royal household, make no mistake. These women were the absolute property of the pharaoh, and with little or no freedom. Tomb reliefs show doorkeepers on duty at harem apartments. And the textual record makes it clear the women were rigorously guarded.'

'Just as I said last night!' Lori Scott said with satisfaction. 'Those women were exploited!'

'It stands to reason,' Natasha Redwood put in unexpectedly. It seemed the morning's events were sparking more Egyptological interest in her. 'The pharaoh surely would have wanted an absolute guarantee that any children born were his.'

Adam nodded. 'While there is no evidence of mistreatment, some scholars have commented that harems were a particularly benign form of slavery,' he said. 'On a sobering note, when excavators cleared the gate area where Miss Harrison was – er – taken unwell – they found evidence that the main entrances to the harem quarters had doors that bolted by means of cords and metal fastenings –' he paused a moment for effect '– on the outside.'

'The outside,' Lori Scott repeated. 'Oh boy! They were locked in!'

'I think we can see why some ancient texts describe the royal harem as a potential powder keg.' Adam said.

'But how the hell did they think they'd get away with it?' Drew Trainer frowned. 'Wouldn't the pharaoh have had bodyguards? Round-the-clock protection?'

'Perhaps not while he was entertaining himself in the harem,' Lori Scott said lewdly and with a meaningful lift of one eyebrow.

'I guess it would depend on who was in on the plot,' Adam answered the question at face value. 'There's evidence the conspiracy extended throughout the ranks of the royal household, involving some of those closest to the pharaoh.'

There was no doubt about it. The conversation had every one of us interested, for all that it was the very last thing I might have expected to spend the morning discussing. Ah well, they had decided to film their movie here, so they might as well learn something of the history of their on-location shoot.

'But why?' Drew Trainer persisted. 'Why would they want the pharaoh dead?'

'The primary motive for murder appears to have been the succession,' Adam said. 'Rivalry between the queens for which of their sons should succeed to the throne once Ramses III was dead.' He went on to explain: 'The position of King's Mother was one of the most revered and powerful roles in the land.'

'One of the pharaoh's *wives* had him killed?' Lori Scott gaped.

'Yes,' he nodded. 'It appears one of Ramses III's lesser queens led the coup d'état to assassinate her husband, no doubt seeking to further her own status and power by securing the kingship for her son.'

A strangled gasp from Skylar Harrison, who had been listening intently and in silence, cut him off. 'Yes! I *know* this!' she exclaimed, squeezing her eyes tight shut and holding her breath. She let it out a moment later in a rush of air. 'Except I don't think you're right that it was one of his lesser queens.'

Adam opened his mouth, no doubt to pursue this cryptic remark, but Mackenzie King cut him off.

'What, in God's name, do you mean?' The director had held his tongue while Adam had been lecturing, mutely taking it all in. Now he frowned at Skylar Harrison. But, despite his choice of words, there was no longer heat in his voice. He sounded more alarmed than impatient. 'How can you possibly *know* this? When you auditioned, you told me you didn't know a fig about ancient Egyptian history!'

'I don't,' she said with a soft sort of whimper, looking frightened again and sounding just about as confused and concerned as he was. 'But as Adam was talking I could just sort of *see* it. I've just kinda got a sense of *knowing* about it. It's almost as if I was *there* when it happened.' Her eyes were wide, and the anxiety was back in them.

'How is that possible?' Mackenzie King asked in exasperation, looking at the rest of us for an answer.

There was no explanation I, or any of the others could think of if the silence was anything to judge by. I remembered her saying yesterday afternoon that this was her first trip to Egypt, so it seemed doubtful she'd picked up her *knowledge* from a local tour guide on a previous visit. Thankfully an ambulance siren cut through the air, finally announcing its arrival having driven over the bridge from the east bank. Skylar Harrison hung her head. 'I don't know,' she said miserably.

Drew Trainer had evidently been turning the question over inside his head. 'Honey; is there by any chance any history of clairvoyance in your family?' he asked her gently.

She looked up at him and her blue eyes blazed. 'Yes! My grandmother on my mother's side! She used to read people's palms at the circus! She had what she called "the sight"!'

Staring fixedly at her, Mackenzie King's expression suddenly transformed from aggravation to something closer to sentience, as if an idea had struck him. I couldn't decide whether he was looking at her rather as if she'd just grown horns, a spiked tail and was covered in red scales, or as if she'd sprouted wings, a shining halo and was dressed in golden robes. As a local ambulance crew jumped out of their wagon outside and exchanged a rapid sentence or two in Arabic with Ahmed who had gone to greet them, I kept my gaze fixed on Mackenzie King as he dropped his head forward into his hands and sat there shaking it slowly from side to side.

'So, we have the violent murder of a pharaoh by one of his queens supported by the women of his harem and other co-conspirators, probably trusted members of his royal household. And we have a Hollywood actor who either has second sight or seems somehow to have been there at the time to witness it!'

He sat up abruptly and addressed the room as a whole. 'Godammit! I'm directing the wrong movie! You can forget about Ramses the Great and Helen of Troy! The whole world knows their story thanks to the global media. But a Harem Conspiracy to assassinate the king while he's pleasuring himself in his palace, with a knife and an axe no less! Nothing so subtle as snakebite or poison in his food! Now there's a story! So, answer me this…! Where the hell is a good script writer when you need one?'

Chapter 6

Neither of the two male medics who jumped from the ambulance and attended to Skylar Harrison spoke a word of English. Even so, it was obvious they knew exactly whom they were treating. Throughout the various medical checks they performed right there in front of us in the coffee shop, their gazes kept swinging around our gathered assemblage. And one of them had a definite case of the shakes. The poor young man's hands were trembling so badly it took him three attempts to put his stethoscope against Skylar Harrison's chest as she helpfully pulled down the loose collar of her tee shirt to grant him access to a patch of bare skin.

Ahmed kept up an enthusiastic running commentary in voluble Arabic, relishing the opportunity to play up his own connection to this drama amongst such exalted company and to act as interpreter when required. It's possible Adam understood much of what he was saying if his occasional raised eyebrows were anything to go by. No doubt things were being exaggerated beyond all proportion. Although, it must be said, given what had transpired, this was hardly necessary.

Mackenzie King observed proceedings balefully. He'd retreated once again into the same rather distant and distracted silence that had characterised him at dinner last night. I couldn't help but wonder if he'd been serious in his recent pronouncement and was indeed wondering if it was too late to upend the movie he'd been here to make and tell a different story.

The rest of us stood around, accepting the hot, sweet coffee the scruffy young waiter brought across to us. He made no attempt to mask his own far from surreptitious glances at the Hollywooders. I observed this with some mild amusement, allowing myself a small mental pat on the back that within the space of less than twenty-four hours I'd swung from being starstruck and dazzled to taking the company of Tinseltown royalty completely in my stride. I sipped the hot treacly coffee, buttering and then nibbling on one of the fresh bread rolls.

Skylar Harrison submitted with good grace to having her heart rate monitored, a temperature gauge stuck in her ear, and lights shone into each of her eyes in turn. But she refused absolutely to accompany the medics back into their ambulance and return with them to the hospital.

'I feel fine now, Mac.' She addressed herself to the director firmly.

'But that was one helluva turn, honey,' Drew Trainer interjected, looking doubtful. 'Don't you think it would be better to get fully checked over in hospital, just to be sure?'

'I get that you all think I'm crazy,' she said a trifle defensively, flicking her blonde hair over her shoulder and looking determined. 'But now I have an explanation for what happened back there – no matter how weird an explanation it might be – I feel kinda better about it.'

It wasn't the kind of explanation that would have made *me* feel any better, but I thought it best not to say so.

'Better enough to have another go at visiting the temple?' Mackenzie King addressed her sharply, looking up from an intent contemplation of the dust on his shoes. 'Medinet Habu is one of our key locations. We can hardly shoot around it.'

80

I sensed a challenge in this, reminded of his earlier remark about her not being his first choice. I thought maybe Skylar Harrison recognised it as one too as she sat up straighter.

'If I can just get to my trailer and rest up a bit, I should think I'll be ok,' she said. 'I want to make a start on the movie just as much as you do. I guess I just need time to come to terms with what happened, that's all.' She looked around at us and squared her shoulders, visibly stiffening her spine, her chin jutting forward. 'I don't suppose there's anything there that can actually hurt me. I think before it was just the shock of suddenly *"seeing"* and *"feeling"* – well, more like *"sensing"* things,' she amended, wrinkling her nose as she groped for the right word, 'that filled me with such terror. And, who knows? Now I know that what I experienced was rooted in something that actually happened here, no matter how long ago, maybe I'll see some more and get a better understanding of what it was all about.'

Even while we all stared at her with varying degrees of consternation, I felt a small knot of respect for her starting to form. While I felt sure there would prove to be a more rational explanation; in the absence of one for now, she seemed determined to make a good fist of things. It couldn't be easy to suddenly confront the possibility of having what some might call psychic or maybe even supernatural powers, and in public too. But she seemed willing to meet it head on.

I wasn't at all sure I believed in ghosts or the paranormal. Had always eschewed tarot cards, Ouija boards and the reading of palms. And scoffed at the occult. But given the evidence of my own eyes and ears this morning it was hard to conclude other than that Skylar Harrison was gifted, or perhaps (given what I'd witnessed) a more apposite word would be *cursed*, with clairvoyance, if such a thing could truly be said to exist. I don't mind admitting I was quite eager to see if there would be any repeat performance should she re-attempt to walk through the Eastern High Gate at Medinet Habu.

'I am *not* going to the hospital,' she said emphatically. And that was that.

The medics insisted on giving her a shot of Serotonin before departing. Accepting that, whatever its cause, a panic attack seemed the most likely diagnosis of her symptoms; this treatment would apparently reduce further anxiety. The young medic with the shaking hands even bucked up the courage before he and his colleague packed up their equipment and left to ask for a *selfie* with her. A little flurry of celebrity madness ensued. Skylar Harrison, Natasha Redwood, Lori Scott and Drew Trainer were each prevailed upon to sign their names on paper napkins and smile into the cameras of the mobile phones the ambulance crew whipped from their pockets and waved in their faces. So much for medical professionalism, I thought with a wry smile. No doubt the medics would dine out on this for months. Mackenzie King was spared, since they didn't seem to know who he was, and he was evidently disinclined to enlighten them. He observed the (no doubt familiar) rigmarole with barely concealed impatience, looking pointedly at his watch and then barked, 'Enough!' at poor Ahmed, who was given the task of sending the excitable ambulance crew packing.

The full heat of the day hit us as we emerged from the fan-cooled interior of the coffee shop into the blazing sunshine outside.

'Take two,' Adam murmured to me under his breath, taking my hand loosely as we walked through the wooden security kiosk and approached the tall *Migdol*-like stone gateway leading to the temple precinct.

Mackenzie King strode ahead; clearly of a mind to snatch whatever productivity he could from the jaws of a so-far wasted morning. Ahmed, as before, brought up the rear. Ahead of Adam and me, Skylar Harrison walked forward with her head up, bolstered between Drew Trainer and Lori Scott, each linking arms with her. Natasha Redwood strolled along on the other side of Drew Trainer, pausing to observe the black granite statues of Sekhmet (the lion-headed goddess of war) that lined the approach to the Eastern High Gate. Once site of the harem belonging to Ramses III, I reminded myself; trying to imagine it.

I looked up at this tall structure as we approached. It was bathed in the golden glow of the morning sun now fully risen in the sky on the east bank behind us. It was an imposing, partially ruined, square-based structure formed of two inter-connected towers constructed of large rectangular-cut sandstone blocks, somewhat reminiscent of a medieval fortress. Huge raised-relief images of the pharaoh were clearly visible carved onto these stones on both sides of the entranceway. Each chiselled image of the man towered about two storeys high. Since the Gateway was originally a three-storey building (its upper storey now largely destroyed, its roof gone), this was clearly pharaoh announcing himself in all his majesty, power and might. In each relief, imposing mirror images of one another carved on either side of the entrance, his outer arm was raised in the act of smiting an enemy. This was an enduringly popular image from pharaonic iconography. It left one in little doubt who was boss, or what would happen should a foe of Egypt dare to transgress.

I wondered a bit at the need for this in what seemed once to have served as part of the king's private lodging, decorated on its interior walls with scenes of the pharaoh at leisure. But then recalled Adam's words about the cloistered and heavily guarded environs where the king's women once lived their lives. Perhaps Pharaoh felt the need to proclaim himself to any brave or reckless suitors who might dare to take a fancy to one of the inmates.

I spared a thought for the women who had called this building home all those millennia ago. I knew enough to know that the temple forecourt, now almost devoid of features, would once have been a beautiful garden. Back then, Ramses III's Theban palace had then been connected to the temple. The entire complex would have been surrounded by vineyards and orchards stretching back to the Nile and intersected by canals. As Drew Trainer had said, no doubt the ladies of the harem had lived in the lap of late Bronze Age luxury. I tried to visualise them looking out from their windows over the grounds and buildings of the temple complex or towards the mighty river. Looking up, I thought the positioning of those windows must also have provided a nice cross breeze essential for cooling the rooms in the torrid afternoons of the Theban summer. Even so, it wasn't difficult to imagine a mix of boredom, seclusion and semi-imprisonment may have served as a toxic breeding ground for resentment, jealousy and intrigue. And here, this hotbed incited a successful conspiracy to assassinate the pharaoh. Literally! Right here!

Looking at the ruins of this ancient construction, I felt I could almost start to picture it and sense the long-dead personalities stirring. But my vivid imagination wasn't the same thing at all as the gift – or curse – of second sight. I don't mind admitting I started watching Skylar Harrison very closely as we approached the spot of her earlier trauma. This time, there was no chance I would cannon into her should she happen to stop dead in her tracks right in front of me. Still unwilling to put down what I'd witnessed to the paranormal, I decided I may as well allow myself to be entertained by the whole thing. This was Hollywood, after all!

Walking between Drew Trainer and Lori Scott, she slowed and stopped. I moved so I could see her face. She stood there motionless for a long moment, eyes screwed shut, breathing deeply. I watched the rise and fall of her chest beneath her tee shirt. Saw the colour drain from her cheeks. Observed her press her lips tightly together and then exhale a long shuddery breath, as her reed-like body seemed to quake.

I thought, had only the cameras been rolling, what a very convincing performance it was. I'd swear she was seeing something playing out behind those closed eyelids, like a movie screening inside her head.

Mackenzie King turned back but didn't speak. Bizarre though it may sound, and whether any of us would have admitted to a belief in extra sensory perception – genuine or not – I think we all recognised we needed to allow her this moment. Speaking for myself, I was watching her avidly and waiting with bated breath to see what may happen next.

Thankfully, there was no repeat of the fully-fledged panic attack.

After a long moment her breathing seemed to regulate. A more natural colour returned to her pale cheeks. She ran the tip of her tongue across her lips to moisten them. Opened her eyes. Looked directly at Adam.

'It was a trap,' she said.

I blinked once or twice at this, looking back at her and trying to discern exactly what she meant, whether an Oscar-worthy performance or something I should take seriously.

'Er – yes,' Adam agreed slowly standing alongside me, also groping for her meaning. 'A trap laid by the conspirators to lure the pharaoh here to the harem so they could catch him unawares, with his guard down, and murder him.'

She shook her head slightly as if clearing it of a vision. 'No. That's not it. It was the conspirators who walked into a trap. But the pharaoh was killed just the same.'

'But – I – er –' Adam started, frowning with confusion.

Skylar Harrison swayed suddenly and put the back of her hand up to her forehead in a dramatic gesture. Drew Trainer caught her as it looked as if she might fall. Oh dear, I thought. Was that just the slightest touch of melodrama too far? She'd had me daring to be convinced until that point.

'Now I need to lie down,' she said weakly. 'I have a splitting headache. Will someone please just take me to my trailer?'

Mackenzie King took charge. He determined the rest of the day would be spent doing sound checks and a series of costume stills to test for camera angles and lighting. Once published, these could also serve as publicity shots to whet the public appetite for the forthcoming release.

I figured this meant he had decided to press ahead with Plan A and make the movie he'd signed up for.

He ordered both Skylar Harrison and Natasha Redwood to their trailers. Their personal assistants and stylists were waiting for them there ready to perform whatever transformation Hollywood producers demanded to turn them into legendary figures from ancient history.

'You go first, Natasha,' he said. 'Let's see how long it takes to turn you into Nefertari. Skylar, you rest up a bit and have something to eat. I'm not sure anyone will believe in you as *the face that launched a thousand ships* with those dark circles under your eyes!'

Whilst a bit bluntly put, I thought, this was certainly true. Skylar Harrison looked somewhat as if a vampire had been feasting on her. I could well imagine she was shaken and exhausted. Trying to put aside the sceptic in me, I could see it had been quite a day for her already. Still not completely willing to take everything I had seen at face value; I could only hope her assistant was a skilled makeup artist.

Drew Trainer, who would need far less time to metamorphose into Ramses the Great, and Lori Scott, whose role in the movie was still far from clear to me, were left at a loose end.

'How 'bout that aborted tour of the temple?' Drew Trainer urged Adam, shrugging out of the lightweight jacket he'd been wearing against the chill of our pre-dawn start. He tossed it to a young man from the movie-making entourage who ran forward. I recognised him as Michael, the chap who had delivered their scanty luggage to the *Queen Ahmes* yesterday. Drew Trainer gave him a brief smile of thanks then turned back to Adam. 'Forget Ramses the Great! This morning's little pantomime has sure got me hooked on learning more about Ramses III.'

With nothing better to do than kick my heels waiting to see the female actors in full costume and make-up, I was more than willing to trail along. Ahmed wandered off to speak to his buddies back at the security gate. It was a dead cert that word was already out that the movie stars were here at Medinet Habu temple; thanks, I felt sure, to the combined efforts of the ambulance crew and coffee shop waiters. I'd hazard a pretty shrewd guess that Ahmed's assignment: first line of defence against fans, groupies and opportunistic happy snappers may get underway earlier than he might have imagined.

So, we toured the temple, the best-preserved of those built in the New Kingdom, otherwise known as the Empire-period of Egypt's mighty past. A huge, magnificent edifice, still with some original colour intact at the top of columns and in the shady porticoes where the bleaching effects of the sun could not penetrate; every inch was covered with painted reliefs and carvings detailing the pharaoh's exploits. I imagined the riot of colour these walls had contained when first built. The whole place must have been overwhelming.

'Ramses III doesn't come across as a man who lacked for an ego,' Lori Scott remarked drily after Adam had pointed out the scenes of the last great warrior pharaoh's military campaigns against Libyans, Syrians, Nubians and the confederation of *Sea Peoples* plastered across the towering walls. We'd contemplated scenes of pharaoh depicted four times the size of anyone else, driving his chariot mercilessly into battle or firing an enormous bow and arrow against fleeing foes. Then frowned at grisly depictions of the counting and presentation to the king of mountains of severed hands and the lopped-off penises of the slain enemy. And gazed at carvings of the pharaoh's sons lined up in two rows making offerings to their father as if he were a god. And further scenes of the king carried on a palanquin high on the shoulders of his sons and other dignitaries. Now, we were standing shading our eyes against the glare of the sun in the middle of the first huge courtyard. It was lined on one side with immense standing statues of the pharaoh set against squared pillars, on the other with columns.

Adam squinted at Lori Scott from beneath his hand cupped over his eyes and nodded. 'It's true,' he said. 'Looking around, his smug self-satisfaction is undeniable, isn't it? But what you must realise is this: Ramses grew up destined for kingship. As the son of a pharaoh, he believed in his own supremacy. His numerous bombastic speeches inscribed here on the walls of his mortuary temple,' – gesturing around us – 'tell us so. And he appears to have had a predilection for assembling his court here in the open to regale them with the wonder that was Pharaoh! He probably spoke to them from the Window of Appearances over there…' He nodded to a gap in the boundary wall of the temple between the columns. '…Since that's the entrance to what was once the palace that adjoined the temple.'

'Surely he was no different in what you describe from any one of the great pharaohs who came before him,' Drew Trainer challenged, looking at the doorway where Adam was pointing. 'I get the impression they were all a bunch of egomaniacs who revelled in their godlike status. He was surely just doing what was expected. Living up to the job description.'

'True.' Adam conceded. 'Let's face it, he modelled himself on the character you're here to play: Ramses the Great, the most egomaniacal of them all. And Ramses III arguably had more cause to boast even than him. His defeat of the multiple forces that threatened Egypt was absolute. It established him as a strong and fearless ruler. He could brag that he'd single-handedly restored peace and secured the boundaries of Egypt at a time when most of the other great empires of the Mediterranean and Middle East were falling. These reliefs reflect a dynamic and illustrious career. Ramses remained at the pinnacle of power throughout his thirty-odd-year reign.'

Lori Scott pulled off her sunglasses and shoved them into her shoulder bag, squinting at Adam from under the peak of her baseball hat. 'But surely a beloved and benevolent ruler is not assassinated by those close to him without good reason,' she argued.

'Whoever said anything about beloved and benevolent?' Adam queried mildly, moving us all into the shade cast by the gigantic entrance pylon. 'There are signs of discontent and decline strewn throughout the surviving records of his reign if you look, although perhaps not immediately evident here in the temple he used to personally proclaim his majesty. But, believe me, there were cracks. And they were beginning to show.'

'What sort of cracks?' she asked interestedly.

'Years of war took their toll,' Adam said with a shrug. 'No amount of bravado could mask the true state of the economy. Fighting off the invasion of the Sea Peoples crippled Egypt financially. And the Libyan wars ravaged the Delta, Egypt's breadbasket. The result was rampant inflation. Fifteen years after the last war, Egypt was in a deplorable condition. A scarcity of grain left many of its granaries empty. Remember, the workers were paid in grain.'

'Yes,' I piped up, feeling I was overdue my turn to contribute to the discussion. 'And I've read about several years of failed harvests towards the end of Ramses III's reign. There's talk in the ancient texts of a strange darkness in the sky. Apparently, it blotted out the sun for almost two whole decades, if you can believe it!' I didn't add that I'd picked up these pearls of wisdom from a particularly engaging series of historical novels that had prompted me to look it all up on Wikipedia. 'Some modern scholars think those years may have coincided with the massive eruption of a gigantic Icelandic volcano. Apparently, it changed weather systems across the globe. So, a combination of war-ravaged finances and year after year of failed crops would have brought the economy to its knees.'

'Hekla 3,' Adam named the volcano from his cavernous memory banks. 'What you say is true,' he concurred, not questioning how I had come by the knowledge. 'And the ordinary people bore the brunt. Oh, and here's a fascinating fact for you: the king's repeated failure to pay the workers their rations led to the first recorded labour strike in history.'

'Wow!' Drew Trainer exclaimed. 'They refused to work? You don't imagine that could be possible in ancient Egypt! Land of slaves and conscripts.'

'There were no slaves in Egypt,' Lori Scott corrected him. 'That's another fiction created in Hollywood.'

In this, to the best of my knowledge, she was perfectly correct. I realised what a pleasure it was spending time with people whose interest in the ancient Egyptian history I loved so much was genuine. This was not what I had expected of the Hollywooders at all. So, I could only be thankful for it.

'The strike happened in year twenty-nine of Ramses III's almost thirty-two-year reign,' Adam said. 'The elite royal tomb builders and artisans from the village we now call Deir el-Medina downed tools and refused point blank to return to work until they were paid. Apparently, it was the first in a series of strikes and minor insurgencies.'

'You have to wonder how they felt observing the pharaoh and his entourage living in the lap of luxury here in the temple and palace, within walking distance of their village.' I mused aloud.

Adam nodded. 'Surviving documents suggest the pharaoh had a lavish lifestyle. He boasted of the riches in his palace in Thebes, with tableware of fine gold, silver and copper, and of a multitude of foodstuffs such as fatted geese and oxen offered daily to the gods.'

'Which of course meant it was distributed among the priesthood and other elite,' I said.

'All of this while the poor of Thebes hungered.' Lori Scott remarked. 'You know, there's a saying that living in the lap of luxury is all very well until Luxury stands up!'

'Oh, I like that,' I murmured appreciatively.

'It perhaps explains the thickness of the enclosure walls around the temple precinct here,' Adam suggested. 'This was the first temple in Egypt to be surrounded by a high mudbrick wall around three metres thick.' He led us across to the doorway and pointed to it, still encircling the temple after all these centuries.

'Holy smoke! It sure makes you wonder about his need for security with an impenetrable barricade like that!' Drew Trainer exclaimed.

'I'm not sure Ramses III was so much beloved and benevolent as blind,' Adam said. 'Blind to the suffering of his people.'

'Yet it wasn't a coup d'état by his people that toppled him,' Lori Scott interjected, also peering through the ancient doorway at the vast enclosure wall, then turning back and frowning. 'You said it was a murder conspiracy conceived and led by one of his queens and the women of his harem!'

'That's right,' Adam nodded. 'Although it perhaps explains why so many people signed up in support.'

'If he wasn't exactly loved and revered by his people towards the end of his reign, one has to wonder if he might also perhaps have been despised by those closest to him,' I suggested. 'Perhaps he was cruel-natured and unkind.'

Adam grinned at me, and then explained for the actors' benefit, 'There's something you have to understand about my wife.' He slipped his arm around my shoulders to take any sting from what he was about to say. 'Merry loves a highly fictionalised version of history. The more sensational, the better!'

I realised I had rather walked into this, despite my earlier unwillingness to admit that much of what I knew came from reading historical novels.

'Don't get me wrong,' Adam went on before I could draw breath. 'We all like to theorise about the gaps in what we know from the textual and other evidence. But Merry takes it to the extreme! She's in her element looking for deep, dark motives to explain historical events and creating character sketches of people whose personalities we can never hope to know since they died millennia ago.'

The squeeze he gave my shoulder and kiss he dropped on my cheek reassured me he was pulling my leg. So, I bit down on the protestation that jumped automatically to my lips and laughed instead. I didn't mind him teasing me since he always did so with such affection. He knew as well as I did that what he called my highly fictionalised version of history was often bang on the money. I might not be in Skylar Harrison's league if her "visions" of the past were for real, but I'd been known to have an occasional instinctive certainty about something. When this happened, I was rarely wrong. But I didn't feel the need to call him out about his ribbing of me. As it turned out, I had no need to, since Lori Scott essentially did so for me.

She tilted her head to one side, removed her baseball cap and contemplated us through slightly narrowed eyes, a small smile playing about her mouth. 'That's no different from making movies,' she observed. 'Folk don't go see a movie for a history lesson. They can watch a documentary for that. They want to be told a story.'

I remembered Mackenzie King saying something similar.

She went on. 'I can see nothing wrong in making up the bits that fill in some of the blank spaces. Besides, what if Merry is right?' she asked. 'You only have to look at what's been going on in America over the last year or so to know her hypothesis is credible. Great men toppled from previously unassailable positions of power in the Hollywood hierarchy because of the tidal wave that built behind the "#Me-Too Movement"! They got away with their abuse of women for years. Thought they were untouchable, invincible even. But it just needed one brave person to speak out, and then another, and then another. And look at the result! A previous giant of Hollywood now languishing behind bars!'

'Right where he belongs,' I muttered with feeling.

'You said there was no evidence the pharaohs mistreated the harem women,' she reminded Adam. 'But what if Ramses III was the exception? Maybe he was a misogynist and a bully,' she shrugged, putting the baseball cap back on again and pulling the visor forward to shield her eyes. 'Maybe he deserved everything that was coming to him.'

Drew Trainer listened to this exchange without comment and then looked at Adam with a small frown on his face. 'But I thought you said the motive for the murder was the succession. One of the pharaoh's queens wanted the throne for her son.'

'That's what scholars believe,' Adam nodded. 'And it seems likely the pharaoh may have been the architect of his own destruction even in that.'

But there was no time to pursue this tantalising comment. We turned at the sound of running footsteps on the flagstones behind us. It was Michael, the harried-looking assistant, sprinting forward from the main temple pylon and gesturing urgently for us to come quickly.

'It's Talia Nolan!' he puffed as he reached us. 'She's turned up on set decked out like the Queen of frickin' Sheba!'

It took a moment for this statement to penetrate.

Talia Nolan?' Lori Scott demanded, aghast. 'She's *here?*'

Chapter 7

Young Michael quite clearly needed a history lesson if he was truly incapable of telling the difference between the Queen of Sheba and Helen of Troy!

Talia Nolan – Academy Award winning actor, screen siren and Hollywood's most bankable female star – was indeed on set; and she looked spectacular! Imagine Elizabeth Taylor in her prime, only if possible, even more beautiful, and with flowing golden blonde tresses braided with glittering gold thread instead of dark hair. Quite tall, nevertheless her figure was about right, with curves in all the right places, a tiny waist and eye-catchingly full breasts shown off to stunning effect in a diaphanous Grecian-style dress in pure white, descending at the front in a deep V from her shoulders to her navel, cinched in at the waist with a burnished gold band that gleamed in the sunlight, and then seeming to float to the floor in silken folds of semi-translucent fabric.

My footfall faltered and I caught my breath as we approached. She was magnetic. Captivating. Stunning. The easy familiarity I'd fallen into so quickly with the Hollywooders abruptly deserted me. I was dazzled. Speechless. Starstruck. *This*… this sense of awed wonderment… *this* was how I had expected to feel yesterday! It was a fully loaded; no holds barred assault of breath-taking Hollywood glamour; although, of course she was "in character" rather than presenting as herself.

The riotous onslaught on the senses, I imagine, was precisely the effect she intended if the slightly challenging expression on her exotically made-up face was anything to go by, confronting us all with her allure. I'm not quite sure what she'd used on her skin, but it glowed as if she'd been dipped in a golden iridescent oil. I heard Adam's sharp intake of breath alongside me and, as one, we came to a skidding halt, recognising, I think, that as hangers-on we were perhaps allowed to observe the drama, but certainly not to take part.

A scant few years ago, I never could have imagined coming face-to-face with a movie star. Now I found myself staring in mesmerised wonder at possibly the biggest female box office draw of our generation. I stood transfixed, openly gaping and breathless to see what would happen next.

But, for the moment at least, was as if we'd pelted headlong into a tableau. Or as if a hidden director had yelled "cut" but told everyone to hold positions for a photograph, a freeze-frame, silent and motionless, vivid and striking in its stillness.

Talia Nolan, decked out gorgeously in full Helen of Troy regalia, was standing in the middle of the wide-open expanse in front of the temple, between the Eastern High Gate, where Skylar Harrison had had her earlier trauma, and the enormous first pylon through which we'd just bolted. She was looking about her with a regal and imperious gaze, shoulders thrown back, chin jutting forwards, hands on hips; a brazen, defiant posture, and clearly a gauntlet of some sort being thrown down, although it wasn't immediately apparent to whom. I had no idea what this was all about, but we'd surely been treated to a grandstand view.

The people in the frame seemed all to have been turned momentarily to stone. I had the strangest sensation I'd stepped into a still life painting of the scene from Sleeping Beauty where the fairies cast a spell to put everyone to sleep.

In that split second of frozen uncertainty, I took it all in. The five massive trailers filled much of the available space. Rigs had been set up for gigantic lights, as if the blazing sun was somehow not bright enough! And I could see at least six cameras from where I was standing; a couple set on the train-track-like rollers I'd noticed earlier, two others mounted on what looked like scaffolding intersected with platforms, and a couple of the more traditional free-standing ones, set up in front of stools on the flagstone temple forecourt.

It lasted for the blink of an eye; that was all. Drew Trainer and Lori Scott ran forward, suffering none of the crippling imposter pangs afflicting Adam and me. This time, it was as if some unseen director cried, "Action!"

Everyone seemed to spring suddenly to life.

'What the hell is *she* doing here?' Skylar Harrison's voice rang out, grabbing my attention. She descended the couple of steps from her trailer wearing what looked to be to be a pale-yellow terrycloth bathrobe tied tightly at the waist, with bare feet visible below its long hemline. Face still devoid of make-up, her hair was netted tight against her head, I could only presume in preparation for a costume wig to be fitted. Beautiful though she undoubtedly was, I couldn't help but think it put her at a distinct disadvantage compared with the vision of loveliness before us.

'Talia! Not like this!' Mackenzie King strode towards the Hollywood star from behind one of the scaffolding structures. He looked decidedly rattled. 'You promised me you wouldn't take matters into your own hands or do anything reckless! As I said, I just need a bit more time to work things out!'

'See, Mac? I *told* you something like this would happen!' Drew Trainer intercepted the director and pushed him backwards, shoving the palm of his hand hard against Mackenzie King's shoulder. 'You should have sorted it out in LA, like you said you would; not let her follow you here. Don't say I didn't warn you!'

I stared agog as Mackenzie King regained his balance and angrily slapped away his leading man's hand.

'You both knew she was here in Egypt?' Lori Scott gaped, looking in open stupefaction from one to the other.

'Mac met her for a secret tête-à-tête yesterday afternoon!' Drew Trainer informed her with a furious glance at the director. 'Why do you think he was late joining us on the boat? He was no more meeting with the scriptwriter than I was gone fishing! That's why he was in such a bitter funk last night at dinner! Sure, he knew she was here!' Then he turned back and angrily addressed the director. 'I told you this morning you needed to get it sorted out before dragging us all out here on set. But you wouldn't listen! And now look!' He gestured around at the film crew. Everyone had stopped whatever they'd been doing, were all openly staring

Ah, I thought. That explained the pre-dawn altercation I'd overheard between the director and leading man.

'I didn't realise she still had an option on the movie,' Mackenzie King attempted to explain himself.

'But how did *you* find out Talia was here?' Lori Scott asked, frowning at Drew Trainer.

'A text came through from my agent overnight,' he said. 'News reached California yesterday that she'd arrived here in Egypt. Honestly! As if the whole sorry drama didn't play out badly enough at the launch party in Malibu, now we have to go through it all again!'

'I thought she was just having a Diva moment back in Malibu,' Mackenzie King attempted once again to explain himself. 'I didn't realise she was pursuing a legal claim until she turned up here yesterday demanding to see me. Then I realised just how deadly serious she was.'

'Yet you still allowed us all to come out here this morning! And subjected poor Skylar to whatever craziness took hold of her!' Drew Trainer accused disgustedly. 'You've been stringing them both along, Mac! And that's not fair!'

'But Talia told me yesterday she wasn't here to cause trouble!' Mackenzie King defended himself then turned and confronted the gorgeous actor directly. 'You told me you wanted to avoid a lawsuit!'

'A lawsuit?' Lori Scott gaped. 'Surely that's going a bit far!'

With his attention drawn away from the screen icon once again, Mackenzie King made yet another attempt to explain himself. 'But – everybody knows Talia was first choice for this movie – the role was originally hers.' He held out his hands, palms upward as if in earnest supplication to say it was all out of his control. 'I'm just the schmuck that stepped into the breach when the shit hit the fan last year!'

'So, she's still saying you had no right to cast anyone else after Victor Bernheim was arrested.' Drew Trainer surmised, naming the disgraced producer now languishing behind bars in America awaiting trial. Funny, I thought to myself; that we'd only just been discussing him.

'But she very publicly turned the role down,' Lori Scott protested, frowning. 'She *can't* still have an option on the movie!'

Exchanging a quick sideways glance with Adam I saw he was as stupefied as I was at how they could carry on this conversation as if Talia Nolan herself wasn't there silently letting it bat back and forth in front of her.

'No;' Mackenzie King corrected her. 'What she actually said was that she wanted nothing to do with any project Victor was involved in.'

'Semantics!' Lori Scott exclaimed.

'Well, you can surely see how folks jumped to the wrong conclusion then,' Drew Trainer challenged him. 'Mac, when you stepped in to direct, you told me yourself there was no producer and no female lead! What the hell were you supposed to do?'

'Thank you!' the director said as if this somehow exonerated him. 'I believed speed was of the essence. All the finances had been raised. The Press was full of Talia's refusal to take the role. At least, that's how they spun it! And now I have Skylar under contract with the studio. Except, Talia suddenly enters Stage Left to tell me her agent was supposed to sort it all out. Accuses me of re-casting the role before she could blink. And get this: announces she never tore up the original contract! So, you tell me! What the hell am I supposed to do?'

The object of this exchange listened to the whole discussion in silence with her head tilted slightly to one side observing the interplay. I had to hand it to her. Even without any lines on the script, she still somehow managed to steal the scene. Simply by standing there, silent and golden and powerful, she was a riveting presence. When she finally spoke, Talia Nolan's tone was every bit as regal as her demeanour.

She held a hand up, stopping Drew Trainer when he might have attempted a response. 'Helen was mine. *Is* mine.' She placed an insistent emphasis on the correction.

I wasn't sure if it was a statement or command. Issued in a calm, softly imperious tone, I rather felt she could have instructed the planets to start rotating backwards around the sun and they would have obeyed her. Put it this way, it would have taken a far stronger person than I to contradict her.

I watched each of the others open their mouths as if to speak and then snap them shut again. Seeing this, I concluded it was game over. Literally, game, set and match to Talia Nolan... or perhaps it was Helen of Troy. I wasn't sure which of them, exactly, had spoken.

Who needed a lawsuit when it was possible to claim the role simply by becoming it? To my way of looking at it, her conviction was more about the way she was dressed – in full character – than in the fact of her being here in Luxor in her everyday persona and confronting Mackenzie King yesterday. As an actor, she was known more for her roles than for herself. Her reputation was as an intensely private person who fiercely guarded her personal life from media intrusion. In truth, I knew almost nothing about her. If put on the spot; I daresay I could have reeled off up to ten of the films that had made her a star. And, of course, she was famous also as the face of one of the most expensive brands of perfume in the world – not that I could afford to wear it. So, all things considered, turning up here as Helen of Troy seemed to me to be a masterstroke.

Impossible to say where the conversation might have gone from there. What happened next took the drama to a whole new level.

I doubted Skylar Harrison could have heard the exchange from her position on her trailer steps a little way away across the temple forecourt. But Talia Nolan's intentions were undoubtedly clear without a single word needing to be said. And it was enough to spur her into action.

Without any of us seeing her, our attention riveted on the interplay between the protagonists closer at hand, Skylar Harrison had climbed into the cab of the lorry to which her trailer was still hooked up. A deafening revving of the engine made any further attempts at conversation impossible. This ferocious engine-revving was soon accompanied by billowing clouds of smoke and dust as the truck's huge wheels started spinning on the loose scree of the forecourt. The lorry was somehow anchored to the ground, and evidently not just with its handbrake pulled up. These trailer trucks were fixed in position, clearly not designed to be moved until it was time to pack up and leave.

'What the hell does she think she's doing?' Mackenzie King yelled over the thunderous roar of the straining engine.

I turned away as dust blew into my face, screwing my eyes tight shut against the tiny loose chippings being blasted in all directions, feeling them sting against my bare arms exposed by my sleeveless top. Adam's arm came around my waist, pulling me away.

'If she thinks she can mow us all down, she's mistaken!' Drew Trainer shouted. 'Those trucks are fixed to mooring plugs.'

'Somebody; get her out of there, for Christ's sake!' Mackenzie King snapped furiously. 'She's taken leave of her senses!'

'You've played both ends to the middle, Mac! This is what you get!'

From the sanctuary of Adam's shoulder now he'd pulled me some way away, I risked a look back. Mackenzie King, with one arm up, elbow bent, shielding his face, was reaching for Talia Nolan to pull her back with the other. Drew Trainer was similarly trying to protect both himself and Lori Scott from the onslaught of dust and debris. Talia Nolan's gorgeous diaphanous dress was blowing in all directions, billowing around her curvy frame and whipping around her legs. Even from here, I could see the dust sticking to the iridescent oil she'd used to polish her skin. No longer glittering and golden, she was caked in grey powder, looking rather as if she'd taken a spin in a cement mixer. If this was the taking down a peg or two that Skylar Harrison intended, she was proving remarkably successful in her intent. I wouldn't have liked to make a choice in the glamour stakes between a woman in an unbecoming hair-net-and-terrycloth-robe combo and a woman smeared in dust with her hair in wild disarray. She'd evened the score rather neatly, I thought.

But I was in full agreement with the director that someone needed to make her stop. The incessant roar of the revving engine straining against its anchors was ear-splitting; the noise and dust joined by the horrible acrid smell of burning rubber as the big wheels kept furiously spinning against the hard-packed earthen ground.

It was Michael, the moviemakers' assistant who darted forward towards the lorry-trailer, with his hand up to shield his face against the loose chippings raining in all directions. But Natasha Redwood beat him to it. Well, I say Natasha Redwood because I knew it to be her … In fact, it was a queen from Egypt's ancient past that braved the noise, dust and air pollution caused by this oh-so modern piece of machinery, a cross between a heavy goods vehicle and a mobile home, to approach the lorry cab. It was an incongruous juxtaposition of the ages. Her Nefertari costume was a long figure-hugging pleated sheath dress in fine linen with voluminous sleeves in pure white. Nipped in at the waist with silken golden cords, it served as a simple base for the dazzling pectoral collar around her neck and shoulders, set with multi-coloured stones intricately laced in gold. Sunlight glinted off it as she moved. On her head she wore a golden headdress of the royal vulture, Nekhbet, its wings framing her exotically made-up face and covering long black tresses, which may or may not have been a wig; impossible to tell from this distance. The top of the headdress was set with two tall upright golden plumed feathers. Honestly, she was Nefertari come to life, and might almost have stepped down from one of the exquisite wall reliefs I'd once been lucky enough to see in the ancient and long-dead queen's tomb.

All of this I absorbed during the short moments it took her to approach the truck where Skylar Harrison was still revving the engine like a thing demented. Luckily for Natasha Redwood-as-Nefertari, the breeze was blowing in our direction, so she was spared the worst of the billowing dust cloud, loose chippings and increasingly noxious-smelling smoke from the screaming tyres.

From my safe distance, I watched her lift her skirts and haul herself up onto the platform from where she could lever open the cab's passenger door and manoeuvre herself inside. Of course, it was impossible to properly see or have any chance of hearing whatever transpired between the two actors once she was seated alongside her protesting co-star.

For a long, headache-inducing moment, nothing happened. The huge tyres continued to spin hideously against the rocky ground sending up clouds of dirt and loose scree. Then they stopped. The truck's engine died. The sudden absence of noise was almost as unnerving as the preceding racket that had had us all covering our ears.

I risked a breath. My throat was dry, feeling as if a good amount of the Western Desert had taken up residence in it. My lips, when I went to wet them, were gritty, like sandpaper. Adam shrugged out of his rucksack, reached in for his water bottle and passed it to me.

'Thank Christ for that!' Mackenzie King said with feeling.

'Hell hath no fury,' Drew Trainer remarked sagely. 'And you have not scorned one woman but two! Double trouble! You've played it badly, Mac, and no mistake.'

Talia Nolan, thunder well and truly stolen, glared furiously at the director. It had to be said she looked neither imperious nor commanding standing covered head to toe in dirt. No question, she had fared worse than the rest of us. With nothing to stick to, I found the dust fairly easy to brush off with a few targeted swipes. But coated in shimmering oil, any effort she made to wipe herself resulted only in smearing the dust into long dirty streaks.

'I think you asked for that!' Lori Scott told her bravely. 'Skylar's not going to take any attempt to oust her lying down. And why should she? She was cast in the role fair and square. It's not her fault there was a mix up over your contract.'

'That's exactly what I said,' Drew Trainer concurred, turning to address Mackenzie King. 'So, unless Helen of Troy had a twin sister forgotten to history, I fail to see how you're going to worm your way out of the hole you've landed yourself in. Honestly, Mac! You should've just handed it over to the lawyers. It was an honest mistake after all. What the hell were you thinking?'

Watching closely, I saw a speculative look come into the director's eyes. I felt I could almost see his brain whirring, wondering perhaps if he could get a creative scriptwriter to come up with a plot twist that might allow him to cast both Skylar Harrison and Talia Nolan in leading roles. I watched the flame go out almost the instant it was lit. 'A story of three warring queens is one thing,' he said in defeated tones. 'Four is stretching it beyond all limits.'

I darted a quick look back at Talia Nolan to see her reaction, but had my attention pulled sharply away by shouts coming from a spot slightly beyond Skylar Harrison's lorry-trailer.

As far as I could tell, Skylar Harrison and Natasha Redwood-dressed-as-Nefertari had not yet emerged from the truck's cab. I couldn't say I was surprised exactly to see Ahmed over there. Our police pal loves a drama. He would have been drawn as if magnetised to observe first-hand the scene that had just played out. What did surprise me, very much, was that Ahmed was the one doing the shouting. He was ordering people high-handedly to stand back and clear a space behind Skylar Harrison's lorry-trailer. The dust had settled now, and the horrible caustic smell was clearing from the air.

And then I realised it was now Adam he was shouting to, waving his arms excitedly, beckoning and demanding for him to come quickly.

'What the hell...?' Adam started, snatching my hand and pulling me with him.

'What's going on?' Lori Scott spun around and trotted along after us.

A single glance back over my shoulder was enough to see Mackenzie King and Drew Trainer also striding forward. Talia-Nolan-Helen-of-Troy was left rooted to the spot, bedraggled but still beautiful, staring after us.

'Come quick! Look!' Ahmed's booming voice filled the air. The movie folk, already interrupted in their morning's work by the drama that had just unfolded needed no further encouragement and crowded around him.

Mackenzie King thrust his way through them, and Adam and I reached Ahmed's side as Drew Trainer brought up the rear.

'What is it?' Lori Scott demanded alongside me, pushing up the peaked visor of her baseball cap. 'What's he shouting about?'

The commotion was enough to draw Skylar Harrison and Natasha Redwood-cum-Nefertari from the lorry cab. I glanced over to see them both pushing their way forward through the throng. The movie crew fell back to allow them through as we gathered at the rear of the trailer. Skylar Harrison's face was suffused with riotous colour, no doubt because of her strenuous and impassioned efforts revving frantically in neutral. She looked somewhat incongruous with her hair tightly netted against her head, with bare feet peeking out from below the hem of her long terrycloth robe. Natasha Redwood-as Nefertari, by comparison was ancient royalty personified. I felt quite awed just looking at her.

But none of this could distract me for long. Ahmed was motioning people to stand back with his long muscular arms, almost as if he was marshalling traffic. 'Look!' he said thrillingly. 'See here...' And he pointed at the ground.

Just behind the trailer-truck's rear tyre, where bucketfuls of loose chippings, stones, dust and scree had been flung heavenwards courtesy of the madly spinning lorry wheels, a gleaming lump of alabaster was clearly visible, hitherto buried beneath the compacted ground of the temple forecourt. More

108

thrilling yet, it was a gleaming lump of alabaster carved with hieroglyphic text.

Adam dropped to his knees in the dust. Reaching forward, he used both hands to scoop away the grit and loose scree settling back against the decorated stone. Then leaned forward and blew the sand and dust from the surface.

'Merry; front pocket of my rucksack,' he instructed, easing it off his shoulders. 'My Swiss army knife...'

I fiddled a bit with the buckle then reached in and pulled out the clever little utility knife.

Moments later, Adam was ever-so-gently scraping away at the tightly compacted bedrock of centuries from around the edges of the alabaster slab. I think it's fair to say the rest of us held a collective breath, staring bug-eyed and unblinking to see exactly what he was uncovering with so much painstaking care.

'Is it a step?' I demanded excitedly, my thoughts immediately flying to Howard Carter and the apocryphal sixteen stone steps he unearthed leading down to Tutankhamun's tomb in the Valley of the Kings. 'Have we discovered a hidden subterranean chamber?'

'No, I don't think so,' he grunted after a bit more concentrated effort. 'I just felt it shift. Whatever it is, I think I can ease it out!'

'Can I help?' Drew Trainer squatted down alongside him. Around us everyone craned forward. I looked up to see Talia Nolan had joined the throng, was standing close behind Ahmed observing proceedings with interest. I noticed a couple of the crew had whipped mobile phones from their pockets, were recording the moment as it unfolded.

'Better not,' Adam said, ignoring them. 'The most important thing is to ensure I can get it out undamaged.'

Drew Trainer rocked back on his heels but didn't get up. 'Whatever it is, you think it's been buried in that hole since ancient times?'

Adam shrugged without glancing up from his labours. 'It's possible.'

'Wow!' Lori Scott breathed alongside me. 'How exciting!'

In the thrill of discovery, it seemed all earlier drama was momentarily forgotten. The actors, director and crew alike watched transfixed, spellbound and largely unblinking as Adam slowly worked the alabaster object free of its surrounds.

Finally, after what seemed an age, he grunted and fell back. 'Ok, I think I've released it. Ahmed, see if you can help me lift it out, would you, my friend? But be careful. It's heavy.'

Ahmed crouched alongside him, rather unceremoniously shoving Drew Trainer aside. I couldn't help but bite down on a smile at this, thinking how star-struck he'd been only this morning. Drew Trainer took it good naturedly enough, merely shifting his position so he could maintain his ringside view. As one, Adam and Ahmed both reached forward. I expelled the breath I'd been holding in a rush of air, feeling light-headed and giddy. My brain was full of images of golden trinkets and precious objects.

The sun was fully up, ferocious in the cavernous sky and beating down mercilessly. I could feel its heat burning my shoulders. But there was no way I was running for the shade right now. I saw beads of perspiration break out on Ahmed's dark forehead beneath his black felt uniform beret.

With straining muscles and grunting at the effort, my husband and our police buddy heaved the object from its subterranean hidey hole and set it gingerly on the floor in front of the big trailer-truck wheel that had exposed it.

Hewn from the palest ivory-coloured alabaster and exquisitely carved with ornate hieroglyphs, its edges were decorated with carved images of rearing cobras.

'Oh! It's a box!' Lori Scott exclaimed as everyone around us exhaled the collectively held breath. 'Can you open it?' Do you think there's anything inside?'

'Not without the proper officials here,' Adam answered her first question.

Now, I feel I should point out here that Adam does not usually suffer such scruples. I can only guess that he was now becoming self-consciously aware of the mobile phone cameras pointed at him recording his every word and deed. And, of course, our further acquaintance over recent years with a certain Director Feisal Ismail from the Ministry of Antiquities had taught us a thing or two. His compunction had no doubt rubbed off.

Adam sat back on his haunches; then turned to address Ahmed. 'Do you think we could get Habiba over here? She's a Ministry Inspector after all.'

But Ahmed was given no chance to respond.

'You don't need to open it for me to tell you what's inside.'

This unexpected pronouncement came from none other than Skylar Harrison. Spoken in low, throbbing tones, it succeeded in drawing all eyes to her face. She was staring at the alabaster box as if one of the carved snakes on its lid had come to life, reared up and was about to bite her. Her face looked like a piece of parchment, pale and pasty, and her eyes had taken on that same distant, other-worldly look I'd seen in them this morning. She'd pulled her robe tightly around her slim frame and looked as if a breath of wind would knock her clean over.

'I've seen that box before,' she said darkly. 'It was used by the scribes at Ipet-Sout to store the transcripts of the trials of the conspirators. You'll find it's full of papyrus.'

And then her eyes rolled back in her head, and she fell at Natasha Redwood-cum-Nefertari's feet in a dead faint.

Chapter 8

I don't imagine it can have escaped Mackenzie King's notice that this latest drama too had been captured on the mobile phone cameras of a couple of the gaping crew members. He cast a goaded look at the fallen actor and started issuing orders.

'Drew! Get Skylar to her trailer. You!' he addressed Ahmed. 'You'd better get those medics back over here! And the rest of you!' he glared around at our staring assemblage. 'Let me remind you you're under contract! No word of this gets out! Stand back everyone!'

To my surprise, the movie crew obligingly dispersed. I figured their contracts must be pretty tightly worded to get such willing compliance. Either that, or they were well paid! As Drew Trainer lifted the unconscious Skylar Harrison into his arms and Ahmed put his own mobile phone to his ear, Talia Nolan stepped forward. She'd dropped the Helen of Troy persona, and now looked what she was: an undoubtedly beautiful woman dressed up in a costume, with grime smeared across her skin and dust dulling the diaphanous folds of her Grecian-style dress. She was frowning. 'What's the matter with Skylar? Is she sick? What was all that talk about seeing the box before?'

'You wouldn't believe us if we told you,' Lori Scott muttered.

'Try me,' Talia Nolan urged, making me wonder if a sick Skylar Harrison might be quite a neat solution to their current dilemma.

'Something about this place seems to be freaking her out. She claims she's seeing visions from the ancient past! Kinda clairvoyant, I guess.'

Talia Nolan's eyes widened. 'Any chance she's hoaxing?'

Notwithstanding that I'd asked myself the same thing, I took exception to this on Skylar Harrison's behalf. She wasn't here to defend herself. But it wasn't my place to speak out.

It was Natasha Redwood who responded. Her shrug suggested she, too, had considered it. But then she shook her head. 'I don't think so.' She watched Drew Trainer carry Skylar Harrison up the shallow steps to her trailer and disappear inside. Mackenzie King followed. 'She had a full-blown panic attack this morning. It was scary to watch. She swears she knows nothing at all about ancient Egypt, but the stuff she's come out with seems to be bang on the money.'

'So, what she said about scribes and papyrus…?'

Lori Scott gave one of her characteristic shrugs. '…Seems to be some kind of genuine second sight. She's sure got me spooked. Adam here is our consultant Egyptologist. He seems to think she's seeing visions of some conspiracy that took place three thousand years ago to kill the pharaoh, right here in this temple.' She waved her hand airily to encompass the forecourt and gigantic pylon with its enormous carved image of the pharaoh smiting his enemies. As Talia Nolan's eyes widened again, Lori Scott turned to address Adam. 'Did you catch all of what Skylar said? Did any of it make sense to you?'

Unsurprisingly to me, Adam was able to quote Skylar Harrison's words verbatim. It's a special talent of his. But I was particularly impressed that he could do so with his – admittedly dishevelled – pinup of choice looking at him in open enquiry. 'She said the alabaster box was used by the scribes at Ipet-Sout to store the transcripts of the trials of the conspirators,' he supplied. 'She said it's likely full of papyrus.'

Adam had pushed his sunglasses up on top of his head while he'd been working to free the box from its burial place. Looking at him, I recognised the expression in his eyes. Deeply blue, they always seemed to change colour becoming an intense violet when he was in the grip of what I'd come to call Egyptological fever. I realised in that moment he was oblivious to the company we were keeping. His passionate interest was reserved solely for the contents of that alabaster box, eager and impatient to lift the lid.

'Ipet-Sout?' Lori Scott made a question of the words.

'It's the name the ancient Egyptians used for the temple complex we now know as Karnak on the east bank,' he said.

'There's no way Skylar could know that, right?'

'Unlikely,' he acknowledged. 'You'd have to have more than a passing interest in Egyptian history to pick up something like that. It's pretty specialist knowledge.' Then he glanced at me and his blue eyes blazed with vivid colour. 'After Ramses III was murdered, the conspirators were rounded up and put on trial. Many of them were executed. But the fate of the queen who led the conspiracy is unknown, lost to history. I wonder if the contents of that box might fill in the gaps!' His excitement was palpable.

'And you know this how, exactly?' Talia Nolan asked with a lift of one eyebrow, as if it all sounded a little too far-fetched to her ears. 'Surely it all happened thousands of years ago. Skylar might claim to be clairvoyant, and I get that you're an Egyptologist, but all this stuff about conspiracies, murders and trials; how can you possibly be so sure?'

Adam met the Oscar-winning actor's gaze readily enough. 'Because, bizarre though it may sound, given the box we've just discovered, there's already a papyrus scroll that preserves a record of the trial that took place after Ramses III was murdered. It's called the Turin Judicial Papyrus, because it's now kept in the Egyptian Museum in Turin, Italy. Believe me; it's sensational stuff. It lists the criminals involved in the coup d'état, the accusations against them in bringing about the plot and the grisly justice meted out to them. But, as I said, we don't know what happened to the queen who raised the insurrection. Significant parts of the surviving papyri are missing, both through accidental damage; also, not helped by the fact that the original finders cut the document into sections, presumably to maximise their profit when they put them up for sale. Many of the fragments have become lost, or only exist now as imperfect copies. So, while historians have been able to piece together a lot of the story, we don't know it all. It's still not clear exactly what happened or how the conspiracy was discovered and foiled. Maybe the contents of that box will fill in the missing pieces!'

This was possibly more information than Talia Nolan either wanted or needed. But I felt my own excitement bubbling up. This was Egypt! "Discoveries" were made all the time. But Skylar Harrison's claim to know the contents of the box before it was opened was in a whole new ballpark. I could feel myself desperately wanting to suspend my disbelief and run with it, especially when I saw Adam's eyes shining like that. 'Skylar Harrison said this morning that the conspirators walked into a trap.' I spoke out despite myself. 'You know, I'm wondering if her visions and the contents of that box might just shed new light on a three-thousand-year-old murder mystery!'

After coming round from her faint and being checked over by another ambulance crew, Skylar Harrison once again refused point blank to return with them to the hospital.

'She doesn't dare leave the set now Talia Nolan's here,' Lori Scott remarked knowingly.

Perhaps realising he had little option but to try to work things out between the two actors jointly cast as Helen of Troy, Mackenzie King determined on a private powwow for just the three of them in Skylar Harrison's trailer. He instructed Natasha Redwood to get some publicity shots in her full Nefertari regalia, handing her over to the photographic team. They would also perform some sound and lighting tests.

Ahmed had put in a call to Habiba. She was currently assigned to the Luxor Museum. A vacancy had opened there a couple of years ago when Director Ismail hauled its previous troublesome curator up to Cairo ostensibly to help prepare for the opening of the brand new Grand Egyptian Museum. In reality, it was so he could keep a watchful eye on him. Still, it had provided a nice opportunity for Habiba to transfer to Luxor after our Belzoni assignment came to an end and smoothed the path towards matrimonial harmony with Ahmed.

Busy supervising the packing of some of the museum's Tutankhamun treasures, which were also being relocated to Cairo to go on display at the swanky new museum when it finally opened (the inauguration kept being put back), she was unable to come immediately. But promised to chivvy things along as quickly as possible – no mean feat in Egypt where time and punctuality are fairly fluid concepts.

It left Drew Trainer, Lori Scott, Adam and me at something of a loose end, especially when Natasha Redwood-as-Nefertari declared that contrary to the events of the day, this wasn't a theatre, and she could do without an audience! With Ahmed tasked with standing protective guard over the alabaster box, now moved to the safety of the security gate, our footsteps turned inevitably towards the massive temple. Lori Scott invited Adam to pick up the threads of our previous conversation.

'All this murder mystery business has got me intrigued,' she said. 'You said earlier that Ramses III was probably the architect of his own destruction in the conspiracy over the succession that led to his death. What did you mean?'

'I'll show you,' Adam said tantalisingly, and led us through the massive entrance pylon into the first open court of the temple.

An hour or so ago, on our first tour, he had pointed out the epic war scenes and the grisly carved images tallying the enemy dead that earned Ramses III his moniker as the last great warrior pharaoh. This time, it was a different set of wall reliefs he took us to see. He led us across the huge square first court, lined on our right as we crossed it with standing statues set against high square pillars, then up the stone ramp, through another pylon into the second court. Like the first, it was open to the dense blue sky overhead, with very little in the way of available shade now the sun was high in the sky.

'Jeez, it's hot!' Lori Scott exclaimed, fanning herself with her baseball cap before plonking it back on her head and pulling down the visor to shield her eyes.

This time, Adam steered us towards the northern half of the portico, behind the second pylon. Here, he stopped and pointed.

We all squinted, and stared at the walls crowded with carved images, many still bearing traces of original colour, faded blues, yellows and reds.

'What do you see?' he asked, drawing his raised finger in a long line through the air to indicate the specific row of images he was referring to.

'It looks like a procession of some sort,' Drew Trainer frowned.

On the wall where Adam was pointing was a long row of carved standing figures wearing what might have been ceremonial robes, with varying headdresses, some appearing to hold staves. Each was depicted with the right hand raised, palm facing forward, as if in greeting, or maybe in praise. Between each standing figure was a set of deeply carved hieroglyphs, some encircled in the oval cartouche that signalled royalty.

'These,' Adam informed us, 'are the sons of Ramses III.'

I lifted a finger to count them: ten in total, separated by the carved hieroglyphs and then a number more trailing along behind them. 'That man had a lot of sons,' I muttered.

'Now what's strange about these images is that, in the pharaoh's lifetime, they all remained unlabelled. Their images were carved, but not their names. Not a single one of them.'

Lori Scott frowned, pointing at the hieroglyphs between each of the first ten figures, 'So, what are *they*?'

'They're their names alright,' Adam admitted. 'But they were added later, during the reigns of his sons Ramses IV and Ramses VI. The texts here tell us so.'

'He had two sons called Ramses?' Drew Trainer queried. 'That's a bit odd, isn't it?'

'Ramses was their throne name,' Adam reminded him. 'Remember, the succeeding pharaohs all self-styled themselves *Ramses* to ape their illustrious predecessor, Ramses the Great,' Adam nodded at Drew Trainer in association since he would bring this giant from history to the silver screen. Then brought us back to the point. 'Not a single one of these images was labelled with its owner's name or titles during their father's lifetime. They were carved with their label texts left deliberately blank where their names should have been. Look, see, there's one here' – pointing to the eleventh figure partially obscured behind a column – 'that's never been given a name. Nor have the ones behind it. And there's a row of fourteen daughters over there,' – jerking his thumb to indicate their approximate location, a mirror image of this processional scene carved on the opposite side of the entrance portal – 'which remain unlabelled to this day.'

Lori Scott was frowning at him beneath her baseball cap, no doubt trying to figure out what this might signify.

'But perhaps even more mystifying than that,' Adam went on, 'is that the very few images we have of Ramses' queens, either have no label texts at all, or the cartouche has also been left blank.'

'What exactly are you getting at?' Drew Trainer asked. 'What are we supposed to make of all that?'

It was Lori Scott who answered. 'What *I'm* making of it is that it's not hard to see how Pharaoh Ramses stirred up a hotbed of rivalry, intrigue and resentment within his royal court.'

'Exactly!' Adam concurred with satisfaction. 'It appears he even held off from naming a crown prince who would be his heir so it's likely his sons and their mothers were pitted against one another, each vying for supremacy. Not exactly a blueprint for domestic harmony.'

Lori Scott wrinkled her nose. 'But wasn't the eldest son automatically the first in line for the throne?'

'All other things being equal,' Adam nodded. 'But that's counting without a high infant mortality rate. There are tombs in the Valley of the Queens for royal princes of Ramses III, sons who predeceased him. And, of course, they are properly named so we know whose they are.' He stepped towards the wall, counted the images, and then squinted at the hieroglyphics, pointing to one of the figures. 'This is Amen-hir-kopeshef. He's widely accepted to be Ramses III's first-born son. This is largely on the basis that Ramses III named his sons after those of Ramses the Great, and Amen-hir-kopeshef was *his* eldest son. This chap,' – indicating the carved figure – 'died young and was buried during his father's reign. As you can see, he's number nine in this procession.'

'So, it's not in order of birth?' I asked, following the conversation with interest.

Adam shrugged. 'It's hard to say. It may originally have been intended to be in birth order but, since the names were left off, we must assume that Ramses III's successors chose some ranking of their own. It's possible they've been ordered by their age at death, or maybe by which queen they were born to. Or more probably by status. The first four princes shown here all acceded to the throne as pharaoh,' he explained. The first is Ramses IV. It appears he actually *was* named Ramses at birth. He's the one who foiled the conspiracy to replace him with one of his younger brothers.'

I stared at the images. 'So how come some of his brothers became pharaoh after he died?' I asked, looking at the other carvings. Adam had said they were all sons of Ramses III, and that four of them had their names inscribed inside the kingly cartouches.

'Because those that had sons to succeed them were short-lived and the sons died young without heirs, so their uncles inherited the throne. The ordering of the others is anyone's guess.'

I was following closely. 'So, four of Ramses III's sons became king?'

'Actually no, that's another somewhat strange thing,' Adam admitted. 'It appears that Amen-hir-kopeshef claimed and labelled two of these figures for himself when he became Ramses VI.'

'Hang on, hang on,' Lori Scott interjected. 'I thought you just said Amun-hir-whatever-his-name-was died as a child and was buried in the Valley of the Queens?'

'That's right,' Adam agreed. 'It appears Ramses III went on to give a later born boy the same name as his dead firstborn son. What's not at all clear is whether this later child was born to the same mother as his earlier namesake who died.'

Lori Scott tipped back her baseball cap and stared at him, her unusual yellow eyes gleaming in the sunlight. 'Let's hope he was,' she said with feeling. 'It's surely the height of insensitivity to demand of another queen that she name her new-born after its dead half-brother!' Then she turned to me. 'I reckon you had it right, Merry, when you said Ramses III had a cruel streak! I can sure see why they wanted to murder him!'

I looked at her keenly, 'Yes, it might be a motive for murder, mightn't it? Especially if he was playing them all off against one another.'

Drew Trainer found a patch of shade, leaned against a pillar and narrowed his eyes on Adam's face. 'It was one of his minor queens, you said, who led the conspiracy to kill the king, planning on securing the throne for her lesser ranking son. I'd sure like to hear the whole story.'

Adam led us across the open court, up some shallow stone steps and into the welcome shade of the enclosed and columned terrace separating the open space from what had once been a hypostyle hall beyond it. With its roof intact, we were shielded from the sun. But I have to say it wasn't a whole lot cooler. We all took a moment to swig down some of the bottled water Adam took from his rucksack and handed around, then sat on the wide stone ledge to take the weight off our feet, ready to hear Adam's lecture.

'We don't know for sure exactly how many queens Ramses III had,' Adam started. 'The consensus is three. The only one definitely acknowledged by him as his Great Royal Wife on monuments during his lifetime, albeit only once, was a woman named Iset, supposed to have been of foreign ancestry. She was mother to Ramses VI who inherited the throne from his nephew, so it's possible Iset became queen later in the reign. There's also a tomb in the Valley of the Queens for a queen named Tyti, known to have been mother to Ramses IV. Given her myriad of royal titles, scholars have established that not only was she Ramses III's Great Royal Wife, but she was also his full sister.'

'Ugh,' Lori Scott exclaimed with a shudder. 'Gross!'

'Brother-sister marriage was pretty commonplace in the royal family in ancient Egypt,' Adam said with a smile at her reaction. 'Not only did they think it would keep the royal bloodline pure; it also replicated the unions of the gods. Isis and Osiris were also a brother-sister marriage.'

Lori Scott wrinkled her nose but said no more.

'And the third queen?' Drew Trainer prompted.

'Ah, that would be the mysterious Tiye. It's Tiye who led the harem conspiracy to supplant the natural heir with her son. We only know about her at all because she is named in the Turin Judicial Papyrus. On the docket of the accused, Tiye is listed along with unnamed women of the harem. They are accused of regicide. But neither the verdict nor the sentence is recorded. It seems Tiye may not actually have gone on trial. It's a notable gap, given that everyone else indicted in the papyri, including her unfortunate son, were found guilty of high treason and given the death sentence, carried out either by execution or supervised suicide.'

'Maybe they didn't like to kill women?' Drew Trainer hazarded a guess.

Adam shook his head. 'I can assure you they had no such qualms. It's clear from the transcripts that six women, wives of the key conspirators were summarily executed.'

Lori Scott shuddered again.

Adam sent her a quick apologetic glance; then went on with his tale. 'Given the remarkable amount of documentary evidence that has survived recording the landmark events of Ramses III's reign, it's frustrating that we know so little about the royal family and their inter-relationships. It's almost impossible to construct his family tree because we're not really sure which of the princes was born to which of the queens, other than in a very few cases. From the evidence of his own tomb, it's clear that Prince Ramses, who became Ramses IV, was Tyti's son. He would have considered himself fully royal, born of a brother-sister union both descended from the previous pharaoh and his queen. Although, he became heir to the throne only after older brothers died. The coup d'état was intended to murder Ramses III and overthrow Prince Ramses in favour of Tiye's son. But we have absolutely no evidence anywhere in the textual or monumental record to cast light on who Tiye actually was. Scholars consider her to have been one of his secondary wives, trying to elevate her own status by promoting that of her son, also a shadowy figure.'

I tilted my head on one side and scratched my ear. 'Skylar Harrison didn't seem to think Tiye was a secondary queen,' I reminded him. 'I don't remember her exact words but wasn't it something about not agreeing it was one of his lesser queens.'

'You're right; it was!' Adam said on a note of enlightenment. 'You know, I always wondered how it was possible for a low-ranking woman of the harem to raise a rebellion against the king. Tiye enlisted the help of senior court officials, including a royal chamberlain and a troop commander. So, either the hatred of Ramses III ran deep, or else Tiye had a genuine grievance and wielded some influence.'

'I read a book about this a while back,' I interjected, wondering whether I should admit it had been a novel. After all, Adam had already regaled Drew Trainer and Lori Scott with my love of historical fiction. 'It put forward the theory that Tiye was a wife of Ramses III's youth, married to him before he became pharaoh, and before he married his sister. So, even as a commoner, maybe she considered herself to have the first claim on the succession for her son. That would be especially the case,' I added, warming to my theme, 'if she was the first queen to have borne Ramses a son. Imagine if her firstborn son or sons died young and were supplanted by the son of a later wife. She surely would have wanted any son of hers to inherit the throne, whether he was the eldest or not!'

Adam smiled at me, a knowing, conspiratorial smile, making clear he knew exactly where I'd read that particular hypothesis. 'I doubt that's right,' he said dampeningly but not unkindly. 'Ramses III was born to be pharaoh. It's unlikely he would have married a low-ranking commoner, unless he was already a grown man and married when his father Setnakht seized the throne.'

'Isn't that possible?' I pressed. 'Setnakht fought his way to the throne through civil war and didn't rule for long.' This much I knew from the history books, not just my preferred novels.

'But believed himself to have a superior claim,' Adam said. 'Again, we don't really know who exactly Setnakht was. The end of the 19th Dynasty is a confusing mess of claims and counter claims. It's probable he was somehow descended from Ramses the Great, possibly through one of the twelve sons who pre-deceased their long-lived father. Having gone to great lengths to secure the throne, I don't think Setnakht would have allowed his son to marry beneath him before becoming pharaoh.'

I'm not sure how much of this Lori Scott and Drew Trainer were following. Adam and I were doing what we do best, what we love to do: debating and theorising about the gaps in the Egyptological record. We could go on all day like this, regardless of what else might be going on around us. I hoped we wouldn't be thought rude or inconsiderate even while I found it impossible to stop.

'What *might* be possible,' Adam offered, perhaps seeking to mollify me having very effectively burst my bubble, 'Is that Tiye was a high-ranking woman from Thebes. We know that the pharaoh and his court governed mostly at this time from Pi-Ramesse, the capital city Ramses the Great built in the north. Thebes was the religious centre where the main festivals were held to honour the gods. The texts of the harem conspiracy strongly indicate that the key players, both inside and outside the palace, were of Theban origin. It is emphatically stated in the indictment of one of the conspirators that messages were being delivered outside to the harem women's families urging them to stand ready to assemble for the revolt. So, it seems the men who joined Tiye in planning to kill the king proceeded with the plot as if sure of local support, in particular for Tiye and her son. We can possibly deduce that the conspirators felt more loyalty to Tiye than they did for a northern-based monarch, who spent much of his time hundreds of miles away.'

'You can start to see how they might have hoped to get away with it,' Drew Trainer commented. 'But do we know what actually happened?'

'It's a rather murky story that emerges,' Adam said, breaking off for another swallow of water. 'Egyptologists believe that the murder and attempted coup d'état took place during the Beautiful Feast of the Valley. This was an annual festival held here on the west bank of the Nile. The divine bark of the principal Theban god Amun – a kind of statue held aloft on a long boat-shaped palanquin on the shoulders of priests – was carried between the primary mortuary temples and religious sanctuaries, including this one at Medinet Habu. It would have been a big celebration, with crowds carousing in the streets to accompany the god's progress. Pharaoh definitely would have attended, staying here at his palace. If it was indeed a Theban plot, it presented the ideal opportunity to catch the king unawares while he was relaxing in the harem at the end of a day of celebrations.

'It seems Tiye and the women of the harem enlisted powerful men from the pharaoh's entourage, including a court magician to cast spells to magically weaken the protections around the king,' he went on.

'Magic?' Drew Trainer frowned sceptically. 'That's a bit far-fetched, don't you think?'

'There's talk in the texts of waxen images being made,' Adam shrugged.

'Voodoo dolls?' Lori Scott exclaimed. 'Jeez!'

'Probably not in quite the way we would understand them,' Adam said. 'But I imagine some kind of spells were cast over them. And potions may have been used on the guards at the entrance to the harem, perhaps to put them to sleep. The magician was tried and executed alongside the other main conspirators, charged with a treasonous use of black magic.'

'The ancient Egyptians believed fervently in magic,' I said. 'Just think about the spells they carved all over tomb walls, the protective amulets they buried with their dead, and the ushabti figures that were meant to come magically to life in the afterlife to serve the dead pharaoh.'

Adam was nodding. 'The distinction between what we term "medicine" and what the ancients called "magic",' he said, making speech marks around the words with his fingers, 'is one of degree. 'In the Ebers Medical Papyrus, magical spells abound side by side with what we today would consider straightforward medical treatments.'

'Anyway, it seems likely the court magician somehow incapacitated the guards,' Drew Trainer brought us back to the point, 'Then what?'

It was Lori Scott who answered. 'Then the conspirators overwhelmed the pharaoh, slitting his throat and swinging at him with an axe, which severed his big toe. Am I right, Adam?'

He nodded. 'It does seem likely he was attacked inside the harem by more than one assailant. They weren't taking the risk of him surviving.'

Drew Trainer grimaced. 'So, the conspirators were successful in the first part of their plot. They'd assassinated the pharaoh. But then something went wrong?'

'We don't know how the attempted coup to oust Prince Ramses was discovered,' Adam said. 'But yes – it's clear something went very wrong for the plotters. They were unceremoniously rounded up and put on trial for high treason. The preamble to the Turin Judicial Papyrus is written as if by Ramses III himself,'

'But he was dead!' Lori Scott broke in.

'Yes, but it's possible his successor, Prince Ramses wanted to wield the full weight of pharaonic power so felt the need to invoke the authority of his dead father before he himself was crowned king. Perhaps he thought it legitimised proceedings.'

'Or perhaps he wasn't popular, and it was the only way he could get compliance from the judges,' I muttered darkly. 'Remember; Skylar Harrison said the conspirators walked into a trap. (I was vaguely surprised to hear myself quoting the Hollywooder, since I had yet to be fully convinced of the veracity of her "visions", but I'd have to admit there was something compelling about the hypothesis she had suggested.) 'Let's face it; the person who stood to gain from the death of the pharaoh and a foiling of the conspirators' plot was the crown prince. It hastened his path to the throne and cleared the court of all dissenters. A masterstroke of cunning, if you ask me!'

'You may well be right, Merry,' Adam allowed, grinning as I confidently espoused this theory. 'The Judicial Papyrus records five lists of rebels. Some were accused of actively participating in the insurgency – forging passes into the harem, providing means of over-powering the guards, using magic to weaken the king and writing to relatives in the army encouraging them to rise up. For others, their crime was failing to report the plot. This was treated just as harshly as actively participating. These people were all executed. The high-ranking conspirators including the magician and army commander convicted of inciting rebellion were condemned to commit suicide in the court, possibly in front of the judges. The hapless prince, figurehead of the conspiracy was charged with collusion with his mother Tiye and the harem women and was also sentenced to suicide but permitted to take his life in private.'

'So, in one fell swoop Prince Ramses cleared the decks of all who might seek to undermine his authority as king,' I said.

'And he even meted out punishment to some of the magistrates who tried the conspirators,' Adam added. 'Get this! Some of them were found guilty of fraternising with the accused – ladies of the harem, no less – during the trial! We can only imagine what these harem women might have been trying to achieve! The misguided magistrates had their noses and ears cut off! Although one found this so humiliating that he took his own life.'

'Gruesome!' Lori Scott shuddered.

'It makes you wonder if I was right and the judges were very reluctant to preside over the proceedings to convict the plotters, who may well have been friends,' I muttered.

'Possibly,' Adam conceded. 'But the very last entry on the list of punishments is of another of the court officials. He was given a stern telling off but apparently no harm was done to him.'

'No mention at all of what happened to Tiye and the harem women?' Lori Scott questioned.

Adam shook his head. 'Tiye is only mentioned in passing in the surviving papyri,' he said. 'The rebels are arraigned for conspiring with Tiye and women of the harem. Her name appears nowhere else in the historical canon. There is no record to say that she herself was tried and punished. I'll grant you this seems a bit odd, since the documents make clear that she was the one to ferment the rebellion that toppled her husband.'

I looked about me wishing the walls of this columned terrace could talk. These ancient stones had borne witness to those long-ago events. These flagstones had echoed to the footfalls of the people we were discussing. Their voices had rung through these columns, just as ours did now. These walls knew the truth of what had gone on here all those centuries ago. Not quite knowing how to put these tumbling thoughts into words, I shrugged.

Adam's blue eyes gleamed back at me. 'Let's hope the details might be sitting in that alabaster box we found,' he said. 'I'd like to think Habiba might be on her way over here by now.'

Chapter 9

I saw the appreciative light in Mackenzie King's eyes from the first moment he caught sight of Habiba Garai – sorry – by which I mean to say Habiba *Abd el-Rassul* – as she arrived on the scene at Medinet Habu.

We'd returned to the temple forecourt and re-joined the reality of twenty-first century moviemaking. Not that there was a whole lot of in the way of moviemaking actually happening thanks to the unexpected twists and turns the day had taken so far.

Natasha Redwood-as-Nefertari was back from her photo shoot. Still in full costume and make-up, she was swiping through digital images of the publicity stills on a computer screen set up under an awning outside her trailer. Another crazy juxtaposition of ancient and modern, I don't think she could have looked more incongruous if she'd tried.

Skylar Harrison had removed the unbecoming hairnet. Her blonde hair was now caught up in a high ponytail swinging down her back. She was still wearing the pale-yellow terrycloth robe. It made her look childlike and vulnerable.

Talia Nolan, I could only imagine, had not thought to bring a change of clothes with her. She was no longer decked out in the ruined Helen of Troy get-up, but was instead wrapped in a terrycloth robe the same as Skylar Harrison's; tightly pulled in at the waist. She'd cleansed her skin of make-up and presumably washed the golden oil from her arms and décolletage. By contrast, I thought she looked older as a result, and no longer as if she'd been let loose in a fancy-dress store. Their matching ensembles definitely evened things up between them in terms of visual impact. It remained to be seen whether one or other of them had secured the upper hand.

The distance between the two and their studied air of indifference towards each other suggested not. It seemed Mackenzie King had, as yet, been unsuccessful in finding a workable solution to his dilemma of having them both cast in the same role. I'd heard job-sharing could work in some professions. But I very much doubted this was one of them.

Since neither movie star was looking her best; and given the watchful way they were both surreptitiously eyeing the director, I figured I could perhaps understand why they greeted Habiba's arrival with somewhat muted enthusiasm.

Habiba's is a wholly effortless and exotic beauty. Her bronze silk headscarf framed her face, drawing attention to the bronze flecks in her eyes. As ever, she looked the last word in stylish desert chic: wearing a crisp white fitted shirt belted into camel-coloured tailored trousers, tucked into flat, brown leather knee-high boots. The slim-fitting ensemble flattered her curves, while being wholly appropriate for the climate and terrain. I happened to know that when she was at the museum, she swapped the leather boots for oriental-style slippers, which added a touch of Arabian-Night's glamour.

Habiba knew, of course, exactly whom she would encounter here on set. We'd talked about the Hollywooders at her wedding mere days ago. And no doubt Ahmed had regaled her at twenty decibels and in microscopic detail about his own somewhat underwhelming introduction to them yesterday.

Whether anticipation accounted for the slight flush on her skin as she approached from the Eastern High Gate, or whether the excited light in her eyes was wholly attributable to the remarkable discovery we'd called her onsite to explore, was anyone's guess.

'*You're* the Ministry of Antiquities official sent over from the Luxor Museum?' Mackenzie King stepped forward. I'm pretty sure I didn't imagine the slight emphasis on his first word. Whatever fusty bureaucratic-type individual he had pictured, I'm sure Habiba wasn't it.

Habiba smiled and reached out to shake his hand. No shrinking violet, she looked the Academy Award-winning director square in the eye, with a twinkle in hers that hinted to me that she was very aware of having ripped away whatever preconceptions he may have had about her. 'Habiba Abd el-Rassul,' she introduced herself, lifting the lanyard that was around her neck to show him her identity card. I was impressed to see this had already been updated with her new name.

Ahmed stepped forward. 'My wife,' he announced. I hesitate to determine whether this was said proudly or boastfully. In truth it could have been either. He'd drawn himself up to his full impressive height and puffed out his chest.

'Lucky man,' I caught Drew Trainer murmur, just out of Ahmed's earshot.

I imagine Adam may have heard it too. He quickly stepped forward to perform the introductions as Mackenzie King, looking keenly at her face for a long moment, returned Habiba's smile, then stood aside. Or perhaps my husband simply wanted to get the formalities over and done with so we could move on to the far more important business of investigating the contents of that alabaster box.

'The artefact was uncovered under the hard-packed earth here on the forecourt, you say?' Habiba looked around, observing the huge trailers and moviemaking paraphernalia. She'd taken her formal introduction to some of the hottest names in Hollywood with remarkable aplomb. But then Habiba is a self-assured young woman, not easily cowed. In truth, I rather think it was *they* who had a harder time being introduced to *her*. Skylar Harrison and Talia Nolan, I felt sure, had seen Mackenzie King's lingering look. This perhaps explained the brevity of their greetings. As for Natasha Redwood, when her turn came to say hello, I rather think that, looking out through Nefertari's kohl-rimmed eyes, must have been something like looking in a mirror. Not much beyond a costume change would be needed to turn Habiba into the living image of the fabled ancient Egyptian queen. 'What exactly happened?' Habiba asked.

Ahmed pointed at the hole behind the rear wheel of the truck Skylar Harrison's trailer was rigged up to. He broke into a burst of rapid-fire Arabic, gesturing first at Talia Nolan and then at Skylar Harrison. The rival stars glanced at each other before they both dropped their gazes to the floor.

I was quite glad Ahmed had chosen to regale Habiba with the tale in their native tongue. While perhaps not entirely sparing the blushes of the two principal protagonists, who must both, I felt sure, feel at least a prickle of unease over the drama they had enacted; it did at least spare us the re-telling in Ahmed's often execrable attempts at colourful English. Whether he had sufficient vocabulary to describe the gauntlet Talia Nolan had thrown down turning up as Helen of Troy, or Skylar Harrison's possible attempt to mow her down with a truck that thankfully was fixed and immovable, could happily remain a matter for conjecture. Ahmed's booming voice and gesticulating hand movements were perfectly adequate for the purpose of enabling us all to mentally re-live the spectacle.

Habiba restricted herself to the merest suggestion of a raised eyebrow. Very commendable, I thought. 'And where is the box now?' she asked in her softly accented English when he had finished, addressing herself to Adam. 'I am very interested to open it up and see what we've got.'

'In the security hut,' he pointed, already striding towards it.

I darted forward to catch him up, as Habiba and Ahmed also followed. Mackenzie King and the five actors trailed in our wake. The other moviemaking folk clearly knew better than to muscle in. Either that or were under strict instructions to mind their own business. For the rest of us the business of filmmaking was temporarily forgotten in the excitement of learning what exactly we had uncovered.

Reaching the hut, the security guard stood aside to allow Habiba, closely followed by Adam to enter. We all huddled eagerly around. I angled myself so I had a good view of Skylar Harrison. Considering she claimed to know the contents of the unopened box, I was especially interested to see her reaction should her premonition prove correct once the lid was prised off.

I caught myself in this thought. Despite my eager impatience, I hesitated, frowning across at Habiba. 'You don't need to take it back to the museum first?' I queried. 'Is it *ok* to attempt to open it out here?'

The look she sent me was full of ironic humour and spoke volumes. It seemed to say, *You Merry? You, of all people ask this?* And I would have to admit that, like Adam, I am not usually given to

136

such scruples. All I can say is that having so recently returned to Egypt and having missed this fabled land of the pharaohs with every fibre of my being for every heartbeat of the time we'd been away, I was especially motivated to want to stay for a good long time this time around. Forever might not be too long. I was starkly reminded that rather a lot of our past discoveries had necessitated some time away and a cooling off period to let the dust settle before we'd been allowed to return.

The fact of the Hollywooders looking on with avid and expectant interest may also have played into my qualms. I wasn't accustomed to doing this sort of thing with an audience, and such a high profile one at that.

I self-consciously registered this thought too as it tumbled through my brain in that infinitesimal meeting of our eyes as Habiba flashed her smile at me. That I was accustomed to it at all was remarkable. All I can say is that I've been fortunate enough to be on hand for some spectacular finds. Doubtful though I would still claim to be about the veracity of Skylar Harrison's so-called clairvoyance, and sceptical of all things mystical and unexplained as I surely was, I would nevertheless be forced to admit that Egypt had whispered secrets to me over the years. For this, I could only be truly grateful.

'I have already spoken to Director Ismail,' Habiba said. 'He has given me permission to investigate the box to determine if it is indeed genuine.'

Something in her tone alerted me to the possibility that the Ministry Director was perhaps wary of this being some sort of bogus media stunt dreamt up by the Hollywood PR agency to drum up publicity for the movie.

'It's genuine alright,' Skylar Harrison's voice throbbed with some nameless emotion. 'Can we please just get on with it?'

Habiba cast her a quick, confused glance. I realised, for all Ahmed's voluble reprisal of events, it appeared there was still a big chunk of the day's surprising happenings he had missed out. But now was not the time to acquaint Habiba with Skylar Harrison's possible psychic powers.

For a long moment we all simply stood and stared at the box, sitting there on a plain wooden desk.

As I have had cause to remark on many an occasion before, there really is something quite literally breath-taking about coming across a genuine relic from Egypt's ancient past. It boggled my brain that this one, quite possibly, had been buried under the forecourt of the temple for something in the region of three thousand years. I didn't think I would ever grow accustomed to this feeling of the distant past colliding with the here and now. As if they had reached across time and space to touch each other. Awed wonder and the most amazing sense of privilege that I should be on hand to experience it came closest to describing how it felt. And even that seemed to fall short.

The box was perhaps the size of a large rectangular briefcase, although deeper. It was fitted with handles at each end. The lid was secured by a series of fixings. They looked a bit like bolts or plugs, although they levered in and out of place in a series of holes made for the purpose; all made of the same alabaster as the box itself. As with most ancient Egyptian artefacts, it was a beautiful objet d'art, irrespective of its primary function as a utilitarian storage box.

Habiba sucked in an appreciative breath, gazing in wonder at the finely rendered hieroglyphics and the carved border of rearing cobras that patterned all four edges of the lid.

'Can you read the hieroglyphs?' Drew Trainer asked eagerly.

Habiba glanced up at Adam, silently inviting him to perform the translation.

He ran a gentle finger across the carved lid, frowning over the symbols. After a long pause, he looked up. His gaze came to rest on Skylar Harrison's intent countenance. 'It's invoking the protection of the god Khonsu,' he said. 'This text here asks for his divine judgement and for justice.'

Skylar Harrison stared back at him with no discernible change of expression. Whether or not she was seeing him at all was a matter for conjecture. I had the strongest impression, confronted once again with the box, that she was watching an inner screen, like seeing a little movie inside her head. Yet again, I reminded myself she was an accomplished actor and silently cautioned myself not to get carried away.

'There's a temple dedicated to Khonsu at Karnak,' Adam went on quietly when nobody spoke. 'It was built under Ramses III, although its decorations and wall carvings were finished by his successors.'

'Ipet-Sout,' I whispered, catching on. I saw that faraway look fade from Skylar Harrison's eyes again and caught myself thinking that maybe she too realised the significance of this affirmation of her earlier outburst. But I suppressed this, since it meant accepting at face value something I was not yet sure I was wholly willing to believe.

'Who's Khonsu?' Lori Scott asked.

'Khonsu was part of the Theban triad of gods with Amun and Mut,' Habiba volunteered. 'He was a god of the moon and of the passage of time.'

Adam was still watching Skylar Harrison's face. 'But that's not all. Khonsu had a darker side. During the early part of Egyptian history, he seems to have been a violent and dangerous god. He appears in a part of the Pyramid Texts as a bloodthirsty deity who helps the deceased king to catch and eat the other gods. And the Coffin Texts describe him as "Khonsu who lives on hearts".'

I think we all grasped the potential meaning of this. Adam's Egyptological knowledge gave a clear insight into why this deity from the ancient Egyptian pantheon had been chosen to preside over the judgement and sentencing of the conspirators. Even so, Lori Scott felt the need to spell it out. 'Ramses III was dead, assassinated by some of those closest to him. Dedicating the trial to the god Khonsu would seem to ensure a divine retribution would be meted out to the murderers.'

The expression on Adam's face as he looked at Skylar Harrison told me he was convinced she'd called it right. The markings on the box clearly indicated the trial of the conspirators had taken place at the Temple of Khonsu at Ipet-Sout. Karnak as we know it today. He nodded his agreement with Lori Scott's remarks, then looked down at the box and pointed. 'The ancient quote is repeated here. Look.... "Khonsu who lives on hearts".' He ran one finger gently over the inscription as he read it aloud.

Habiba leaned closer, studied the hieroglyphics. After a moment she nodded confirmation of his translation. 'Adam,' she invited, standing back. '*Very* carefully please; see if you can free the fastenings.'

I swear we drew a collective breath. The air seemed to grow hotter, felt suddenly heavy, as if with the weight of centuries. Fancifully, I imagined the god Khonsu drawing closer to observe proceedings. The nape of my neck prickled. The moment had come.

Adam pulled his Swiss army knife from his pocket. Without opening it out to reveal its many blades and gadgets, he used one end to tap ever so gently at the row of little alabaster plugs securing the lid to its base. For a long moment it seemed nothing would happen. 'I daren't put any more force into it,' he muttered. 'The plugs might splinter or crack.'

Persistence paid off. A few more gentle taps and one of the fixings shifted, then another. Finally, they were all loose enough for him to use his fingers to ease them out of their plugholes.

Adam glanced up at me, and then moved his gaze to skim across the faces of our assembled audience. They each stared back at him with barely concealed excitement. All that is, except Skylar Harrison. Being honest, I'd say she looked a little bit sick. The pallor of her face made her skin appear translucent. Her throat was working convulsively as if she were swallowing acid. I found myself thinking if she was acting, it was an award-worthy performance. I saw Lori Scott slip a steadying arm around her. 'Ready?' Adam asked. 'Habiba, do you want to help me lift it?'

Habiba stepped forward and handed Ahmed her mobile phone. 'We should record this,' she said, indicating the video button.

Ahmed was only too happy to play cameraman. It meant he could shift closer, so he had an uninterrupted view. Yet again, I noticed he shouldered Drew Trainer out of the way. Even in the breathless anticipation of the moment, I couldn't help but smother a smile. Ahmed does not lack for looks, but he's not in Drew Trainer's league. And of course, he's not Hollywood's hottest beefcake.

Again, Drew Trainer took it equably. In this, I couldn't fault him. It proved his good humour was on a par with his good looks.

Habiba stood opposite Adam so they had the alabaster box between them. They each clasped the outer rim of the lid nearest them and with painstaking care eased it slowly upwards. It lifted away from the base readily enough. With infinite caution they set it alongside the box on the tabletop.

Habiba gasped and Adam expelled the breath he'd been holding in a rush of air as they both gazed down into the box.

'There's papyrus, alright,' Adam breathed on a note of wonderment. 'But that's not all.'

I shot a lightning glance at Skylar Harrison. She looked as if a strong gust of wind might blow her clean off her feet. The incongruous pale yellow terrycloth robe strangely looked to be the only thing holding her upright as if stiffened with starch. Her gaze was fixed, unblinking, on the contents of the ancient box.

'It's the genuine article?' Mackenzie King asked, a definite catch in his voice. He was forced to break off to clear his throat.

'It's genuine,' Adam nodded, still in that same awed tone. But he didn't look up; seemingly unable to tear his gaze away from the relics of Egypt's ancient past.

Habiba pulled a pair of lint-free gloves from the pockets of her tailored trousers and slipped them on. She wore a look of rapt but scrupulously professional concentration. 'Let's see what we have in addition to papyrus,' she said, reaching into the box.

I felt my breathing stall, watching her. In that moment of rapt wonder, I forgot Skylar Harrison and her improbable revelations. Yet again, we were traversing the millennia – the first to look on and touch the contents of the box since its original owners stored them inside around thirty centuries ago. It was an unimaginable passage of time. Despite the practise I'd undoubtedly had, my brain never proved sufficiently agile to do the mental gymnastics necessary to truly comprehend it. A thousand years before Christ; long before the fall of the Roman Empire, or the Greek. Aeons before William the Conqueror invaded British shores; before America was discovered; before Tudors and Stuarts rampaged through the British royal family; before Hollywood was ever thought of, and before a myriad of other events school children to this day learn about in their history lessons. This box had sat there, undiscovered, bearing witness to a chapter in ancient Egypt's past that pre-dated them all. It sent a shiver snaking down my spine. Goose bumps rose on my skin. The tiny hairs on my forearms stood on end.

It's fair to say everyone jostled forward at Habiba's words, craning for a view of what else might be in the box.

What is it about the glint of gold that so mesmerises the senses? I've had cause before to note its almost magical, enthralling, one might almost say *hypnotic* properties. The gasp that went up as Habiba lifted a glittering object between her hands subsided almost immediately into a silent stupefaction.

The other thing I've noticed about moments like these is that there are no words to do them justice. We all stared. It might have been in awe or perhaps in wonderment. But these fail to capture the heart-stopping *majesty* of the moment. It drew out to a full minute; perhaps more.

'What is it?' Drew Trainer croaked at last.

'Jeez!' Lori Scott exclaimed; her favourite word, it seemed, of the day.

'*Bea-u-ti-ful!*' Adam breathed, perhaps not realising he'd pronounced every syllable.

I saw the tremor hit Ahmed's big, brown hand, and had no doubt the video recording would have a definite wobble at this point.

Sharp intakes of breath betrayed the sentiments of the others.

Speaking for myself, I understood the meaning of the expression about one's eyes coming out on stalks. I swear, looking at that dazzling, colourful, golden object, my eyes shot out of my head, only retracting when I forced a blink.

But Skylar Harrison's reaction was more physical still. Despite the supportive arm Lori Scott had around her waist still, she sank slowly to her knees. She was staring at the glittering object as if trying desperately to place it. She looked at once confused and reverent – almost as if she couldn't quite dare to believe the evidence of her eyes.

'It's a pectoral collar,' Adam said, sparing Habiba, who looked at Skylar Harrison and then at me, as if I could somehow and by osmosis furnish her with the knowledge to understand what had caused such an extreme reaction in the Hollywood star.

I shrugged; knowing explanations like this one would have to wait.

And then I couldn't help it. My gaze flew to the pectoral collar around the neck and shoulders of Natasha Redwood-dressed-as-Nefertari. What can I say? The Hollywood costume-and-prop department was sparing no expense on this movie. Even so, when compared to the real thing, the mock-up around Natasha

Redwood's neck looked cheap and tawdry; a bit like a street vendor knock-off of a top-end designer original.

The semi-precious stones of the ancient collar winked brightly: jasper, carnelian, turquoise; alongside faience, jade and pure yellow gold. It was exquisite, intricate and delicate. Natasha Redwood's by comparison – beautiful and finely made though it was – looked what it was: a theatrical prop.

'I'm confused,' Lori Scott said a trifle breathlessly; reaching forward and trying to pull Skylar Harrison back onto her feet. She managed it once Drew Trainer lent his muscular strength to the task. 'I thought Skylar said the purpose of the box was to store the transcripts from the trial of the conspirators. What the hell is a gorgeous and no doubt priceless object like that doing in there?'

It was an unanswerable question. The pectoral, quite clearly, was fit for royalty. Rather than attempt a response, Habiba put it back with consummate care, and started to lift another item from the box. This time, I watched the gentleness with which she was handling the ancient artefacts give way to anxiety and downright panic. 'I daren't lift it!' she murmured. 'It's too fragile.'

'What is it?' Everyone crowded around.

Leaving the item in the box, Habiba reached in and very gently ran the tips of her gloved fingers over it. 'I believe it's a sheath dress,' she said wonderingly. 'Oh, wow! We have almost no examples of these surviving from antiquity. It's made from the finest, sheerest linen.'

Adam leaned forward. 'It's almost transparent, it's so fine,' he breathed. 'Just like the examples we see on the tomb-and-temple wall reliefs!'

'A woman's sheath dress?' I questioned. I was starting to get an inkling of what we might have discovered here.

Breathless with wonder, Adam simply nodded. In its sheer, gossamer-thread quality it was, once again, as far removed from the undoubtedly fine linen-pleat of Natasha Redwood's Nefertari costume as night from day.

Habiba reached forward again, lifting another object from alongside the folds of the desperately fragile sheath dress and holding it aloft in one hand so she could study it in the light.

'It's a bangle, isn't it?' Lori Scott exclaimed, looking intently at the golden circlet. It was shaped in the curling image of a snake, wrought in pure gold, meant to encircle the lower arm; with the head, set with obsidian eyes, at the wrist and the tail snaking up towards the elbow.

'It has engravings on it!' Adam pointed to the hieroglyphic symbols carved onto the wide golden surface of the ancient adornment.

Habiba held it towards him so he could see it more clearly. Since Adam was bereft of a pair of lint-free gloves, there was no way she could hand it over to him for his closer inspection. All he could do was squint at it as she turned it slowly in front of his face.

I watched that tell-tale stillness creep across his features. Adam always has these little freeze-frame moments when struck by something significant.

His voice sounded constricted when he finally spoke, rather as if someone had taken a cheese grater to his vocal cords. 'It's engraved for the Mistress of Upper and Lower Egypt,' he rasped.

'That's the title of a queen,' I breathed as the pieces started to slot together inside my head. 'A great royal wife, no less!'

'Yes,' he nodded, tearing his gaze away from the golden bangle to meet my eyes. 'Bloody hell, Merry! Her name is engraved here, too! This bangle belonged to Mistress of Upper and Lower Egypt; Queen Tiye!'

I stared back into his deep blue-turning-violet eyes. 'Tiye was no more a secondary wife than I am,' I murmured. And, believe me, while it is certainly true that I am Adam's second wife, I have never for a moment been in doubt that I rank first in every single way that matters.

Sadly, looking at that bangle, and knowing what I now knew about her husband Ramses III, thanks to the blank labels on the temple wall reliefs, I wasn't quite sure Tiye had been able to say the same. But that wasn't the point. Taken together, the pectoral collar, sheath dress and bangle – all of the very highest quality imaginable – pointed to me towards a queen of a supremely exalted rank. The big question was what they were all doing inside that alabaster box.

I flicked another lightning glance at Skylar Harrison, standing propped between Lori Scott and Drew Trainer, still in her improbable terrycloth bathrobe. 'They put her on trial, didn't they?' I asked her softly and against my better judgement as a woman with no belief in the occult.

Staring at ghosts, the Hollywood actor nodded. She seemed incapable of speech. That is, her mouth moved, but no sound came out.

Adam gently nudged Habiba. 'The papyrus,' he prompted.

'I'm not sure I dare.' She admitted. 'I can't take the risk of it disintegrating. We need to properly preserve it. When Director Ismail gave me permission to open the box, I don't think he was imagining *this*.'

The agony on Adam's face as she said this was excruciating to observe. It was a bit like having the pot of gold at the end of the rainbow snatched away.

'But look!' I cried, pointing into the box at the single scroll of papyrus, faded tea-coloured and brittle-looking, nestled alongside the fragile folds of the exquisite linen sheath dress. Wrapped around it was a label-tie, also covered in a carefully drawn text – cursive this time, the joined-up letters written in the hieratic script of the more everyday written records of the ancient Egyptians, used by scribes and administrators. 'What does that say?'

Adam caught the excitement in my voice. He darted a glance at me. In that moment I knew we were as one. Regardless of the Hollywooders looking on, Adam and I were experiencing this as we had so many wondrous moments in the past, unlocking Egypt's ancient secrets as a twosome. I'll exclude Ahmed, and even Habiba, from the sense of being in a crowd. Ahmed, after all, was a fellow musketeer. And Habiba had been there for enough of our previous adventures to be considered an insider.

I think in that moment we both forgot the staring eyes of the moviemakers and the incredible claims of our would-be clairvoyant. Forgot even the iPhone camera pointed at the interior of the box. This was just Adam and me, and the thrill of discovery.

Adam's gaze followed the line of my pointing finger and he squinted at the text. That characteristic stillness settled over him again.

'What does it say?' I asked eagerly.

'It reads "Testament of Hori",' he said sounding breathless.

'Hori?' Mackenzie King broke the spell of our shared moment.

Adam whipped his mobile phone from his pocket, punched in a few letters and started scrolling. 'Yes! I thought so!' he exclaimed triumphantly after a moment.

All gazes flew to his face.

'Hori was one of the trial judges,' he informed us, eyes bright and gleaming with excitement. 'He was the one to get off with a harsh reprimand when the others had their noses and ears cut off after they were found fraternising with the harem women during the trial! It looks as if he may have kept his own independent record, buried here. And it's possible it may have had to do with the trial of Queen Tiye, who conceived and led the harem conspiracy! My God! I'll bet it's the missing piece of the puzzle and tells us what happened to her!'

Before he'd even finished, Skylar Harrison snatched her arms away from the grasp of both Lori Scott and Drew Trainer, physically holding her upright. 'Hori was devoted to Queen Tiye,' she said. 'He was appointed by Setnakht himself to watch over her. They didn't dare touch him!' And then her eyes rolled up in her head and she fell forward in a faint that was just like an action replay of the one earlier. The only difference this time was that Drew Trainer caught her before she hit the floor.

Chapter 10

A few hours later Drew Trainer looked the Academy Award-winning director in the eye, 'I'm tellin' you straight, Mac; you were speaking truer than you knew when you said we're making the wrong movie. You gotta hear this story. It has all the hallmarks of a sure-fire hit. A three-thousand-year-old murder-mystery!'

We were back onboard the *Queen Ahmes,* sitting up on the open deck as the night swept in to claim the last vestiges of sunset, enjoying a pre-prandial drink in the warm evening air. Skylar Harrison had been delivered back to us from her trip to the hospital. Mackenzie King had insisted on it this time after what he described as her "third funny turn". So, yet again, an ambulance had arrived. She wasn't gone long. Physically, there was quite clearly nothing wrong with her. Psychologically, it was quite possibly a different matter. But I doubted the Luxor medical team in the international hospital – especially treating a world-famous actor – were qualified to deal with Skylar Harrison's "funny turns"; should they prove to be real or of some deep and mysterious devising of her own that I couldn't begin to guess at. So, after giving her a thorough check up and pronouncing her fit and well, they'd discharged her.

Talia Nolan had returned to her hotel, a sophisticated hostelry tucked away in the foothills of the Theban mountains on the west bank. It was known for discretion, privacy and luxury, away from prying eyes, and was where all the famous names stayed these days when visiting Luxor. All those, at least, who didn't exclusively charter a private dahabeeyah for the duration of their stay, I thought a trifle smugly.

I was relieved all our cabins were taken. It meant I was prevented from extending an invitation for Talia Nolan to join us even if I'd wanted to – which I emphatically did not. The place for the sort of drama she'd brought with her was on set. I had no desire to bring it home with me.

So, we were the same grouping we'd been last night: Adam and me and the Hollywooders. Rabiah and Khaled were unobtrusively on hand to ensure all refreshment needs were catered for. Ahmed had accompanied Habiba back to the Luxor Museum. They'd taken the alabaster box along with them so it and its eye-watering contents could be properly studied, conserved and securely stored. Speaking for Adam, I'm quite sure, given the choice; he'd have preferred to go with them. Playing host to some of the hottest names in Hollywood was all very exciting all other things being equal. But it paled to nothing compared to the chance to learn more about what Drew Trainer quite rightly described as a three-thousand-year-old murder-mystery. Adam, of course, wanted to study the papyrus. But was Egyptologist enough to know that the unrolling and preservation work needed to happen first. It was a specialist job requiring expertise he didn't have and would take place in a thermostatically controlled and sterile environment in the behind-the-scenes part of the museum. So, biting down on his impatience, he accepted that reading the Testament of Hori would have to wait. In the meantime, there was Drew Trainer's assertion that they truly were making the wrong movie to ponder.

Mackenzie King nursed his drink of choice, a Coca Cola. But tonight, Drew Trainer opted for whiskey. I wasn't sure what, if anything, I should read into this given his abstemious behaviour last night.

Drew Trainer sat back against the cushions, sipped his drink and looked upwards for a long moment at the stars winking brightly overhead in the velvety night sky. Then he brought his gaze back and let it skim across the director and his co-stars as he said, 'As Adam tells it, the end of Ramses III's reign is like something straight out of an orientalist melodrama: an elderly and tyrannical warrior pharaoh, fighting to hang onto power having protected his nation's freedom from would-be invaders for years; a series of failed harvests caused by an explosive volcanic eruption on the other side of the planet; an ill-fed populace seething with resentment and refusing to work; scheming ambitious queens at war with each other over which of their sons should succeed to the throne; scantily clad, nubile and idle young women of the harem, forcibly secluded from the world in an environment of indulgence, rivalry and intrigue; a plot against the king's life aided by black magic; open rebellion in the land; a last minute foiling of the conspiracy, which somehow fails to prevent the pharaoh being killed; a hastily convened trial led by judges whose moral compass is questionable at best; a verdict that ensures the evildoers get their just desserts, put to death through a gruesome series of executions and suicides; mutilations of those who step out of line; all before the presumably rightful heir seizes the throne!'

Put like that, I could absolutely see where he was coming from! It was a plot crying out for the Hollywood treatment!

Mackenzie King watched his leading man steadily. I felt I could almost sense the cogs of his brain whirring. But he didn't speak. So, after a moment, Lori Scott piped up.

'Add to the mix that we don't really know who the leads in this ancient soap opera actually were thanks to the wily old king refusing to name his queens or children on any of his monuments, and you can start to see why it's such a mystery! I'm sure a good scriptwriter could characterise it and pull all the threads together into a coherent story.'

It did seem to me that a whole new movie might be a very neat solution to Mackenzie King's casting problem. But, speaking for myself, I didn't want some clever and creative screenplay team to dream up a series of plot vignettes and personality profiles to fill in the gaps of everything we knew from the historical record. I wanted to know the real story.

It suddenly occurred to me that we had someone sitting in our midst, if she was to be believed, that might very well be able to tell it. My gaze alighted on Skylar Harrison's wan face. She was dressed in her normal clothes once more. It was warm up on deck: Egypt's early evenings at this time of year provide a cloak of blanket-like heat. But she'd wrapped her cardigan tightly about her, hugging her arms around her midriff, almost as if warding off evil djinn. As well she might be. It was a closed, protective posture. Even so, I desperately wanted to test out what more she might be able to tell us. Her pronouncements today, if credulous, had started to lift a veil on the past. Impossible though I found them to accept at face value, it seemed everything she'd said had been spot on so far.

'Er – excuse me,' I started hesitantly and, I hoped, politely, to get her attention. I really didn't feel comfortable to address her by her first name. To me, each of these screen sirens, as well as the heartthrob actor and Academy Award-winning director would forever have their first and last names lumped together. I mean; one could hardly grow up thinking of Julia Roberts, say, as – well – Julia Roberts, and all of a sudden start calling her Julia. It just didn't seem right. It might be ok among her closest friends and peers. But I assuredly was not one of them. So, to me, Skylar Harrison, Lori Scott, Drew Trainer, Natasha Redwood and Mackenzie King would forever remain just that.

Skylar Harrison's gaze lifted to meet mine. It was hard to tell how Drew Trainer's re-telling of the essential storyboard version of the historical events she claimed to be able to *see* had landed with her. Her shuttered expression and closed-in body language gave nothing away. It seemed to me to be as good a place to start as any, as I groped for how to go about asking her what I really wanted to know.

'Forgive me,' I said, not wanting to overstep the mark. 'But do you mind me asking…? When he –' gesturing towards Drew Trainer – 'er – I mean – listening to that summary just now of the story of Ramses III,' (I realised I had almost cornered myself in knowing how to refer to the actor sitting right in front of me). 'Um – did you recognise it? Did any of it seem like something you could, you know, add some detail to, or corroborate in any way?' I hoped I sounded genuinely intrigued rather than disbelieving.

Lori Scott's gaze snapped between my face and Skylar Harrison's. 'What a great question!' she exclaimed. 'Skylar, honey; I guess you've had a traumatic day, all things considered. But I sure would like to know more about this second sight thing you've got going on! How exactly do you know the stuff you've come out with today?'

This wasn't exactly what I'd been getting at. But I reckoned I had little choice but to run with it.

Skylar Harrison bit down on her bottom lip and stared back at her. 'I'm not sure I know,' she said haltingly. 'It all just seemed to kinda *come* to me.'

Then her gaze moved to meet mine. 'The honest answer is no,' she said. 'Not really. Sure, there's something vaguely familiar about what Drew just said. But nothing I could pin down. It's like he was talking about the storyline of a book I read once a very long time ago, but I don't remember the plot or how it ended, or who any of the main characters were. Not like the clarity I had today at the temple, when I just seemed to *know* stuff.'

I had to hand it to her: she was very believable. As such, I bit down on a little puff of disappointment. It was clearly unrealistic to have hoped Skylar Harrison might be able to sit here and fill in the gaps from history. Or else, she was faking, and this was a bridge too far, I thought with a touch of cynicism. If I'd wanted to give her the benefit of the doubt, then maybe I'd have said she had to *be* there where the original action took place to experience her second sight. But Lori Scott had got the bit between her teeth, clearly not of a mind to let her so easily off the hook.

'Clarity,' she repeated, pouncing on the word Skylar Harrison had used. 'Isn't that what clairvoyance is?' She looked around at the others. 'Literally translated from French it means "clear seeing".' Then she snapped her gaze back to Skylar Harrison's face. 'You said you *saw* the knife and the axe that were used to attack Pharaoh Ramses. Was it like seeing a proper scene play out in front of you?'

Skylar Harrison wrinkled her forehead in concentration, not seeming to mind being asked a question that invited her to re-live the trauma. 'More like a series of flashing images,' she said slowly. 'That's what was so terrifying about it. I wasn't sure what I was looking at. And I felt the pharaoh's shock and fear; almost as if the person ambushed with the weapons was me!'

We all stared back at her; I'll admit with some disbelief on my part. I was quite willing to accept that Skylar Harrison had never visited Egypt before. But as a lover of historical fiction myself, I could easily see how certain ideas might have come to her. Natasha Redwood whipped out her phone and tapped on it. 'That's called clairsentience,' she informed us. 'I looked up what clairvoyance was all about while you were being checked over in the hospital, Skylar. See? It says here clairsentience is having clear feelings, emotions or physical sensations that have nothing to do with where you are in reality. That sure as hell seemed to be what was going on for you when you had your panic attack first thing this morning!'

I remembered the apparently very real terror on Skylar Harrison's face; the way her body had convulsed, the awful dry, choking retching as she'd struggled to draw breath.

She looked calmer and in control of herself now. It didn't seem to upset her to talk about it. In fact, having some labels to apply to her experiences looked to be helping. That awful, haunted look had left her face.

Natasha Redwood waved her phone at us. 'There's also something here called clairaudience. It means "clear hearing". It's like an inner voice whispering intuitive messages.'

Skylar Harrison was nodding. 'Yes, I had that too,' she said slowly, wrinkling her brow. 'Kinda like the hearing queen who led the plot to kill the king saying she was NOT a junior wife,' she explained. 'It's like she, well, like she *told* me. I mean, obviously it wasn't in English or anything. But it was as if I heard a voice and could understand what it was saying. She was quite categorical about it. The same thing happened when you read out the label on that papyrus, Adam.' She glanced across at him. 'It was as if the same voice informed me that the man who wrote it had been her protector.'

We all took a moment to let this sink in. I felt my eyebrows inching towards my hairline. It was quite something to admit that a long-dead ancient queen was directly communicating with her.

'And what about the stuff about the conspirators walking into a trap?' Lori Scott questioned after a moment, looking at her with a bright avid gaze, clearly relishing the chance to learn more about Skylar Harrison's occultist powers. 'Did she tell you that too?'

'No, I –' Skylar Harrison broke off, biting down on her lower lip again. 'I don't think I heard that... I feel as if I just sort of *knew* it. I didn't see any clear images like I did when I saw the box and knew it once stored the trial transcripts on papyrus. And I didn't hear voices, like I did about the queen. I was just sure, totally certain in fact that they were tricked.'

'That's called Clair cognisance,' Natasha Redwood nodded, pointing at her phone again. 'It means "clear knowing"; an inner unshakable intuition.'

Mackenzie King had listened to all of this in a profound silence, his dark, brooding gaze shifting from one face to the next as the conversation batted back and forth. 'So, what you're telling us,' he drawled at last, addressing Skylar Harrison, 'is that you actually are gifted or afflicted – whichever you prefer – with, not one, but *all* of these psychic powers.' There was no doubting the scepticism, or maybe it was sarcasm, in his voice, nor the challenge implicit in the words or the way he levelled his gaze on her flushed face.

I'll admit I could kind of see his point.

'You think I'm hoaxing!' Skylar Harrison accused hotly, immediately defensive.

To my way of looking at it, he was simply pointing out a self-evident truth: these people were skilled actors, had made their names and their fortunes in pretence, making us all believe in whatever role they were playing, no matter how far removed from reality. I couldn't claim to know how Skylar Harrison had apparently taken the crash course in early 20th Dynasty Egyptology that furnished her with the specialist knowledge she'd revealed today. But surely all things were possible; and it was the logical explanation. I'll acknowledge her "funny turns" and "insights" were unnerving, but I couldn't yet make the leap to accept them as wholly genuine. I had no idea how the Hollywood publicity-machine operated. For all I knew, this could be something they had cooked up between them and were putting on as a show especially for Adam and me so that when the story went viral, we would corroborate it. Sure, her "visions" appeared to have shocked her as much as the rest of us. But I was still hanging on to my scepticism. I'd watched enough movies to know it was possible to act that sort of stuff.

But calling into question the veracity of her observations didn't seem to be Mackenzie King's objective. 'I'm not questioning your word,' he said. 'Or your soundness of mind,' – holding up his hand when she started to interrupt him. – 'I'm merely questioning whether, with so much – er – extra sensory *interference* to deal with, this is really the right movie for you.'

I was glad to have some time alone with Adam at the end of the day. Mackenzie King's statement, delivered in that flat tone laced heavily with irony put a dampener on the evening. Nobody seemed comfortable pursuing things further. The Hollywooders all opted for dinner on a tray in their cabins, perhaps eager for some time apart. And that was the last we'd seen of them.

I wasn't sure if there was a veiled threat implicit in the director's words. But I couldn't help but wonder if Skylar Harrison's days on this project were numbered. To be honest, it had shaken my theory that they might all be colluding in whatever was going on. It would make Mackenzie King as talented an actor as the rest of them, and that was assuredly not what he was known for.

But Adam wasn't interested in talking about moviemaking or the interplay between the stars once we were alone. 'What an incredible day!' he said, kicking off his shoes and flopping on the bed. 'Did you see the quality of that pectoral collar? A fabulous work of art!'

'It was the sheath dress that got to me,' I admitted, willing enough to go along with the change of subject.

'Yes, unbelievable!' he agreed. 'I wonder if Habiba has had a chance to unroll the papyrus scroll yet.' He looked at me with shining, hopeful eyes. 'Imagine, Merry! What might Hori have recorded in his testament that was so explosive he felt the need to bury it hidden away from prying eyes!'

'He was taking a risk,' I remarked drily. 'Considering his fellow judges had their ears and noses cut off, he was lucky to escape with a reprimand. I wonder why he was treated differently. There's no question the pectoral collar, bangle and sheath dress in that box belonged to the disgraced queen. I wonder what the relationship was between them.'

Adam sat up, swung his legs over the side of the bed and pulled his mobile phone from his pocket. He tapped on the screen for a moment. 'Yes, it is strange that he got off so lightly,' he said. 'We know almost nothing about Hori besides him being one of the trial judges appointed to try the conspirators by Ramses IV and that he was a standard-bearer. It says here that the final group to be tried by the judicial commission included some of their own members, punished by mutilation because they "abandoned the good instructions given to them".'

'Wouldn't you love to know what they did?' I mused aloud.

'Well, quoting from the Turin trial transcripts,' he said, reading from the screen, 'it seems the harem women made something called "beer-hall" with them and with the condemned army general.'

I felt my eyes widen in surprise. 'The judges were caught drinking with one of the ring-leaders of the plot to assassinate the king?'

'Yep,' he nodded. 'They were pulled up on charges of disorderly fraternisation with a key defendant and for carousing with the women. Those punished by having their ears and noses cut off included the chief of police, a soldier, two judges, a scribe and a butler. Hori, although convicted of being "as one" with the participants, clearly escaped severe corporal punishment. It says here that the butler – which was a high-ranking court position in ancient Egypt – was so affected by his mutilation he took his own life.'

I stared at him trying to imagine what might have made Hori different from the other high-status jurors, even as I asked myself what on earth we'd done in the days before Google and mobile phones. 'You do have to wonder how many of the so-called magistrates were actually party to the conspiracy.' I speculated.

'And were either acting to save their own skins in signing up to convict those caught, or else were acting, possibly against their will, under the strict instructions of some higher authority to bring in the verdicts that they did,' he agreed.

'If there hadn't been a trap that somehow foiled their coup d'état, I'll bet they'd all have willingly served the unfortunate prince, Queen Tiye's son when he was proclaimed pharaoh. I get a strong sense they were devoted to his mother.'

He grinned up at me from the bed. 'Not you too, Merry!'

'What do you mean?'

'Don't tell me you're developing psychic powers as well! I know you have a sixth sense where this stuff is concerned. I've had cause to stand in awe of it on more occasions that I care to count. But there *are* limits!'

'The contents of that box, I can believe in!' I defended myself hotly. 'About the telepathic testimony of a Hollywood actor, I am perhaps more inclined to reserve judgement.'

'Merry!' he exclaimed, disbelieving. 'I thought you, of all people, would be rapt and wondrous about what Skylar Harrison revealed today!'

'I might be more inclined if I didn't suspect the cogs of a Hollywood publicity stunt in full motion,' I dissembled.

He ginned at me. 'Meredith Pink: practical to the last!'

Pretending to be affronted, I swiped at his arm playfully. The truth was, Adam was the one with the romantic soul. I could see he wanted desperately to believe Skylar Harrison's unexpected revelations were for real. I decided I loved him enough to humour him. 'Practical until proven wrong,' I smiled.

He reached out, grabbed hold of me and pulled me down on the bed beside him, slipping an arm around me and pulling me close.

'So, how does it feel,' he murmured against my hair, 'to be in company with someone whose telepathic senses outstrip your own?'

'Intriguing,' I said, perfectly happy to let the conversation end there. All of a sudden, I found myself much more interested in the here and now than in the fantastical claims of a Hollywood star.

He kissed me, then pulled back and smiled into my eyes. 'You do realise what's going on here, I suppose?'

I looked back, thinking I certainly hoped so. When Adam's eyes fired signals like that it usually meant I was in for a fun night. 'What?' I asked, playing along.

He laughed. 'We've stumbled into another ancient Egyptian mystery-adventure,' he announced happily. 'God, Merry! It's good to be back! I've missed this!'

This time his kiss was long, deep and lingering. I surrendered to it completely, feeling a supreme sense of wellbeing and fulfilment. I'll concede (privately) that I'd harboured a secret fear that being in close proximity with three such beautiful Hollywood stars might turn Adam's head – especially when one of them seemed – pretended? – to hold the key to unlock a three-thousand-year-old murder-mystery. Catnip to the spirit of Boy's Own adventure that drives my husband. But when his hand reached up to unfasten the buttons of my sleeveless blouse and he looked at me with that focused intensity, I'd have to admit my world righted itself. I sank back on the pillows with a deep sigh of contentment. Only to be interrupted by the sound of a light knocking on our cabin door.

'What the –' Adam broke off from kissing me and grunted, frowning. 'What was that?'

'Someone's at the door,' I sat up and tidied myself up a bit.

'Well, they can go away,' he said grumpily. 'We're busy!'

But I was already getting up. 'It might be important.'

I wasn't especially surprised to find Skylar Harrison standing in the corridor outside our cabin door. And was perhaps rather more forgiving of her intrusion than I might have been a few minutes ago. Even so, I was somewhat astounded by her request.

'Please,' she entreated, eyes burning into mine. 'Will you help me?'

'Of course,' I said automatically, noting the flush on her cheeks. It had to be said, she looked very beautiful, blonde hair tumbling loose around her shoulders and with that intent expression on her face. I glanced back at Adam, hoping I might be the only one to notice.

'Mac will throw me off this shoot if I keep having these paranormal – er – episodes.' She asserted, clearly unsure how to describe them. 'But there's nothing I can do to stop them. It's completely outside my control. And it's scary as hell! So, I got to thinking… what if we hire a hypnotist?'

'A hypnotist?' I parroted, grasping for her meaning and trying not to look suspicious. If this was the next step in a carefully crafted subterfuge then I, for one, had not seen it coming.

'Yes!' she said emphatically. 'I'm thinking he could put me under and maybe the whole story would come out, and then perhaps I'd be free of it.' Her eyes were wild and desperate looking.

'Mac thinks I'm crazy. *I'm* asking *myself* if I'm crazy. I don't want to *see* visions, or *hear* voices, or *know* things I have no rational way of knowing. I just want it to *stop*. I can't lose out on this role. I just can't!'

I have to say, it was a convincing performance.

Speaking from behind me, Adam, unexpectedly, sounded equally doubtful. 'Not meaning to pour cold water on your idea,' he started. 'But if you're channelling ancient spirits, I'm rather wondering if a Medium might be more the thing. But hypnotist or Medium, it's not straightforward. This is Luxor, not LA. I'm not sure we can magic someone skilled in the mystic arts out of thin air – certainly not one who speaks English.'

Ok, maybe not doubtful. More pragmatic.

'But I thought you'd want to see if a professional might be able to help me tap into this second sight thing I seem to have going on,' she appealed. 'It might be the best chance you have of finding out what really happened three thousand years ago.'

If she was indeed playing a game, it was certainly the teaser to hit us with, especially since I'd been so eager earlier to ask her if she could fill in any gaps in the evidence. But, looking into her eyes, seeing the naked and transparent appeal on her face, I had to ask myself if I was being unfair in my persistent inclination to doubt her honesty and look for a more down-to-earth explanation for her behaviour.

'Please,' she begged. 'This thing has me scared half out of my wits. How can I go on set every day at that temple not knowing what kind of ancient supernatural force is going to hit me next? Twenty-four hours ago, I was normal. Well, as "normal" as anyone in my profession can be,' she qualified, attempting some levity. She was immediately serious again. 'Now I'm confronting the fact that I'm very probably clairvoyant, at least where that temple is concerned. Yes, and I'm quite possibly the other "clair" things Natasha reeled off from her cell phone too! Please! You have to help me!'

I'm not sure which part of her plea appealed to Adam the most. There's no doubt she'd dangled an irresistible bait with the suggestion of learning more about what actually happened all those millennia ago. Equally, Adam is a sucker for a damsel in distress. And, as I may have mentioned, she did look remarkably beautiful with her blonde hair cascading down her back. Really, what man could resist?

'Well,' he said slowly, 'I guess we could ask Ahmed.'

'Or his sister,' I said, struck by a sudden brilliant idea that might just prove her veracity or out her as a fraud once and for all. 'If anyone knows someone versed in spiritualism it's surely Atiyah!'

Which is how come we were approaching a ramshackle dwelling in one of the dusty back streets of Luxor the following afternoon. And when I say "we", I don't mean just Skylar Harrison, Adam and myself. We were joined by Ahmed; dressed in a long dove-grey galabia instead of his police uniform, with a white turban wound around his head and leather sandals on his feet; and his eldest sister Atiyah. This lady I had met only a handful of times before; most memorably when she'd believed herself afflicted with an ancient curse. It's a strange thing about some modern Egyptians that they still believe in magic spells, hexes and malevolent enchantments.

In this, it must be said, I had placed my faith, or my disbelief: take your pick. I think I was approaching this outing with a healthy dose of scepticism.

Atiyah had chosen to accompany us dressed in full traditional garb of long black robes and a hijab headdress with only her face showing. I knew she was not averse to wearing pretty dresses, modest in design as befitting a devout Muslim, so could only imagine her choice of attire was intended to underline the gravity of our mission. What Ahmed had told her; I could only guess at. Atiyah had a few words of English, no more.

Adam was, I think, more willing to suspend his disbelief than me. But my husband is a romantic. A single glance at his face was enough to see he was thrilled to be caught up in another adventure, happy to go with the flow and see where it led us.

So, we made an incongruous grouping for sure as we left the taxi and walked the last few streets to our destination. Very aware of whom we were accompanying on this excursion, we'd agreed in advance to keep the lowest possible profile. Skylar Harrison had a black silk scarf over her head, tied securely in a knot under her chin, a pair of dark glasses covering her eyes. I thought it a poor disguise, drawing more attention than it sought to divert, it was such an obvious attempt at a cover-up. In black jersey leggings, black loafers and a black silk shirt, her goal was that she might have been anyone. Really, she looked almost as bat-like as the local women in their enveloping black robes. As I'd had cause to note before, I could have passed her on the street and not known I was within a hair's breadth of a superstar.

Ahmed and Atiyah looked like the locals they were. And I guess Adam and I most probably resembled tourists, him in tan chinos and a white, brushed cotton shirt and me in navy, cotton crops with a motif tee shirt. Still, I preferred to think of us as locals – adopted perhaps, but locals, nonetheless.

Thankfully, the people of Luxor, going about their business, paid us scant attention. The caleche drivers, felucca vendors and sellers of trinkety souvenirs were all down on the Corniche that bordered the Nile, ready to ensnare the unwary. Here in the back streets almost nobody showed our little party any interest. We arrived at the wooden door set into the mudbrick wall without anyone having cast us so much as a second glance.

Luxor, for all that I love to call it home, is not the cleanest city in the world. Refuse littered the roadside, stinking horse dung piled against the high, chevron-painted kerb, buzzing with small black flies. Stray cats and dogs roamed free, mangy-looking and no doubt riddled with fleas.

I risked a glance at Skylar Harrison to see what she was making of the general malodorous squalor. To give her credit, she appeared to be taking it in her stride; merely watching her feet to ensure she didn't step in anything to risk consigning her shoes to the bin.

We were right on the outskirts of the city behind the railway line, where the hotchpotch sprawl of crowded suburbia – mostly rough, brick-built apartment buildings with washing-strewn balconies above shops – gave way to the more tumbledown dwellings of the agricultural land beyond. Answering most closely to the description of shacks rather than houses, these were the poorer quarters. Donkeys stood mournfully in doorways, and chickens and goats ran loose. The smell of stale garlic hung heavy in the air.

'We arrive,' Ahmed said importantly, reaching out to rap soundly on the door he'd stopped in front of. Peeling, pale green paintwork detached itself from the rotting wood at the motion and fell to the join the dirt at our feet.

A long moment passed. Then came the sound of a metal bolt being drawn back. The door opened a crack. An old woman peered out. Crinkled, rheumy eyes shifted between us. It would surely have taken only a black pointed hat, a broomstick and a black cat to transform her into the archetypal witch of children's fantasy horror stories. Wizened was only the half of it. She had that deeply lined, parchment skin that comes from living a lifetime in a bone-dry climate. Like Atiyah, she was decked out head to toe in voluminous black robes.

I heard Skylar Harrison suck in a breath.

Atiyah murmured something in Arabic. It might have been a prayer for deliverance, or maybe just a simple hello.

The old woman's mouth drew back in a toothless smile – it really was like looking at a cliché of a soothsayer – and she held the door back for us to enter.

Chapter 11

The word "hovel" best described the dwelling we crowded into. But looking beyond the packed earthen floor covered with reed mats and bare brown plaster walls, it was spotlessly clean. A broom was propped against the wall in one corner. Light filtered through a high window with what looked to be a tea towel draped across it. There were no concessions to comfort. Invited with a gesture to sit, our only option was the unrelieved wooden bench that ran at right angles along two walls. Without a single cushion it was hard on the buttocks. I was grateful to be wearing cropped trousers in thick cotton in case of splinters. There was nothing to look at, not a picture, not a TV, not a single ornament, nothing. Perhaps the ability to commune with the spirit world relieved one of any need for earthly trappings or creature comforts, I thought a trifle acerbically as my eyes adjusted from the brightness outside.

To my astonishment, the old lady hitched up her skirts and squatted down nimbly on the floor, peering up at us myopically and nodding to herself. Then she addressed Atiyah in a thin reedy voice.

Of course, I had no idea what she said, but it became obvious when Ahmed's sister indicated Skylar Harrison, and nudged her forward.

'She wants me to sit on the floor with her?' Skylar Harrison protested, baulking at the prospect.

The old lady crooked a gnarled finger at her, making it clear this was exactly what she wanted. So poor Skylar Harrison really had little choice but to comply. She removed the black scarf covering her hair and passed it to me along with her sunglasses.

Then she too got down on the floor, sitting cross-legged facing the old woman with obvious trepidation.

They really did make the most incongruous sight: the wizened old witch and the Hollywood movie star. I blinked a couple of times but stopped short of pinching myself because I was perfectly well aware this was not a figment of my over-active imagination.

There was another short exchange between the old woman and Atiyah, who then turned to Ahmed.

'She asks for your language,' Ahmed translated.

'My language?' Skylar Harrison frowned confusedly. 'Doesn't she know I'm American, so I speak English?'

It was perfectly possible the old woman knew she was American, given that Atiyah must have said *something* to arrange this appointment. Beyond that, I doubted very much she had the first clue as to the beautiful blonde's identity or fame.

Another little burst of Arabic.

'Yes. It is not to speak. It is to write.' Ahmed said.

'I don't understand –'

Neither, in truth, did I; looking on in open fascination and wondering how on earth they would penetrate the language barrier if attempting some form of hypnosis really was the plan. But *in writing*…? I failed to imagine how that might work!

My astonishment was complete when the little old lady reached into a cavernous pocket of the robes swathing her from top to toe and pulled out a large, rather crumpled sheet of paper and a pencil. The paper appeared to be covered in empty grid boxes, rather as if she was about to invite Skylar Harrison to join her in a big game of Battleships. There looked to be literally hundreds of little blank boxes on the sheet.

Skylar Harrison accepted the sheet and pencil when they were offered to her, looking at them in obvious confusion, and then up into those rheumy old eyes for some clue as to what was going on.

Ahmed translated the instructions as they poured forth.

'You are to fill the boxes with the letters,' he directed.

'Letters?' Skylar Harrison asked, puzzled.

Ahmed turned to Adam for help. 'What is it called in English when you write out letters in order?'

Adam looked every bit as bewildered as Skylar Harrison, gazing back at him with a blank expression. 'I wish I could help, buddy, but –'

Ahmed looked to me in frustration. 'You know; the letters that children learn in school to help them to read and write –'

'You mean the alphabet?' I hazarded.

'Yes!' he pounced on the word, and then addressed Skylar Harrison once again. 'Write out the letters of your English alphabet as many times as they will fit. Take your time. Your alphabet should repeat often in the space.'

The old witch nodded along while he issued these instructions, smiling her toothless smile, looking perfectly at ease squatting on her haunches on the reed-covered floor.

Skylar Harrison stared at her in open mystification, then shrugged. 'Does anyone have something I can lean on?' she asked, looking around for a non-existent table. 'I'm guessing I could be some time.'

Adam undid the buckles on his rucksack, propped on the floor at his feet. Reaching in, he passed her an old notebook.

She took it gratefully, propped it on one knee and started to fill in the blank boxes. I watched rows and rows of ABCDEFG-and-soon gradually fill the sheet. Ahmed was correct. There was room enough for our alphabet to fit possibly a hundred times over.

A single fly circled lazily overhead as Skylar Harrison concentrated on her task, sitting cross-legged and hunched over on the floor. We all watched silent and stupefied as the tiny boxes filled with letters. I knew in a million years I couldn't have dreamed this bizarre scene. Conversation was out of the question. This was clearly some deeply mystical technique. How it worked – supposing it did – I couldn't begin to imagine. I sat staring in what I hoped wasn't too open disbelief, pondering a bit about spiritualism and Ouija boards and the occult. None of it had ever appealed to me. But I knew of people who believed absolutely in the ability of professional mediums to channel messages from those beyond the grave. I wondered dispassionately whether there was any time limit on it; whether three-thousand-year-old ghosts might take longer to reach and tune into than the souls of the more recently departed.

The whole thing was starting to spook me out. Intuition was one thing. As Adam had pointed out just last night, I could claim personal experience of hunches, gut-feelings and moments of quite uncanny insight. I'd always thought of these as having exceptional instincts, a natural feel for things. Yes, maybe a sixth sense. But I had never perceived anything paranormal in it.

Looking at the wrinkled and withered old woman watching Skylar Harrison with a bright, avid gaze, I found myself questioning if it was all perhaps just a matter of degree. If maybe instinct and intuition could be trained to become something we might call extra-sensory perception, or any of the "clair" powers Natasha Redwood had educated us about by reading from her phone last night. I felt my deeply held cynicism start to waver.

Finally, Skylar Harrison was done filling in the little grid boxes over and over with all the letters of the alphabet. She put down the pencil. 'Now what?' she enquired, looking expectantly at the witchy woman.

Our enigmatic hostess reached once more into the deep pocket of her enveloping robes. The object she pulled out this time looked like a hatpin, long and with a sharp point, encased within a protective sheath. She spoke to Ahmed as she pulled it free.

'Now you are to fold the sheet of paper as many times and in as many different ways as you like,' he translated. 'You may fold it in half, or turn in the edges, or turn it over and over from one edge, whichever you choice.'

'Choose,' Adam murmured automatically, correcting him.

'Or you may do all of these,' Ahmed clarified, ignoring the correction. 'It is up to you.'

We all watched riveted as Skylar Harrison set to work, folding over and again, apparently at random, frowningly intent on her task. Finally, when the big sheet was reduced to the size of a playing card nestled on her palm, she looked up for further instruction.

The old woman grinned gummily at her and passed her the pin.

'You are to stab the pin into the paper,' Ahmed said. 'It should pass right through from one side to the other.'

'Anywhere?' Skylar Harrison asked.

'Anywhere,' he nodded confirmation. 'She says the pin will direct you.'

With this surprising statement hanging in the air, Skylar Harrison rested the wad of folded paper on Adam's notebook to avoid using herself as a pin cushion and took a stab at it, putting enough force behind the movement to ensure the sharp point penetrated right through to the bottom.

'Now unfold three times and stab again,' Ahmed instructed.

This process was repeated a number more times until the paper was once again fully unfolded and resting across the Hollywood star's knees.

Ahmed concentrated as the old witch issued another burst of reedy Arabic. 'She asks how you read your language.'

'Huh?' Skylar Harrison asked, confused. 'I learnt to read when I was small.'

'She's asking if it's to be read from top to bottom, from left to right,' Adam stepped in, evidently having followed some of what had been said.

'Oh,' Skylar Harrison said. 'Yes, that: what Adam said,' she confirmed.

'Then she says you are to read the sheet in the same direction and note down all the letters with a pinhole through them in the order they appear left to right and top to bottom.' Adam said, taking over as interpreter as he came to a full understanding of what was being asked.

We all traded glances as Skylar Harrison put down the pin, picked up the pencil, opened Adam's notebook to a blank sheet and started slowly to transcribe letters onto it, one at a time. Her concentration was absolute, hovering the pencil above the sheet a grid row at a time to ensure she didn't miss any of the pinhole letters.

I wished I could read it over her shoulder, but she was sitting hunched in such a way it was impossible to get a clear view.

Finally, with a long sigh, she relaxed her shoulders; sat back and stared at the notebook, transcribed now with her own handwriting.

The old woman rocked back on her haunches, smiling that toothless grin and looking supremely self-satisfied.

'Does it make sense?' I asked eagerly. I wasn't quite sure what I had just witnessed; knew only that it was beyond my wildest imaginings. It was a curious, breathless moment waiting to see if it delivered on the promise of something otherworldly, or was just an elaborate and rather theatrical farce, perhaps befitting of a queen of Hollywood.

Skylar Harrison looked at what she had written and started to read aloud. '"King's Daughter, King's Sister, King's Great Wife, Lady of the Two Lands, God's Wife, Mistress of Upper and Lower Egypt",'

Forget queen of Hollywood!

'Those are queenly titles from ancient Egypt!' I exclaimed, unable to stop myself jumping in as all my scepticism took flight. I'd seen the same magic shows as anyone else, streamed on YouTube or TV. But I failed to see in a million years how she could have faked that with all of us watching so minutely, and not having known in advance where she was coming or what she would be asked to do.

'But very specific queenly titles!' Adam added in similarly excited tones. 'Not many queens of ancient Egypt can claim to be daughter, sister *and* wife of pharaohs.' He whipped out his phone as he spoke. 'I'm pretty sure...' – scrolling as he spoke – '...*Yes*! Those are Tyti's titles! She was a great royal wife of Ramses III! As his full sister, would have been the daughter of pharaoh Setnakht and his wife Tiye-Merenese.' Then he stopped and frowned. 'But hang on a minute! Tyti was also titled "King's Mother". Ramses IV was her son!' Then his expression cleared as he added, 'Although, of course, that title didn't come until later…'

I tried unsuccessfully to fit the pieces together. 'So, this is *Tyti* trying to make contact…?' I groped incredulously, still hanging on to my reservations for all I was worth, reluctant to take what we'd witnessed at face value.

'You didn't let me finish!' Skylar Harrison cut crossly into our debate. 'You broke in before I could read the rest.'

Realising this was directed at me; I subsided into silence, guiltily aware that I had been the one to cut her off. 'Sorry,' I mumbled.

'There are two more lines,' Skylar Harrison said thrillingly. 'They read: "eldest royal child" and "eldest sister".'

And then it was as if the pin she had used to stab through the folded paper had somehow been turned inwards upon herself. She deflated as if she'd been popped: slumping backwards and only avoiding the injury of striking her head against the unforgiving wooden bench because it happened to land on the soft lap of Ahmed's sister Atiyah.

Quite what this lady made of having a siren of Hollywood nestled, quite literally, in the folds of her traditional robes, I could hardly imagine.

The old witchy woman nodded, smiled smugly, revealing her gums and cackled something.

'She says you have been visited and now the spirit has departed,' Ahmed intoned, reaching out a big hand to gently help the movie star lift her head from his sister's lap, then offering both hands to pull her up from the floor. 'You are feeling better; yes?'

Skylar Harrison nodded as he lifted her to her feet, then apologised to Atiyah, who smiled shyly back at her.

'It did work; yes?' This was about as good as Atiyah's English got.

Skylar Harrison sat back down on the bench and sent a questioning glance at Adam.

He turned his head to look at me. In our shared glance I knew we were silently asking each other what exactly we had just witnessed. If I hadn't seen it play out with my own eyes, I never would have believed it. Still wasn't sure, in fact, that I dared believe it. But I'd watched the whole process, start to finish; seen the random nature of the paper folding, and pin stabbing. There was no way that could be faked that I could see. Once again, the messages the alphabetical letters had spelled out required an Egyptological knowledge of ancient queenly titles I doubted the Hollywood movie star was likely to have. A shiver snaked down my spine. Railing against my better judgement, I decided I had no option but to conclude there was more in heaven and in earth than I could hope to explain. And I saw in Adam's eyes that, against whatever scientific and practical instincts lurked beneath his more romantic preferences, he was reaching the same conclusion. Perhaps the spirit of a centuries-dead ancient queen really had paid a visit.

That being the case, all we could do was believe in it and try to figure out what it meant. Silently, his hand reached for mine. In the moment of connection as it joined with mine, I knew we shared a single thought. 'It's not Tyti,' he said. 'It's Tiye!'

'They were sisters!' I proclaimed, my voice overlapping his. 'Of course! Tiye was named for her mother, Tiye-Merenese! Fully royal and descended, we have to presume, from Ramses the Great, she would have out-ranked her younger sister!'

'And, of course, she was never "King's Mother" because her plot to put her son on the throne failed,' Adam added.

'But are we any further forward with knowing why I had those visions?' Skylar Harrison cut across us desperately.

'I think it's quite clear Queen Tiye is trying to settle the score,' I asserted, deliberately suspending my disbelief. 'You know; there was another Queen Tiye further back in history. She was Great Royal Wife to the pharaoh Amenhotep III who ruled at the height of ancient Egypt's Empire period. She was one of the most powerful queens in Egyptian history. It's possible our Tiye, if I can call her that, was named for her predecessor as well as for her mother. If so, it was quite a pedigree she was inheriting. If we can place any credence on it, I think your sheet of paper is proof that she was no junior-ranking wife of the harem. She was, in fact, the most senior of all of Ramses III's wives. And, if "eldest royal child" is to be taken literally,' I said, quoting from the sheet of paper Skylar Harrison had left on the floor at our feet, 'then she was the firstborn of pharaoh Setnakht and queen Tiye-Merenese, older even than her husband Ramses IIII!' Even as I said it, I couldn't be sure I truly dared believe it. I was simply interpreting the information as presented.

'It makes sense,' Adam nodded slowly. 'With status like that, you can see why she would have wanted a son of hers to inherit the throne. Wow! Those visions of yours,' – looking at Skylar Harrison (I guess he wasn't comfortable addressing her by name either) – 'would seem to have the potential to set the historical record straight!'

So, it seemed my husband was willing to believe. All I could say was, if true, it was assuredly a piece of the puzzle. But we were still a long way from knowing how it all fitted together. And what perhaps inclined me towards a more sympathetic view was that I wasn't at all sure Skylar Harrison had got what she'd come looking for. But our hostess made it clear she was done.

Atiyah and Ahmed voiced our thanks to the wizened old woman as she hoisted herself lithely up off the floor to see us out. But when Skylar Harrison tried to give her a generous handful of Egyptian notes to show her appreciation, the old lady threw up her hands in horror, stepped backwards, slammed and bolted the door.

'She doesn't want payment?' Skylar Harrison asked in surprise.

'It is a gift she freely shares,' Ahmed responded.

Skylar Harrison shrugged. 'Will you take the money for your sister instead?'

Ahmed shook his head, and Atiyah joined in, having understood. 'No, no,' she said and touched her chest. 'Happy.'

'We want to help you,' Ahmed said gruffly. 'I hope it has given you some more clearness.'

'It's not enough to stop me getting thrown off the movie,' Skylar Harrison said dully. We stepped away from the dim interior of the mystic woman's dwelling and into the wall of heat and brightness on the street. I didn't notice the stale garlic smell so much now, which probably meant I'd grown used to it. 'Filling in gaps in the historical knowledge you guys are so passionate about is all very well,' she went on. 'But I learned nothing today to tell me why this ancient, doomed queen appears to have chosen me as her channel. What do I have to do to make her stop?'

It truly did count as one of the most bizarre conversations I'd ever had, discussing how to exorcise an ancient Egyptian royal ghost. 'I guess we need to get the whole story out,' I hazarded.

She looked at me in some desperation. 'But I can't sit about for hours on end sticking pins into sheets of paper! It will take forever! I'm here to make a movie!"

'I have high hopes of the papyrus Testament of Hori,' Adam said. 'I'm guessing, judging by what we've just witnessed, that it was no accident you uncovered that box yesterday.'

'You think she's guiding my actions?' Skylar Harrison asked wildly.

I had to agree that it sounded far-fetched; especially given the role Talia Nolan had played in the dramatic events yesterday. I could see exactly how the movie star felt about the suggestion. As an actor, she was used to being directed, of course. But there was a world of difference between the likes of Mackenzie King and the ghost of a queen of the ancient world, dead for three millennia.

Adam shrugged. 'After what I've just seen, I'm ruling nothing out! Sadly, it's likely to be a while before we can properly study the papyrus.'

'It's a slam-dunk that Mac thinks I'm nuts!' she complained, sounding very American. 'He made it perfectly clear he wanted me to stay away from set today.'

'He thought you ought to rest,' I reminded her. 'You had a traumatic time of it yesterday.'

'But the rest of them are carrying on without me,' she lamented. Then her eyed blazed. 'If I find he's shooting with Talia Nolan instead of me, I'll sue the pants off him!'

There was nothing any of us could say to reassure her on this point. I had no clue how the director would attempt to wriggle out from the rock and hard place he found himself squeezed between. The making and breaking of movie contracts were mysteries to me.

Skylar Harrison looked at us in open frustration. 'I said all along that my best bet was a hypnotist,' she said. 'Someone who speaks English,' she qualified.

I looked at her as a thought struck me; although I rather thought it was my own credulity we'd be testing, as opposed to her own belief in her telepathic powers. 'Well, if you're up for it, there is something else we could try…?'

Barely an hour later we approached the mighty Karnak Temple across an expansive paved area between the ticket office and the security gate.

Ahmed and Atiyah were no longer with us. Atiyah had decided to go home, and Ahmed had been sent by Adam on a mission to see his new wife at the Luxor Museum promising to report back any progress on the unrolling of the papyrus.

I was quite glad about this. I could never pass the security kiosk at Karnak without a shudder. This was where Ahmed had been on duty a while ago when a suicide bomber attempted to gain access to the temple. Our police buddy and his colleagues had mercifully foiled the attempt. But not without some collateral damage. Ahmed still bore scars from the burns he'd sustained to his hands and forearms.

Skylar Harrison had once more donned her disguise of headscarf and dark glasses. Nobody paid us the slightest attention. But I was forced to keep pinching myself. There was something about being in company with a screen siren of Hollywood on her own that was strangely overwhelming, in a whole different way from being with an entire contingent of them. It was more intimate somehow; almost as if we were friends – which, given her worldwide fame was too head-spinning a concept to get to grips with.

And, of course, our reason for being here was about as far removed from a married couple taking a friend sightseeing as it was possible to get!

'Wow!' Skylar Harrison said as we descended shallow steps, walked between two rows of ram-headed sphinxes rising high on both sides of us on stone plinths, and approached the truly massive entrance pylon, made of gigantic blocks of hewn rock.

Karnak is actually a collection of temples built over hundreds, thousands even, of years, the largest religious structure on the planet.

'You're definitely ok about this?' I checked in with her.

'I don't see what could be worse than seeing flashing images of a pharaoh being murdered right in front of my eyes!' she assured me. 'It's gotta be worth a try. Like you say: if being in the places where the ancient drama played out brings on my particular brand of clairvoyance, then it makes sense to come here and see if anything happens. And, if it does, I'd sure as hell prefer it to be in front of just you two! I can totally do without Mac and the others looking at me as if I've changed shape!'

'Well, if you're certain,' Adam said, leading us forward between the huge stone gateway and into the first court.

There were a few tour parties about, crowding around their guides, and peering at columns, sphinxes, statues and shrines.

Skylar Harrison pulled her headscarf tighter around her face and gazed around her, taking it in.

In my opinion, the most fascinating thing about the open first court of Karnak is the massive remains of a now-crumbled mud-brick ramp still in situ behind the towering structure of the first pylon. It gives a clue to how the ancient workmen hauled the gigantic stone blocks to such dizzying heights during the construction.

But we weren't here to point out the normal tourist highlights.

Adam led us diagonally across the open court towards the right-hand side. 'This,' he said, indicating a much smaller entrance pylon flanked on each side by two striding statues of a king mounted on plinths, 'is the House-of-Ramses-in-the-House-of-Amun, built by Ramses III. It's literally a temple within a temple, which is true for a lot of this place. Amun was the principal god of Thebes. Karnak is dedicated to him.'

'Ipet-Sout,' Skylar Harrison whispered.

'Yes, exactly,' he nodded. 'That's what it was called back then.'

He led us through the entrance gateway between the two raised statues. We entered a peristyle court, open to the sky, lined on one side with more standing statues of the pharaoh. This time standing feet together with arms folded across the chest and holding the crook and flail, they were set against tall pillars, reminiscent of the ones at Medinet Habu. The first few were reasonably intact, but the three at the end of the row were missing the top part of their torsos and heads. Beyond the courtyard, we stepped into a four-columned portico and small hypostyle hall, with three chapels at its rear. All were closed to the public and cordoned off with chicken wire, just possible to peer through into the dark interiors beyond.

'Anything?' I asked Skylar Harrison.

She took off her sunglasses and closed her eyes for a moment. 'This temple was used for a festival of some sort,' she said slowly. 'These three chapels were used to house statues of a trio of gods before and after they went on parade through the streets.' She opened her eyes and looked at Adam. 'That's all I've got.'

I could see from his expression that it was quite enough to be going on with. 'You're absolutely right,' he said, sounding awed. 'This is most commonly known as the barque temple. Ramses III built it to accommodate the divine barques – think of them as a kind of carnival float – of the Theban triad, Amun, Mut and their son Khonsu when they were kept at the temple between events such as the Beautiful Feast of the Valley.'

Skylar Harrison proving once again, I thought, that either she had a doctorate in Egyptology, or else her clair-whatever-Natasha-Redwood-had-called-the-*knowing*-one was as possibly genuine as the late afternoon sunshine radiating down into the peristyle court.

'Nothing more?' I questioned. 'Nothing to fill any gaps?'

She closed her eyes again, then sighed and shook her head. 'I have a feeling this temple was built in the latter half of Ramses III's reign, but outside of that, I think it had no part to play in the harem conspiracy.'

'Then we move on.' Adam said.

We retraced our steps out of Ramses III's temple-within-a-temple back to the main Karnak open court. The tour parties looked to be wrapping up as the shadows started to lengthen, mostly heading for the exit.

'Ready to be impressed?' Adam said, and led us through another massive pylon flanked by statues, this time of Ramses the

Great, into the world-famous hypostyle hall. The majestic chamber of gigantic sandstone pillars took my breath away every time I visited; surely a feat of ancient building and engineering to rival the pyramids of Giza. Some of these colossal pillars thrusting up into the sky all around us were so huge it would take ten men joining hands to span their circumference.

Skylar Harrison stopped and stared. 'Not as impressive as it used to be,' she said at last. 'It was fully painted: a riot of colour.'

Of course, I thought; wondering if, however sceptical, a part of me had expected a pronouncement of this sort. The hypostyle hall had been commissioned by Seti I and completed by his son Ramses the Great. So, it was still relatively new when Ramses III ascended to the throne, possibly upwards of half a century. Now, more than thirty of them had passed. Unsurprising that the columns were mostly golden-toned stone, bleached in the sun with passing millennia; many of them patched with buff-coloured concrete where they had fallen and been repaired. But, looking upwards, at the remains of what had once been the stone roof, it was still possible to see remnants of original colour on the underside of some of the stones where the sun's fearsome rays had not been able to reach.

That Skylar Harrison had the ability to *see* rather than imagine the way it had once looked had me thinking, for the first time, her clairvoyance, if it was to be believed, more a gift than a burden.

'And the obelisks were here back then, of course,' she said, gesturing at them as we moved beyond the Hypostyle Hall. 'But they were blinding to look at in full sun. Their tips shone with electrum.'

Seeing how Adam hung on her words, I could see he was way way way beyond doubting that Skylar Harrison and her inner visions were for real. And, I must admit, it was starting to get to me too. In the past I had only been able to guess at what this remarkable place might have looked like in its heyday. Being here now, in her company, was somehow like being able to experience it through ancient eyes. I felt almost that I could *see* it too.

Adam steered us to the right, and we passed the sacred lake where the ancient priests had once bathed to purify themselves.

'This has changed,' Skylar Harrison said, without elucidating.

But I guessed I could see how the modern café with its tourist book carousel and ice-cream-and-cold-drink stand might strike a jarring note. (I have to say, passing this particular spot; I couldn't help but indulge in a moment of reminiscence. This was where Adam had first told me his life had burst into Technicolor on meeting me. It was a treasured memory, a little hazy now with the passage of time, but no less poignant.)

The fact that he took my hand as we passed told me he remembered it too. I squeezed tight to convey how much I loved him and relished all the adventures we had shared since that first moment when it had occurred to me that I could stay in Egypt and choose a different future from the one mapped out for me back at home in England.

While Adam and I shared this nostalgic moment, I saw Skylar Harrison take over to lead our steps. Clearly, she knew where we were headed. This; the woman who claimed never to have set foot in Egypt before now!

She steered us towards the right, past the sacred lake and through then crumbled remains of three more pylons, some with partially reconstructed statues in front of them. The modern cranes rising against the sky betrayed the effort going into rebuilding these ancient structures from the tumble of carved blocks set out on either side of the path we were walking.

'Oh! It's all fallen down,' she remarked as we continued on. 'What a mess.'

Adam and I exchanged a glance. In that shared look was an acknowledgement that, against our better judgement, we'd seen things today and yesterday that had shattered our preconceptions about what was real and what was not. I was quite sure he'd been quicker to accept the extraordinary turn of events than I had. But I was catching up fast. Against my better judgement, I was starting to think sometimes the most far-fetched, seemingly impossible explanation really might be the one to believe.

A short walk further between rows and rows of ancient stone blocks set out in neat columns, brought us to the temple of Khonsu. Anywhere else, this structure might have looked like an impressive and majestic temple in its own right. The trouble was, having just traversed such magnificent sights within Karnak's many precincts; it seemed rather plain by comparison. Its exterior walls were undecorated; just the usual temple shape fronted by a pylon and tall entrance gateway, all built from big blocks of sandstone. Which perhaps, together with the long walk from the main touristy Karnak structures, explained the lack of visitors. We had the place completely to ourselves.

'Yes!' Skylar Harrison said as we walked through the entrance pylon into the pillared courtyard, open to the sky. 'I know this place! Although it was plainer inside then.'

Adam watched her steadily. 'Although laid out under Ramses III,' he said, 'scholars believe only three subsidiary rooms in the innermost part seem to have been decorated in his lifetime. The wall carvings here weren't added until years later.'

'I know,' she nodded. 'Just through there…' And she indicated towards the spot. 'That's where the trial took place.'

And then she started uncontrollably to shake.

Chapter 12

Adam and I looked at each other in alarm.

'Maybe this wasn't such a good idea,' he muttered as convulsions took over Skylar Harrison's body. 'Should we get her back outside?'

'No,' I said, detaining him when he would have reached for the movie star. 'She was very clear she wanted to try this. As long as she's not actually in danger, I think we have to stick with it and see what happens.'

He looked at me doubtfully. But I was determined to see it through or else call it out for the hoax it might still conceivably be.

'I don't pretend to understand all this extra sensory stuff any more than you do,' I pressed on. 'But it seems to me her only hope of freeing herself of it and being able to carry on with the movie is to put herself in the way of having more visions – which seem to me to happen when she's physically on the spot where it all played out in ancient times. And Mackenzie King plans on filming here; remember? He said this was going to be one of his location shoots. I think her only chance is to confront the place here, now, with us; and let it speak to her.'

Watching the actor apparently in the grip of whatever terrifying force seemed to have hold of her, Adam didn't look any happier. But I knew he could see the sense in what I was saying as he made no further attempt to pull her outside.

'Think back to yesterday,' I carried on. 'She was much calmer the second time we approached the Eastern High Gate at Medinet Habu. She didn't have the awful panic attack twice; although it's clear she was still able to close her eyes and sense stuff.' In truth, I was seeking to reassure myself as much as him. It wasn't at all comfortable watching the Hollywood star taken over by what, if real, I could only think of as supernatural forces; or to sense that she was no longer aware of Adam and myself standing worriedly alongside her; deaf to our urgent back-and-forth debate. 'If she can get the worst of it over and done with now, she might be ok to film here,' I finished, fervently hoping it was true or that this might be the moment to expose her as the consummate actor she undoubtedly was.

But my persistent reluctance to let go of this jaundiced view didn't make it any easier to witness that faraway look in her eyes give way to an expression of abject horror and fear. Or to listen to her laboured breathing, seeing her chest rise and fall with the effort. All the colour drained from her face, and she swayed unsteadily on her feet.

That was the point at which Adam stepped forward and caught her. There was no way he was letting her fall smack on her face on the uneven flagstones.

The touch of his hands on her upper arms seemed to cut through the trancelike state she'd fallen into. She let out a long shuddering breath and the focus came back to her eyes. She slumped forward into Adam's outstretched arms, and they automatically came around her in a protective gesture.

'It's ok,' he soothed, as if he were holding a small child awakening from a nightmare. His gaze met mine over her shoulder as he cradled her, and her breathing started to return to normal. 'You're going to be just fine.'

I wondered if in our wildest dreams a week ago, say, we could have conceived of a moment like this: Adam holding a world-famous movie star in his arms with me looking on not in the least bit perturbed (at least; not by the holding bit. I remained thoroughly perturbed by Skylar Harrison's visions).

Seeming, finally, to return to herself, she flushed, stepped hastily back and dropped her arms back to her side, 'I'm sorry about that,' she murmured sounding abashed.

'Forget it,' he said. 'Are you alright?' he looked at her concernedly.

'I could sure use a glass of water,' she said. 'And I'd like to sit down for a bit.' She looked decidedly shaken. But it was good to see colour returning to her cheeks.

'Let's go to the refreshment stand,' I suggested, glancing at my watch. 'It should still be open.'

We left the Khonsu temple with some relief and retraced our steps past the partially reconstructed pylons and sacred lake. Skylar Harrison still seemed turned in on herself somehow, walking along between Adam and me but not really *with* us. We made no attempt at conversation as we went, sensing she needed time to come to terms with whatever she may have *seen*.

Thankfully, I was correct, and the little café was still serving customers. A few tourists sat at the plastic tables, fanning themselves, flicking through their guidebooks and sipping soft drinks. While Adam went to the drinks cabinet and paid for three bottles of water, I found us a small table at some distance from anyone else and pulled out the chairs. I motioned Skylar Harrison into the one that meant she could sit with her back to anybody who might glance casually over. This was partly to keep her incognito, but also so that she might feel more comfortable telling us about her experience without feeling she was drawing attention.

Adam re-joined us and we both looked at her expectantly as she unscrewed the cap from her water bottle and poured some into a glass with hands that trembled ever so slightly.

'I'm guessing it worked,' I prompted after a moment, watching her take a small sip. She'd stuffed her sunglasses into her shoulder bag. That haunted look I'd first seen yesterday was back in her eyes. 'You certainly seemed to be witnessing something Adam and I were unable to see.' I hoped I sounded more supportively enquiring than openly challenging. In truth, I was a mixture of both.

'Yes,' she said at last. 'It was more than just a jumble of impressions, flashing images, voices and sensations this time. Some of it was quite clear and distinct. My overwhelming feeling was horror. I don't think the conspirators were given what you or I might call a fair trial. They knew they were coming here to be condemned to a violent death. The place reeks with it.'

That's what she'd said about Medinet Habu, I recalled. If true, it was clear that amid the sophisticated trappings of art and culture that made up the glory days of ancient Egypt, there was a much darker side. I knew that sanctions for criminality were severe and rigorously applied. It was hard to imagine crimes more serious than treason, use of sorcery to assassinate the pharaoh and a coup d'état to replace the rightful heir with one of his younger brothers.

'Can you piece any of it together?' Adam asked her gently.

I watched her lovely face while she marshalled her thoughts, seeing pain and distress flit across her features, and felt the walls of my resistance crumbling brick by brick.

'The low-ranking conspirators were flogged before they were even brought here for trial,' she said with a shudder. 'It was a way of beating a confession out of them. The guilty verdict was a foregone conclusion. They weren't permitted even to speak.'

Adam nodded, 'There were no defence lawyers or representatives for the accused in the ancient judiciary. The plaintiff argued his or her own case.'

'Except they couldn't because the first set of accused were all brought before the court bound and gagged,' she frowned. 'I saw this quite clearly. These weren't the ringleaders but were accused of aiding and abetting and failing to report what they knew. They were brought into the pillared Hall of Judgement. At the far end of the hall, the magistrates were seated behind a row of court scribes. One at a time, bailiffs ushered the plotters in, bending them forward by the scruff of their neck. They were thrown to the floor, accused of crimes against the gods and told the deity would sit in judgement on them.'

'Divine judgement at its most literal,' I remarked wryly, picturing the scene quite vividly as she talked.

'It meant the new pharaoh could absolve himself of any responsibility,' Adam repeated what he'd said yesterday. 'Gods found the plaintiffs guilty; and gods pronounced the death sentence. A nice, neat way for the new pharaoh to avoid any pangs of conscience.'

'But how?' I frowned. 'How did the deity pass judgement?'

'The statue of the god of the temple "spoke" to them,' Skylar Harrison said with a deep frown, the as if trying to figure out what she had *seen* and make sense of it.

Adam nodded. 'Oracular consultation,' he said. 'A golden statue of the god was held aloft on a model barque carried by priests. The physical and textual evidence suggests that a movement of the statue or the entire litter such as a forward or backward thrust would be deemed a judgement, a way of saying yes or no to a specifically worded question: I guess something like "do you find the accused guilty as charged?"'

'But surely the use of oracles is a load of hokum!' I protested. 'One of the priests must have made the statue move!'

'A rationalist would certainly think so,' Adam conceded. 'But remember the ancient Egyptians were ardent believers in the gods, magic and the occult. They described oracular responses as miracles. It's very unlikely deliberate physical prompting would have been tolerated. It was the ancient equivalent to the modern use of Ouija boards.'

I'd been about to argue but this called me up short. I'd thought about Ouija boards more than once over the last couple of days, witnessing the strange phenomena of Skylar Harrison's "funny turns". The memory of her stabbing a pin into a folded wad of paper flashed in front of my eyes. There was no way I could think of to explain *that*. The protest died on my lips, and I subsided, taking a sip of my water. Just because there was no rational way to account for something did not necessarily make it untrue. Another brick in my armour of resistance crumbled to dust.

'The prosecutors made sure the gods would impose eternal damnation on the accused,' Skylar Harrison added, frowning again as if puzzling out the message she had been given. 'The conspirators were tried and convicted under pseudonyms.'

'Huh?' I said, not following.

'Ah, yes!' I'd forgotten about that!' Adam exclaimed. 'But you're right!'

'They changed their names?' I questioned.

Adam had pulled out his mobile phone again and was madly scrolling with his thumb on the screen. 'Here!' he said, finding what he was looking for on the magic search engine. 'The names of the plotters were altered to be a negative variant of their own name. For instance, Kha-em-waset, which means "arisen in Thebes" became Bin-em-waset, "evil in Thebes'. Another example is Mery-ra, meaning "beloved of Ra" which was changed to Mes-ed-sura, "Ra hates him".'

Then he explained, 'Changing their names was a way of ensuring the condemned criminals were recognisable in the records but that their names could not live on after they were dead. The ancient Egyptians believed that to speak or write someone's name granted them eternal life. And that would certainly not have been tolerated in this case. Putting an end to a criminal's days on earth clearly wasn't enough to satisfy offended Egyptian sensibilities. Eternal damnation really was what was demanded.'

Skylar Harrison nodded, and her face paled again. 'Once the statue of the deity had affirmed the sentence of execution,' she said, 'the convicted men and women were taken from the court hall to a place just outside the temple gate where a blazing furnace had been erected.' Her eyes filled with horror and her voice cracked on a whisper as she re-lived her inner vision. 'There, in front of their children, their relatives, and crowds of curious onlookers, they were burned alive.'

We sat in silence for a moment, reflecting on the gruesome nature of this punishment. Adam had said yesterday that the ancient Egyptians had no compunction about executing women. But knowing it and hearing it described were two very different things.

'It was horrific,' Skylar Harrison choked, tears in her eyes. Watching the very real emotion on her face I felt myself creep towards a final acceptance of her clairvoyance. Surely nobody in their right mind would subject themselves to the type of trauma I'd seen her experience here today and at Medinet Habu yesterday all for the sake of some dubious publicity stunt, or whatever other unthinkable motivation may be at play. There was acting, and then there was masochism.

'No mercy,' I murmured, thinking about what she'd said and finally accepting it at face value. 'They were beaten after they were captured, had their names cursed by the gods as they came before the court, then sentenced to a grisly death.'

'With their ashes scattered on the streets for the donkeys to trample,' Skylar Harrison finished looking thoroughly sickened.

Adam's expression was grim. 'Egyptians believed preservation of the physical body was needed for the individual to go to the Afterlife. It was a thorough job they did, and that's for sure.'

It was hard to believe such a grisly episode had played out just a stone's throw from where we were now sitting among tourists from all corners of the globe come to gawp in awe at the ancient ruins. It made me wonder how many of these visitors really tried to picture this place as it had once looked, and to imagine what human dramas were once enacted among the now-sun-bleached stones.

'What happened to the bodies of the higher-ranking conspirators who were forced to kill themselves rather than be executed?' I asked at last, forgetting for a moment that she hadn't been there yesterday when Adam had told Drew Trainer, Lori Scott and me about the trial. 'And do you know by what means they took their lives?'

She didn't miss a beat. 'They were made to drink from a poisoned cup,' she said with another shudder. 'I think it was mixed from a plant of some kind. They writhed and convulsed on the floor while the judges watched. It was hideous. Their contorted bodies were also tossed into the burning brazier.'

If it was indeed the spirits of these long-dead unfortunates channelling their story to a modern-day movie star, they'd evidently spared her no detail.

'Mandrake, most probably,' Adam said prosaically. 'It's a poisonous plant depicted in tomb paintings of Egyptian gardens. It was administered in wine as a cure for sleeplessness. But taking an overdose would surely induce a sleep the victim would never wake up from! The mandrake plant produces a fruit that can be eaten safely but eating the plant itself is lethal; fatal in about thirty minutes. But those thirty minutes would be agonising.'

'Only the puppet prince was allowed to take his own life in private,' Skylar Harrison said. She broke off to sip from her almost empty glass, frowning and tilting her head to one side as if in concentration. 'I know about that on some level, but I don't feel that I actually *saw* anything about him. I don't have any images of his trial or death.'

I was starting to think that what she *had* seen was more than enough to be getting on with. If anything, it fleshed out the bare bones of the story Adam had sketched out yesterday in rather more detail than I might have preferred. But there was one part of the ancient murder mystery still missing.

'And what about Queen Tiye?' I asked, looking at her enquiringly. 'Did she speak to you again today?' Of course, now I was willing to take the leap of faith and believe her, this was what I wanted to know most. To learn the fate of the high-born queen who devised and led the plot to murder her husband. Adam had said she wasn't mentioned at all in the Turin Judicial Papyrus other than in a passing reference. Her name survived because other conspirators were accused and convicted of collusion with Tiye and the women of the harem. 'Perhaps she was of such an exalted rank they couldn't put her on trial,' I speculated, pondering what we now knew about the ancient queen's lineage thanks to our paper-and-pin process. 'Maybe she continued to have status or influence even after she conspired against the pharaoh. It may have set her above the law.'

Skylar Harrison narrowed her eyes on my face and shook her head, dismissing these conjectures. 'Oh, they tried her alright,' she murmured, that faraway expression glazing her eyes again. 'I thought I told you that yesterday.'

She had, I remembered. But I'd been disinclined to believe her.

'So why isn't there any record at all of what happened to her?' Adam asked, frowning. 'Surely as the instigator of the plot her fate was sealed! I don't imagine for one second Ramses IV would have allowed her to get away with it. I'd have thought she would be top of his list for retribution.'

Skylar Harrison met his eyes and stared into them for a long moment. 'There are worse forms of punishment than being forced to take your own life or to be summarily executed,' she said darkly.

But, beyond that, she'd refused to be drawn. Announcing that she was exhausted, we'd had little choice but to leave Karnak and hire a taxi to bring her back to the *Queen Ahmes*. Once on board, she headed directly to her cabin to rest. I sent Rabiah to fuss over her, feed her and fix her a favourite drink. I thought she might have need of something stronger than water and hoped she gave in to it.

Adam and I speculated madly on what she'd said, of course.

'So, you're inclined to believe her now?' he asked as we sank into the cushioned recliners on the upper deck to enjoy the sunset.

I shrugged. 'Having found no other way to explain what I witnessed today, I guess I'm willing to run with it,' I conceded.

'So, what did you make of what she said about the queen, and the way she clammed up?'

'Maybe they made the queen watch while her son took his life,' I said. 'That would surely be unbearable.'

'Yes; or perhaps she was exiled,' he shrugged. 'A tomb was started for her in the Valley of the Queens, where Ramses III's other two principal queens, Tyti and Iset were buried. But it was never completed, and she was certainly never interred there. Being stripped of her royal titles and sent away from Egypt might have seemed a fate worse than death to someone of her royal lineage.'

I thought of the sheer linen sheath dress, stunning be-jewelled pectoral collar and engraved golden snake-bangle found inside the alabaster box. It seemed to me they might have stripped her quite literally. But this was too unpleasant a thought to voice aloud, so I squashed it.

We'd learned a lot today. But, like Adam, I could only keep my fingers crossed that the Testament of Hori might fill in the blanks, and perhaps provide the final proof that the Hollywood star was for real. Unless Skylar Harrison had more visions – entirely possible, of course – it seemed our best hope of piecing together the whole story. Either that, or we really would have to put out an advertisement for an English-speaking hypnotist.

I was interrupted in this thought by the sound of a violently slamming door. Adam and I jerked our heads to look at each other. 'Sounds like the others are back,' I said.

'And someone doesn't sound happy,' he remarked.

We opted to sit it out rather than go and investigate. We didn't have to wait long. Minutes later, Drew Trainer bounded up the spiral staircase. In shorts, a tee shirt and training shoes, he raised one hand at us in a salute of greeting but headed straight for the gym equipment the indispensable Khaled had already arranged to be delivered and set up on the rear upper deck.

Natasha Redwood came too. Dressed in one of the fluffy robes we leave in each of the guest bathrooms, she too waved but chose not to join us. She moved towards the front of the deck, pulled a rattan chair close to the lamp lit in readiness for the onset of nightfall, spread what I took to be the pages of her script across her lap and started to murmur softly to herself.

Lori Scott trailed them up the staircase. Looking elfin and delicate in a short denim skirt with a plaid over-shirt tied into a knot at her minuscule waist, and bare feet, she came forward. 'Ok if I make up a threesome?' At my nod she opted for one of the deeply padded armchairs, curling up on it with her legs drawn up underneath her.

'Everything ok?' Adam enquired mildly.

She gave one of her expressive shrugs, watching Drew Trainer as he warmed up through a series of stretching exercises. I'll admit my eyes were drawn too. It's no hardship to watch a fit, good-looking man work out!

'I guess I can tell you,' she said with one of her airy hand gestures. She glanced over at Natasha Redwood assuring herself her co-star was out of earshot. 'Mac's gone to his cabin to cool off his temper. Talia Nolan turned up on set again at the end of the day. Same old rigmarole as yesterday, except without the extraordinary get-up. She'll disrupt filming until Mac gives in. Drew and I couldn't believe he didn't just send her packing. But it seems maybe I'm not alone in having a hold over him. When Drew and I attempted to take him to task in the minibus on the way back here, he lost his temper and told us we had no idea what we were talking about. Then he stormed off.'

Adam and I exchanged a glance. Discord among our guests was bad enough. But what had my eyebrows inching towards my hairline was her cryptic comment about having a hold over the director. That surprised me very much indeed, and that she'd admit it. I thought back to some of the remarks she'd made during dinner on their first evening on board: the way Drew Trainer had seemed to want to gag her, the awkwardness I'd sensed among the others, the way Mackenzie King had told her she'd made her point and should now let it drop. I recalled her saying she'd fought hard to land the role. Perhaps whatever she was alluding to was an open secret among her co-stars. And now her breezy declaration that maybe she wasn't the only one! I had no idea at all what to make of that! But it didn't sound too good for Skylar Harrison if Talia Nolan truly had some hold over the director, she could leverage to win the part.

By silent, mutual agreement, I think Adam and I saw instinctively it was probably best not to comment on what Lori Scott had shared or question her further. The interplay between the Hollywooders was really none of our concern. If harmonious living arrangements stood any chance of being restored, then letting things run their natural course was surely our best bet.

Lucky for us our inestimable housekeeper proved once again that she was worth her weight in gold: choosing that moment to come up on deck carrying a tray loaded with a jug of her homemade lemonade, ice, glasses, a bowl of skin-on peanuts and a bottle of beer for Adam. We smiled our thanks as Rabiah dispensed these welcome refreshments, including Natasha Redwood in a glass of poured lemonade. Then watched as she retreated back down the spiral staircase with a cheeky swish of her long black robes.

Saved by this timely interruption from the need to make any sort of response, Lori Scott's words drifted off on the airwaves over the endlessly shifting waters of the Nile. We sat in silence, sipping our drinks and letting the warm Egyptian dusk work its magic. Curbing my habitual curiosity, I reckoned I could place my faith in that old expression about things coming out in the wash. They usually did.

Drew Trainer was pumping iron now. I allowed it to distract me. It wasn't hard to see how he came by his muscular physique watching him lift such heavy weights. Adam's exercise of choice was an early morning run. Speaking for myself, a bit of yoga when I could be bothered was about the extent of it. I doubted myself capable of picking up even one of the weights the actor was hoisting with such apparent ease.

Lori Scott seemed not to notice, or maybe care, that we hadn't interrogated her further. Her attention drifted away from her co-star's exertions with the weights. She gazed out across the darkening waters of the Nile, watching sunset turn the riverbank a mural of soft colours. I've never been much of an artist, but I'd always thought if I'd been moved to try to capture this scene that charcoals and chalks would be far more the medium to use than watercolours.

'This place really does have a mystical beauty all of its own, doesn't it?' she commented at length. 'There's something almost gauzy about the light quality. It's as if a soft-focus lens has been dropped over it.'

I glanced at her approvingly. It always scored high marks in my books when someone else showed the same appreciation for this ancient land that I felt. The tension seemed to have dropped from her shoulders. She looked relaxed and content, and very pretty without the baseball cap hiding her features.

'Something to do with the quantity of sand and dust in the atmosphere,' Adam said with a smile. 'It makes for some of the best sunsets on the planet.'

'I'll bet this view hasn't changed for centuries,' she said, looking beyond the nodding palms lining the riverbank to the Theban hills beyond, darkening to a deep purple as the fiery sun sank behind them. 'It's strange to think the characters we're here to play might still find it familiar all these centuries later. It brings them closer, somehow; less fabled names from history books, more real people who once sailed this mighty river, gazing out over the same scenery we're looking at now.'

Her words reinforced that I liked Lori Scott. I let go of the strangeness of her earlier remarks. She thought about Egypt the same way I did.

We sat in a companionable silence for a while, enveloped in the warm evening air, listening to the frogs and crickets strike up their evening chorus. The dahabeeyah rocked slightly as waves lapped gently against the hull. The only slightly jarring note was the procession of brightly lit modern cruise boats that drifted down the centre of the Nile, heading for Aswan. But I couldn't be sorry about this. The tourism industry in Egypt had been badly hit over recent years for one reason or another. It was great to see its resurgence.

Natasha Redwood kept on rehearsing her lines, speaking them quietly to herself, oblivious to us, or her surroundings. She looked very beautiful pooled in the lantern light, quietly intent on memorising her words.

'How's Skylar?' Lori Scott asked at length as the final vestiges of hot colour in the sky were swept away by dark navy nightfall and silver pinprick stars appeared. 'It was good of you guys to stay here with her today. We really didn't need you out on set.'

Adam and I exchanged another glance. 'She's resting in her cabin,' I spoke the literal truth about her current whereabouts. It was not our place to divulge the details of her co-star's second traumatic day in a row.

Thankfully, timing once again proved to be everything. We were spared any further interrogation by Drew Trainer coming across with a towel draped around his neck and slumping into the armchair alongside his co-star. Rabiah appeared in an instant – I'd swear that woman must have the place bugged! She took his order to join Adam in a beer. She was back moments later to deliver it.

Drew Trainer took a long swallow and smacked his lips together in appreciation. 'Local brew?'

Adam nodded. 'Egyptian beer is very good.'

'I'm thinking it's rather a nice set up you've got here.'

Adam nodded again. 'We're living the dream.'

'He means that quite literally,' I added with a smile.

'And anyone with eyes in their head could see what it meant to you guys yesterday: being on the spot for that awesome discovery! I imagine it's not the sort of thing that happens every day! You must be blown away!'

There was really only one way to respond to this. To admit to some of the other discoveries we'd been on the spot for would stretch his credulity beyond all limits. The hard-to-admit truth was that Adam and I had possibly become frighteningly blasé about unearthing ancient Egyptian treasures. 'It really was remarkable,' Adam agreed readily.

'I've never seen anything like it in my life!' the actor enthused. 'It's possibly the most exciting thing that's ever happened to me! Did you get a load of that jewelled collar? Spectacular! Do you think your associate at the Luxor Museum would be willing to arrange a private viewing of the items – in particular that dress and the papyrus – once they've been properly stabilised?'

Adam's hesitation was infinitesimal. But it told me he'd been hoping for a private viewing that was truly private, i.e., just for the two if us.

'I'll see if we can arrange it,' he murmured.

'That'd be great!' Drew Trainer grinned, oblivious to the fractional pause. 'And I imagine our PR team will want to make something of it. I mean – c'mon! A genuine pharaonic haul turning up on location on a movie set! It's every publicist's fantasy!'

Adam's rather strained silence told me exactly what he thought about this. But, in truth, it was no different from the way we'd had to submit some of our other finds to media frenzy. I consoled myself with the thought that it was putting Egypt very firmly back on the tourist map, which was all to the good. But sadly, it seemed our days of being able to keep our discoveries to ourselves – even if only temporarily – were well and truly behind us. (All except one glorious discovery, which remained a closely guarded secret. I cannot begin to tell you how much better it made me feel to remind myself about our tomb still hidden and safely secure, awaiting Director Feisal Ismail's pleasure.)

'I sure would like to learn more about that crazy queen who stirred up the rebellion.' Drew Trainer addressed Adam, 'You said she was a minor wife, right? With a dazzling pectoral collar like that? Jeez!' He borrowed Lori Scott's favourite word. 'Makes me wonder what his most senior queen would have been decked out in if that's an example of a bauble he gave a junior one!'

'Actually, we're working on a theory that Tiye may have had a higher status than scholars originally thought,' I chipped in, although without giving away what had prompted our re-think. Let him think it was the quality of the pectoral collar, which did indeed accord with a queen of exalted rank. It was clue enough.

Lori Scott sat forward and replaced her now-empty lemonade glass on the occasional table in front of her. 'You know, I think the royal women of the harem may have wielded more power than we might imagine,' she said. 'It got me interested: everything you told us yesterday, plus that miraculous find, and not forgetting,' – pulling a face – 'Skylar's crazy visions. So, during the downtime I had on set today I started scouring the Internet. From what I learnt online there was more to the royal harem than simply being the institution where the royal women and children lived and the place the pharaoh went to take his sexual pleasure. The ladies of the harem weren't simply sitting idly about eating sweet treats and trying to catch the pharaoh's eye. The royal harem was run like a full-blown business empire. The finest linen in the country was made there.'

'I think we saw a perfect example of that yesterday,' Drew Trainer interjected, listening with interest. I nodded; immensely gratified to see the genuine Egyptological fascination our experiences yesterday had sparked. But I wasn't especially surprised. I defy anyone to spend time in this ancient and fabled land, learn a bit about its epoch-scorning history and not want to unlock more of its secrets.

Lori Scott acknowledged his words with a brief nod and carried on. 'Despite the barred doors, the royal harem had estates if its own. Under the auspices of the queen, it had administrative and governmental functions. The children of the elite – probably future administrators of the state – were educated there. Far from being some backwater, the harem seems to have been a second centre from which the country was run, parallel to the pharaoh's court. It sounds like it was a powerhouse second only to the throne and perhaps the priesthood of Amun. There was more to those women than might meet the eye.'

Listening to this I figured I could start to see how Tiye had been able to raise rebellion against the divinely anointed pharaoh.

Especially if, as Adam had suggested, she continued to run the harem from Thebes while the king and his entourage, possibly including his other queens, lived most of the year up in Pi-Ramesse, in the northern Delta region.

I was about to open my mouth to say so, but the thought was destined to go forever unspoken. Our intriguing and enlightening discussion was cut short in the most thoroughly unnerving way imaginable.

I'm not sure I'd ever heard real, genuine, terrified and prolonged screaming before. But I heard it now, echoing up through the wooden beams of the dahabeeyah. The blood-curdling sound chilled me to the bone, stiffening the tiny hairs on my forearms, making my nape prickle and my stomach muscles clutch in tight knots of panic.

All four of us leapt up as if scalded. Natasha Redwood also jumped to her feet as if her chair had been suddenly electrified. The small bowl skidded off the table, sending peanuts flying in all directions. We cast shocked, dread-filled glances into each other's eyes. It sounded as if someone was being brutally attacked right here onboard the *Queen Ahmes*!

Chapter 13

'What the...!' Adam and Drew Trainer were already halfway down the spiral staircase.

As the screams continued to shatter the limpid night air, Lori Scott and I hastened after the men. Natasha Redwood dropped her script and rushed across the deck to join us. There were only two females below deck. One was Rabiah, who appeared from the kitchen onto the little landing platform at the bottom of the spiral staircase looking like a startled rabbit as Adam yanked back the door into the lounge-bar. The other of course was Skylar Harrison. And it was assuredly a female doing the screaming. Surely, I thought wildly, this couldn't be Talia Nolan come to stake her claim on the part of Helen of Troy by removing her rival in the most savage way possible! It was a crazy, random thought; probably undeserving of the space it took up in my brain, but I won't deny I had it. I had no reason not to like the Oscar-winning actress (actor; sorry); but there you have it.

But when we hurtled across the lounge-bar and into the corridor beyond with our six cabins lined along either side of it, it was to find Mackenzie King and our skipper Khaled standing in open alarm outside Skylar Harrison's room, from which the bone-chilling screams still emanated.

'Spare key?' the director was demanding urgently. 'The door's locked!'

'At the reception desk, sir; if you permit me...?' Khaled tried to squeeze past him.

'Forget that!' Drew Trainer took command. There was no time to stop him; even though his intent was obvious. He braced himself then gave the closed door a single mighty kick. I watched in some distress as it flew off its hinges, slamming back against the interior cabin wall. It wasn't the first time our beloved dahabeeyah had suffered similar damage. But I knew well enough that doors could be replaced. So, I accepted this sight with as much equanimity as I could muster.

I'd thought, given the ear-splitting crash of the door breaking open, the screaming might stop. It didn't. There was clearly no attacker. From my position in the doorway with light from the corridor spilling into Skylar Harrison's darkened cabin, I could see her tangled in the sheets of her bed. I'd swear she was fast asleep, twisting and turning, and screaming.

Drew Trainer strode into her cabin, closely followed by Mackenzie King and Adam. Lori Scott also darted forward, leaving Natasha Redwood and me hovering by the door, while Khaled and Rabiah exchanged concerned, anxious glances, pressed closely alongside us in the confined space.

Mackenzie King picked up a glass of water from her nightstand in readiness to throw it into the movie star's face. Drew Trainer stepped between them. I thought at first, he intended to slap her. Instead, he reached forward, pulling her upwards into his arms as he sat alongside her on the bed, all in one fluid movement. He cradled her close, crooning and murmuring, and stroking her damp hair back from her perspiring face, 'Skylar, honey; you're ok. Everything's gonna be ok; it's just a bad dream. Hey, it's all ok.'

His soothing voice or the rhythmic touch of his hands, or maybe a combination of the two reached into her subconscious.

She stopped thrashing about. Mercifully the screams died on her lips, replaced by a soft sort of whimper. She opened her eyes, looked wildly about, disorientated and breathing heavily. I watched the rapid rise and fall of her chest beneath the simple nightshirt she was wearing.

'Where am I?' she asked confusedly.

In that moment, I felt a profound and heart-wrenching sympathy for her. One thing was for sure: she'd got a whole lot more than she'd bargained for signing up for this motion picture.

'Skylar, sweetie; it's Drew. We're in Egypt, on the sailboat; remember? We're here to make a movie.'

I saw the breath leave her body in a sudden rush. She sagged in his arms like a rag doll with all the stuffing knocked out of her. 'Oh, thank god!' she breathed, and started to cry, huge wracking sobs that seemed to erupt from the pit of her stomach.

Drew Trainer continued rhythmically to stroke her blonde hair, meeting the director's frowning gaze across the top of her head. 'It was just a bad dream, Sky,' he repeated. 'You're fine now; everything's just fine.'

Perhaps feeling he was intruding, Adam re-joined me, and we stepped away from the doorway. Seeing the poor woman in such a vulnerable state was gut-wrenching but not meant for our eyes. She deserved privacy, not to have us all gawping at her as if she was some kind of freak show.

But the absence of a door still enabled me to hear her words, uttered in a husky, rasping voice as if she were forcing the words past a mouthful of broken glass. 'Suffocating! Pitch black! Airless!'

'Just lie back and rest, honey. You'll be ok.' Drew Trainer attempted to soothe her.

'No!' The terror in her voice was plain for all to hear. 'I'm afraid to close my eyes! I don't want to go there again!'

'Go where?' he asked gently.

'That room!' she cried out. 'The walls closing in on me! I couldn't breathe!'

'Skylar, sweetheart; you were dreaming. You're safe. Nothing here can hurt you. It was just a nightmare.'

Adam and I exchanged a glance. Psychic vision, more like.

I hadn't noticed Rabiah had disappeared until she returned and thrust past us. I spun back and watched agog as she pushed her way into Skylar Harrison's cabin. Our usually timid housekeeper dared to nudge Mackenzie King out of her way and held out a glass full of yellow liquid to the distraught star. 'Drink,' she said firmly. 'You will sleep. No dreams. I will sit.' To my astonishment, she took hold of one of Drew Trainer's arms and pulled him up off the bed, deftly taking his place at Skylar Harrison's side and squeezing her hand. 'You drink,' she invited again. 'I stay. You sleep. All ok.'

I wondered if perhaps Rabiah was possessed of the much-vaunted hypnotic powers as the movie star obediently took the glass and raised it to her lips, immediately calmer. Rabiah looked up from her place at the bedside. 'You leave now,' she instructed the Academy Award winning director and his leading man. 'I stay and keep safe.'

I was amazed to see Skylar Harrison's eyelids already starting to droop. 'Let's leave her to sleep,' I said softly. 'Rabiah will keep a close eye on her.' I smiled my heartfelt thanks at this redoubtable lady and thanked my lucky stars for the day Khaled had brought her into our lives.

We gathered in the lounge-bar. Khaled stood at the bar dispensing drinks. This evening I noticed every one of our usually abstemious guests opted for alcohol: a gin and slimline tonic each for Lori Scott and Natasha Redwood, whiskey for Drew Trainer. Mackenzie King chose a shot of rum to enliven his coca cola. Adam had a beer, and I opted for a small glass of wine.

'Rabiah had the dinner ready prepared,' Khaled said when he'd finished pouring and mixing. 'I'll bring it in so you can help yourselves when you're ready. Just give me a shout.' And he left us to it.

'What in the name of God was *that* all about?' Mackenzie King slumped onto one of the patterned divans looking morose. There was no way of misunderstanding him. A single glance around at everyone's faces told its own story. The quiet, relaxing evening we might have fondly hoped was in store had been shattered.

'I think the visions she saw at Karnak must have upset her,' The words were out of my mouth before I'd engaged my brain sufficiently to judge the sense in voicing them. My only excuse, I think, was that I was as thoroughly unsettled by Skylar Harrison's terrified screaming as everyone else – and perhaps feeling guilty since I was the one who'd suggested the trip to see if her psychic antennae picked up any further telepathic wavelengths. It had proved more successful than I might have dared imagine. But the dramatic scenes she'd tuned into had been traumatising to say the least. It had been bad enough having them described to us. Skylar Harrison, from what she'd told us, had actually *seen* the conspirators tried and put to death. A grisly but largely abstract historical event to me must have been all too real for her. I could well imagine the flashbacks she might be susceptible to every time she closed her eyes. Yes, I could see how it might bring on nightmares.

I was unprepared for the fury that swept into Mackenzie King's face. 'You took her to Karnak? What the hell were you thinking? Are you crazy?'

'No. I – er – we – I mean – she – thought –' I started to dissemble.

Adam reached for my hand to silence me and spoke on my behalf. 'Miss Harrison was upset last night,' he explained levelly. 'She asked for our help. We agreed that going to the places where the ancient drama played out – and where your movie is set – might enable her to confront the – er – the – well, whatever it is that seems to be happening to her.'

The director narrowed his eyes on Adam's face. 'You think she is really seeing visions and channelling spirits from Egypt's ancient past?'

Adam met his gaze without flinching. 'If there's another explanation, I'm yet to find it, sir,' he said respectfully but firmly while Mackenzie King continued to stare back at him, black brows drawn down, a prominent crease in his forehead.

(I think by silent, mutual understanding we both knew we wouldn't be mentioning our trip to see the old witchy woman.)

Adam went on, 'We believed the best chance Miss Harrison had of being able to continue with the movie was to see if –'

'Instead, you frightened her half out of her wits,' Mackenzie King cut across him. 'By rights I should sue you for sabotage.'

'– she saw anything more –' Adam trailed off as the director's words sank in.

'But I won't bother, since this picture is clearly cursed! I think, all things considered, I have no option but to close down production – at least for a few days. Maybe that will give her time to sort herself out before the Media scents blood and descends on us like a pack of hungry wolves!' With a last disgusted took at us, Mackenzie King got up. 'I'll take dinner at one of the hotels in town,' he said. 'If you can ask your skipper to call me a cab. I'll wait on the jetty.' And with that, he turned and stalked to the door.

Natasha Redwood stared after the director as the door closed behind him. 'Oh,' she said. 'I didn't see that coming. I think I might just go to my cabin and watch some YouTube on my phone. And maybe call home. Could you ask your guy to send me in something to eat on a tray?' And she, too, got up and left us.

Once more, it was just Drew Trainer, Lori Sott, Adam and me. I looked at my shoes for a while, feeling awkward. 'Sorry,' I murmured. 'I never should have let the cat out of the bag.'

'Don't mind Mac,' Lori Sott said kindly. 'His bark is worse than his bite. He's had a bad end to the day, and this has just set the seal on it. When he calms down, he'll see Skylar's probably just done him a favour. She handed him the excuse he needed to halt things for a bit. A few days might buy him time to decide what to do about Talia Nolan.'

Drew Trainer got up and approached the bar. 'Mind if I fix myself a refill?'

Adam jumped up to play host, but the actor waved him back into his seat, and he subsided alongside me again.

Lori Scott shook her head as Drew Trainer waved the gin bottle at her. She looked at us with bright, inquisitive eyes. 'So, you guys have spent the day with Skylar at Karnak,' she said. 'I'm looking forward to seeing it.'

'But not through Skylar's eyes, by the sound of it,' Drew Trainer said ruefully. He waved the wine bottle at me, and I accepted a small splash as a top-up. 'If her performance just now was anything to judge by, she saw something that freaked her out good n' proper.'

In a few short sentences Adam filled them in about Skylar Harrison's visions of the trial and execution of the conspirators. Lori Scott pulled faces to express her revulsion at what he described.

'Poor Skylar,' she murmured. 'I'm not sure any of this is what she thought she was signing up for on this contract.'

'We tried to get her to open up about what happened to the queen who led the insurrection.' Adam went on.

'Tiye,' Lori Scott put in.

Adam nodded. 'She confirmed the queen *was* tried for her crimes,' he said. 'But then she clammed up. Just said there were worse ways to punish someone than to execute or force them to take their own life.' Then he turned his head, and it was to me to whom he addressed his final words, although ostensibly still speaking to the actors. 'I don't know what you thought ...? But I was listening to her words just now. It seems to me that it's the queen's spirit she's channelling the most.' His meaningful look reminded me of the "visitation" she'd had during the paper-and-pin-performance. 'I think it was the queen her nightmare was about.' I stared back into his mesmerising navy-turning-violet eyes as he said, 'I reckon she knows exactly what happened to Tiye. And I don't think Tiye will rest until it's out in the open.'

I felt a deep shiver snake down my spine. That my usually rational husband and I were engaging in this crazy conjecture showed just how deeply held was our new belief in Skylar Harrison's psychic powers.

Perhaps understandably, Drew Trainer was less susceptible to the chills than I. Maybe he didn't have that spine-tingling feeling that the ancient queen was somewhere just beyond the periphery of our vision, orchestrating things. 'It's the hapless prince I feel sorry for,' he stated, then lifted his whiskey glass to his lips. 'His mother surely knew the risk she was taking. But you have to wonder if her son colluded in her scheming: power hungry and eager for advancement whatever the cost; or whether he had his strings pulled like a puppet. A pawn in the game, played for the highest stakes, and its victim. His mother gambled with his life and lost. He paid the ultimate price. It doesn't seem much consolation that he was permitted to commit suicide in private. It still meant he wound up dead, surely cut down in his prime.'

'Pentaweret,' Adam said.

'I'm sorry?' Lori Scott enquired, as if unsure she'd heard him.

'Pentaweret,' Adam said. 'That was the name of the unfortunate prince. Except, it wasn't his real name. In common with many of the conspirators, he was tried and convicted under a pseudonym so his name would die with him.'

'And what does his name mean?' I asked, thinking back to the changed names of the other plotters that meant they remained recognisable even though cursed by the gods in their new derivatives. Maybe we could identify him among Ramses III's vast progeny of sons.

Adam looked at me and scratched his ear. 'Well, Taweret was the ancient Egyptian hippopotamus goddess of childbirth and fertility. It's hard to say what his name might mean, but some have translated it as "he of the great, fertile female".'

Lori Scott's unusual eyes were brighter than ever. 'You said you thought the queen, his mother, was of higher rank than many previously believed,' she said. 'Maybe that's the proof.'

Adam flashed a quick glance into my eyes, for of course we already knew, thanks to Skylar Harrison, that Tiye was the foremost among royal ladies. Then he looked at Drew Trainer. 'There are a few oddities about Prince "Pentaweret",' he said. 'First, of course that he was permitted to take his own life in private. Perhaps this was simply because of his status as the pharaoh's son. But, I agree, it begs the question about the extent to which he may have been a puppet of his mother and her fellow plotters. Perhaps more interesting, is that he was never given the epithet of "great criminal", which was the label applied to most of the accused rebels. And he was arraigned with offenders of the third level, whose crimes were principally failing to report the conspiracy rather than active participation. But, most fascinating of all, is that his body was preserved, rather than being cast into the burning brazier like the others. Preserved in somewhat unusual fashion, I'll grant you. But, preserved, nonetheless. It's on display in the Cairo Museum, if you're ever minded to go and take a look.'

Lori Scott stared at him as if he'd suddenly changed colour. 'The body of the prince *survived*?' she exclaimed, tiger-yellow eyes widening.

'Yes, but he's not a pretty sight,' Adam said. 'He's often been dubbed "the screaming prince".'

Considering the unnerving noise we'd just been subjected to, I thought this rather apposite.

Drew Trainer was looking at him in open disbelief. 'The more you tell us about it, the weirder this ancient murder-mystery gets!' he remarked. 'But I'll admit you've got me hooked. I still think Mac is shooting the wrong movie. So, tell us about this "screaming prince".

'Ok, you may have heard about the discovery in 1881 of a cache of royal mummies hidden in the Theban hills by priests during the 21st Dynasty. Our friend Ahmed Abd el-Rassul – your driver and security man –' (in case they were struggling to place him) '– is descended from the local family who stumbled across this treasure trove.'

'Another example of fact being stranger than fiction,' I put in, and quickly qualified my meaning. 'The discovery of the royal cache, that is; not Ahmed being descended from the infamous Abd el-Rassul family; although it does give him a claim to fame, he's ever so proud of. Pretty much all the A'list pharaohs were there: Ramses the Great, Seti I, Thutmosis III, and poor, murdered Ramses III, to name but a few.'

Adam took a long swallow of his beer and took up the tale. 'Inside a plain cedar-wood anthropoid coffin was the mummy of a young man. Rather than being wrapped in linens, his body had been sewn inside a goatskin – ritually unclean to the ancient Egyptians. When the men of the Antiquities Service removed him from it, a sickening, putrid odour filled the room. His body was stretched rigid, stomach tightly contracted, with both his hands and feet bound. But it was his agonised facial expression that earned him his nickname:

head thrown back and mouth wide open in a hideous silent scream. Their conclusion was that he'd died a violent, terrible death.'

'Sounds like something out of a horror story,' Lori Scott grimaced.

'For years, he was referred to as "Unknown Man E". There was no clue to his identity on his animal-skin shroud, and his unfinished coffin was left blank and uninscribed. But the priests who hid the mummies of the ancient royals must have had an idea he'd been someone notable to bother moving him at all – especially keeping him in such exalted company. So, he was put on display in the Cairo Museum along with the other royal mummies, but with a question mark instead of a name on his label.'

'How appropriate,' I murmured thinking of the blank princes' label texts at Medinet Habu.

'How was he identified as the unfortunate prince caught up in the harem conspiracy?' Lori Scott asked.

'In 2012, Zahi Hawass, then head honcho for the Supreme Council of Antiquities, published the results of DNA testing and CT scanning carried out on a number of the royal mummies. It was explosive stuff. The CT scans revealed the deep gash in Ramses III's neck that proved he'd had his throat slit. The investigation also showed that "the screaming prince" shared a Y-chromosome DNA sequence with the mummy of Ramses III consistent with a father-son relationship.'

'Could the tests establish a cause of death?' Drew Trainer asked.

Adam shook his head. 'Not definitively. Suggestions made were that a compressed fold of skin around the prince's neck might indicate suffocation by strangulation or hanging.'

'But I thought he was permitted to take his own life in private,' I said. 'So, strangulation can't be right. Although, I suppose he might have thought hanging himself a quicker option than poison if he'd witnessed the tortuous deaths of those who drank the mandrake potion.'

'Whatever his method, I think we can say the poor prince paid a terrible price for being caught up in his mother's conspiracy,' Drew Trainer concluded. 'A traitor's death and a ritually unclean burial, sewn inside an animal skin. Yuck! I can only imagine his mother rued the day she first thought of challenging the succession! I can sure see why you're interested to know what they did to *her*.'

We decided to go back outside to the upper deck to eat. There's something about sitting out under the stars on a warm, Egyptian evening that settles the soul. Just what we needed after our traumatic start to the evening and rather unpleasant discussion.

Rabiah had prepared a simple tagine of lamb, chickpeas and spices, served with freshly baked crusty bread, ideal for mopping up all the fragrant juices. Lori Scott ate a minuscule portion, of course. Although I was pleased to see Drew Trainer tuck in with rather more gusto.

'Mac sure is missing out, storming off into town like that,' he remarked between mouthfuls.

'Do you really think he'll close down production?' I asked.

Lori Scott gave one of her trademark shrugs. 'Probably. But it will only be for a few days at most. He was just being melodramatic saying the movie is cursed.'

'Do you mind?'

She shrugged again. 'It gives us more time to go over the script. And, who knows? Maybe there'll be time for a little sightseeing. I'd sure like that.'

'So long as it includes a visit to the museum to get another eyeful of those stunning artefacts,' Drew Trainer reminded us.

But I didn't want to be diverted back onto a discussion about what we'd found. I felt rather that we'd done our ancient murder-mystery to death. No pun intended! 'Tell me more about the movie,' I prompted, looking at Lori Scott. 'I don't even know what role you're here to play. Obviously not Helen of Troy or Nefertari.'

'My character is someone called Iset-Nofret,' she said. 'Apparently she was Ramses the Great's second Royal Wife after Nefertari. The script portrays her as a devious minx who stirs up trouble between Ramses and his favourite wife insinuating that Helen is trying to seduce the pharaoh while sitting out the Trojan War in Egypt. She creates an atmosphere of rivalry, hostility and intrigue. Although, of course, there's a happy-ever-after for Ramses and Nefertari in the end, and Helen goes back to Mycenae with her husband Menelaus once Troy has fallen to the Greeks.'

Adam rolled his eyes at the heavens, then looked at Drew Trainer. 'The director and you had it right about making the wrong movie. If the producers wanted to tell the story of three rival queens, look no further than the court of Ramses III. Forget Ramses the Great! There's no historical evidence that Nefertari and Iset-Nofret jostled for position. And, of course, Helen of Troy was the pharaoh's cousin, not his queen, and doesn't seem to have disrupted marital relations during her sojourn in Egypt. But, from everything we've learnt, Ramses III appears to have been a tyrant who positively pitted his wives and sons against each other!'

'So, find us a script writer,' Drew Trainer said, getting up and excusing himself to go to the bathroom.

'You know, I think it's a cool idea,' Lori Scott mused. 'And it might be a way of solving Mac's problem of having two Helens. Of course, he'd have to break contract with all of us... but if it was for a better offer...' She trailed off for a moment, looking out across the dark, shifting waters of the Nile towards the twinkling lights of Luxor in the distance. The call to prayer started up on the far riverbank, an exotic if rather tuneless background accompaniment to our conversation. 'You know, I quite fancy the idea of playing this Queen Tiye who managed to incite an open rebellion and arrange for the assassination of her jerk of a husband! She sounds like my type of woman!'

Try as we might, we didn't seem able to stop discussing her! I made a valiant attempt to steer us back to moviemaking. 'But you said you fought hard for your role in the film,' I reminded her. 'You said it was a role you were born to play.'

She gave one of her airy hand gestures. 'That's because I wanted to be in a movie set in ancient Egypt. I told you, it's been an enduring fascination. And who doesn't want to play a troublemaker, however much of a departure the characterisation might be from reality? That's what I love about acting: the chance to become a different person and explore all the shades of light and dark. Sure, I fought hard. But in the end, Mac knew he had no choice but to cast me.'

Adam and I both let our silence be an invitation for her to go on. It was easier than asking a direct question. With a gin and tonic inside her, and having got to know us a bit, I rather think Lori Scott was inclined to open up.

'Mac owes me,' she said. 'And he knows it. I could have made life difficult for him while the #Me-Too Movement was raging across the world, but I didn't.'

I looked down at my lap and felt Adam shift uncomfortably beside me. I recalled the way Drew Trainer had laid one hand across her wrist during dinner on their first evening on board and that I'd overheard Mackenzie King telling her she'd made her point and should let it go. Whatever it was, it seemed an open secret among the Hollywooders. I remembered also that Drew Trainer had never joined in whenever the #Me-Too Movement had cropped up in conversation. But he wasn't here to stop her talking now.

'Oh, it's not what you think,' she said, interpreting our facial expressions. Her words drew our eyes back to her face. 'Mac has never been guilty of harassment, sexual or otherwise. There's no way Talia Nolan would have anything to do with this movie if that were the case. She made that crystal clear when Victor Bernstein was outed. But it's possible to be vicariously guilty.'

'You don't have to tell us,' Adam said, sounding uncomfortable. 'It's none of our business.'

She rested her gaze on his face for a moment. 'It's because women never talk about this stuff that certain types of men get away with it,' she said at last. 'Lots of brave women came forward to tell their stories. But I only told part of mine.'

'What happened?' I asked gently.

She met my gaze directly, her eyes looking like molten gold in the soft light from the hurricane lamps. 'I was one of the young actors Victor groomed. Remember, I was fresh into Hollywood from Ozzie soap land, trying for my first break. I was one of the lucky ones. He never tried anything serious with me. But Mac inadvertently walked in one day when I was in Victor's office. Victor was asking me to unbutton my blouse – not that I have much to look at!' She attempted a laugh that didn't quite come off. 'Mac saw what was going on. But Victor put pressure on him not to report it. Lucky for me, it meant Victor didn't come near me again, and I still got my break. I think he realised Mac could have made him squirm. And it probably did Mac's career no harm either since he agreed to stay silent. But I guess I saw it as a betrayal. Mac's a powerful man now in Hollywood. He could have spoken out last year but didn't. I've been pissed with him ever since.'

'Does Drew Trainer know?' Adam asked.

'Sure,' she said. 'Drew and Mac go way back. They were at college together. Drew knows about it, and says it changed Mac. He says Mac felt soiled by association. But that if he'd spoken out last year, everyone would've asked why he didn't say something sooner. He saw it as a no-win. But he gave me the role, even though this was one of the hottest movies being cast. So, I figure I got even. Although I like to put a shot across his bows every now and then.' Her eyes gleamed and I knew I had my explanation for that strange conversation on the first night.

I thought about the young director who had so sensitively animated my favourite fairy-tale. I guessed maybe I was starting to see how something had changed in Mackenzie King because of the experience Lori Scott described. It perhaps meant he'd lost his soft centre, become somewhat more hard-bitten; more of the man he was today. Maybe there were more casualties than the obvious victims of Victor Bernstein's behaviour.

'On behalf of all men, I'm sorry you had to experience that,' Adam said sincerely. 'We're not all cut from the same cloth.'

Lori Scott looked across the table at us, smiled at Adam and shrugged again. 'I know that,' she said. 'It was a long time ago. Victor Bernstein got what he deserved.' She picked up a crust of bread and nibbled on it before going on. 'Like we said the other day; you have to wonder if Victor Bernstein and Ramses III had something in common. It took a strong woman to stand up to them, and possibly good men got caught in the fallout. Except, poor Tiye and her co-conspirators paid a terrible price.' She looked up as Drew Trainer re-joined us. 'So, yes, all things considered, I would very much like to bring her to the silver screen and tell her story. I'll get onto Mac about it when he gets back; always assuming he's in a better mood.'

Except Mackenzie King didn't come back. Not later that evening, and not the following morning either.

Chapter 14

Skylar Harrison was immediately suspicious when Mackenzie King failed to appear at breakfast and remained absent when Rabiah plated up a fresh chicken salad for lunch.

I sincerely hoped our inestimable housekeeper had been able to snatch some sleep, having sat all night at the troubled movie star's bedside. But she looked bright and alert, smilingly brushing off my attempts to get her to take some time out to rest.

Skylar Harrison, by comparison, looked pale and wan, with dark, violet smudges under her eyes. When I enquired whether she had slept ok, she confirmed she'd had a deep and dreamless sleep. (I made a mental note to ask Rabiah what the yellow liquid had been.) So, it was clearly mental trauma putting those bruise-like shadows under her eyes – and not without cause. What with violent psychic visions, the melodramatic and scene-stealing appearance of Talia Nolan on set, and Mackenzie King's increasingly bad temper, the poor woman had every reason for the paranoia I sensed in the way she kept pulling her mobile phone out from a pocket to glance at the time. Natasha Redwood had already told her that the director had threatened to cease production for a while.

Drew Trainer's attempts to reach Mackenzie King on his mobile phone proved unsuccessful. 'He must have it switched off,' he muttered.

'He's gone to see a lawyer,' Skylar Harrison prophesied. 'He wants to know how to break the contract with me. He's decided I'm a fruit loop!'

Adam attempted to reassure her. 'I doubt that's it,' he said, his tone of voice an obvious attempt to bolster her flagging spirits. 'This is Luxor, not New York or Los Angeles. I doubt there's anyone within three thousand miles of here who could give him that sort of advice.'

'So, where *is* he?' she demanded. This, of course, was the unanswerable question. Mackenzie King had been in a foul mood when he left, but that was no explanation for why he had failed to return. I couldn't imagine his motivation was a desire to subject one of his leading actors to the mental torture writ large across her strained features. But, of course, this still left him absent and unaccounted for.

'The trouble is,' Lori Scott murmured to me as an aside, 'all the time Mac doesn't make a decision between Skylar and Talia, he's replicating the behaviour of your anti-hero of the moment: Ramses III. Mac might not intend it, or even be aware of it – he's not deliberately cruel – but it's pitting them against each other.'

'Mac said he was going to take dinner in one of the Luxor hotels,' Drew Trainer reminded us. 'He asked your guy Khaled to call him a cab. Is it worth seeing if we can track down the driver and ask where he went?'

I glanced at Adam. 'Is Khaled back yet?' Our skipper had gone into Luxor this morning to buy the fixtures needed to repair the shattered door to Skylar Harrison's cabin.

Adam nodded and Khaled was duly called into the lounge-bar as we finished lunch. When I say, "finished lunch", I speak only for Adam and myself. The four actors picked at their food and moved it around their plates a bit but rarely lifted their forks to their mouths. They all looked grateful to have a reason to put down their cutlery as Khaled presented himself. 'Mohammed was y'rr man,' he said in his distinctive and incongruous Scottish brogue.

I'll admit I couldn't help but roll my eyes skywards at this. My fingers and toes were insufficient for counting the number of local taxi drivers called Mohammed. It's Egypt's most popular male name, although Ahmed comes a close second.

'Can you call him and find out where he took Mac?'

'Of course, sir.'

I wasn't sure I was especially surprised, sipping a cup of peppermint tea a few minutes later, to learn that Mackenzie King had, in fact, remained on the west bank and asked Mohammed (the one with the cheeky, gap-toothed smile and excessive fondness for Paco Rabanne aftershave) to take him to the secluded and exclusive hotel where Talia Nolan was staying.

Skylar Harrison's reaction to this news was predictable but possibly did her no great credit. 'The snake!' she spat. 'If he's given her the role, I'll sue him midway into the next century!'

Natasha Redwood looked over at Drew Trainer. 'Is there any chance he could still be there?' It seemed a bigger question she was asking.

'What do you mean?' he frowned back at her.

'Y'know; could – er – could Mac still be with – ahem – with Talia, at her hotel?' There was no mistaking the innuendo.

I noticed Lori Scott sit up straighter, her tiger-eyes bright and alert.

'What are you gettin' at?' Drew Trainer's frown deepened.

'C'mon, Drew!' Natasha Redwood said, flicking glossy, dark hair back over her shoulder and fixing smouldering eyes on him.

'I'm sure you're not the only one to know about the pash Mac had for Talia back in the day.'

Drew Trainer shifted uncomfortably.

'Word on the street was he asked her to marry him,' Natasha Redwood pressed. 'They had a hot affair, but then she went and married Tim Craven. Although, of course, they divorced last year.'

Lori Scott flashed a glance into my eyes that seemed to say "Aha!". Ah, ok, I thought, so this hold she suspects Talia Nolan has on the director is that he's still in love with her. My sympathy for Skylar Harrison ratcheted up a notch. Now I understood the altercation I'd overheard between Drew Trainer and Mackenzie King a couple of mornings ago. Mackenzie King knew he'd cast Skylar Harrison fair and square after his old flame pulled out, but all his emotional instincts went to war with the decision once it became clear she was still set on the part.

'Call her,' Lori Scott said unequivocally. 'Find out if he's there.'

It really left Drew Trainer no choice, for all that I could see he would rather not. I have to say, I was finding all the revelations intensely interesting. It was a bit like having exclusive personal access to a red-hot Hollywood gossip column. Of course, the confidentiality agreement Adam and I had signed when arrangements were being made to have the Hollywooders stay onboard the *Queen Ahmes* during location filming ensured our discretion. Lucky for them, as it turned out. When the contracts were drawn up, I don't suppose for one minute they could have imagined the stories we would be able to tell. The gagging order ensured our silence, had our personal integrity proved unequal to the task! Speaking as someone well practised at keeping secrets, I won't deny being mildly affronted by the requirement to sign their legal disclaimer. But, right now, I guess I could understand why their people had demanded it.

The exclusive credentials of the hotel where Talia Nolan was staying were such that it was not the work of moments to be put through, even if you happened to be Drew Trainer; heartthrob, hunk and Tinseltown's man of the moment. None of the Hollywooders had her personal mobile number: Talia Nolan living up to her extremely private reputation. The hotel reception staff did an impressive job of screening the call. But finally, after much to-ing and fro-ing, Drew Trainer had the world-famous Oscar-winning actor on the line.

He omitted to put her on speakerphone, so we were unable to hear both sides of the conversation. Party only to his question about whether Mac had shown up there last night (of course, we already knew he had) and – more hesitantly – whether he was still there now.

After several moments, Drew Trainer pressed the red button to end the call and glanced around at us all, looking perplexed. 'Mac was there last night,' he confirmed. 'But Talia sent him packing. He offered to get the scriptwriter to go back to the story board and invent a whole new part for her. She said it was Helen or a lawsuit.'

Lori Scott let out a long breath. 'Phewee! Mac must want to smooth things over pretty bad to go to lengths like that!'

'She's deadly serious about wanting Helen.' Natasha Redwood said.

Skylar Harrison chewed her bottom lip and studied the oriental rug at her feet but made no comment. It sounded to me as if Mackenzie King had done his best to find a workable compromise that would enable him to keep her in the role she'd successfully auditioned for. I hoped this made her feel better. My opinion of the absent director crept upwards.

Drew Trainer went on as if he hadn't been interrupted. 'They argued and Mac left Talia's hotel around 9pm. He was on foot.'

'He should have been able to walk back here in about forty-five minutes,' Adam said, glancing at me for confirmation. 'It sounds as if we need to get Ahmed to come over.'

But Drew Trainer vetoed this eminently sensible suggestion. 'No, it's too soon to start involving the local police. We don't want to blow the whole thing out of proportion. It's possible Mac simply hit a local bar, downed a few too many and checked into some local hostelry to sleep it off.'

'So, why isn't he answering his cell phone?' Natasha Redwood frowned.

'It's probably out of juice,' the actor shrugged. 'The last thing Mac will thank us for is overreaction, especially if the Media gets wind of it. I can see the headlines now. If Mac was in a funk last night, he'll flip out completely if we screw up.'

Lori Scott fixed a level gaze on him. 'So, what do you suggest? We just sit about and wait? He might have fallen in a ditch or been bitten by a snake!'

Natasha Redwood intervened. 'Let's not panic,' she advised, then looked over at Adam. 'Would it be possible to walk from Talia's hotel to the temple where our trailers are set up? I'm thinking, he might have wanted some time to cool off after his spat with Talia and before seeing the rest of us. His trailer would be a comfortable place to spend the night.'

Adam tilted his head to one side. I could see he was calculating the distance. 'Yes, I would think so,' he said at length.

It's probably a similar time in the opposite direction, upwards of half an hour's walking. But it's mostly straight lines, down to the canal road from the hotel, along it through Gurna, and then inland again past the Colossi of Memnon. He'll be pretty familiar with the route having been driven there and back a few times now.'

Natasha Redwood looked back at Drew Trainer. 'Surely the obvious place for Mac to be is on set, albeit without his cell phone charger.'

Drew Trainer's clearing expression told me he could see the sense in this suggestion. 'We should check it out,' he agreed.

So, Adam got his wish to call Ahmed. But just to be our driver. And under strict instructions to say nothing to reveal Mackenzie King was missing.

There was an air of barely suppressed excitement about our police pal from the moment he jumped down from behind the wheel of the minibus he brought to a dramatic stop in a cloud of swirling dust on the riverbank above our landing platform. Ahmed does so love to make a dramatic entrance. He respectfully pulled back the passenger door on its rollers to allow the Hollywooders to climb onboard, way too pre-occupied to bother counting heads or register that we were one person short.

As Adam and I brought up the rear, ready to step up into the bus and join the others, he pulled us aside with an urgent gesture. 'Afterwards, Habiba, she says you are to come to the museum. The papyrus we finded, it is now laid out flat and ready to be readed!'

Holding Adam's hand, I felt a buzz go through him as if he'd been wired up to the national grid. Suddenly our search for the absent movie-director became a matter of supreme indifference to us both. I was quite sure we'd have happily hopped on our scooters there and then and made a beeline for the Luxor Museum had good manners allowed.

Groaning with frustration, Adam said, 'Ok, let's get to the temple set and back as quickly as we can.'

The sun was high overhead as we made the familiar journey to the temple of Medinet Habu. Usually, this demanded travelling with the minibus curtains pulled tightly closed across the windows. Air conditioning did its best to counteract the fearsome afternoon heat but allowing the aggressive sun to radiate through glass was usually not to be tolerated. Today I noticed we all kept the curtains open a crack or wider. Our gazes scoured the scenery we passed, hunting for any sign of the missing moviemaker. Of course, it was perfectly ludicrous to think we'd spot him lying in a ditch by the roadside this late in the day. This route had been traversed by donkey carts, tourist buses, taxis and locals on mopeds, camels or their own two feet since first light. But I guess it was human nature to keep our eyes peeled just in case we should happen to spot him sharing a hubble-bubble pipe in an open doorway, hunched over an impromptu game of dominoes so beloved of Luxor's men, or assisting one of the be-robed local women to beat dust from a carpet on the open balcony of one of the rustic red-brick dwellings lining the canal.

Unsurprisingly, when Ahmed brought the minibus to a standstill in the parking lot adjacent to the Medinet Habu complex, none of these sightings had been made. It was just the usual rural and semi-urban scenes of chickens, donkeys and big-horned cattle standing among bullrushes and raggedy, brightly clothed children playing barefoot in the dust beneath nodding palm trees.

Unclipping my seatbelt, I remembered the anticipation with which I'd approached that first morning here only a couple of days ago. Impossible now, to imagine how things might have progressed had Skylar Harrison not proved herself the Hollywood manifestation of Mystic Meg and had Adam's Hollywood crush not turned up hoping to snatch back the role she openly discarded. I felt vaguely robbed of the chance to see a movie in the making, especially as it looked as if I would have to wait awhile for it to recommence. But oh, so grateful to have been on the spot to witness the miraculous discovery of the alabaster box. I could only hope it may yet prove to be the key to unlock the truth behind the so-called harem conspiracy.

'Right, shall we crack on?' I urged brightly to chivvy everyone along.

I noticed Drew Trainer and Lori Scott move to flank Skylar Harrison as we approached the Eastern High Gate, now entrance to the temple complex.

'You ok, honey?' Drew Trainer asked.

She hooked an arm through his. 'Yep; fine; thanks.'

Either this were true, or else she was determined to put a brave face on it and not give in to another case of the heebie-jeebies. But I saw her knuckles showing white as she gripped his arm, as if he alone might keep her standing upright. We made it through into the forecourt where the five trailers were anchored to the ground without any repeat of her hallucinations, so I dared to let out the breath I'd sucked in.

The temple remained closed to the public. A few movie crew folks were milling around. I recognised some faces from the other day.

Michael, the young assistant-gofer-whatever came rushing forward, wiping a film of perspiration from above his top lip with the back of one hand. 'I wasn't expecting to see you guys today. I got a text from Mac last night to say he wanted to pause things for a day or two. He asked me to ensure the camera rigging was secure and get all the costumes properly labelled for the scene changes.'

Ah, I thought, so the director was in possession of his mobile phone.

'Have you seen him?' Drew Trainer asked shortly, cutting across him.

'I'm sorry...?'

'Mackenzie. Have you seen him today? Has he been on set?'

'Er - no. I wasn't expecting him – or you people, for that matter. I hope there isn't a problem. Is everything ok?'

'Perfectly,' Natasha Redwood interjected smoothly, reaching out to lay a lightly restraining hand on Drew Trainer's tanned wrist. 'We just wanted to check everything was being done according to Mac's instructions and to look around the temple, since we didn't all get a chance the other day.'

Michael cast her a somewhat harried look, as if not at all appreciative of an interruption he appeared to interpret as being checked up on.

But I wondered if her words hadn't been perhaps a bit inspired when I noticed Skylar Harrison walking as if in a trance along the central causeway leading to the temple entrance pylon between the grand façade of towering, deeply carved outer walls. Ramses III smiting his enemies was prominent on the left-side.

What stopped me in my tracks as I caught up with the beautiful blonde bombshell, was realising her eyes were screwed tightly shut.

It was as if she were being pulled gravitationally by some unseen force. I failed to see how someone could traverse a whole – enormous – temple with eyes shut, despite the uneven floor, and still, apparently, have all the unswerving direction of a heat-seeking missile. A temple moreover she had never set foot inside before. Yet that appeared to be her intent.

It was only Adam and I, initially, who joined her, perhaps more attuned to her extra-sensory abilities since our experiences with her yesterday. Drew Trainer, Lori Scott and Natasha Redwood, presumably, were checking out Mackenzie King's trailer – and perhaps theirs too – for any signs of overnight occupancy. Ahmed had told us he would wait in the coffee shop opposite the temple entrance.

Skylar Harrison walked directly across the first courtyard without looking right or left. She ignored the statues of Ramses III standing against the square pillars on our right and the Window of Appearances that once led to the mudbrick-built royal palace on our left. She walked on through the second open courtyard, with both Adam and me anxiously trailing her in case she should trip and fall on the uneven flagstones, past the unlabelled processions of royal princes and princesses that Adam had pointed out a couple of days ago. Up the ramp, through the shaded, columned portico, still with so much of its ancient colour preserved, and we were out in the open air again, this time less of an open court, but what remained of what was once a hypostyle hall, which must originally have been a densely packed ensemble of columns, now broken to stubs, surrounded on the outer perimeter by small individual shrines and dark chambers.

Skylar Harrison walked, eyes closed and purposeful, all the way to the back outer wall of the temple. Here, she stopped. Opened her eyes. Looked about her, confused and disorientated. 'Oh!' she said. 'Where is the doorway?'

I looked at the carved solid stone wall and then back at her, blank and uncomprehending. 'There should be a doorway here,' she frowned. 'It led to another high gate on the outer perimeter wall.' She was emphatic. 'Very much like the Eastern High Gate we came through earlier to access the site, but at this end of the temple.'

Adam was nodding thoughtfully. 'I don't pretend to be an expert on 20th Dynasty architecture,' he said, 'but I have a feeling she's right. I'm sure I've read somewhere that there was a mirror-image gateway on this side of the temple that may also have been used to house part of the royal harem. It's now ruined, of course; and no attempt has been made to re-construct it.'

With no warning, Skylar Harrison reached out and gripped his forearm. She looked wildly into his eyes. I've never seen a woman deranged before but, in that moment, I think I discovered what one looked like. *'She's here!'* she breathed.

'I'm sorry?' Adam looked at her in alarm. 'I'm not sure I follow...'

Her knuckles showed white as she clung to his arm. 'I can feel her presence!'

I looked about me at the stubby, bleached-white bases of what were once proud standing columns, many with their broken-off circular stumps carved exquisitely with reliefs of rearing cobras looking quite jaunty in their royal crowns of Upper and Lower Egypt. There was nobody here that I could see. Looking back at her wild eyes staring fixedly at something beyond the periphery of my vision,

I felt my blood run cold. A deep shiver snaked down my spine as all the tiny hairs on my forearms stood on end. Watching her staring in that fixed yet at the same time rather vacant way, I had a sense if I concentrated hard enough, I might see the ghost of the long-dead ancient queen materialise out of thin air in front of us. It must surely be Tiye she meant. I felt myself succumb to a bad case of the chills, notwithstanding the furious heat and blinding sunshine.

Skylar Harrison let go of Adam's arm and put both hands up to her temples. '*Here*! Inside my head!' she moaned. 'She's calling to me!' And then, she did what she appeared to do best. Her breathing stalled, her eyes rolled back in her head, she sank to her knees and then toppled forward onto her front in the dust at our feet.

Adam and I looked at each other in consternation. 'This is becoming a bad habit,' I muttered as together we reached forward to scoop her back up again.

The sound of running feet behind us made me turn as we got her upright, propped limply between us. It must be said, for a woman as slender as a papyrus stem, she was a dead weight. Drew Trainer and Lori Scott jogged forward along the central causeway between the broken-off columns.

'What happened?' Drew Trainer demanded.

'Oh, God; has she had another telepathic visitation?' Lori Scott's voice overlapped his. She looked anxiously at the wilting actor being held up by Adam and me.

Gently this time, we eased her down again, so she was sitting slumped on the bleached stone, still with one of us on each side of her as ballast. I scarcely knew how or where to begin in trying to describe this latest episode.

'It was creepy,' I tried to put into words that sense of watching someone commune with a ghost but broke off as Skylar Harrison groaned and started to come to.

'She walked through the entire temple with her eyes closed, as if she were being pulled on an invisible thread.' Adam said as she sat up.

Drew Trainer dropped to one knee on the dusty stone in front of her, reached forward and lifted her chin with one hand so, as she opened her eyes, she was forced to look at him. 'Skylar, honey, this is getting scary. You can't keep blanking out like this. You might get seriously hurt.'

Lori Scott also plopped down onto her knees, facing her co-star. 'What did you see this time?'

But Skylar Harrison was shaking her head. 'Please... tell her to stop,' she begged, turning her head to look beseechingly first at Adam, then me. 'I just want her to go away and leave me alone!'

'Who?' Adam asked gently. 'The ancient queen? Tiye?'

Skylar Harrison nodded miserably. Her eyes were wet, and her voice splintered. 'I thought I could cope with it at first. But I don't *want* to *see* these *things*! I don't want to close my eyes and *picture* her! I don't want to hear her *calling* me! Please... what must I do to make her *stop*?'

I saw the glance Drew Trainer and Lori Scott exchanged. It didn't take a psychic to interpret it. They were starting to seriously doubt her mental health and ability to continue with the movie. I guessed I couldn't blame them. Coming to Egypt to play a character from ancient history was one thing. Channelling the spirit of a long-dead Egyptian queen was quite another.

Adam and I also exchanged a glance. Ours was a bit different to the actors. In it, I read our shared determination to help Skylar Harrison if we could. Of course, we were passionately interested in what her visions might reveal about a grisly chapter of pharaonic history shrouded in the mists of time. But it didn't seem fair that a modern movie star should have to suffer so much just to furnish us with new knowledge.

Adam shifted sideways so, like Drew Trainer, he was propped on one knee looking intently at her. Skylar Harrison stared back, a hunted expression on her beautiful face. 'I think you need to tell us what you saw,' he urged. 'If this really is Queen Tiye using you as some sort of vessel to get her story out, then I'm guessing she won't stop until it's been told.'

Skylar Harrison looked back at him with a wobbling bottom lip. 'You doubt me?'

'No,' he admitted. 'I don't doubt you. I keep telling myself I should. That my rational brain should reject absolutely what is going on for you. But I've seen with my own eyes things I can find absolutely no logical explanation for. I want to help. The only way I can think of to do so is for you to let us know what you meant yesterday when you said about worse ways to punish someone, what made you – er – scream in bed last night, and what you experienced just now when you said you could feel her presence.'

Lori Scott and Drew Trainer traded glances again.

'I think she saw her ghost,' I murmured, skin prickling.

But Skylar Harrison was shaking her head. 'No,' she whispered. 'It's not that clear. It's more a sense of what I can *feel* than what I can hear or see. I just know they did something terrible to her.' She looked around her, agony on her face, visibly wilting again.

Adam tried again. 'Can you tell us anything?'

'Darkness,' she said, starting to shake. 'And no air. I feel as if I can't breathe.'

She'd said similar last night, I recalled.

Drew Trainer and Lori Scott looked at their co-star wearing matching expressions of concern. 'She can't go on like this,' Drew Trainer muttered. 'Mac will blow a gasket.'

'Maybe you're right,' Skylar Harrison lifted her head and looked at him with red-rimmed eyes. 'Perhaps I should just give up and go home. I was never meant to have a part in this movie in the first place.'

'Don't say that!' Lori Scott instructed. 'That's defeatist talk!'

'But if this keeps happening, I'll have no choice! It's making me sick. And it's only a matter of time before it leaks. If that happens, I'll never work again!'

Drew Trainer's frowning silence suggested she had it about right.

'But if you really can't piece together any of your sightings into anything coherent,' Lori Scott said gently, 'then I don't see how any of us can help you.' She turned her head to look at Adam. 'There's really *nothing* in the historical record to tell us what happened to the queen?'

'Nothing,' he confirmed. And then I saw the thought catch hold of him at the exact same moment it hit me. Impossible to think that for a moment we'd forgotten it in the extremity of this latest episode.

'The papyrus!' we exclaimed as one, voices overlapping. Adam's gaze locked with mine across the top of Skylar Harrison's bent head.

'The one we found yesterday?' Drew Trainer's gaze snapped between us.

'It's looking like our only hope,' Adam nodded grimly.

Excitement bubbled up inside me. 'We need to translate the Testament of Hori and see what light it might shed on what happened to the queen.' I looked at Skylar Harrison's eager face with a determined optimism. 'Maybe then she'll set you free.'

Chapter 15

We had established that Mackenzie King had not spent the night in his trailer. Beyond this, we were no further forward in finding out where the taciturn director had disappeared to.

Natasha Redwood was waiting with Ahmed in the coffee shop on the other side of the road when we emerged from the temple precinct. A single glance told me how our police pal felt about this private one-on-one time with the gorgeous Hollywood screen goddess. I don't think he could have looked more starstruck had a genuine goddess – Hathor perhaps – metamorphosed in front of him and sat down to chat.

They stood up as we approached; perhaps on Natasha Redwood's part a teensy bit more quickly than she might have done. I caught the quick exchange of glances between Drew Trainer and his co-star. It was enquiry from him and confirmation from her that she had not told Ahmed about the missing director. I imagined our friend instead had enjoyed himself immensely, bombarding her with all manner of questions about her life in Tinseltown. Whether the Hollywood star had had quite such a good time, was impossible to say. Well, good for Ahmed, I thought fondly. It was a treat he could tell his grandchildren about one day.

'We'll see if Mac's back at the dahabeeyah,' Drew Trainer said to her in an undertone. If not, we'll have to have another think about what to do.'

But when we got back, he still wasn't there. Adam asked Ahmed to wait in the minibus on the riverbank above our jetty while we ducked inside with the three actors to see if the director had returned.

'We'll give it until dinnertime,' Drew Trainer decided.

'What do we do in the meantime?' Natasha Redwood asked.

'Speaking for myself, a couple of hours relaxing up on deck wouldn't go amiss,' Lori Scott announced. 'What's the point of all this beautiful hot sunshine if we don't get to enjoy it?'

I thought about what Skylar Harrison had said on that very first day about how wonderful it must be to have time to kick back, chill out and enjoy the Nile. It was a lesson in being careful what you wished for, I thought wryly. I looked at Skylar Harrison's pale face, seeing the uncertain way she looked back at me. 'Adam and I are going to the museum,' I answered her unspoken question. I caught Drew Trainer's eager expression and added quickly, 'We'll speak to Habiba about arranging a private viewing for you of the treasures we found. Today, I suggest you stay here and look out for Mr King. We'll be back in time for dinner. If he still hasn't returned, then we can get Ahmed on the case.' Then a thought struck me. 'If you want to start your own investigations, you could maybe ask Khaled to call the local hospitals, just to check nobody answering to Mr King's description has been admitted with temporary amnesia. Khaled's fluent in both Arabic and English, if you can penetrate the Scottish brogue. He signed the same confidentiality clause we did, and of course, already knows Mr King has gone AWOL. Khaled doesn't have to name any names. But it might help to put your minds at ease.'

I'll admit I registered the way they were all staring back at me. I don't suppose they were used to being bossed around. Nor, in truth, was I wholly comfortable being the one doing the bossing. But

I was overcome with Egyptological zeal, keen as mustard to get to the museum and see what we might learn. Of course, this was largely for the sake of Skylar Harrison's health and mental wellbeing, I assured myself. But I couldn't deny I wanted to know the content of the papyrus for its own sake. To see if it could shed light on what had happened to Queen Tiye after her rebellion failed. So, while I saw the looks on their faces, I didn't falter. 'Please, help yourselves to anything you want. Rabiah will be delighted to look after you.'

Thus satisfied that I had satisfactorily fulfilled my duties as hostess, I took hold of Adam's hand and went to re-join Ahmed in the minibus so he could drive us to the museum.

'Careful, Merry,' Adam chided with an eloquent lift of one eyebrow. 'You'll have them wishing they'd checked into a hotel after all.'

I thought it a shame the Tutankhamun treasures until now on display in the Luxor Museum were being packaged up and transported north to Cairo for the much-vaunted opening of the brand spanking new Grand Egyptian Museum. There, I rather felt, they risked becoming lost among the multitude of other artefacts from the boy king's tomb. Whereas, here, in this charming local museum they stood out: the gilded cow head of goddess Hathor that used to welcome visitors from its position just inside the entrance, the assembled chariot in its big glass case in the second gallery, and, upstairs, a bolt of linen sewn with fist-sized golden star emblems. Here, these were stunning objects each in its own right. Items to dazzle, wonder at and spark the imagination.

If I'd had any say in the matter, I'd strenuously have resisted their relocation. But Habiba had received her instructions and knew better than to argue. I could only hope the treasures we had unearthed from the temple forecourt at Medinet Habu might fill the gap and prove an equally enthralling lure for tourists and those with more than a passing interest in history.

As ever when visiting, it was impossible for me to walk past the statue of Thutmosis III – now moved close to the entrance to replace Hathor as the treasure to welcome people to the first gallery – without pausing to reflect that the first words Adam and I exchanged were to comment on the war exploits and illustrious career of Egypt's greatest warrior pharaoh. The statue does him justice: a beautifully carved and perfectly preserved work of art. Adam and I had been casual strangers back then, with no idea about the many adventures Egypt had in store for us. We'd exchanged pleasantries and gone our separate ways, only to run into one another again a few days later.

But today we weren't here to admire the statuary on display in the first gallery. I quickened my pace as Ahmed strode towards the security door leading to the behind-the-scenes part of the museum.

We entered a brightly lit, sterile environment reminiscent of a hospital. This was perhaps appropriate considering what went on here was very much like treating the sick. This was the conservation and preservation work necessary to care for and restore damaged, sometimes shattered artefacts ready for public display. I daresay a better description would have been a laboratory, especially given the white coats the staff tended to wear while working. A good idea, given the quantities of dust they encountered.

Ahmed threw open the door to a room I'd visited before, which I knew to contain a special glass press for protecting papyrus once unrolled. Adam stood aside to allow me to enter ahead of him. Full of eager anticipation I stepped through the doorway. The first thing to catch my eye was the stunning pectoral collar from the alabaster box, glinting under the lights. Now cleaned, it dazzled, a multi-coloured mix of tiny semi-precious gemstones in jasper, carnelian, turquoise and gold, set in an intricate design. But this wasn't the sight that made me choke as my breath caught in my throat.

Turning from his contemplation of the sheath dress I spied on a special sort of mannequin behind him, Director Feisal Ismail of the newly merged Ministry of Tourism and Antiquities stepped forward to greet me. I wouldn't have cared, or maybe dared, interpret the expression on his face. No doubt, mine was a mask of frozen shock.

'Meredith, my dear,' he held out his hand. A tall, urbane man, always immaculately turned out in a suit and tie with razor sharp creases in his trousers, he had closely cropped black hair turning silver at the temples and a single gold molar, which glinted when he smiled. As it was now, I noticed.

But I still couldn't quite bring myself to place my faith in that smile. On our last encounter, down at Abu Simbel, he had invited Adam and me to call him Feisal. As well he might, considering my husband had just rescued him from possible attack by deadly crocodiles. Yet, try as I might, I still couldn't get his name to trip easily off my tongue. 'Director Is – er – Feisal!' I exclaimed, allowing him to take my hand and raise it to his lips; a gentlemanly gesture I'd have scoffed at if just about anyone else performed it, but which befitted his character down to the ground.

'And Adam!' he shook Adam's hand. He spoke with only the merest suggestion of an Arabic accent.

'Sir,' Adam said respectfully, perhaps similarly unsure of our current standing with the man we hadn't seen for so many months, who had once invited us, politely I'll grant you, to leave his country for a while. All the arrangements for the Hollywooders coming to stay had been made by his staff.

Coming forward from across the room, Habiba greeted us warmly. She looked stunning as usual, wearing one of her long oriental tunics in soft green patterned silk over nipped-in-at-the-ankles trousers in the same fabric, with what I can only describe as slippers on her feet, and her usual headscarf – this one an almost iridescent pale gold colour wrapped around her face. I rather imagine this was what Scheherazade may have looked like. 'Merry. Adam. I'm so glad you could come.' She kissed us each lightly on the cheek, enveloping us in the wonderful, exotic scent she wore.

Director Ismail shook hands with Ahmed, then looked back at me. 'You have been back in Egypt, what is it? Less than a month? And already, you are up to your old tricks: making discoveries of the kind archaeologists would spend years of backbreaking labour to turn up.'

I searched for a critical note. Saw instead the definite twinkle in his eyes. And breathed a heartfelt sigh of relief. Maybe we hadn't been invited here for a stern ticking off after all.

'Well, strictly speaking, we can take neither the credit nor the blame.' This was Adam, setting the record straight, perhaps unsure if the twinkle was wholly to be trusted. 'We just happened to be on the scene at the time. We really have Skylar Harrison to – er – thank.'

'Ah yes, the Hollywood contingent, come to put our last adventure together onto the silver screen. How is it going? Habiba tells me there was some – um – altercation on set at Medinet Habu that led to the uncovering of the alabaster box,' – indicating it resting on a workbench close by – 'containing these remarkable treasures.'

'I'm not sure you'd believe us if we told you,' I muttered. 'But I think it's fair to say it has thrown a bit of a spanner in the works. There's not been a whole lot of moviemaking going on. One of the actors has been a little – er – unwell.' I stopped short of divulging the current unknown whereabouts of the film's director.

Director Ismail nodded sagely, 'Yes, I'm led to believe Egypt can have that effect on some. It's the combination of sunshine, heat, air-conditioning and unfamiliar food, I'm told.'

In my experience, the affliction to which he was referring had more to do with forgetting to use purified water when brushing one's teeth. But safest, I decided, not to correct him, either in this or his assumption about what ailed Skylar Harrison.

'And Talia Nolan, she showed up, looking like a million-American-dollar-notes!' Ahmed announced grandly. 'That was how the box, it came to be finded. Never have I seen such a thing with my own two eyes!' But he stopped short of regurgitating the whole trailer truck episode, for which I was thankful. I wasn't at all sure I wanted to re-live that particular drama all over again! Nor was I wholly sure whether he meant seeing Talia Nolan in full Helen of Troy regalia or Skylar Harrison's attempt to mow her down, which had revealed the alabaster box.

'A remarkable find, for sure,' Adam repeated Director Ismail's assessment, steering us back to the treasures we'd come to see.

'We've been longing to take a closer look. We didn't dare touch them too much when we opened the box.'

'Allah be praised!' Director Ismail murmured. 'For once, you did the right thing and contacted the authorities.' His golden molar gleamed again as he indicated Habiba standing alongside him. 'Rashid Solomon at the British Museum trained you well. Suppressed your Indiana Jones instincts, hmm? I must remember to send him my compliments.' The twinkle was very much in evidence in his nut-brown eyes.

Speaking for myself, Indiana Jones hero-worship was one of the things I loved best about Adam. But, on this occasion, I'd have to admit he'd made the correct judgement call. I doubted very much the golden molar and twinkle would be quite so prevalent in this encounter had that not been so.

'Tell me, have you formed any conclusions about what you found inside?' Director Ismail looked from Adam's face to mine.

Thus invited to propound our theories, I didn't hold back. 'The gold snake-bangle is inscribed for Queen Tiye,' I offered. 'Given where it was found and the other contents of the box,' – not to mention Skylar Harrison's psychic commentary, I added silently to myself – 'We're daring to believe this is the ephemeral Queen Tiye, one of the wives of Ramses III, rather than her more famous forebear, consort of Amenhotep III.'

'The richness and exquisite detailing of the pieces is leading us to think Tiye may have had a higher rank than scholars hitherto have thought,' Adam chipped in, also holding back from mentioning the additional insights we'd been granted, thanks to our visit with Skylar Harrison to the witchy woman.

Ahmed, standing stolid and immovable as a granite boulder could be relied upon, I knew, to take his lead from us. I had no idea how much of what he'd witnessed of Skylar Harrison's "funny turns" – by no means all, but enough of them to be getting on with – he had shared with Habiba. For now, it seemed safest to stick to the facts as they presented themselves and not stray into the realm of clairvoyance. I trusted the lightning glance I flashed each of them was telepathic communication enough. We could fill in Director Ismail later about the otherworldly aspects of what had been going on should it prove necessary. For now, I rather thought the Hollywood gagging order we'd signed enough of a deterrent had the risk of ridicule for our undoubted belief in what we had experienced not been an equally strong disincentive to spill the beans.

'We're hoping the papyrus will be the key to unlocking the truth of the harem conspiracy and what happened to Queen Tiye,' I added. 'Adam translated the inscribed tie around the scroll as reading "Testament of Hori". We know Hori was a royal standard bearer, one of the original judges appointed to try those arrested for rebellion and assassination of the king. The contents of the box seem to have belonged to the disgraced queen. We very much hope a translation of the papyrus will shed light on this horribly violent chapter of ancient Egyptian royal history.'

Director Ismail's eyes gleamed every bit as brightly as his golden molar. 'You have made a study of our famed pharaonic murder-mystery?' he enquired.

'The harem conspiracy is one of the most fascinating stories to emerge from the New Kingdom,' Adam said. 'And this, precisely because so much and yet so little is actually known about it.'

'So, you are here to translate the papyrus.'

'With your permission, I'd love to try,' Adam nodded respectfully. 'Although I may need some help from my old mentor back at home. I was hoping to take some pictures to send him, should it prove a challenge too far for me. Er – again, if you'll allow it, sir?'

'Ted Kincaid,' Director Ismail named Adam's teacher, once leading light and lecturer of philology at the Oriental Institute, Oxford. 'How is the professor?'

'Enjoying retirement and doting on his three-year-old granddaughter,' I smiled, thinking how glad I was to have been able to spend time with him in the months before our recent return to Egypt. 'But this is exactly the kind of thing that might, perhaps, entice him away from Peppa Pig!'

I doubt Director Ismail understood the reference, although I'm sure he got the gist as he smiled. 'Please do give him my regards when you speak with him.' And, with that pronouncement, I knew we had his seal of approval and could continue our investigations unabated.

'One day, my dear,' he pulled me aside a few moments later as we moved to study the artefacts, and murmured in my ear, 'you really must tell me how you do it. How do you manage to be on the spot when so many of our ancient treasures are found?'

I glanced up at him and responded with perfect truth. 'It's as much of a mystery to me as it is to you, Dir – er Feisal. But I can't help but be grateful for it. It makes life one hell of a lot more exciting than it is back at home.'

He fixed me with a gimlet gaze. 'Hmm, I am seriously considering if I should have you fitted with a security tracking device. That way, I could keep tabs on your whereabouts at all times.'

I glanced at him askance, not entirely sure he was joking. He looked back at me benignly enough, so I judged it safe to smile and dimple at him. This brought a bark of laughter. 'And I have to say, Meredith, that I share your sentiment. Life is more interesting in Egypt when you are here.'

Feeling immensely gratified and far more settled, I wondered perhaps if Director Feisal Ismail was a man much like my husband with just a touch of the Indiana Jones about him. He'd joined in some of our earlier adventures with a dramatic flair of his own. I realised I should perhaps have expected him to turn up rather than be perturbed by it. Smiling, I turned away.

Noting that Adam had made a beeline for the papyrus secured within its glass press, I felt myself magnetised by the sheer linen sheath dress. Feeling a bit like Skylar Harrison pulled by an unseen force, I moved across the sterile lab-like room to study it. And caught my breath. Having only ever seen ancient textiles displayed flat, I was surprised to see it on a mannequin; one especially designed for cleaning and preservation though this undoubtedly must be. Given human shape like that, it was uncannily as if the ancient queen was standing before me. I stared in astonishment and unexpected reverence. My goodness! She was *tiny*! Knowing she'd incited the revolt against her husband and his chosen successor, I'd imagined her larger than life, a strong, commanding figure. But looking at the minuscule, whisper-thin garment she once wore, I could only gape and ask myself how on earth she had been able to stand upright with the weight of that pectoral collar around her neck.

'You can almost picture her, don't you think?' Habiba murmured, moving to stand at my side. 'Wearing this dress, with the pectoral, her gold snake-bangle wound around her lower arm, a crown and woven sandals.'

'It brings her to life in a way the other objects don't,' I agreed, mesmerised by the delicate fabric. Knowing the way women the world over felt about clothes, it was quite a unifying experience across the centuries to stare at such an intimate piece, to know it had touched her skin, perhaps borne traces of her perfume. I leaned closer and sniffed.

'Yes,' Habiba said. 'There is still a delicate scent attached to it. Although sadly I think the preservation fluid with which we're treating the fabric will take it away.'

Yes! I did imagine I caught a very subtle and elusive drift of something heady and intoxicating. A deep shudder ran through me. Call me fanciful, but like Skylar Harrison I could almost sense the spirit of the ancient queen, lost for millennia to the shifting sands of time, stirring as we discussed her. Although perhaps this wasn't so strange considering the ancient Egyptians believed that to speak a dead person's name was to grant them eternal life. 'I wonder what she looked like,' I mused. 'And how she was able to command such an uprising.'

A loud exclamation from Adam brought us both spinning around.

'See here,' he shouted excitedly from the other side of the room. He leaned forward over the glass press protecting the unrolled papyrus. With one finger, he traced the text he was translating as he started to read aloud, his voice filled with a thrilling timbre. 'Listen to this! "I Hori, son of Setnakht, brother to king and queens, do make this, my most solemn and faithful declaration". What do you make of that then?'

My eyes popped. 'Hori was Tiye's *brother*? Er – *Ramses III*'s brother?'

'It would seem so,' Adam concurred, straightening up to look at me with a bright, avid gaze. 'Although as a royal standard bearer, I'm guessing he's more likely to have been born of a concubine from the royal harem than the Great Royal Wife, though perhaps we shouldn't rule it out. But the fully royal princes were more usually destined for the military or priesthood.'

'Well, that would certainly explain why he escaped with a warning when his comrades suffered the humiliation of having their ears and noses lopped off,' I announced with satisfaction.

We all crowded around him and gazed in awe at the papyrus secured firmly between two glass plates. It really was the most wondrous thing to look on a relic from Egypt's ancient past, knowing we were the first to do so since the brittle scroll was rolled up and hidden away three millennia ago. The ink was barely faded, courtesy, I guess, of its thousands of years secreted inside the alabaster box. Something of a time-slip moment, it took no great leap of imagination to picture a man sitting hunched over it with his reed pen and ink pot, setting down his testimony of the violent events he had witnessed.

No matter how many times I had this experience of stepping across the centuries, it never failed to overwhelm, leave me feeling strangely small and insignificant in the cosmos, my lifetime but the blink of an eye. Even so, I knew I would never tire of it.

'Is it written in hieratic script?' I asked, noting the more cursive form that distinguished it from the hieroglyphics. I'd seen previous examples, and thought I recognised it although, no expert, I couldn't be sure. And there was no way on God's green earth I could read it.

Adam nodded. 'I studied it for my degree and translated a few examples at The British Museum under Rashid's watchful eye. But I'm not in Ted's league. Nowhere close. I'm going to need his help.'

It wasn't hard to see why. A long scroll, the colour of iced tea, it stretched sideways for at least two metres, structured into columns densely packed with writing.

Adam glanced at Director Ismail, 'Is it ok if I take some photographs?'

I let out a small puff of disappointment before the director could respond. 'Can't you read any more?' Now he'd started, I didn't want him to stop. As I've had cause to note before; patience may well be a virtue, but it's not one of mine. Adam's winged brow told me he was thinking the same.

Feisal Ismail extracted a pair of glasses from the inside breast pocket of his jacket and secured them to his nose. He leaned forward and studied the text for a few moments with focused concentration.

'By my reckoning, this next bit reads something along the lines of, "I remain the loyal and devoted servant of my beloved sister, our fallen queen".' He looked at Adam for confirmation as I felt a shiver ripple down my spine. Skylar Harrison had described Hori as protector to the queen, if I remembered rightly. 'So, Tiye was also sister to Ramses III?' Feisal interpreted the evidence of his eyes.

Ah yes, I thought. He wasn't party to that particular insight, learned by us through Skylar Harrison's pin-stabbing exercise.

Adam nodded slowly and frowned once more at the text. 'It would seem so,' confirming both the director's translation and its meaning. 'And this part here,' – pointing – 'says, "She ruled our land like a lioness, maintaining Maat", that is the proper order of things,' he explained unnecessarily, since we were all, even Ahmed, I suspect, familiar with this.

'Yes,' I nodded. 'Go on.'

'"She ruled our land like a lioness,"' he repeated. '"Maintaining Maat while our Lord defended the Two Lands against all foes".'

I stared at him, but Habiba got there first.

'Hori is saying that Tiye took over the reins of domestic government while Ramses III was off fighting the Libyans, Syrians and Sea Peoples?'

Adam nodded dumbly; his gaze still fixed on the ancient writing.

Feisal Ismail looked up and met her eyes. 'That's power almost beyond imagining. Especially for a woman.'

'Bloody hell,' Adam breathed, straightening to look at me. 'We suspected she ran the business of the harem like a national enterprise, but to govern the whole country?!?' This was far more an exclamation than a simple question. 'Wow, Merry! Our Queen Tiye was no royal ornament!'

'She was following in illustrious footsteps,' I pointed out. 'Just think of Hatshepsut.'

'Ah, yes, but Hatshepsut wrested the throne for herself,' Feisal Ismail said, scratching his chin. 'From everything we know, Tiye determined to seize it for her son, the one we know as Pentaweret.'

'Perhaps so she could rule through him,' I hypothesised. 'It explains why she was able to rally so many powerful men to her cause. If the king was losing his grip and she'd proven herself capable of running a tight ship...' I didn't need to finish. The rest was self-evident.

Director Ismail acknowledged this with a nod. 'It is certainly true that CT scans of the mummy of Pentaweret – our "screaming prince" have aged him at around eighteen at the time of death, a young man. Whereas Prince Ramses was a man in his forties when he ascended to the throne.'

Adam was bending over the papyrus again, studying it intently. After a moment he let out a low whistle. It brought Director Ismail forward alongside him, so their heads were bent close together. It was Feisal who stepped back to translate for the benefit of the rest of us. 'I can't be sure of the exact wording, but the next part seems to say, "Now she is no more,"'

'"Cut down" is how I'd read it,' Adam interjected.

'Ah, yes,' the director allowed equably. Then they turned back to the papyrus, their heads almost touching, voices overlapping as they translated together, '"The great queen, my revered sister, whose only crime was birthing too many daughters".'

We greeted this in a somewhat stupefied silence. I pictured the ceremonial procession of royal princesses carved onto the wall at Medinet Habu. Almost a mirror-image of the long line of king's sons depicted opposite, it differed only in that these royal daughters of Ramses III had never had label texts added to name them, not during the reign of their father, not even when various of their brothers came to the throne and promptly filled in their own blank labels and those of some of their brothers. Fourteen royal princesses remained unidentified to this day. Many, it now seemed certain, daughters of Queen Tiye.

Thoroughly aggravated, I couldn't stop myself bursting out indignantly, 'What is it with this idea of male supremacy in royal succession? Haven't there been enough women who've proved they are every bit as competent to rule as their male counterparts? Think of Elizabeth I. Hang that! Think of Elizabeth II, her majesty The Queen! My God! It's only in the last few years that our own country has seen fit to change the line of succession so a woman can come to the throne by birth right!'

I'm not sure whether Feisal, Habiba and Ahmed got the reference to Elizabeth I. It was probably unfair to expect them to be well versed in British royal history. But everyone had heard of The Queen. And I'm quite sure they got my drift.

Lucky for them, they were rescued from the need to respond. The telephone on the desk in the corner rang shrilly, a very twenty-first century intrusion. I jumped out of my skin.

Habiba muttered something in Arabic and started moving across the room to answer it. At the same time, the door opened. A vaguely familiar individual popped her head around it. I searched my memory banks to recognise her face swathed in the black hijab. Ah yes! This was Jamira, once personal assistant to the museum curator Director Ismail had whisked off to Cairo after he proved himself rather a liability, certainly regarding the winkling out of secrets. I was glad to see Jamira had hung onto her job here at the museum. I have no idea if she recognised or even registered Adam and me. It had been a while. She fixed her gaze on Habiba, gesticulated at the still-ringing telephone and let out a volley of urgent, rapid fire Arabic. Among all of this, I recognised two words: Talia Nolan.

'*Talia Nolan* is calling?' I gasped.

A charge of sudden energy seemed to electrify us all.

'She wants to speak to *me*?' Habiba asked in surprise and Jamira frantically nodded.

'Please to put her on the loudspeaker,' Ahmed begged. 'My ears want to hear what she will say.'

I could only applaud this sentiment, very much intrigued by a call from the Oscar-winning actor.

Habiba reached for the receiver and pressed a button on the desk-phone's modern dash. 'Er – hello? This is Habiba Gar – I mean Habiba Abd el-Rassul.' In her confusion, I thought it perfectly natural and forgivable that she should stumble over her new name.

Ahmed stared at the telephone as if the Hollywood star might perhaps metamorphose right there on the desk. Instead, Talia Nolan's husky voice filled the room.

As it turned out, she was calling with a disappointingly prosaic request. Like Drew Trainer, she wanted to arrange a private viewing of the treasures we had unearthed, and to bring a publicist along with her – being clear that this absolutely MUST take place at a time when no members of the public would be present. She wanted a world exclusive.

But it wasn't this that brought Adam's and my gazes in search of each other. Yes, I thought! He'd heard it, too. A faint, far off cry for help in the background. A male voice, shouting to be heard.

Chapter 16

'Could it be Mac?' Adam pulled me aside and whispered in my ear, unconsciously using the nickname by which the Hollywooders referred to the director.

I looked at him in consternation. 'But Talia Nolan told Drew Trainer they'd argued, and that Mackenzie King left on foot,' I protested, also in a whisper.

'She might have lied?' he shrugged.

'So, what are you suggesting? That she kidnapped him?' It was too ridiculous for words.

Adam shrugged again. 'She's ruthlessly determined to secure the role in the film. Let's face it; if he'd turned up in one of the local hospitals after a drunken brawl or a bump on the head, we'd have heard by now. He must surely have ID on him.'

I looked at him a bit helplessly, feeling at a loss. 'So, what do we do?'

'I don't know yet,' he frowned. 'But I'm sure we'll think of something.'

In the meantime, Habiba was still conversing with the screen siren on the phone. Feisal Ismail and Ahmed were all ears, rapt at the opportunity to eavesdrop on a conversation – however mundane – with a global film star. If they picked up on the distant shouting in the background, it's possible they attributed it simply to background noise in a public space. But knowing how fiercely Talia Nolan guarded her privacy, I suspected she was calling from her hotel room.

Habiba handled Talia Nolan's request rather neatly, I thought. She promised to speak to her superior, failing to divulge that he was standing right here in the room alongside her, listening in on their exchange.

And that was that. The call ended with Habiba agreeing to let her know but making no promises. She looked around at us. 'Did I say the right thing?'

I nodded firmly. 'Talia Nolan is not alone in wanting a private viewing of the artefacts we found. Drew Trainer and Lori Scott have asked for the same. To give them credit, I think this is more from genuine fascination than as a publicity stunt. Although, of course, that may follow.' I had no idea whether Natasha Redwood and Skylar Harrison – or Mackenzie King – would wish to be included in this excursion, should it come off. Speaking for Skylar Harrison, it was possibly unnecessary. She might need only to close her eyes to "see" the treasures secreted until now in the alabaster box.

'Perhaps we should arrange a special viewing for them all, Talia Nolan included,' Director Ismail said decisively. 'And turn it to the advantage of the Ministry of Tourism and Antiquities. Publicity cuts both ways, after all.' His golden molar glinted as he bared his teeth in what might have been a smile.

I doubted this was what the screen goddess had in mind at all but managed not to say so. I glanced at my watch. 'We should be getting back,' I said to Adam. 'We promised to be home in time for dinner.'

'I will speak to the Minister,' Director Ismail referred to his boss, the top dog at the Ministry for Tourism and Antiquities. 'We will see about arranging a little Reception for our visiting Hollywood guests.

A chance to bring this latest fabulous discovery to the world Media at the same time, eh?'

'Yes, and hopefully restore Queen Tiye to her proper place in history if we can manage a full translation of these texts,' Adam said, not for a second forgetting the primary purpose of our visit. With a quick look to Director Ismail for consent, he pulled his iPad from his rucksack and started taking pictures of every column inscribed onto the papyrus, and then of each of the precious artefacts in turn, so we had a complete pictorial record of our find.

We took a taxi back to the dahabeeyah. There were any number of local drivers we could call upon at short notice, and it relieved Ahmed of the need to take us in the minibus, so he and Habiba could enjoy their evening together.

Feisal Ismail told us he planned on sticking around in Luxor for a few days. I think he was as eager as us to get a full translation of the papyrus. Like Adam, he wasn't in Ted's league in reading the ancient hieratic. He too would need to wait for the professor's help. They had both done well to interpret the first few passages, but Ted would confirm if they had it right. Then there was the prospect of the celebrity "private viewing" to contemplate, another reason for Feisal to sit tight for a bit. I'm sure he'd spied an opportunity for a bit of mutual back scratching and would go all out to secure it. So, all things considered, Luxor was obviously the place to be. I had no doubt he would want to keep a close eye on us too as part of his plan, but we bid our farewells cordially enough.

Back onboard the *Queen Ahmes*, we made a quick detour via our cabin so that Adam could put in a call to Ted, and then zap off the papyrus images to him. Outside of that, we found things very much as we'd left them. The Hollywooders were up on deck. They were rehearsing, or rather performing a read-through of the script. Although, performing was a poor choice of word. There was little in the way of actual acting going on that I could see. They were sitting around the dining table as the sun sank over the Theban hills, sending fiery rays to light the scene, each with a glass of Rabiah's homemade lemonade at their elbow, simply reciting their lines.

They didn't notice Adam and me as we ascended the spiral staircase. We were able to creep across the deck and sink into the cushioned chairs unobserved with the drinks Rabiah had pressed into our hands as we'd come through the lounge-bar.

The closest we'd come so far to gaining an insight into the movie, I was perfectly content to sit quietly, listen and watch. I might have wished for them to be in costume. Ramses the Great, dressed in white shorts, red polo shirt, trainers and with a baseball cap turned backwards on his head was not quite the thing. Although, I suppose, it did have the advantage of drawing one's attention to his nose. Still, Drew Trainer pulled off the commanding presence I imagined was a prerequisite for the role, sitting upright with his shoulders squared, wearing an imperious expression as he glanced at his script, then up at the three gorgeous women paying him court.

Equally incongruous: Nefertari in a turquoise swimsuit and sarong, Iset-Nofret in teensy denim shorts and a pink bikini top, and Helen of Troy wearing a sky-blue halter neck and pant combo; all three of them with bare feet and sporting broad-brimmed hats. I wondered idly what the ghosts of the ancient queens would think if they could see this tableau and hear the words the scriptwriter had put into their mouths.

It seemed to be a scene involving Helen of Troy demanding quarters of her own at the royal palace, that she might entertain in private and keep out of the public eye. Certainly, Skylar Harrison had most of the lines. Good, I thought, if it was helping take her mind off her real-life dramas.

The contribution of Lori-Scott-as-Iset-Nofret was largely restricted to meaningful looks, implying the type of *entertaining* the Greek queen had in mind was open to interpretation. Inspired casting, given the Ozzie actor's unusually expressive tiger-yellow-eyes. I imagined the camera would be set to capture a highly-zoomed-in close-up as she let them do the talking.

Nefertari, on the other hand, was characterised as an innocent, adoring of her husband and blind to the apparently seductive intentions of the foreign queen during her sojourn in Egypt while the Trojan war raged on the other side of the Mediterranean. Speaking her lines, Natasha Redwood pitched her voice a little lower than her normal tones and added a breathy quality I felt sure would have her male fans swooning in the aisles in movie theatres the world over.

Listening in, I couldn't help but wonder how Mackenzie King would direct them to inject life into the scene. Four world-class actors, their read-through sounded wooden and stilted to my ears. The need for, and role of the director in moviemaking became all too clear to me. Which brought me back to noticing the absence of the fifth of our paying guests.

Turning my head, I glanced at Adam, also observing the actors with an eloquent lift of one eyebrow. Adam's view was clear. The ancient story was sensational enough without characterising its queens as players in a soap opera. I recalled Lori Scott saying similar. Mackenzie King had his work cut out, his role to coax out a *performance* from each of his leads that was more than just saying the words as written in the script.

Perhaps feeling my gaze on him, Adam looked sideways at me. 'He clearly hasn't returned,' he whispered, his thoughts running along similar lines to mine as they so often did. 'Do you think we ought to say something?'

'What if we're wrong?' I murmured, frowning at him. 'Natasha Redwood said Mackenzie King had a – what did she call it? – pash? – for Talia Nolan back in the day?' – realising I was frighteningly out of touch with the language of today – 'I really have no desire to get caught up in a lovers' squabble. Let's leave that for the film.' I nodded at the actors rehearsing their scene.

But he couldn't let it go. 'I'd accept that if only one of us had heard it. But we both did. What did it sound like to you?'

'Like a man calling for help,' I admitted quietly.

'So, what if Talia Nolan is somehow holding him against his will at her hotel?'

'Then we should maybe call the police?'

He looked at me askance. 'Merry; these people are Hollywood royalty. I don't think we can ask Ahmed or one of his squad to go over there and smash the door down! You've heard how protective Drew Trainer is towards the director.'

'Yes, although happy to take him to task himself,' I pointed out softly.

'The point is, I don't think he'd thank us.'

'So, what do you suggest?'

'I'm wondering if we should do a little recce for ourselves...'

Frustratingly, this was the point at which Lori Scott noticed us. Perhaps we hadn't kept our voices as low as we'd imagined. 'Hi,' she called brightly, making the others look up. 'How long have you guys been sitting there listening in?'

'Just a couple of minutes,' Adam said with perfect truth.

'And what do you think?'

Not knowing what Adam had in mind and wanting to steer the topic to the absent director, I decided honesty was my best policy. 'Seems it needs a bit of direction to inject real energy into it. Right now, it sounds a bit flat.' And I rushed on lest I had caused offence. 'I'm guessing you haven't heard from Mr King?'

Drew Trainer got up, leaving his script open on the table, and came to join us. 'Nothing,' he said.

The others followed, flopping into the cushioned armchairs so we were sitting in a loose sort of circle.

'Did you learn anything at the museum about what happened to Tiye?' Skylar Harrison fixed Adam with an intent gaze. Clear what was uppermost in importance to her, although hard to blame her.

'Not yet,' Adam let her down as gently as he could. 'It's not the work of moments to translate the ancient texts. But we're getting the best in the business onto it, so I'm hoping it won't be too long.'

I allowed this diversion and then brought us back to the point. 'You know, I'm wondering if you should put in another call to Talia Nolan,' I said as casually as I could, looking at Drew Trainer, although I didn't miss Skylar Harrison's frown out of the corner of my eye.

'Why would I do that?' he asked, baffled.

'I'm just thinking if you do decide to get the police involved in searching for Mr King, the first place they'll start their investigation is at his last known sighting. It might be only fair to warn her?' Of course, I was also thinking it might serve as a shot across the bows and encourage her to think twice if she were indeed keeping him against his will and may just be the jolt she needed to set him free.

'Then I imagine she will tell them exactly what she told me,' he said shortly. 'Talia Nolan, right now, is someone I would rather have as little to do with as possible. She's caused quite enough trouble following us all out here. I think I'd rather not be the one to let her in on the secret that Mac hasn't come back yet. Who knows what she might choose to do with information like that?'

Exchanging a glance with Adam, I realised I couldn't pursue it without drawing uncomfortable questions. It didn't seem the time to mention the call she had put in to Habiba at the museum, yet again perhaps hoping to steal her rival stars' thunder. So, there was no way easily of divulging what Adam and I suspected we'd heard.

Drew Trainer went on, 'Your man Khaled did as you asked and put in a call to the local hospitals – there are two in Luxor, it seems. Nothing. So, we must assume Mac is off on some mission of his own devising. It's still only twenty-four hours since he left here yesterday evening. I'm not sure we should call in the bloodhounds just yet. It's possible he simply wanted space to clear his head and has checked in somewhere else. But if he's not back by morning, we'll have a re-think.'

And with that pronouncement, I had no choice but to accept the matter closed.

Conversation was inconsequential and superficial throughout the light dinner Rabiah served up on deck. She'd evidently learnt that her feasts were rarely done the justice they deserved by the Hollywooders. The plates other than Adam's and mine often returned to the kitchen barely touched. So, this evening she had restricted herself to a delicately spiced broth and a grilled Nile perch served with steamed fresh locally grown vegetables (an inspired choice for the Keto diet this lot appeared to be following). Nobody bothered to get changed, although Natasha Redwood slipped a shawl on top of the turquoise sarong. The evenings remained warm and balmy, with just the merest suggestion of a breeze to stir the palm fronds swaying atop their tall stems along the riverbank.

There was really very little we could tell Skylar Harrison that she didn't already know; certainly nothing to quell her earlier fears that the ancient queen would dog her footsteps throughout filming – if it ever started again. And the subject of where Mackenzie King had mysteriously vanished to was very clearly closed. At least, until I could get Adam alone.

'One of the top directors from the Ministry of Tourism and Antiquities turned up at the museum today,' Adam informed the actors conversationally. 'He was excited to see our discovery. We asked about a private viewing, and he promised to speak to the Minister.'

But that was about it for around-the-table conversation. After Rabiah cleared away the plates and accepted the – genuine, I think – thanks of the Hollywooders for the – far more appropriate – meal she had prepared, the actors drifted away, each to his or her own cabin or, in the case of Lori Scott, to ask if she could look at our library of books in the lounge bar. I reminded myself they were here as work colleagues, not friends indulging in a Nile cruise, and told myself I shouldn't be surprised at this desire for some time alone.

As soon as they were gone, I turned to Adam. 'When you said "recce", what exactly did you have in mind?'

A little over an hour later, we approached the luxury Al Moudira hotel, where Talia Nolan was staying. From the front, it looked like something out of an orientalist fantasy. Styled on a sprawling Arabian Nights palace, complete with Arabesque domes, regal arches, roaming bougainvillea (petals closed for the night), intricate wooden latticework screens, and ornate lanterns. It welcomed visitors through a lush, ivy clad, beautifully tiled interior courtyard, the hub of the hotel, complete with colourful architecture, rising pillars and beautiful hand painted murals.

I figured if one wasn't fortunate enough to be able to hole up on board a luxury dahabeeyah, but still wanted privacy and seclusion, this romantic boutique hotel on the west bank was probably the next best hideaway. Adam and I had been here for a meal once or twice over the years, and I knew the hotel's reputation for discretion and exclusivity.

Ahmed and Habiba accompanied us. Adam and I had debated this furiously. Adam's plan had been to borrow one of Ahmed's uniforms and present himself as an officer of the law; although don't ask me how he'd thought to pull it off! Given their relative disparity in size, I rather think he'd have looked like a schoolboy playing at dressing up in a grown-up's suit! Not that Adam is small. But Ahmed is BIG. Not to mention the problem of nationality!

As I'd pointed out, we had a tried and trusted police officer as our closest friend, one who had joined us, I might add on many a hare-brained scheme in the past. So, it seemed unnecessary to go to the extreme lengths he was suggesting. His protestations about Drew Trainer's insistence on keeping the police out of things for now, I'd waved away as irrelevant. For the recce we had planned,

Ahmed would be there "unofficially", to lend credence to the madcap plan we were devising.

Habiba, too, was necessary for the ruse we planned to enact. She was, after all, our "in" to the glamorous Hollywood star. And possibly our biggest stumbling block, given her historic insistence on protocol.

However, the willingness of the newly married couple to join us in putting into action our hastily cobbled-together mission suggested to me very strongly that they had missed us terribly while we'd been away. Love each other they undoubtedly did. But, given the choice of a quiet evening enjoying newly wedded bliss, or joining us on a risky adventure, the contest was over before it began; even, it seemed, for normally risk-averse Habiba. She raised a few token objections, for sure. But it took no great effort to persuade her in the end. Naturally, we had to fill them in on a few essentials, swearing them to secrecy and silence. But they were well used to this by now, a typical bedrock of the sort of schemes we hatched. It turned out they had both heard the shouting in the background of the earlier call but, as we'd thought, put it down to other guests at the hotel being raucous. With no reason to search for a more sinister explanation, they'd dismissed it.

So, there was no need for us to creep into the extensive hotel grounds under cover of darkness, darting between shadows, which I suspected may secretly have been Adam's preference. We were able to bowl up to the reception desk as bold as brass and announce that Talia Nolan was expecting us. That is, she was expecting Habiba and Adam.

Habiba, once persuaded, had telephoned ahead, using the number Talia Nolan had given her, and got straight through to the screen legend. She could say with perfect truth that she had consulted her superior, a Ministry Director about arranging a "private" viewing of the artefacts we'd uncovered. And then add that there were some papers to sign: just disclaimers, but allowing for the attendance of a publicist, and to get the wheels in motion. (Easy enough to mock-up if you had years as a communications specialist under your belt, as I did. We could tear these up afterwards, we agreed). Explaining that she was extremely busy packaging up the museum's Tutankhamun treasures for transportation to Cairo, Habiba asked if there was any way she might please visit Ms Nolan at her hotel this evening, bringing along with her the movie's Egyptological consultant in case of any questions, since he had a full photographic record of the treasures on his iPad, which Ms Nolan might wish to be the first in the world to see.

With the carrot thus dangled, Talia Nolan had agreed readily enough. So, part A of our plan was in place.

Lest you're wondering, as Habiba did, about the dubious integrity of our scheme, I should reassure you our sole objective was to see if Mackenzie King did indeed need rescuing. If it should happen to turn out that he wasn't there after all, then it seemed the simplest way of leaving again with the minimal collateral damage done. I was pretty sure we could find a way to square things for the rather-less-than-exclusive private viewing of the artefacts, involving ALL the Hollywooders, should such a thing prove necessary, even if it meant bending Feisal Ismail to our collective will.

I was also heartened beyond words to have overheard Adam admit to Habiba, 'I've worshipped Talia Nolan from afar for years. But I have to be honest; up close and personal I'm finding her a hard woman to warm to.'

So, maybe the ends justified the means.

As agreed in advance, having made ourselves known to the reception staff alongside Habiba and Adam, Ahmed and I stepped aside into the obscurity of a shadowy enclave, obscured by trailing plants and carefully positioned antiques. In truth, Ahmed was well-known to the staff of the Luxor hostelries. A man with his local pedigree could hardly be otherwise. For all that Luxor is a modern city, its generations of occupants are still firmly rooted in their relative genealogy, one to another. In this knowledge, for this evening, I had placed my faith.

Talia Nolan, of course, was staying here incognito. I saw her step into the courtyard. The lengths these world-famous and instantly recognisable stars went to in order to disguise their true identity was extraordinary. And yet, so simple. All it took was a pair of loose-fitting jeans with a denim shirt, loosely tied at the waist, a pair of sliders on her feet and her hair caught up in a wide band a bit like those ballerinas wore, and she presented as someone you might have noticed and thought looked a bit like the movie star Talia Nolan. But would probably never have guessed was the multi-millionaire, Oscar-winning individual herself.

She spotted Habiba and Adam sitting beneath a skilfully drawn pharaonic mural and swayed (yes! That really was the only word) towards their low-slung table and grouping of chairs.

Ahmed and I watched from our vantage point for a few minutes. If anyone wondered what we were doing, we had our mobile phones at the ready, looking as if we were taking photos of our luxurious surroundings, or apparently texting friends. Ahmed was in uniform but had thrown a dark jacket over the top to disguise the fact. I saw Habiba engage Talia Nolan in earnest conversation. Then watched Adam draw out his iPad and tap on the screen.

This was our cue. Adam and Habiba had chosen their seats carefully, so that when Talia Nolan joined them, she would have her back to the reception desk.

While I remained out of sight, Ahmed approached the reception team. This was the moment we had gambled on. Of course, they knew him. And respected his police badge. So, when he told them Talia Nolan had asked him to collect a cardigan from her suite, all we could do was wait and see if they could accept it.

The biggest risk in this whole enterprise was whether the reception staff could be prevailed upon to hand over a room key. Of course, the obvious question was why Talia Nolan had simply not given him her own key to perform this little errand on her behalf.

From my position behind a trailing pot plant, it was impossible to say what swung it. But the next minute Ahmed approached me brandishing the little card that served as a key these days. 'I telled to them that she had locked herself out!' he informed me proudly.

So, part B of our plan – amazingly – was also in place.

Approaching the door to Talia Nolan's suite a few minutes later, I don't mind admitting to a severe case of the jitters. If we were wrong, then all of this was for nothing and we'd no doubt have some explaining to do. Adam and I could have spent a pleasant evening aboard the *Queen Ahmes*, leaving Habiba and Ahmed – and Talia Nolan – in peace.

I held my breath as Ahmed used the key-card to gain access to Talia Nolan's suite. The door clicked open at his first attempt.

She was a messy occupant. Whereas some of us unpack our suitcases straight into our hotel room wardrobes, Talia Nolan appeared to favour the floor and every other available surface to store her clothes. Strewn everywhere, amid leftover room-service hot plates and sheafs of paper that might have been a copy of the screenplay, the stunning domed room looked as if a bomb had hit it.

Ahmed coughed loudly as we entered. 'A-hem; is anyone here?'

In that moment, I couldn't honestly have said what I expected. A big part of me thought this was a wild goose chase; that Adam and I had been hearing things and making two and two make four-hundred-and-sixty.

But then, as Ahmed called out, I heard the answering shout from an adjacent room. And knew we'd called it right.

The messy room and uncollected room service crockery suddenly made sense. Talia Nolan had clearly dispensed with the hotel's housekeeping services for the day.

Mackenzie King was locked in the bathroom, a stunning vaulted room with another domed ceiling, enormous ornate gilded mirrors and beautiful wall-and-floor tiles. With a traditional keyhole, Talia Nolan had simply taken the key and locked it from the outside. The windows were fixed, presumably so as not to interfere with the air conditioning. Escape was impossible.

Everything until this point had gone exactly as we had – optimistically – envisaged it. But we had reckoned without Mackenzie King's reaction to being set free. His momentary look of relief as Ahmed opened the door changed in the instant it took him to recognise us to a fury that might just have measured on the Richter Scale!

'What the hell do you think you're doing?' he glared at us both as we threw open the bathroom door.

Taken aback by this unexpected apoplexy, Ahmed stepped hastily backwards and looked at me. I opened and closed my mouth a couple of times, wondering what had happened to the relief and the heartfelt thank you I had expected.

'Er – Adam and I were at the museum when Ms Nolan called earlier to speak to Habiba,' I stammered. 'We, well, we had the phone on loudspeaker. We – er – we heard you, that is, we heard someone – a man – shouting for help in the background and – well – since you had gone missing, we – er – we presumed it might be you.'

This was not me at my most articulate. But it was incredibly difficult to string together a coherent sentence with him glaring at me like that. Ahmed, I noticed, had moved to stand behind me. Now, Ahmed is a brave man. He could usually be relied upon to stick up for me. But I guess there are limits. For him, perhaps this was it. It occurred to me that usually when people called out for help, help was exactly what they hoped for. In Mackenzie King's case, it seemed he was determined instead to give us a thorough grilling. I could only deduce from this that perhaps it was me he objected to as his rescuer, thinking maybe I should have let Ahmed do it alone.

'How did you know I'd come here?' the director demanded; eyes narrowed on my face; brows pulled down in a deep scowl.

'Er – Khaled asked the taxi driver where he had taken you last night.'

'You know the taxi driver?' he asked in astonishment, brows lifting then dropping immediately back into his frown.

'Er – yes; this is Luxor, not LA. Everyone knows everyone. Well, at least, the locals do.'

'And who else knows you are here?'

'Er – nobody. Just Adam, Ahmed, Habiba and me.'

'You didn't tell Drew and the others?'

'No. We weren't sure there was anything to tell.' I could feel my confidence returning, determined to stand my ground. I knew we'd acted out of good intentions and didn't deserve lambasting for our rescue attempt. I guessed I could see that he was maybe embarrassed; a powerful man mortified to be found like this, but even so... 'We just came to check it out and – er – release you if you did happen to be here.'

'I suppose you expect me to be grateful for that much, at least,' he muttered.

Yes! I thought. At the VERY least! I could feel my temper starting to ignite. 'Mr Trainer wanted to hold off from letting anyone know you hadn't come back,' I explained tautly. 'But assuming you'd still failed to return in the morning he knew he'd have no choice but to call in the police. As I told him, they would start their enquiries at the last place you were known to be. That is – er – here.'

'Drew knows I was here?' he snarled.

'Er – yes!' I could feel myself losing a grip on this conversation. Surely, we'd already established that. 'I told you, the taxi driver –'

'Yes, yes –' he cut me off with a goaded gesture. 'I didn't realise he had trumpeted my visit here to my entire cast!'

I made no attempt to hide my exasperation. 'They were worried about you! Anything could have happened. You could have been mugged or run over or fallen into the canal or bitten by a snake...'

I might have gone on, but he cut me off again. 'Yes; I get the picture. Instead, I was kidnapped by a crazy woman!' He caught himself immediately. 'Forget I said that!' he instructed. 'She's having a tough time.'

I decided it politic not to comment. 'Mr Trainer spoke to Ms Nolan this morning,' I said. 'She told him you'd left here on foot. Mr Trainer believed her – er – still believes her.'

Ahmed – beautiful man that he is – decided this was the moment to intervene. Stepping forward and dwarfing me with his physical bulk, he pulled himself up to his full impressive height, puffed out his chest and chose his words with care. 'Sir, I am sorry that you are not happy to be set free. We did believe it to be your wish when you shouted out for help. We can depart and leave you here if that, now, it is your choice. But please to believe, Meredith and Adam, they wanted only to help you. In time, I think, you will come to see that this is a true thing. Your anger, it is not good. You should say that you are sorry, I think.'

It's not often that Ahmed uses his stature to intimidate. I couldn't say for sure that I could think of another example of when he had done so. But he'd chosen his moment to perfection.

The director seemed to shrink in direct proportion to my friend's brazen effrontery. 'You misunderstand me,' he said, 'if you think I am not grateful.' He strode from the bathroom into the main lounge area of the suite and snatched up his mobile phone sitting where he had obviously (ill-advisedly) left in on a low table. Then he spun back to face us and exerted his authority. 'But understand this: three things are about to happen. One: I am going to see Talia before I leave. I don't think it would serve any purpose for me to re-enact *The Great Escape*. Two: you are going to call me a cab –

preferably an anonymous one, so I can return to the dahabeeyah on my own. Three: you are going to swear never to breathe a word of this. Believe me when I say I will sue your asses from here to Kingdom Come if you dare to –'

This time I was the one to cut him short. 'Mr King, sir; please don't insult us! And if that's your idea of an apology then I think you could do with some lessons in how to do it properly!' I was getting properly fired up now. 'When we agreed for you and your "cast", as you call them, to stay on our dahabeeyah, it was not to be on the receiving end of threats like that!'

He looked at me for a long moment and I watched the anger drain from his face. It left him looking tired and hollow-cheeked. 'You're right,' he said at last. 'I'm sorry. It just, this movie has been nothing but trouble from day one.'

Looking at him, I saw a man very much used to calling the shots, from whom all sense of control had slipped. I nodded and stepped towards the door. 'There are some taxis outside the hotel,' I said. 'Any one of them will take you back to the *Queen Ahmes*. Ms Nolan is in the courtyard with Adam and Habiba. What you tell Drew Trainer, and the others is up to you. I promise they won't hear of it from us. And I know I can speak for Ahmed and Habiba too when I say, neither will anyone else.'

He gave me a long, searching look. 'Thank you,' he said at last. 'I believe you mean it.'

'Because it is true.' Ahmed solemnly joined the pact. 'We are good at keeping silences.'

Mackenzie King nodded a few times, as if taking in the fact that he could trust us, possibly a rarity in Hollywood circles. 'Right,' he said. 'Let's go. I want to see the look on Talia's face when she sees me...!'

Chapter 17

'You tricked me,' Talia Nolan said waspishly, fixing Habiba with a reproachful stare.

Adam stepped into the breach. 'Yes, and we're sorry about that. It was the only way we could think of to be able to check whether Mr King was in your room.'

'Short of dressing up as housekeeping staff,' I murmured at his elbow.

'Talia, we need to talk.' Mackenzie King held out one hand to help her up from the low-slung divan she was sitting on.

'Shame,' she said as she got up, ignoring his proffered hand. She swept a withering glance across our assemblage, managing to encompass each of us, and leaving no room for doubt about depths to which her opinion of us had plummeted. 'I would have enjoyed seeing those treasures on display. But I guess that won't happen now. I suppose I must thank you for the world exclusive of viewing them on screen.' She reached forward and picked up the single sheet of paper with her signature on it from the coffee table and tore it cleanly in two and then into quarters, which she dropped into Habiba's lap. Treating us to one last look of bitter contempt, she followed the director into a shadowed alcove, where they could talk privately while still being, for his sake, very much in the safety of a public space.

I hung my head a moment, surprisingly chastened.

'Did you see her face?' Adam exclaimed as soon as they were out of earshot. 'Actually, I felt like a total rat! I thought her eyes were going to fall out of her head when she saw Mackenzie King striding towards her with you two bringing up the rear.' He looked at me. 'So, did the ends justify the means, Merry?'

I thought about it for a moment. When I had run the rescue scenario in my head, it hadn't included coming face-to-face with the screen siren herself in the aftermath and being called to account for our actions.

'Well, Mackenzie King could have been more grateful,' I muttered. 'For a man presumably locked in a bathroom for twenty-four hours, he had a very bad temper about being set free!'

It was quickly told. 'I expect embarrassment and humiliation were the driving forces,' Adam remarked, reinforcing what I'd thought. 'She dented his male pride. It may not have been so bad had some anonymous staff member released him, or even Ahmed and maybe Habiba on their own. But you're part of the crew. He can't escape it.'

'He seemed more worried that we'd blag.'

'I rest my case,' Adam said. 'A world-famous man sitting on his dignity, knowing exactly how it would look if the story got out. The Press would have a field day. I doubt that's the kind of publicity he wants for the movie.'

'And Talia Nolan? What was she like?' Ahmed asked eagerly, looking at Habiba.

His new wife looked at the quarters of torn paper she'd rescued from her lap and put on the low table in front of her. 'I feel sorry for her,' she said at last. 'Her actions are not those of a woman fully in command of herself.'

'She has an unflattering propensity to lay down the law,' Adam added. 'Before you came back, she was issuing all sorts of demands. All staff at the museum to be stood down to avoid unauthorised photographs, a guarantee of exclusivity, her own publicist but no Egyptian journalists, that sort of thing.'

'Diva,' I murmured.

'But I agree with Habiba,' Adam said. 'I get the sense of a woman losing her grip. I hope someone can help her. There's desperation behind her actions. And a bitterness in the way she looks at the world. I think she knows she's played the whole thing wrong.'

Mackenzie King said she's having a tough time,' I said, remembering.

'She went through a very public divorce last year,' Adam nodded. 'It got nasty by all accounts.'

'Yes,' I recalled. 'And famously resulted in her losing custody of her six-year-old son to her ex-husband. That must be tough.'

'It's been a while since she had a really meaty role to sink her teeth into,' he added. 'She won the Oscar over a decade ago.

'Perhaps that accounts for the brittleness in her manner,' I surmised. 'Talia Nolan was at the top of her game for years. But she's getting older and losing out on prime roles to younger actors. She has just learnt a bitter lesson that she is replaceable. Skylar Harrison was cast in her place. It must rankle. Especially when she was stupid enough to throw the role away in the first place.' I looked across at Talia Nolan and Mackenzie King heads bent close together in their shadowed alcove. 'I wonder what they're talking about. He was determined that he wasn't going to skulk out of here without seeing her first.'

Adam shrugged. 'I guess that's between them, something we'll probably never know.'

By the time Adam and I got back to the *Queen Ahmes* it had been a very long day indeed. As far as the Hollywooders were concerned, we had simply been out for an evening with our friends. No questions were asked at all. Possibly this was because they had no interest in how we spent our free time. Or maybe because Mackenzie King made a grand re-appearance just a few minutes after we got back aboard the dahabeeyah.

He called out as he approached along the jetty and stepped onto the gangplank Adam had left lowered, just in case. 'Ahoy there! Where is everyone? Did y'all miss me?'

Adam and I were in the lounge bar, enjoying a late evening cocktail. Lori Scott looked up from the novel she was reading and flashed an amazed glance at us. I heard cabin doors being flung open in the corridor.

'Mac?' Drew Trainer's voice rang out. 'Is that you? Where the Hell have you been, man?'

I reached for Adam's hand, waiting with interest for the explanation. The others joined us in the lounge-bar. Rabiah rushed in to dispense drinks.

I had never seen Mackenzie King in such a good mood. Gone was the incandescent fury that had greeted Ahmed and me when we sprang him from Talia Nolan's bathroom. Gone too, the withdrawn, moody, taciturn character I'd come to expect. In his place, a man full of beans and bonhomie. Given the last twenty-four hours of his life, I don't mind admitting I found the about turn a little hard to square.

His explanation was also a bit thin, if you ask me. He announced that he had gone to see Talia Nolan at her hotel last night, hoping to sort things out. He admitted they had argued. This much, I guess, he had no choice but to divulge, since we already knew it. But then he added that he'd needed time alone to think, so had taken a room of his own. Given a certain slant on things, I supposed this was as close to the truth as he dared get. He had indeed spent the night at Talia Nolan's hotel in a separate room. The bit about leaving on foot was glossed over, indeed not mentioned. This was a subterfuge, after all, of Talia Nolan's making. Today, he claimed, he had needed to look over contracts and figure out options. And then he dropped his bombshell.

'Talia is flying back to LA tomorrow,' he announced. 'I have made her an offer and she has promised to go home to talk to her agent about it.' But he refused point blank to be drawn on what this mysterious offer might be. 'Filming is paused until I hear back from her. In the meantime, Skylar, make sure you know your lines.' Then, declaring himself shattered – as well he might be – he took himself off to bed.

Adam and I did the same. It had been a long day. Since his return, Mackenzie King had treated us as exactly what we were: hired help, sending barely a glance in our direction. I understood. As far as he was concerned, the episode was over; chapter closed. Fine by me, I decided. We'd done our bit, and we'd keep his secret. Hopefully things could get back to whatever passed for normal around here.

'Well, it sounds as if Skylar Harrison might have won out after all,' I said as we pulled back the covers and climbed in. 'I wonder if his "offer" will stop Talia Nolan pursuing the role of Helen with such ruthless determination?'

'Whatever it is might be just a way of buying her cooperation and getting her out of his hair, at least for now.' he shrugged. 'I'm sure we'll find out soon enough.'

Deciding he was correct, I curled cosily alongside him, head tucked on his shoulder.

He dropped an absent-minded kiss onto my temple. 'I'm not tired, Merry,' he confessed. 'You know, I'm seeing parallels between the whole Talia Nolan situation and the events led by our mysterious Queen Tiye.'

I turned my head to see his face. 'How so?'

'You described Talia Nolan as a woman at the top of her game for years. From what we learned today; I'm thinking Tiye was similar. Perhaps with diminishing influence as she aged.'

'Married to a tyrant, losing a grip on how to rule, more like,' I muttered. 'But I can see how, if she'd held the reins of power for years, the prospect of the pharaoh's natural death and then being put out to pasture by her nephew when he succeeded might have rankled.'

'Exactly,' he said. 'And maybe in the same way it sounds as if Mackenzie King failed to take Talia Nolan seriously when she challenged him in Malibu, Ramses III might have dismissed any legitimate proposals Tiye made. So, maybe the harem conspiracy was a last-ditch attempt to hold onto her status and rule through her son. By the sounds of it, she only had the one after a string of daughters. If she was the senior ranking queen, it must have stuck in her craw that her younger sister's son was set to inherit the throne now she had a boy of her own.'

'But she lost her son, much as Talia Nolan did; and in a much more terrible way.'

'So, you're seeing the similarities,' he surmised. 'Talia Nolan, by all accounts, lost custody of her son through her own actions. Fame and beauty are not great prerequisites for motherhood. And Tiye's actions led directly to her son's execution.'

'She must surely have believed she had a strong chance of success,' I said.

'Just as Talia Nolan must have believed that turning up on set dressed as Helen of Troy would somehow swing it.'

'I keep wondering about the trap set for the conspirators.' I admitted. 'It sounds to me as if someone tricked them to. Somebody wanted Tiye out of the way, and Pentaweret too.'

'Yes; poor Pentaweret,' Adam murmured. 'Whose name was taken away so he would die a permanent death and never cross to the afterlife.'

'I wonder who he was really,' I mused.

'Lost to history, I expect,' he said. 'We can guarantee he's not one of the princes named on the processional list at Medinet Habu since the label texts were added after his traitor's death.'

'Are all the sons of Ramses the Great accounted for on that list?' I asked.

He pulled away slightly to look at me in the soft glow cast by our bedside lamp. 'What do you mean?'

I looked into his eyes, thinking it through. 'You said Ramses III aped his more famous forebear, copying his temple design and naming his sons after those of Ramses II. So, maybe if we cross-reference them, we'll find a son of Ramses the Great missing from the processional list and be able to hazard a guess at Pentaweret's real identity.'

Adam's eyes glinted darkly. 'I like the way you think, Merry.' He kissed me again and then rolled away and swung his legs over the side of the bed and reached for his iPad sitting on the bedside table. 'And you've set my brain on fire. I don't reckon I'll sleep until those texts are translated,' he admitted.

'But what about Ted – surely…,' I started to protest.

'Yes, I have no doubt Ted will burn the midnight oil too. He was beyond intrigued when I filled him in. But I'd love to have a go myself and see if I can be a match for him.'

I knew there was no point trying to persuade him to stay in bed. In truth I was just as eager to know what extra light the Testament of Hori may be able to shed.

'I'll take the iPad to reception so I can stay out of the Hollywooders' way.'

Which explained why Adam and I approached from different directions when Skylar Harrison started screaming the place down again in the early hours of the morning.

'This is getting beyond ridiculous!' Mackenzie King raged after Rabiah had soothed the blonde and encouraged her to take another dose of her yellow sleeping draught. It hadn't taken long for his temper to return. But the provocation was admittedly extreme. 'What the hell's the matter with her this time? Surely she's not *still* having nightmares about whatever it is she imagined she "saw" at the temple the other day! How in God's name am I supposed to make a movie with all this nonsense going on?'

Thankfully, he didn't hang about waiting for an answer but stomped off back to his own cabin, leaving the lounge-bar door swinging on its hinges as he slammed through it.

'That's two nights in a row,' Natasha Redwood pointed out. 'It does rather make you wonder what you have to do to get a good night's sleep around here.'

I stopped myself from suggesting a drop of Rabiah's magic potion.

Flicking her long, dark hair over her shoulder and pulling her robe more tightly at the waist, she too got up. 'I wonder if he'll regret whatever his "offer" is to get Talia to go home. If Skylar's going to keep carrying on like this, it strikes me his better bet would simply have been to give Helen back to Talia. She was his first choice, after all.' And she too made for the door, closing it behind her with a click almost as pronounced as the director's stormy exit.

Adam and I looked at Drew Trainer and Lori Scott. 'She has a point,' Drew Trainer said, stifling a yawn. 'What was she shrieking about this time?'

Adam glanced at me. He had reached Skylar Harrison first since her cabin was closest to the reception area, and he'd had the presence of mind to bring the spare key with him to save the door from being kicked in for a second time. I suspect he'd heard more than anyone while we all came running. Making no attempt to hide his discomfort, he said, 'She wants to be found.'

'Huh?' Lori Scott enquired inelegantly.

'I presume Queen Tiye,' he shrugged, looking uncomfortable. 'Your – er – co-star wasn't making a great deal of sense.' His glance at me told me he wasn't sure he'd picked the right word to describe her, but he carried on regardless. 'She was just thrashing about wailing "but I don't know where to find you"!'

The four of us exchanged glances for a long moment absorbing this and trying to decipher what it might mean. I wished

I had a glass of something strong and intoxicating in my hand as I rather felt I might need some Dutch courage for what I was about to say.

'If we accept that – er – your – er – Skylar –' I called her by her name for the first time, '– is experiencing something genuine that none of us can explain ... and if we're willing to run with that scenario ...' They were all looking at me with various degrees of expectancy as I paused before going on. '...Then do you think it's possible the ancient queen is asking literally to be found?'

'You mean...?'

'Yes! I mean, to discover her burial?'

Given that Skylar Harrison was adamant she had no idea where to search, The Valley of the Queens seemed the obvious place to start. Adam accepted my reasoning that since Pentaweret's body had been sewn inside an animal skin and buried in an anthropoid coffin that had somehow found its way into the royal cache alongside his father's mummy; a similar fate may have befallen the queen. That is to say, her body had been buried.

'They can't have tossed her into the burning brazier or thrown her to the crocodiles,' I surmised. 'She was way too important for that.'

'But scholars think the tomb that may have been intended for Tiye in the Valley of the Queens was re-cycled.' Adam frowned. 'Ultimately it was used for burial of one of the royal princes.'

'I'm not suggesting they gave her a nice ceremonial burial as originally intended,' I pointed out. 'It's more likely they dug a pit for her coffin and simply tossed her in.'

'So, what are you suggesting?'

'That we take Skylar Harrison over there and see if she "*feels*" anything that might give us a clue where to start digging.'

'"*Digging*", Merry?' That softly indulgent look was on his face, as if I was a bit barmy and needed humouring. It was a look he reserved for the moments I crossed the line from madcap to downright foolhardy. 'You think we can take a spade and shovel, or maybe a pickaxe, into the Valley of the Queens in the dead of night and start chipping away at the bedrock?'

'Well, maybe not that exactly,' I said regretfully, thinking it something I might quite enjoy. It had been a while since we'd done something truly thrilling like that. 'But we do know a Ministry Director who might just be prevailed upon to help...'

In the end, Director Feisal Ismail proved a necessary accomplice to the plan we cooked up.

Adam suggested over breakfast – fruit and yoghurt with lots of hot, strong coffee – that Natasha Redwood might like to visit the exquisite tomb of Nefertari now open in the Valley of the Queens after decades closed for preservation and restoration.

'It's stunning,' he said. 'I can think of no better way for you to get up close and personal with the character you're playing.'

'I'd sure love to see it,' Drew Trainer jumped on the bandwagon, possibly playing along to add some verisimilitude, possibly for real.

'Me too,' Lori Scott piped up.

'Mac sent me a link so I could take a virtual tour online,' Natasha Redwood said, making a question of the look she sent across the table at the director. 'It sure does look beautiful.'

'Possibly the finest tomb to survive from antiquity.' I put in.

Mackenzie King looked around the table at us all, his gaze snagging on the dark smudges under Skylar Harrison's eyes. 'Oh, why the hell not?' he said at last. 'This project has already turned into a circus. Filming is on-hold. I don't suppose a bit of sightseeing will make a whole lot of difference. I presume you can get us a private viewing?'

Which was where Feisal Ismail came in. A chance, too, for him to have a private meet-and-greet with the Hollywooders, it was a win-win. And since he had been the man to preside over the tomb's grand re-opening a couple of years ago, he was the obvious choice.

The viewing was set for late afternoon, after tour parties had departed and just as the sun started to set over the western horizon, sending lengthening shadows into cracks and crevices and cooling the air. This gave Adam time to read up on everything he could find about the early 20th Dynasty tombs and burials in the Valley of the Queens, and for Lori Scott and me to approach Skylar Harrison with our plan.

Reluctant at first, eyes shadowed with fear at what she might "*see*", she came around to Lori Scott's persuasion.

'Honey, if you – or any of us – want to get a good night's sleep on this location shoot, and if you want to have any chance of being a convincing Helen of Troy, you need to exorcise the queen's ghost. Merry here,' – with a nod at me – 'thinks if you can get a sense of her burial place and then hand the whole thing over to the authorities to investigate –'

'Adam will help with that, so you don't have to admit to your part in it.' I said quickly, seeing another sort of fear leap in her eyes.

'– then maybe you'll be free of her.'

I'd never thought of myself as a ghostbuster. It occurred to me our mission into the Valley of the Queens might just be the start of a whole new career!

Ahmed was once again at the wheel of the minibus, doubling as our driver and security guard. This time, Director Feisal Ismail was on board. We had performed formal introductions on the *Queen Ahmes* before setting off. Feisal's height, sartorial elegance and effortless air of authority impressed the Hollywooders that here was a man with gravitas and an exalted position in the Egyptian Ministerial system. I gathered that in setting up the arrangements for filming in Egypt, Mackenzie King's people had dealt with Director Ismail's people. So, it was nice that they could meet in person, perhaps a little unsure which party should be the more impressed by the other.

The route from the dahabeeyah to the Valley of the Queens was the familiar one: along the road running parallel to the canal on the west bank, then the sharp left-hand turn inland in Gurna, past the Colossi of Memnon, sitting grand and silently observant at the roadside, and onwards towards the Medinet Habu Temple, where filming had so far been sabotaged.

At the crossroads, rather than take the left-hand fork leading to the temple, Ahmed steered ahead, up into the Theban hills, past the turning leading to the ancient workmen's village of Deir el-Medina and onwards to the junction leading to the Valley of the Queens.

The Valley of the Queens lacks the grandeur of that of the Kings. The cliffs into which its tombs are cut rise less steeply, although the shale, sand and loose scree are equally sun-bleached, blown across the buff-coloured rock; an arid, desert landscape, unrelieved by so much as a solitary blade of grass. It also lacks the pyramidal shape of the mountain of Meret-Seger – she who loves silence – rising steeply behind it. Nevertheless, the basic layout is similar, though smaller: a design reminiscent of an oak leaf, with a central pathway or stem, from which slim walkways branch outwards to the tombs, some defined by low-slung walls constructed of the same tawny-beige rock. There are also a number of simple burial pits with metal grates over the top to prevent the unwary from taking a tumble. I wondered if one such might be the final resting place of Queen Tiye, although without the benefit of having been excavated or having a metal grate installed.

We had agreed between us in advance that since Feisal Ismail would accompany the Hollywooders on their private tour of Nefertari's tomb, Adam and I would stay above ground with Skylar Harrison, taking in the terrain and seeing if her subconscious tapped into anything that might give a clue as to the ancient queen's burial place. Lori Scott and Drew Trainer agreed to join Natasha Redwood and Mackenzie King on Feisal's viewing, keen to see for themselves this glory from the height of Egypt's ancient civilisation.

I rather envied them, having only been inside Nefertari's tomb once myself. As a testament to a man's love for a woman, I rather imagine it stands alone in all of art and architecture. Descending steeply into the rock beneath the modern concrete dome built above it, it opens out into brilliantly painted and coloured outer chambers before descending steeply again into the large, pillared burial chamber. Images of Nefertari abound, captured beautiful, slim, with kohl-rimmed almond-shaped eyes, a whisper blush on her cheeks, in a form-fitting linen sheath dress and wearing a golden-plumed, feather headdress. There was nowhere else that brought Nefertari to life with such vigour. Richly decorated with religious and ceremonial scenes depicted in olive green, mustard yellow, russet red and black-and-white, I knew it had plenty to keep our guests in thrall while we performed our little experiment with their co-star to see if there might be a repeat of her experience at Karnak.

We stood back while a local guide dressed in the ubiquitous galabia, turban and sandals, led the way down the outer staircase and unlocked the heavy door installed at the tomb's entrance. Drew Trainer was the last to enter, holding back like a true gentleman to allow Feisal Ismail, Natasha Redwood, Lori Scott, and Mackenzie King to make the descent ahead of him. He glanced back as he negotiated the steep steps, holding up crossed fingers to say "good luck" to his co-star.

Ahmed wandered into the shade of the rest house built alongside the tomb to chat to a couple of his buddies, the guards. They had watched the Hollywooders' arrival with avid interest but, in company with a Ministerial bigwig, knew better than to badger them, as might have been their usual approach. Ahmed could be relied upon to ensure they allowed Adam, Skylar Harrison and me to make a tour of the Valley in peace.

'The tombs of Ramses III's queens and the princes who died young are at the western end of the Valley,' Adam said, glancing at Skylar Harrison before leading the way. The shadows lengthened as the sun started to sink below the hills as we walked. Director Ismail had done a great job of ensuring privacy. The place was deserted. Despite the warmth of early evening, I succumbed to a chill. There is definitely something creepy about an ancient necropolis as dusk descends.

'The tombs of queens Tyti and Iset are over here,' Adam indicated, walking forward. 'Although they're closed to the public and there's not much to see. They're relatively small. Iset's tomb comprises only an axial corridor leading to the burial chamber and two subsidiary chambers. The decoration shows Iset with various deities. Tyti's next door is decoratively similar in both composition and style but has a third subsidiary room off the burial chamber, perhaps denoting her more senior rank as the king's sister; although Ramses himself is not named on the wall reliefs.'

'Where is the tomb originally intended for Tiye?' I asked, cutting into his lecture.

'Over there,' he pointed to the other side of the Valley. 'Scholars agree QV42 was the tomb most likely initially quarried for the queen. Apparently, her image is still visible on the wall, although without any trace of her identity, of course. The sarcophagus had also been made for a woman, with her name and titles all erased.'

'Wow, they really did want to ensure there was no way she could live on in the afterlife,' I murmured.

'Her tomb was used ultimately for the burial of Prince Pre-hir-wenemef.' Adam managed to wrap his tongue around the unusual name.

I looked at Skylar Harrison, walking with us in a kind of daze. 'Anything?'

She closed her eyes. I watched in mute distress as a single fat tear squeezed out and rolled slowly down her cheek. It dripped off her chin and splashed onto the front of her light khaki jacket, leaving a visible stain. 'Aching sadness,' she whispered. 'An agony of loss.' Then she opened her eyes and looked helplessly at Adam as more tears spilled freely down her cheeks. 'This is where Tiye's son is buried.'

Adam looked at her in confusion. 'No,' he said gently. 'Pentaweret - or whatever his name was before he was put on trial – wasn't buried here. His remains were found in the mummy cache. Well,' he qualified, 'it's possible he was interred here before the priests moved him. But, if so, it's not clear.'

She listened to this, shaking her head. 'Not him,' she said. 'Tiye's first-born son. The eldest child. The crown prince. The one who died first.'

Adam stared at her. 'That was Amen-hir-kopeshef,' he said. 'But I don't think you can have that right. Egyptologists believe he was Tyti's son. And, from everything we've learned so far, it seems Tiye had only daughters, until the boy re-named Pentaweret came along.'

'Amenhirkopeshef was Tiye's son,' Skylar Harrison said with clear and calm certainty, managing to pronounce the tongue-twister name without needing to split it out the way Adam had done. 'He died as a teenager.'

Adam and I exchanged a glance.

'Why would scholars believe him to be Tyti's son?' I asked. 'I thought nobody could be sure exactly which princes were born to which queens.'

'While his mother isn't named in his tomb,' Adam said, 'Amen-hir-kopeshef was born to a queen whose titles match Tyti's so closely historians have been reasonably confident about calling him her son.'

'Those would be, "King's Daughter, King's Sister, King's Great Wife, Lady of the Two Lands, God's Wife, Mistress of Upper and Lower Egypt",' I reeled off, also having learnt them by heart.'

'Yes,' he nodded, looking impressed. 'Although you're forgetting King's Mother and God's Mother".'

Not allowing myself to be put off by this rather dampening correction, I glanced at Skylar Harrison's wretched expression. I'd heard the conviction in her assertion, seen the all-too-real emotion. 'Remember, those were Tiye's titles too,' I said, recalling the outcome of our visit to the old witchy woman. 'She was the elder sister and could claim the same pedigree.'

Adam was staring back at me as it clicked. I watched the expression in his eyes change at the exact moment the same thought struck me. 'My God, Adam! Tiye was mother to the first Amen-hir-whatever-his-name-was. The senior-ranking queen with the succession secure. Tragically, he died young. She had more children but only daughters, until Pentaweret-whatever-his-original-name-was came along. In the meantime, she had to stand by and take it while her husband had another son by one of her rival queens, calling him by the name of her dead child! And then see another of the sons elevated to crown prince! It must have been agonising!'

I broke off at a sudden movement from Skylar Harrison. 'Tiye wants to visit his tomb,' she said in a strange, distant-sounding voice. Breaking away from us, she starting to walk up the scree-covered incline ahead.

I moved to follow her, but Adam caught my wrist and held me back. 'Wait,' he whispered. 'If Tiye is somehow directing her, she'll know where to go. Amen-hir-kopeshef's tomb is QV55, that one over there.' He pointed. 'It will be locked as all the visitors have gone,' he added softly. 'If she really wants to go inside, we'll have to ask Ahmed about getting the key from one of the guards.'

'This is spooking me out,' I admitted. 'Taking instructions from a ghost!'

Skylar Harrison looked neither right nor left but walked with measured steps towards a tomb entrance with a shaded portico built across the top of it. She'd shown no hesitation in making for the correct sepulchre.

We both watched her a moment as, trance-like, she stepped towards it. I think we both saw the movement at the same instant. At the top of the steps as she approached. Adam dropped my hand and let out a shout. 'Stop!' He ran forward, urgently calling out to her. 'Miss Harrison – Skylar! Please! Stop! *Stop*! Don't go any further!'

Chapter 18

The snake was about two-and-a-half metres long, big for an Egyptian cobra. It was writhing in a last patch of late sunshine close to the top of the steps leading down to the tomb of Prince Amen-hir-kopeshef. The sun was sinking fast. Splashes of sunshine were all that remained as it dropped behind the western hills. As Skylar Harrison approached, the big black snake reared up, spreading its hood, swaying hypnotically and hissing, observing her with evil obsidian eyes.

I'd run forward too, hard on Adam's heels, but skidded to a halt at this sinewy movement, gripped by primordial terror of the deadly creature. I couldn't believe Skylar Harrison deaf to Adam's frantic shouting. But still she walked forward, literally into the path of Egypt's most venomous snake. A single bite enough to kill a fully-grown elephant within three hours; God alone knew what it would do to a willow-the-wisp of a woman wearing cropped cotton trousers and a light jacket. I screamed out her name. '*Skylar*! *Stop*! *Snake*!'

And then I realised her eyes were shut. It was a dreadful action-replay of her bewitched progress the other day through the Medinet Habu temple. She was being pulled as if hypnotised towards the tomb with the lethal snake writhing angrily at its entrance.

Adam wasted no more time. He rugby-tackled the Hollywood screen icon from behind, grabbing her around the waist, literally hurling her aside with every ounce of his strength.

Skylar Harrison flew through the air and fell heavily onto the loose scree with a grunt, then tumbled sideways, rolling away from imminent danger. Leaving Adam in a deadly face-off with the snake. My heart leapt into my throat, choking me. I wanted to scream. But when I opened my mouth, no sound emerged. It felt as if my oesophagus was stuffed with sand. Could only watch, round eyed with terror. Skylar Harrison more than made up for it. Opening her eyes, jolted from her reverie dumped so unceremoniously out of harm's way, she sat up, turned, caught sight of the rearing snake, opened her mouth and screamed. And screamed. And screamed.

I did the only thing I could think of. I snatched up a fist-sized stone and hurled it at the snake with all my might. I missed; sent the stone bouncing off a boulder, to ricochet down the stone steps and glance off the metal door to the tomb with a loud crack.

The long snake reared sideways, almost half its length raised from the ground, following the motion of the stone. With a cry, Adam leapt backwards, stumbling and losing balance. As he fell, I sprung forward without thinking, grabbed his shirt to haul him away. We both fell heavily on the stony ground. I was up again in an instant, pulling him with me. These snakes could move like lightning. We needed to get away.

It took me a moment to realise Skylar Harrison had stopped screaming. Had got to her feet. Was standing where Adam had flung her, staring at the snake and – well – the only word for it really was – *swaying* – her upper body moving as if in time to a rhythm I was unable to hear. All this I took in during the lightning glance I sent her; terrified to take my eyes from the snake lest it should seize its opportunity to rear up, lunge forward and sink its deadly fangs into one or other of us while we remained within striking distance.

'It wouldn't have hurt me,' she said, still swaying and drawing the cobra's evil black eyes to her. At least, that's what I *thought* she said. The sound of shouts and running feet on the loose stones swallowed her words, left me doubting my ears.

'Adam! Merry!' This was Ahmed, running forward with his police issue gun unslung. He spied the cobra and came to a skidding halt, throwing out one arm to stop the galabia-clad guard running with him, come to see what the screaming was about. Stopped in their tracks, they took in the scene at a glance: Adam and me still within range of the venomous fangs of the snake, the Hollywood movie star, trancelike once more, a faraway look in her eyes, swaying almost as sinuously as the snake; and the deadly cobra itself, hood spread, blinking black eyes, rearing aggressively, poised to strike.

Ahmed removed his black beret. Held it at arm's length and started moving it in a slow circular motion to attract the snake's attention.

The cobra reared sideways, seemed torn about where to look. Arced towards Skylar Harrison, still matching its sinewy movements with her swaying; then leaned towards Ahmed and his slowly circling beret.

Adam's arm clamped around my waist, using the distraction to edge slowly and cautiously backwards, not wanting to draw the cobra's attention.

Alongside Ahmed, the guard started stamping his sandalled feet on the ground, letting forth a volley of guttural Arabic. Ahmed joined in with the stamping. Adam and I used the distraction to dart back until safely out of striking distance.

'Snakes, they do not like the vibrations,' Ahmed shouted, still heavily stamping his black-booted feet and waving his beret.

The cobra reared side to side twice more, as if undecided, choosing between Skylar Harrison and our rescuers, unsure which movement to follow. Then, in front of my astonished eyes, it flattened its splayed hood against its head, dropped its full length to the floor and, as the sun finally disappeared behind the western hills, slithered away behind the boulder.

I needed all of Adam's strength to hold me up. The adrenaline surge left me weak-kneed, shaking and feeling sick.

More shouts warned us the Hollywooders, and Feisal Ismail had been alerted to something amiss. They converged on us in the gathering dusk.

'Is everything ok?' Lori Scott demanded urgently. 'We heard screaming.'

'There was a cobra,' Ahmed announced grandly. 'It is gone now, but we should go quickly from the Valley, as the night-time it falls.'

Now the extremity of the moment was over, it was quite comical to observe the way the Hollywooders leapt backwards onto the main path, casting anxious glances about their feet. I heard the guard mutter something to Ahmed, pointing towards the spot the snake had disappeared.

'What did he say?' I asked Ahmed.

'That he has heard stories of a royal cobra protecting this tomb,' he said, 'But he has never seen it for himself. It is Wadjet, the cobra goddess, she of the royal diadem.'

'She of the arm-bracelet we found,' I murmured aloud to no-one in particular, feeling another shiver ripple down my spine. In the lengthening shadows, with the imperishable stars starting to wink in the darkening sky, it wasn't hard to imagine the spirit of the ancient queen incarnate in a modern reptile come to protect the everlasting resting place of her firstborn son.

I looked at Skylar Harrison as we made our way out of the ancient graveyard of the royal queens. 'Did you find her?'

'No.' She gave me a long look. 'Tiye was not buried in the Valley of the Queens.'

'I've said it before, and I'll say it again,' Mackenzie King complained when, back onboard the dahabeeyah, it became clear Skylar Harrison had a badly sprained wrist that needed strapping. 'This picture is cursed. It's been more stop than start from the word go! I'm starting to think we should all just give up and go home. Or else forget about the location shoot and film the whole thing at Elstree.'

'Better a sprained wrist than a snakebite that would have shut down her nervous system and put her in a coma within an hour!' I retorted hotly, feeling the need to defend Adam from the implied criticism of his actions. 'She almost stepped on it!'

He looked at me balefully from the chair he was sitting in on the other side of the lounge-bar but said nothing, so I subsided.

I wouldn't have minded seeing a cobra in the wild,' Drew Trainer mused, sipping a whiskey and soda. 'Another story to tell the grandkids someday, huh?'

Natasha Redwood shuddered, making Lori Scott giggle.

'Are we any closer to figuring out what's causing Skylar's – er – episodes?' the director asked wearily. 'I noticed she didn't come with us into the tomb of Nefertari. I imagine you were undertaking an experiment of some sort, like the day you took her off to Karnak without my say-so.' His sour look left me in no doubt this time of his low opinion. Whether of me, the situation or, more probably, a combination of the two, was less clear. I think it's fair to say any chance I'd had of counting the Academy Award-winning director among my friends disappeared the night I had the temerity to rescue him from Talia Nolan's hotel bathroom. I daresay he thought it safe to ask such a question since the actor herself had been passed into Rabiah's tender care to have her wrist and the abrasions on her hands tended to.

It was Lori Scott who responded. 'There are two possibilities,' she said. 'Either Skylar is a complete fruit loop, and should be sent to a clinic for care, or else she is somehow channelling the spirit of the ancient queen who led the harem conspiracy to murder Ramses III.'

'We discounted the possibility that she could be faking ages ago,' Drew Trainer put in. 'She knows too much detail and has absolutely nothing to gain by playing a charade. Hell; we've all seen the torture it's put her through.'

Electing not to comment on Skylar Harrison's mental acuity, I joined in. 'We were hoping that by exposing her to places the ancient drama played out, we might be able to get the whole story out and set her free.' I attempted to explain our actions with a small apologetic shrug.

'And maybe fill in the plot holes for your next movie,' Drew Trainer added with a wink sideways at me.

Adam looked up at this point. He had been staring intently at the screen of his iPad propped on his knee, paying no attention to the conversation as it batted back and forth around the lounge-bar. I knew he was snatching every spare moment to study the Testament of Hori. Although how he was managing to keep his eyes open after his almost sleepless night, don't ask me. 'There's an email here from Ted,' he said excitedly. 'He's been working night and day on the translation. He reckons he'll have a transcript for us by tomorrow evening!'

To give absolute credit to the Hollywooders – Mackenzie King included – this news was exciting enough to push thoughts of stop-start moviemaking into the background. To be on hand for a discovery such as this, the first to learn the contents of the ancient texts, was a world exclusive even movie stars couldn't resist.

Adam got straight on the phone to Feisal Ismail, who took control and made all the arrangements. He would host a private reception at the Luxor Museum the following evening on the understanding that a press conference could be held the next day with our Hollywood guests in attendance.

It was a publicist's dream. And Feisal upped the ante. If Talia Nolan could be prevailed upon to attend, he would consider it an honour to meet her since he had learned of her unexpected trip to his country.

I was quite sure Mackenzie King would prefer to know she was safely onboard her flight home, but since word was clearly out that the Oscar-winner was here in Luxor, he determined his best bet was to ask her to delay for a day or two and to speak to her agent on a video-call about his mysterious "offer". I raised an eyebrow at this, hoping it was a judgement call he wouldn't come to regret. But I knew better than most how persuasive Director Ismail could be.

The hours leading up to the reception passed with agonising slowness. Mackenzie King took the actors, including Skylar Harrison this time, strapped wrist notwithstanding, back to Medinet

Habu for a photo shoot to ensure there would be some stunning stills to accompany the publicity material. As advance movie hype went, having film stars make a momentous ancient Egyptian discovery was off the scale. I could see why Mackenzie King wanted to max it out.

While I took this as a positive sign for Skylar Harrison's confirmation as Helen of Troy, I was uncertain how she would cope with another trip to the ill-fated temple. But Lori Scott promised to watch out for her, and Drew Trainer said he would stick to her like a limpet.

Not needed on set, Adam spent the day glued to his iPad. His first chance to test his skills against those of the mentor he idolised, he refused even to break at lunchtime. Remained ensconced in one of the deeply padded rattan armchairs up on deck in the deepest part of the shade cast by the wide canvas awning. Bolted down the plate of sandwiches Rabiah pressed on him with barely a glance up from the screen. Refused absolutely to give me any clue how the Testament of Hori was unfolding, no matter how hard I entreated.

'Wait to hear the whole story, Merry, oh-impatient-one,' he instructed.

Left at a loose end, I offered to carry Rabiah's shopping bags on a trip to the nearby market. The hustle and bustle of the local women in their bat-like black robes, some with wicker shopping baskets propped atop their heads, riotous squawking of chickens in big wooden cages, and pungent, brightly coloured baskets of spices lining the kerbside masking the somewhat more malodorous scent of horse dung took me to another world and reminded me why I loved this place.

The Hollywooders returned around the same time we did. Lori Scott confirmed that Skylar Harrison, other than succumbing to a bad case of the shakes, had been able to get into costume and through the photo shoot without mishap. So, we could all return to our cabins to prepare for the evening ahead.

I took special care with my appearance for our private reception in the company of Hollywood royalty, hosted by a senior-ranking Ministry official, and with my gorgeous husband set to reveal the contents of Hori's papyrus scroll, counting myself fortunate to be part of a world-first. I blow-dried my hair into a sleek bob and even used my straighteners to ensure a smooth finish, made up my face with subtle colours to emphasise my eyes, put on the slinky dress in bronze crushed silk I'd bought in Selfridges not long before our return from London and strapped my feet into high-heeled sandals. Talia Nolan had lost her opportunity to lay down the law about how the event should be conducted but would be there. I'll admit to feeling a tad awkward about this, since she was fully cognisant of our part in busting Mackenzie King from imprisonment in her hotel bathroom. Although I thought it very much in her interests, and those of the director to keep it our secret. Still, I imagined she might very well hold a grudge, possibly with justification. So, I thought it as well to look my best – even if only for the confidence boost it gave me to attempt to hold my own among such glamorous women and for such an important event.

Because, of course, the Hollywooders looked stunning, knowing they would have their pictures taken for the publicity machine. Feisal Ismail had graciously allowed the official movie photographer to attend for the welcome, although not for the whole event. I had no doubt images from this evening's soiree would be splashed all over the Internet after the press conference tomorrow.

Michael, assistant to the stars and general movie-land dogsbody turned up at the dahabeeyah with an armful of dresses, trailed by stylists and makeup artists to transform the actors into bombshells of the red carpet. To be fair, they kept it simple. This wasn't a night at the Oscars. There were no ballgowns. But nobody watching as we left the dahabeeyah for the limousines Feisal had sent to the riverbank to collect us, could be in any doubt that the toast of Tinseltown was heading out for a special evening event in Luxor.

The men, Adam included, wore black tie. Naturally, Drew Trainer carried this off with consummate ease, jacket emphasising broad shoulders, while the fabric strained at his biceps. But Adam, I thought, looked sexier, taking in his very slight self-consciousness. Mackenzie King looked less than comfortable in his. He kept running one finger around the collar of his shirt as if the starch was cutting in. I wondered how he felt about the prospect of an evening in the company of the woman who had locked him in her hotel bathroom for twenty-four hours.

Ahmed, present in his official capacity as the police officer assigned to the location shoot, was in his crisp white uniform complete with gold epaulets, black boots polished to mirror-shine, black belt and with his black beret tilted at a jaunty angle above his brightly snapping eyes. Suffering none of Adam's self-consciousness, it was clear he was all set to have the time of his life.

But, of course, it was the three female stars who drew audible gasps of admiration from Rabiah and Khaled, come to our small reception area to wave us off. And made me doubly glad of my efforts in front of the mirror.

Natasha Redwood wore a figure-hugging knee-length, off-the-shoulder creation in deep crimson, with the highest stiletto heels I have ever seen, colour matched to perfection. Her long, dark hair was swept forward over one shoulder, secured at the nape of her neck with a diamond clasp. It matched the bracelet, her only jewellery.

Lori Scott wore yellow. A high-necked, straight-fitting number to just above her knees, it had a plunging back, cutaway literally to the top of her pert little bottom. Her hair was pulled up in a high ponytail to make the most of this backless feature. With her captivating tiger-eyes, it was an inspired colour choice, setting off to perfection the golden tones of her skin. Her legs seemed to go on forever, feet in the strappiest of strappy sandals in gold. Jewellery, she eschewed altogether. She didn't need it, eyes like gemstones, looking huge in her face thanks to the skilful application of kohl.

But Skylar Harrison was the revelation. I think with all the traumatic drama of her last few days with us, I had rather forgotten to look at her as a beautiful bombshell; seen only a frightened woman in the grip of inexplicable and possibly supernatural forces. Of course, she had hardly been dressed to impress. Now, a single glance was sufficient to see why she had been cast as the face that launched a thousand ships, famously a woman so beautiful men lost all sense around her. And why Talia Nolan was so torn up about it.

Her pale skin was so luminous as to be almost translucent; blonde hair piled loosely on top of her head, a few curling tendrils allowed to tumble freely and frame her face; made up to perfection to deepen the blue of her eyes, sharpen the line of her cheekbones, sculpt her jawline and moisten her lips. She looked ravishing. It was really the only word. She'd removed the wrist strap, claiming Rabiah had given her a magic ointment to reduce the swelling, and looked none the worse for her close encounter with an Egyptian cobra. In a powder blue strappy dress shot through with a shimmering silver thread in a tiny crochet-type pattern, with a tight skirt that skimmed her ankles, her feet in high-heeled silver sandals, the outfit set off slender curves I hadn't realised were there in what was a truly fabulous figure.

'Helen of Troy, eat your heart out,' I murmured under my breath.

Luckily the number of men and women in our party evened out when you included Adam and Ahmed, so each of these screen sirens could be helped to negotiate the crumbling stone steps leading up from our jetty to the riverbank where the limousines waited to whisk us off to the Luxor Museum. Drew Trainer partnered Lori Scott, and Mackenzie King Natasha Redwood. Which left Skylar Harrison and me looking rather uncertainly at each other. I saw her hesitate between my husband and our big, burly police pal, and did the decent thing. I took Ahmed's arm. On such little gestures are the strongest of marriages built, I told myself, watching with the best smile I could manage as Adam offered his hand and led the most beautiful woman in the world along the causeway.

But I had reckoned without two other beautiful women.

Talia Nolan had gone all out in the glamour stakes. Perhaps the pure white, knee-length dress nipped in at her tiny waist with a statement piece gold belt, the golden choker at her throat and stilettos on her feet, also in gold, didn't have quite the visual impact of her Helen of Troy costume, but it still packed a mean stylish punch.

And then there was Habiba. Joining Director Ismail in hosting this evening's reception, she had chosen to wear a traditional Egyptian costume. Her long-sleeved cream robe, elaborately embroidered in taupe silken thread was simple, modest and elegant. Falling straight from her shoulders to her ankles, where her feet peeked out in little oriental slippers, also in cream, it merely hinted at her shape beneath while still managing to convey slenderness and femininity. Her headscarf, wound artfully to frame her face and secured with a bronze-tipped pin, was of the same cream silk.

I have never been able to figure out if Habiba wears make-up or is just naturally exotically beautiful. If she does, it's so subtle as to be invisible, used merely to highlight perfectly arched eyebrows, darkly lashed eyes, curving cheekbones and upward tilting, full lips.

To my way of looking at it, she was the most stunning woman in the room. Mackenzie King clearly thought so, too. I didn't miss the moment, shortly after our arrival, that he passed her his card and murmured, 'If ever you fancy a career change, please don't hesitate to give me a call. Hollywood would adore you.'

Sadly, for him, Ahmed didn't miss it either. Perhaps the director had forgotten that our security man was recently married to the gorgeous Ministry Inspector-turned-museum-caretaker. 'My wife, she is already adored,' he declared stoutly. 'By me!'

I couldn't help but smile inwardly as the Academy-Award-winning director, put firmly in his place, flushed and turned quickly away.

As things turned out, I needn't have worried about Talia Nolan. She completely ignored me. Although now I come to think about it, to ignore me, first she would have had to notice me. And I can't say for sure that she did. Not that she paid all that much heed to any of her fellow Hollywooders, beyond a scant few words of greeting and a muttered conversation with Mackenzie King. This, presumably to check that their bizarre lock-in at the Al Moudira hotel remained under wraps. Perhaps, with whatever her new "offer" was on the table, she considered herself above such things as mingling. Or maybe, as Adam suggested, she was embarrassed by her behaviour but didn't know how to stand down from the high-handed position she had taken and make a fresh start. You see; Adam is always looking for the best in people. I wish I could be so generous.

But the screen siren did seem very impressed by Feisal Ismail. He was especially dashing tonight in his tuxedo, complete with a dark red bow tie, matching cumber band, which showed off his toned torso and washboard stomach, with the usual razor-sharp creases down the front of his trousers. Like Ahmed, his shoes were polished to a glass-like shine.

The Ministry director was a good-looking man, I noticed, wondering vaguely why I had never taken the trouble to really look at him before. Perhaps because I had always seen him as holding sway over us, with authority to determine our future and power enough to enact whatever he deemed fit.

To his credit, he had gone all out this evening. The private viewing of the antiquities we had found took the form of an exclusive cocktail party. Mindful of the killer heels his female guests were wearing, there was no plan for a tour of the Museum itself, although he did point out one or two of the choicest pieces as he guided us through the first ground floor gallery towards the door leading to the behind-the-scenes part of the building. But not to the laboratory-style room we had been in previously. Instead, the treasures had been moved for display to a special, windowless, artfully lit room, decorated with soft fabric drapes. I took it in with one long sweeping glance: chairs set around small round tables topped with the finest linens and exquisite, fragrant floral centre pieces, a long side table set with dainty and delectable looking canapés and several magnums of genuine French champagne cooling in silver ice buckets. I raised an eyebrow at this, knowing the astronomical cost of imported fizz. Feisal was clearly sparing no expense. In truth, it looked like a rather lavish wedding reception was about to take place.

Given the privacy the Hollywooders had insisted upon, there were no serving staff. Director Ismail himself popped the corks on the champagne bottles, pressing a glass into the hands of each of our guests in turn.

I accepted the crystal flute he handed me and stood aside to allow the photographer to get busy with his camera. Feisal explained this gentleman had been granted special permission to photograph each of the artefacts before we arrived and under close supervision. All were now shrouded under cloth or behind screens for the big reveal later. The photographer was under contract to keep the pictures similarly under wraps until after the press conference tomorrow, when he would get his world exclusive, since no other photographs of the ancient treasures would be allowed.

Talia Nolan held back from the camera-posing. It made me wonder afresh about what was going on between her and the mercurial film director. She stood off to one side, deep in a conversation with Feisal Ismail that I was too far away to be able to eavesdrop on. That he looked utterly captivated by her was perhaps enough to be getting on with.

The Hollywooders submitted to a few minutes of red-carpet-like happy-snapping. They were more than used to this, evidently well versed in just how to stand to get the most flattering angle, the correct tilt of the chin, the ability not to blink as the shutter clicked, and all manner of other tricks of the trade. It was all a bit of a circus and, I hope not unkindly, rather put me in mind of performing chimps.

Adam's thoughts were clearly running along similar lines. He leaned towards me and whispered in my ear, 'Aren't you glad we're not famous?'

I gave a single, emphatic nod. 'Yes, and very grateful it will be Feisal fronting the press conference tomorrow, not us. But I have to say, it's quite good fun to watch. Just look at Ahmed!'

Adam glanced over at our police pal, openly drinking it all in and perhaps enjoying it all the more since it was the only drinking he would be doing. Adam chuckled. 'I was about to say he looks as if all his Christmases have come early,' he murmured. 'But you know what I mean.'

I did indeed, and exchanged a smiling glance with Habiba, clearly of a mind to indulge him in this moment as the Hollywooders put on a show.

'I keep pinching myself,' Adam whispered. 'Does this all seem as crazily surreal to you as it does me?'

'Bonkers,' I admitted, and took a moment to actually take it in that I, Meredith (Tennyson) Pink, was here in the company of some of the most famous, instantly recognisable people on the planet; and that our shared purpose in being here this evening was a miraculous discovery that would make front page news across the planet!

Finally, it was over. The photographer left, Feisal topped up the champagne glasses and the much-vaunted private viewing could begin. As the Hollywooders distributed themselves among the tables and sat down, he started by giving a little speech.

'Never before have I had the honour to welcome world-famous film stars to my country. It is exciting enough that you should all be here in Luxor, come to make your epic movie dramatising our glorious ancient history for audiences across the globe to enjoy. But, to learn from Habiba here,' he smiled at her, 'that on the very first day the cameras started to roll, you were instrumental in making a discovery to rival some of the greatest treasures ever unearthed in Egypt, this, my friends, this is real drama!'

While he was essentially correct, I couldn't help remembering there had not been a whole lot of camera rolling going on during that first day. Probably just as well given some of the – well – drama – leading up to the discovery. I glanced at Talia Nolan, sipping her champagne and staring at the Ministry director with a rapt sort of fixation as he spoke, perhaps to mask any discomfort reminded of her part in events.

I noticed Mackenzie King similarly observing the way the troublesome screen siren was gazing at our tall, dashing host, but had my attention drawn away as Feisal went on with his introductory speech.

'Tomorrow the world will come to know of it. But for tonight, these astonishing artefacts are ours alone. You are here this evening to see the treasures you uncovered in all their remarkable glory. And to find out whether there is more we can learn about a fascinating and violent period in pharaonic history. Events that led to the assassination of the divinely anointed king, an uprising intended to subvert the royal succession. A story that has come to be known as the harem conspiracy.'

Despite myself, I felt the little hairs on my nape and along my forearms prickle. I hadn't noticed it before in all the hullaballoo of the photo shoot, but there was a sound system set up, piping an appropriately stirring music score into the room. It set the scene and the atmosphere to perfection; the Ministry director playing the Hollywood director at his own game, I thought with an appreciative smile.

'And now,' Feisal announced. 'The moment has come. I will introduce to you each of these magnificent treasures in turn.'

He proceeded to do so, starting with the golden-arm-band-snake-bracelet. Drawing the black cloth from the display case, he invited the Hollywooders forward and gave a short lecture on Wadjet the cobra goddess, protector of royalty whose rearing image on the royal crown was the Uraeus, symbol of sovereignty and divine authority over Egypt. I listened with polite interest; head full of ghastly images of yesterday's encounter with the deadly snake, recalling the guard's assertion that it was protecting the prince's tomb and Skylar Harrison's strange pronouncement that it wouldn't have hurt her; relieved beyond words not to have seen this put to the test.

Feisal moved next to the sheath dress, still carefully arranged on its special mannequin but protected now in a purpose-built glass cabinet from which he again melodramatically swished away its cloth covering. The dress drew similar reactions from the female stars as it had from me the other day.

'Jeez! But the queen was *TINY!*' Lori Scott exclaimed. The furthest thing from being a strapping woman herself, there was no way on God's green earth she would fit into the ancient costume. Not that she would ever be allowed to try it on, of course; or so much as touch it.

This time, the Ministry Director's lecture confirmed the actor's earlier information about the harem being run like a business enterprise, its looms producing the finest linen in the land. 'I consider this may become among our most prized possessions,' he said. 'So rare is it.'

When everyone was done exclaiming over the whisper-thin gossamer fabric, Feisal whisked away the next protective cloth covering. This time from the display case covering the dazzling pectoral collar. It winked and gleamed provocatively in the carefully angled lighting, a magnificent example of ancient artisans' skill.

'Hard to believe that thing is three-thousand years old!' Drew Trainer asserted. 'Holy smoke! Would you just look at the workmanship! Looks like it was made just yesterday! But Hell! It sure must have been heavy around the shoulders of a teensy little woman like the queen! You sure it was hers?'

It was Habiba who answered, stepping forward. 'Like the arm bracelet, it was inscribed for Tiye,' she said. 'Her titles and name are on the gold counter-balance weight that would have hung at the back securing it around the queen's neck, worn over the top of the sheath dress.'

'What are the stones?' Talia Nolan asked, leaning closer to where the Ministry director was standing to admire the exquisite, patterned design.

'Turquoise, carnelian, lapis lazuli, jasper and faience.' Feisal informed her. 'All set in gold. A stunning piece, is it not?' He did a great job, I thought, of keeping his eyes averted from the very impressive cleavage so openly on display in front of him.

'It makes the one I'm wearing for the movie look like a tawdry fake,' Natasha Redwood murmured, voicing my thoughts when I first clapped eyes on it.

'That's because that's what it is, honey.' Drew Trainer smiled. 'Even a multi-million-dollar budget won't stretch to genuine Egyptian treasures in the costume department!'

I watched Skylar Harrison closely throughout the viewing. Displayed in glass cabinets and under electric lights, it seemed the ancient artefacts had lost their power to speak to her. She stood back from the others, quiet and perhaps a bit pensive, but suffered no repeat of her harrowing visions. I wondered if perhaps her stunning Hollywood makeover was an effective armoury of sorts, anchoring her firmly in her own persona, less susceptible to psychic intervention.

Director Ismail let them have their fill, answering questions and giving as much information as he could about how the antiquities – especially the sheath dress – would be preserved and cared for. I waited as patiently as I could, glancing at Adam, also shifting his weight from one foot to the other and barely touching his champagne.

Finally, the moment I had been longing for arrived.

'And now,' Feisal started. 'I will invite you to sit and enjoy some canapés as I top up your glasses. I am about to hand over to Adam. As you are aware, perhaps the most intriguing of the items discovered hidden inside the alabaster box was the papyrus scroll, labelled as the Testament of Hori.' As he spoke, he pulled aside a simple screen, revealing the papyrus displayed in a long wall mounted glass frame. 'Hori was a royal standard-bearer for Ramses III, an important role in the court. He was appointed as one of the magistrates to preside over the trial of the conspirators after the plot to subvert the succession and murder the king was uncovered. Disgraced for being caught alongside some of his fellow judges carousing with women of the harem and some of the convicted conspirators during the trial; unlike them, he escaped the punishment of having his ears and nose cut off and was instead released without harm. We are hopeful that the translation of this papyrus undertaken by Adam with reference to a world-renowned English professor of ancient languages, will become the greatest gift in Egyptology: the gift of knowledge. Tonight, we will listen to a voice echoing from antiquity, telling us the story of the harem conspiracy. Sit back, my friends, and let us hear the Testament of Hori.'

Chapter 19

Adam stood up, squared his shoulders and cleared his throat. I'm not sure he could have imagined this moment in a million years. When we had agreed to host household names of Hollywood aboard our dahabeeyah, it was never for a second thinking it could come to this: that Adam would be called upon to present a hitherto murky chapter of ancient Egyptian history to a rapt movie star audience. The more normal way of things would have been for us to be sitting in a darkened cinema, a bucket of popcorn propped between us, staring up at *them*.

'I'm not going to read you the transcript word-for-word,' he said, his bright blue-eyed gaze sweeping the room. 'It is written in the typical opaque style of the ancient Egyptian texts where sensitive matters were recorded in often cryptic language. But there is enough detail in what we have been able to interpret that, between us, my Oxford professor and I have been able to piece together the story I'm going to tell you this evening.'

I felt a thrill go through me. Looking at him, so handsome in his black-tie dinner suit, about to reveal new insights into an ancient Egyptian murder-mystery, I couldn't help but remember the "thwarted Egyptologist" who had introduced himself to me on the forecourt of Hatshepsut's funerary temple a few years ago, come to Egypt after his divorce having called time on a career he loathed. Well, he was the real thing now, respected enough to be given the floor by a man of Feisal Ismail's exalted Ministerial status. Swelling with pride, I sipped my champagne reminded afresh of how very very lucky I am.

'Hori was a royal prince,' Adam started. 'He was sired by the pharaoh Setnakht, who seized the throne after a period of civil war at the end of the 19th Dynasty. It is not clear who Hori's mother was, but we suspect not Tiye Merenese, the Great Royal Wife. Hori gives his title as "standard-bearer" as opposed to "fanbearer on the king's right", which was a more often-used princely title. Nevertheless, he was a man of significant standing in the royal court. Brother, or half-brother, to the pharaoh Ramses III and also to not one but two of the pharaoh's principal wives who were, of course, pharaoh's full sisters.'

I sensed a ripple of distaste run around the room. Incest was such a taboo in our modern society but was commonplace among the royal family of ancient Egypt, although apparently not among the populace. The intention was to keep the royal bloodline pure – although it seemed clear all the royal in-breeding often had the opposite effect. And perhaps it served to mop up the royal women who, safely married to their brother, couldn't make alliances with anyone who might mount a rival claim on the throne.

'Egyptologists have known for some time that Ramses III was married to his full sister, Tyti,' Adam went on. 'But Hori's testimony reveals that Tiye, an elder sister, was also a great royal wife of the pharaoh. It appears Tiye was the eldest child of Pharaoh Setnakht and his wife Tiye-Merenese. Hori does not tell us, but scholars believe Sennakht may have been directly descended from Ramses the Great, possibly a grandson by one of the elder sons who predeceased their long-lived father. And some historians think Tiye-Merenese was a daughter of Merenptah's old age, Merenptah being the thirteenth son of Ramses who succeeded his father to the throne,' he explained. 'It seems our Tiye, if I can call her that, was named for her mother and possibly in memory of one of the most formidable of Egyptian queens to have gone before: Tiye, wife of Amenhotep III, who ruled at the height of Egypt's mighty Empire period. So, she had quite a pedigree.'

I glanced across at Skylar Harrison, sitting stock still and breathlessly beautiful, listening as Adam validated and confirmed the findings of her paper-and-pin stabbing exercise with the mysterious old crone Atiyah had taken us to visit. She'd told us from the start that Tiye wasn't a minor queen of the harem. And now we knew it to be true. Tiye was, in fact, the most senior-ranking queen of all three of Ramses III's wives.

'Hori tells us Tiye was fiercely intelligent, fully royal of course; and ran the government while Ramses was away fighting his military campaigns by land and sea against the various forces who would have invaded Egypt. I'll say that again.' Adam said, just in case we hadn't cottoned on to the critical importance of this statement. 'Tiye didn't just preside over the business of the royal harem, she ran the entire government in the pharaoh's absence. That was a quite remarkable achievement. And, by Hori's account, she did it well. Tiye was a powerhouse. Her younger sister Tyti, by contrast, comes across as something of a "pretty princess", spoilt, indulged and privileged.'

I wondered if Mackenzie King was taking notes, could sense the plot of his alternative movie starting to take shape.

'Their royal brother, the pharaoh, seems to have taken a malicious sort of pleasure in this. Ramses III comes across in Hori's writings as a narcissist and egoist, who played his sister-wives off against each other, and brought a foreign queen into the mix, whom he flagrantly paid court to and flaunted in front of them. Iset, as some of you are aware, is the only one of his three principal queens to appear on a statue of the king. Ramses deliberately omitted images of his sister-wives from his monuments and left the label texts of the children of all his wives blank on his temple walls. He relished seeing them vie for supremacy. It made him feel powerful.'

'Now, there's a character worth playing,' I heard Drew Trainer murmur. 'The bastards are always the best parts.'

'It's possible none of this rivalry would have mattered,' Adam went on. 'Tiye's first child by Ramses was a son. He automatically became Crown Prince, the first-born son of pharaoh and his senior-ranking great royal wife.' He glanced over at Skylar Harrison as he said this, once again verifying one of her apparently clairvoyant pronouncements as fact. 'His name was Amen-hir-kopeshef.'

'Nice little tongue-twister,' Lori Scott remarked.

'Tragically, the boy died as a teenager. He was bitten by a snake.'

My eyes widened at this, thoughts flying to the cobra writhing near the steps of the young prince's tomb. So, Wadjet, protector of royalty, had stolen Tiye's firstborn son from her. It seemed a cruel irony. My shiver was nothing to do with the air conditioning. But it did make me wonder about the superstition about the snake we'd seen protecting the boy's tomb.

I caught myself in this conjecture and gave myself a mental shake. It was just a snake! Egypt does have rather a lot of them. Honestly! All this supernatural stuff was sending me loopy!

'Naturally, Tiye was devastated,' Adam continued. 'The prince was interred in the Valley of the Queens, in the tomb where we encountered the – er – the snake the other evening.' It was the first time he had faltered, his eyes flashing to mine, and I realised our thoughts were hurtling along twin tracks as usual. I sent him an encouraging smile. 'The tomb shows Ramses introducing his dead son to various deities, but nowhere on its walls is Tiye mentioned.'

It was hard not to interpret this as a deliberate slap in the face, especially since the boy had survived beyond infancy. I mentally contrasted it with the wall carvings in the royal tomb at Amarna, showing the pharaoh Akhenaten and his great royal wife Nefertiti all-too-visibly grieving the loss of a daughter. I'd always considered the tombs of the royal princes in the Valley of the Queens unbearably sad before. Now, the absence of his mother's name in teenage Amen-hir-kopeshef's tomb seemed the act of a cruel, egomaniacal tyrant.

'Hori tells us that Tiye had more children by Ramses, her crime being that they were daughters, who clearly counted for nothing in the court of Ramses III. In the meantime, her sister Tyti was giving birth to sons, the eldest of whom, Ramses, became next in line to the throne. It's possible Tiye would have stomached this. Child-mortality in ancient Egypt was a sad fact of life. But Hori tells us two events tipped her over the edge. First, as he reached maturity Prince Ramses was married to his full sister, the princess Tentopet. In Queen Tyti's eyes, as mother to the future pharaoh and his great royal wife, this gave her superior status, and she started lording it over her elder sister. Second, and in what Hori saw as an act of great cruelty and betrayal, when Queen Iset gave birth to a boy shortly after the death of Tiye's only son, Ramses named him Amen-hir-kopeshef.'

'As if his dead son was instantly replaceable!' Lori Scott frowned. 'Pig!'

I had to agree with her. It seemed to me cruel to both women: that Iset should have the name of her dead stepson foisted on her new-born baby, like some sort of dreadful talisman (although I recalled the second Amen-hir-kopeshef had grown to maturity and gone on to become king). But particularly so for Tiye.

'But then Hori tells us a miracle happened. Towards the end of her child-bearing years, Tiye gave birth to another son. She saw him as a gift from the gods.' Adam glanced over at me. 'His name was Nebenkharu. Yes, Merry,' he answered the question he could read in my eyes. 'You had it right. That was indeed a name previously given to one of the sons of Ramses the Great and is missing from the label texts at Medinet Habu.'

'So, that's what gave her the idea of a coup d'état?' Drew Trainer surmised. 'Another son to elevate to the kingship.'

'As he grew to maturity, yes. The glory years of Ramses III's reign as a mighty warrior pharaoh were over. His military victories against foreign would-be invaders were behind him. By the time of the harem conspiracy, he'd been on the throne around thirty-one years. He'd celebrated his *hed seb* jubilee, a kind of ceremonial rejuvenation event performed in front of great crowds in year thirty. Hori suggests the king was losing his grip on government and refused all the advice and guidance Tiye offered him. By now, he was a man in his late fifties and, remember, she was slightly older. Hori records the years of bad harvests and the strange, dark skies that blocked out the sun.'

'From a massive volcanic eruption on the other side of the world,' Drew Trainer recalled.

'And notes also the recurring strikes of the workmen of Deir el Medina, employed in cutting and carving the king's tomb. They downed tools and marched on the grain stores of the Ramesseum on at least three occasions, demanding the payment they were due.'

I saw Mackenzie King's eyes widen at this, reminded that he had not been with us when we'd discussed it. I was sure it would make for a cracking movie scene, full of stick-waving, shouting and scuffles.

'Tiye watched the reins of government come apart in horror. She despised her husband for his propensity to feast behind the thick boundary walls of the palace while the poor of Thebes hungered.'

'Let them eat cake,' Lori Scott murmured as an aside.

'And, of course, as a terrifically intelligent and astute woman, she was fully aware of her country's recent history. The terrible example of the chaos that followed the death of a long-lived king, pre-deceased by many of his sons, as had been the case with Ramses the Great. It led to the years of civil war by which her own father wrested the throne for himself. Hori tells us that at least four of Ramses III's sons were already dead by the time of his jubilee. Tiye knew herself to be a strong and capable administrator. Her husband was a selfish tyrant. Worse; while Hori is not explicit, what comes across in his text is that Ramses III treated the women of his harem with a casually cruel, almost ritualistic abuse. Tiye raged against this mistreatment but was unable to stop it.'

I shuddered. When we'd speculated that the pharaoh was a misogynistic bully, I hadn't gone quite so far as to imagine sexual abuse. Now it was clear exactly what the women of the harem stood to gain by dispatching the pharaoh.

'Tiye saw herself as the only chance for righting things. Her younger sister little more than a royal ornament. And her nephew, the Crown Prince Ramses is described by Hori as a man with a monumental ego the size of the Great Pyramid, a massive sense of entitlement and a tendency towards brutality.'

Exactly! I thought. A chip off the old block!

'Tiye watched her youngest son grow up while all this was going on and saw a chance to act. She knew she could count on support from the powerful men of Thebes who had served under her leadership while Ramses was off fighting his wars and bankrupting the economy. Many of them were fathers and brothers of harem concubines and knew exactly how their women were being treated. Tiye wanted to install her son on the throne while she still had power and perspicacity to rule, and coach him in the skills of good government, and perhaps the respectful treatment of women. And so, the harem conspiracy was conceived.'

'Brave lady.' This was Talia Nolan, listening intently. I wondered if perhaps, recognising Tiye as an older woman, she spied an opportunity for the role of a lifetime. Another Oscar-winner, maybe. I saw her eyeing the sheath dress in its protective glass cabinet, hearing the story of the queen who had once worn it, perhaps imagining herself in a replica.

'Tiye recruited men from among the king's inner circle and all the key state departments to her cause. Hori was aware of her plot and stood full square behind it. He shared her views of the rack and ruin the once mighty empire of Egypt was falling into in the later years of their brother's reign. The assassination and coup d'état were timed to take place during the Beautiful Feast of the Valley, one of the key celebrations of the Theban ritual year when everyone at court would be drinking and merry making. The king's chamberlain, high-ranking butlers, a number of senior priests, the court magician, an army general and a troop commander from Kush were all in on the plot.'

'The ability to make use of Nubian troops would have been extremely useful to the conspirators.' Feisal nodded. 'A general uprising to secure the rebellion.'

'Hori states the plan was to remove – er – that is, to murder – not only Pharaoh but also Crown Prince Ramses,' Adam informed us. 'And then to quickly get young prince Nebenkharu crowned – which was where the priesthood came in. They were primed and ready to perform the ceremony before anyone could object. Once it had been sanctified by the gods nobody would be able to reverse it. But something went horribly wrong.'

'They walked into a trap,' I said, recalling Skylar Harrison's words on that very first morning at Medinet Habu.

Adam nodded. 'Somehow - Hori does not say how, perhaps because he does not know – Crown Prince Ramses got wind of the plot. Rather than intervene beforehand and perhaps save his father's life, he instead raised troops of his own and had them installed in secret, hidden within the harem quarters. As heir apparent, Prince Ramses' primary duty was as "commander in chief of the army". As such, he was well placed to quash the uprising. With his men in place, he stood back and let it go ahead, ensuring he himself was safely out of harm's way.'

'You bet he did!' I said tartly. 'As a man already approaching middle-age, it was in his best interests to clear his own path to the throne. You know, I've always wondered about those accounts,' – (ok, they were novels, but I wasn't about to admit that in front of present company) – 'representing Prince Ramses as the wronged victim of an evil conspiracy who heroically rounded up the conspirators and brought them to trial and then got his happy ending, coming to the throne as Ramses IV.' I looked over at Feisal Ismail not feeling quite brave enough to lecture to the Hollywooders but wanting to make my point, nonetheless. 'As you know, The Harris Papyrus, commissioned by Ramses IV sets out in great detail the towering achievements of his father's reign. It has always smacked to me of protesting too much! That man had a guilty conscience. He quite clearly stood to gain the most from his father's early death. Let's be honest! Queen Tiye did him the most enormous favour!'

A small cough from Adam alerted me that I had probably said enough about Prince Ramses. I subsided and sipped my champagne. But it was nice to have my long-held theory proven correct.

'Bringing the conspirators to trial, Prince Ramses – now Ramses IV – selected trial judges from among those he knew to be loyal to his aunt's cause to preside over the sentencing of their co-conspirators as their only hope of saving their own skins. He was an early proponent of the aphorism that "to divide is to conquer".'

I managed to bite back my comment that I had guessed as much, thinking maybe I should do as Adam had so often suggested: write historical fiction. I'd nailed the true character of the "wronged" prince!

'Tiye and Prince Nebenkharu were placed under house arrest in locked quarters within the Eastern gatehouse, where the murder of the pharaoh had taken place. Guards were placed on the doors. The low-ranking conspirators were put on trial, found guilty and summarily executed.'

I noticed Skylar Harrison shudder. This, of course, she had "*seen*" in gruesome detail.

'Since everyone knew who stood accused among the senior-ranking officials, they were not imprisoned during the trial. That's how Hori and some of his fellow judges were able to meet with them and Tiye's loyal women of the harem while the judicial proceedings were underway. They were desperately trying to figure out a way to break Queen Tiye and Prince Nebenkharu free and get them away to safety, knowing the death sentences they were expected to deliver on them. But, of course, Ramses IV's spies were everywhere, and caught them. Realising they had to cover up the true purpose of their meeting, they pretended to be wildly drunk, indulging in a kind of "last supper" with the accused – although, of course, they wouldn't have known that analogy a thousand years before Christ,' he qualified quickly.

'I'd have thought a better bet might be for the harem women to put on a bit of a show,' Drew Trainer put in, winking. 'If you get my drift...? I thought you said they were caught "*fraternising*". Isn't that suggestive to you of something with sexual connotations? They were, after all, an ancient-world type of hooker, weren't they?

Adam smiled at him. 'That might work in a movie. But remember, the harem women – concubines, yes – were the absolute property of Pharaoh, there solely for his – er – pleasure. There's no way they could indulge in that type of activity with anyone else and expect to live. Besides which, they were related to the judges and convicts, sisters, cousins, nieces. So, pretending to be roaring drunk was their best bet.'

'Ah,' Drew Trainer said. 'Shame. It was just starting to get juicy!'

'As we know,' Adam went on, easing his collar with one finger in the way Mackenzie King had done earlier, 'this wasn't enough to get the judges off scot free. Most suffered the indignity of facial mutilation.'

'But why not Hori?' I frowned.

'Hori was the new pharaoh's uncle,' Adam reminded us. 'Something of a court elder by his own admission. He tells us he was hauled in front of the king himself to account for his actions.'

'And?' I prompted.

'Hori says he told the king the drinking session was intended to be a final farewell that went a bit far, then begged for the queen and prince not to be put to death. From what Ted, I mean Professor Kincaid, and I have been able to work out, Hori came to regret his plea, feeling that he had made a bargain with Set himself.'

'Set was an evil god in the ancient Egyptian pantheon,' Feisal put in for the Hollywooders' benefit. 'He murdered his brother Osiris.'

'So, a bargain with the devil,' Lori Scott translated.

'But why did Ramses IV allow Hori to go free?' I asked.

Adam looked back at me in open frustration. 'That, Hori does not explicitly record. But I think it is wrapped up in that word "bargain". My guess is that he was agreeing to something he hoped would be in exchange for the queen and prince's lives.'

'How strange,' I muttered. 'He's recorded everything else.'

'And, as we know, it made no difference to the tragic fate of Prince Nebenkharu,' Adam stated. 'He was brought before the judicial court set up in the Khonsu Temple at Karnak, charged under a pseudonym for colluding with his mother, Tiye, when she plotted rebellion against the Lord of the Two Lands.

'Pentaweret,' I murmured. 'I wonder how they arrived at that...? Oh, I see!' It struck me at once. 'It was a cruel joke, an ironic jibe.' I looked back at Adam. 'You said Taweret was a goddess of fertility. The one thing his mother was NOT was fertile with sons. Perhaps that was her tragedy not her crime. So, "he of the great, fertile female" is a horribly sarcastic name to convict him under; and must have been a dagger in the heart to her.'

'Nebenkharu/Pentaweret was found guilty of course. We know he was allowed to kill himself rather than be executed. We're told this happened in private. But Hori goes into a bit more detail. Poor kid! He was only eighteen. It wasn't the most dignified suicide you can imagine. Terrified, screaming and crying to his mother who had been forced to watch his sentencing. He broke away from the guards and ran up the interior staircase onto the temple roof. He took off his robes, tied them into a makeshift rope, which he dangled over the temple wall, secured to a flagpole, hoping to escape by climbing down to safety. But he tripped, got caught up in his own improvised rope and hung himself.'

'Well, that explains the folds of skin at his neck on his mummy hinting at strangulation,' I murmured. 'But clearly it wasn't by choice.'

'Hori records his disgust at the royal decree for the prince's body to be sewn inside a goat skin. He himself provided the anthropoid coffin and managed to persuade the mortuary men to use it, although it was unfinished, and they refused to add labels to name the prince.'

'And what of Tiye?' I asked, glancing across at Skylar Harrison, sitting still-beautiful but pale-faced and visibly trembling. I noticed Lori Scott reach out to lay a hand over hers resting on the tabletop. 'Was she put on trial?' I remembered Skylar Harrison had said so, for all that the records were silent on the subject.

'Yes. Hori tells us she was brought before the hall of judges, men who had been her faithful servants, remained loyal to her still. Many openly wept. It was the one and only time the new pharaoh attended the court room in the Khonsu Temple. Tiye faced him proudly and regally, every inch a queen. She made no attempt to defend herself but calmly pleaded guilty to each of the charges read out against her: that she had incited rebellion, plotted the assassination of her husband the king and planned a coup d'état to dispatch the appointed Crown Prince, replacing him with her youngest child. Then, fully in command of herself, she waited, head bowed, for them to pass sentence.'

I caught myself holding my breath.

'The pharaoh deliberated. He said it spoke in the queen's favour that she admitted to her crimes, that there were those who had begged for her not to be put to death and that he was minded to grant this wish. We can only imagine that Hori had a moment of genuine hope, thinking maybe his plea had been heard, that her life would be spared after all. A couple of the judges even shouted out in triumph. But Ramses IV's was a sadistically clever kind of cruelty. He delivered his malicious verdict. Instead of being "put to death" by execution or supervised suicide, Tiye would be bricked up, incarcerated without food or water in an airtight room from which there could be no escape. Eventually, by neither her own hand nor his, death would find her.'

The silence that fell over our exclusive little assemblage was somehow heavy, weighed down with revulsion at the queen's fate. I felt suddenly claustrophobic, in need of fresh air. I think all our gazes were drawn to the tiny sheath dress, almost as if the ancient queen was standing before us re-living her dreadful sentencing. After a moment, I pulled mine away to glance again at Skylar Harrison. It provided an explanation for her night-time horrors, that was for sure. She was pressing her lips together, looking as if she might be channelling all her effort into keeping herself in her seat, when I'm sure all her instincts were to get up and flee.

'Yes,' Adam said, seeing where everyone's gazes were fixed. 'Tiye was de-robed, and her personal possessions taken from her. Hori was given the task of handing the jewels over to the royal treasury and burning her dress, but he hid them in the trial transcript box instead and swapped the alabaster box for another one while the pharaoh wasn't looking. Tiye was taken away there and then to have her horrific punishment enacted. Hori and the members of the judicial panel were not permitted to know where she was being incarcerated. They were held at barracks behind the Temple of Khonsu at Karnak for a full month under armed guard, so there could be no chance of any rescue attempt. Tiye was bricked up by members of Ramses' personal guard, men he knew he could count on, possibly through fear and coercion to carry out his instructions to the letter and show no sympathy for the queen.'

I shuddered, not really wanting to imagine it.

'Hori emerged from the whole experience a broken man,' Adam said. 'Assigned the queen's protector by his father, her devoted servant and a loving brother, he had no desire to live on without her; believed, in fact that he himself may have been instrumental in consigning her to such a slow and tortuous death. In total thirty-eight people were executed, many of them friends and associates. He dedicated months to transcribing this document,' he indicated the long papyrus scroll displayed in its glass case. 'Months during which the new pharaoh sought vengeance on all those remaining who might have hoped to thwart his succession to the throne. Ramses IV requisitioned several thousand men for a gruelling mission to the stone quarries of Wady Hammamat, in the desert to the east of Thebes. Ostensibly this was to provide stone for an ambitious building agenda intended to rival that of his illustrious predecessor Ramses the Great.   But he sent administrators, priests, military officers and their troops in addition to the stone cutters. Hori states that nine hundred men perished on the hazardous mission. Of course, being sent to the mines or quarries was a punishment throughout most of Egyptian history, so, no matter how much the new pharaoh boasted about his intended building programme, it was Hori's belief that Ramses was deliberately ridding himself of men loyal to Queen Tiye. Hori states it will be his final act to hide the box where it will never be found by the new king, so that one day the true events of the fate that befell his sister the queen at his nephew's decree may come to be known.'

'Ramses' revenge,' I murmured.

We sat contemplating everything we had heard for a few moments. I realised I had forgotten entirely about helping myself to the canapés; thought about rectifying this oversight but found I was unusually lacking in appetite. I wasn't sure I even wanted to finish my glass of champagne.

'I'm sorry,' Adam said at last, sensing the gloom that had settled over our exclusive little party. 'It would have been lovely to read all the way through and discover a happy ending, that somehow Hori found out where they imprisoned Tiye and broke her free just in time. But I guess this isn't Hollywood, right? I think it's clear the queen was bricked up just as the pharaoh ordered and died there, possibly through suffocation as the air gave out, or maybe starvation.'

'Indeed, it is not the most uplifting story,' Feisal Ismail stood up. 'But for the Egyptologists among us,' – I was immensely gratified to be included in the gaze that also swept up Adam and Habiba – 'it is knowledge priceless beyond words.'

'You have your plot,' Drew Trainer murmured to Mackenzie King. 'Now you just need someone to turn it into a screenplay.'

'Thank you, Adam,' Feisal shook his hand. 'And I will be sure to call Professor Kincaid and pass on my appreciation for his labours in helping you transcribe the papyrus so quickly. Tomorrow we can tell the world the whole story of the harem conspiracy and reveal also the true characters of those involved; something, I think, never before achieved in the whole of Egyptology and archaeology. That, I believe, calls for another glass of champagne!'

I was pleased the Ministry director was happy. Speaking for myself, there was still something somehow - I groped for the right word – *unfinished* – about the story Adam had told us.

I got up as Feisal set about topping up the glasses, and went to join my husband in contemplating the papyrus. 'Well done,' I congratulated him, reaching up to kiss him lightly on the lips. 'You held everyone in thrall. It was a bit like a night at the movies, just without the big screen. Still, you painted the picture vividly enough.'

He grinned at me. 'I enjoyed myself, Merry. But I don't mind admitting I was nervous. I just wish I'd been able to tell a happier tale. I hope I didn't depress everyone too much!'

'It's not your fault it's such a dark story,' I said staunchly. And then I had to ask: 'Did your translation match up to Ted's?'

'Well, I didn't get as far as he did,' he admitted. 'I managed a pretty good fist of it up to the part about the poor prince's sad demise. But not the bit about the men of Thebes being sent off to perish in the desert stone quarries. And certainly not the part about the sadistic fate that befell our tragic Queen Tiye. Ramses IV may not actually have had her blood on his hands but he sure as hell made sure she'd suffer. Skylar Harrison was right when she said there were worse ways to punish someone than to execute them or force them to take their own life. No wonder the queen has a restless spirit,'

'How differently history might have turned out if only she'd pulled it off,' I said. 'I wonder how Prince Ramses got wind of the plot.'

'Hori is silent on that point,' he shrugged. 'Perhaps he didn't know.'

I hadn't realised Skylar Harrison had come to join us until I caught a subtle drift of exotic-smelling, no doubt fearfully expensive fragrance. 'The queen will tell us, if we can find her,' she said cryptically.

'I'm sorry?' I thought I'd heard her correctly but didn't dare interpret the words.

'The queen,' she said, looking intently me and then at Adam. 'She's still there, where they bricked her up alive and left her to die. She wants to be found.'

Chapter 20

Adam and I did not attend the press conference. There was no reason for us to go. Given Skylar Harrison's remarkable claim last night, I couldn't honestly say I was sorry to be left behind. There was plenty to discuss.

We watched them go from the upper deck. Once again dressed to the nines like the Hollywood royalty they were, they'd dialled down the all-out glamour of the outfits they'd worn last night. Opted instead for a chic and stylish vibe, no doubt from America's finest fashion houses. An eye-catching assortment of designer daywear, they left the dahabeeyah looking ready for a full-on Tinseltown assault on the good people of Luxor. The locals would, I felt sure, turn out in droves hoping for a glimpse of them now Director Ismail had put out the word.

I had no idea whether Talia Nolan was to be included among their numbers for the media event. Found myself vaguely surprised that the private reception last night had ended without further dramatics on that score. Given the way she had been making eyes at Feisal Ismail in the early part of the evening, I'd rather thought she might be building up to something. But she'd seemed strangely quiet and withdrawn after Adam had finished reprising the harem conspiracy and its consequences. Perhaps it had been drama enough for her. Whatever, she had made her excuses shortly afterwards and had her private driver collect her early. And, right now, there were more important matters uppermost in my mind than thinking about the troubled and troublesome screen siren.

As soon as Ahmed closed the door on the minibus to drive the Hollywooders into Luxor, I turned to Adam. 'It's all very well Skylar telling us the queen wants to be found – is demanding it, in fact – and won't stop haunting her until she is. But it's of absolutely no use if we don't have the first clue where to start looking!' (I think since the snake incident we were both more comfortable referring to the movie star by her first name).

Adam nodded. 'She seems pretty clear that she doesn't want to be the one to find her,' he said. 'But it's hard to see how we can proceed – always assuming we should – if we don't have Skylar there to guide us. We've established Tiye is not in the Valley of the Queens, and now we know why. Ramses IV ordered her bricked up in a living tomb. But it could be anywhere!'

Gazing at him in frustration, it suddenly struck me how bizarre this whole thing was. I surprised myself by starting to giggle.

'What is it, Merry?' he looked at me in bewilderment.

'I can hardly believe we're having this conversation!' I managed. 'I mean, just listen to us, Adam!' I brought myself under control, still smiling. 'You say, "always assuming we should", when the simple fact is that quite obviously, we should not. We'd be hunting for the mortal remains of a queen who was killed – in a roundabout way, I'll grant you – around three thousand years ago! There's probably nothing left but dust! And all on the say-so of a Hollywood movie star with psychic powers! It's beyond far-fetched! It's downright ludicrous!'

His face split into an enormous grin, eyes sparkling. 'But it's the most enormous fun, don't you think?' Expanding his chest, he tipped his face up to the sunshine. 'God, Merry! It's great to be back! I've missed this!' He looked back at me and draped one arm across my shoulders. 'And you've just given a very convincing rundown of all the reasons we shouldn't tell Feisal Ismail. At least, not until we've established whether there is actually anything to tell.'

I rested my head on his shoulder, looking out over the broad expanse of the Nile, noticing the way the sunlight cast diamonds onto its surface. Despite the rather grisly story we'd unearthed, a sense of supreme wellbeing stole over me. In Egypt my life was one big crazy rollercoaster adventure. The things that happened to me here were as far away from the humdrum little life I used to lead in England as the moon from the sun. Madcap it might be, but I loved every second. To have Adam as my partner in crime in all of this was almost more happiness than I knew what to do with. Almost, but not quite! 'So, we really are going to see if we can find her?'

'Why the hell not, Merry?'

I got serious again. 'It's just, if Hori didn't know where they incarcerated her, I don't see how we have a hope of figuring it out. All Skylar has been able to give us is that awful sense of darkness and suffocation as Tiye felt the life ebb out of her. That's what her screaming night-time horrors were all about.' I shuddered. 'God, Adam; it must have been horrific. I know he saw Tiye as his bitter enemy, but Ramses IV was cruel beyond words. To think of her walled up all alone, somewhere no one could hear her cries, with all that time to reflect on what might have been and re-live the awfulness of her son's death; all the while staring her own in the face with each agonising moment; it gives me the heebie-jeebies!.'

Rather than pull me closer as I might have expected, his arm dropped from my shoulders. He spun me instead to face him, eyes blazing. 'You've given me an idea!' he exclaimed. 'Remember that saying about keeping your friends close and your enemies closer? Well, that might have been exactly the new pharaoh's thinking. And, reflecting on it, I reckon Skylar has already told us exactly where to look! We just didn't realise it at the time.' He glanced at his watch. 'How long do you think we have until the Hollywooders get back?'

A scant half-an-hour later, we left our scooters in the Medinet Habu temple car park. Khaled had ensured these were ready and waiting for our return to Egypt. Other than the ubiquitous temple guards, colleagues of Ahmed's from the Tourism police, the place was deserted. The movie location shoot had been shut down for a few days. I guessed the moviemaking folk were enjoying the unexpected time off lazing by their hotel pools, sightseeing, or else perhaps attending the press conference. With everybody otherwise occupied, I guessed we had no need to hurry. I could enjoy the time out with my husband the way I liked it best: just the two of us. Adam flashed his Egyptologist's ID card, but the guards recognised us and waved us through the security kiosk without looking at it.

The sun was high in the sky overhead making the airwaves shimmer. There is something physical about the air in Egypt, like nowhere else I have been. It hangs hot and heavy; a presence you feel you could reach out and touch. We'd dressed appropriately for our excursion, both in long sleeved cotton shirts. Adam favoured sand-coloured chinos and hiking boots, whereas I had on navy-blue cropped cotton pants and plimsolls – closed-in shoes being essential given the quantities of sand and dust. He sported his battered old Indiana Jones-style hat, and I wore a broad-brimmed straw hat to protect me from the fierce rays of the sun.

Adam took my hand as we entered the temple precinct through the Eastern High Gate, where Skylar Harrison had the first of her psychic visions. A scant few days ago, so much had happened since, it seemed longer ago than that. He led me on past the ruins of ancient stone chapels on either side of us as we entered the temple forecourt, then beyond, where the massive Hollywood trailers were parked and various moviemaking paraphernalia, cables, cameras, scaffolding poles and the like littered the space. I stared at all of this in fascination, thinking how much I'd like to peek inside one of those trailers. But it wasn't what we had come to see, and they were undoubtedly locked anyway. With the gigantic first pylon rising steeply in front of us, Adam led us to the left, so we skirted the outer wall of the mighty memorial temple.

'You really think Ramses IV bricked her up *here*?' I asked.

Still leading me forward, he shrugged. 'It stands to reason. Remember I said about keeping your enemies close. And you said something about nobody being able to hear her cries. Well; what if they could? What if she knew they could? But that nobody was coming to help her? Just how cruel would that be? I'll bet Ramses IV took a sadistic pleasure in hearing her weaken. And he may well have enjoyed the fact that some of those who remained loyal and sympathetic to Tiye could also hear her but could do nothing. It was a further punishment for them too. I expect he put armed guards on the place and instructed them to kill anyone who came near, probably on pain of their own death.'

It was rather too vivid a picture he was painting for my liking. Speaking as someone with a highly tuned appreciation of historical fiction that was saying something. 'So, why didn't Hori know where she was?' I frowned and asked the obvious question.

'Remember, Merry; Hori wasn't permitted to leave the Temple of Khonsu at Karnak for over a month after the trial verdict was delivered. By that time, Ramses IV was press-ganging the men of Luxor into their suicide mission to the stone quarries of Wadi Hammamat. And Tiye was probably dead. I imagine Hori wanted to give Ramses and, by definition, this place, the widest possible berth. He can't have thought for one moment the new pharaoh would bring her back here. I'll bet he avoided the place like the plague.'

'But he buried the alabaster box here.'

'Well, yes; although not until some months later. I imagine it was after Ramses moved the court north again, back to the new capital Pi-Ramesse. Remember, Ramses III had mostly ruled from there. The whole court was only here in Thebes for the Beautiful Feast of the Valley celebrations.'

He had an answer for everything, seeming filled with the spirit of Boy's Own adventure, his blue eyes bright, sparkling and full of life. It made him irresistible. And I'll admit I was starting to think maybe he was onto something. We were now among the excavated foundation stones of what had once been the royal palace, abutting the temple on its southern side. Built mostly of mudbrick, the palace itself had not survived the passage of three millennia. Looking about me as we picked our way between the low stone foundation deposits, it was impossible to imagine what the ancient structure must have looked like when Tiye had known it.

'You think he had her walled up inside the royal *palace*?' I asked in disbelief as he led me forward.

'No, Merry; I don't. Come on.' And he pulled me onwards.

I glanced back at the rear outer wall of the first pylon as we passed. I'd always thought it among the most impressive of all temple wall carvings in Egypt: a towering edifice deeply etched with hunting scenes, with two huge images of Ramses III driving his chariot, bow and arrow drawn, trampling oxen under the thundering hooves of his horse. The lowest register showed a squadron of army troops marching in perfect sequence, the front lines with bows and arrows cocked, pointing at the sky, the men behind them marching with shields up. It was splendid for sure but now I found I couldn't look at it without a shudder. I could suffer the ego-maniacal nature of the pharaohs and how they had themselves depicted. As Drew Trainer had said, it went with the job description. But now knowing the vindictive and spiteful nature of the man, I found Ramses III was no longer a pharaoh I could look on with admiration, for all that his wall art was spectacular.

We were inside the temple boundary, walking between the southern outer temple wall and the impenetrable three-metre-thick mud brick barrier that still circled the perimeter of the temple precincts. When we reached the end, we turned right so we were behind the back outer wall of the temple itself, at the furthest end from the entrance.

I watched with interest as, dropping my hand, Adam walked the length of this back wall, minutely studying its surface. 'Didn't Skylar say something about a doorway?' he said, frowning at the ancient stone.

Getting my bearings, I realised where we were. On the other side of this great wall was the jumble of broken stubs of pillars and ruins of chapels and shrines where Skylar Harrison had passed out after her eyes-tight-shut hypnotic walk the other day from one end of the temple to the other.

I caught on in an instant. 'Yes! She said there used to be a doorway at the back of the temple.' I joined him in staring at the stonework. It looked intact to me. 'You think it's possible he had Tiye walled up in the outer enclosure wall of the temple itself?' I asked doubtfully.

'Can you remember exactly what Skylar said?' he looked at me, tipping his hat further back and mopping his brow with the back of his hand.

I tilted my head to one side, trying to recollect. 'Something that made me think she'd seen the queen's ghost,' I recalled. 'I remember it gave me the creeps and sent the biggest shiver down my spine.'

'She said, "*she's here*",' he reminded me. 'Like you, I thought she was channelling the queen's spirit, or whatever the hell it is that she does. And I daresay she was. But what if she was also speaking the literal truth? What if that whole walking with her eyes shut stuff was the queen leading her – and us by extension – to the place they incarcerated her?'

My spine was tingling this time around. I looked at the solid outer wall of the temple, thinking if she was inside there, we had no hope of ever finding her. Built as Ramses III's Mansion of Millions of Years, I knew Feisal Ismail would never in a million of our own years grant permission to investigate the ancient masonry. 'But the temple was dedicated to the gods,' I objected. 'As a mortuary temple, it surely had a special function. Even if they closed-up a doorway that was once here, I find it hard to believe they could do so with Tiye inside without giving offence to the whole pantheon. Besides, didn't you say it was a room they put her in?'

'That's how Hori described her sentencing,' he acknowledged with a frown, staring at the wall in frustration.

'Well, this wall is surely not thick enough to have a room built inside it,' I pointed out. 'It's not wide at the base, like the pylon at the front.' To prove my point, I picked up a stone and tossed it over the top, hearing it rattle to the ground on the other side. The motion, watching it arc upwards before falling over the wall made me notice something else. 'God, Adam! Look at the sky!'

He joined me in looking up and let out an exclamation. Livid purple clouds were rolling in above the Theban hills behind us.

'Wow! Is it going to rain?' I was unsure whether to feel excitement or dread at this prospect. Rain here wasn't like the persistent gentle wet stuff we got back at home in England. A rare event in and around Luxor, the sudden cloudbursts could result in torrential downpours and had been known to flood the tombs in the Valley of the Kings.

The air took on a still, limpid quality as, while we watched, the sunlight turned hazy, then, with the speed of someone pulling down a visor, the skies darkened to the colour of a blood orange, as if full of sand.

The implication of this struck us both at once.

'Sandstorm!' Adam shouted; his voice carried away by the sudden gust of wind that literally smacked into him as he spoke, made his shirt billow and blew off his hat.

I reached up and held mine on my head, feeling little pinheads of sand sting my face and hands.

'We need shelter!' he yelled urgently, grabbing my hand again and pulling me with him, snatching up his hat as he went. 'These things blow up in an instant.'

I whipped off my own hat and held it in front of my face, shielding my eyes as we ran forward around the side of the temple and along the length of its northern wall this time. Glancing back, I could see a roiling wall of orange-and-purple cloud gathering momentum, seeming to hurtle towards us on the strength of gathering winds. It buffeted us as we ran, hurling sand at our backs that hit with the force of a machine gun fired at close range.

Knowing the movie trailers to be locked, and with the guards' security kiosk a bit too far further on to be sure of reaching safely, the temple seemed our best bet. There was a measure of protection once inside its thick walls. Adam pulled me through the first pylon and together we pelted across the first courtyard, up the ramp, on through the second courtyard, up another ramp and into the relative sanctuary of the roofed colonnade. This, where he had lectured to Drew Trainer, Lori Scott and me about the Ramesside rivalries the other day. Here, we stopped and hunkered down.

'Our first sandstorm, Merry!' the excitement in his voice gave away how he felt about it.

'I don't fancy our chances of riding our scooters home,' I looked on the pessimistic side, raising my voice to be heard.

He laughed aloud. 'Khaled will be glad to have something to fix.'

'I hope he and Rabiah have the presence of mind to cover the furniture on the upper deck with something they can pin down,' I shouted anxiously.

'Don't worry, Merry; they're used to this sort of stuff. They'll know exactly what to do. Although, it's an odd time of year for a sandstorm. Usually, the Khamsin blows in springtime.'

We sat in the safety of the colonnade listening to the violent sand-filled windstorm rage around the temple.

'You can certainly see why the Egyptians worked hard not to anger the gods,' I muttered as darkness obliterated what had, mere moments ago, been middle-of the-day broad and bright daylight.

He grinned at me, determined to enjoy the experience. 'I can think of worse things than to be holed up here with you in the middle of a tempest.'

His good mood was contagious. 'Well, I suppose it might add a bit more drama to the Hollywooder's press conference! As if it needed it!'

No sooner were these words out of my mouth than the wind dropped away to nothing. The sudden lack of noise was almost as unnerving as the howling maelstrom that preceded it. I looked at Adam in surprise, saw the mirror of my own shock on his face, magnified tenfold as a sudden almighty crack rent the air.

I bit back a scream. 'What the...?' I jumped as if electrified, as maybe I had been. The atmosphere seemed to buzz with static.

'Thunderbolt?' he hazarded.

'My God! It sounds as if the temple is being bombed!'

More crashing and banging overhead harkened a thunderstorm more brutal than any I had experienced. Adam and I stared at each other while the heavens exploded. I covered my ears, thinking it must be literally right on top of us, understanding for the first time what it meant to be in the eye of a storm.

Rain came then. A torrential, lashing monsoon-like deluge. We moved hand-in-hand to stand at the top of the ramp and watch as it formed huge lake-like puddles on the flagstones and splashed up the walls of the courtyard we'd just crossed, washing away the piling sand.

'My God, Merry; this is apocalyptic!' he yelled.

It did indeed feel as if the end of the world might be nigh.

And then it was over. Almost as quickly as they had blown up, the great black clouds lightened and cleared. The rain stopped. Sunlight broke through the dispersing thunderclouds and burnt off the mist that rose as the water vaporised.

'That,' Adam proclaimed, 'was surreal! I thought for a moment there we might have to call to be rescued! I didn't expect it to be over so fast!'

'We should call Khaled and Rabiah,' I suggested, glad to be able to speak in my everyday tones. 'Check everything's ok on the *Queen Ahmes*.'

Adam pulled out his mobile phone and tapped the screen, putting it on speaker. A moment later Khaled answered in his broad Scottish brogue.

'Hey,' Adam greeted him. 'How are you doing in the storm? Quite a cracker, wasn't it? I think I'll have a job for you later fixing our scooters!'

'Call that a storm?' Khaled's voice sounded faintly amused. 'We've been through worse'n that guvnor.' (He loved calling Adam this). 'Sure, the wind blew up a bit and I thought I heard a far-off rumble of what might have been thunder. Rabiah said there were a few spits and spots of rain. But nothing to write home about.'

Adam rang off and we stared at each other in open perplexity.

'Maybe it was just a localised storm?' I hazarded. Unless… Well, I hesitate to say this… but... are you sensing something other-worldly in what just happened?'

'I wish I'd thought to film it,' he said, looking bemused. 'But given how weird everything else has been recently – let's face it, I don't have a rational explanation for anything that's been going on – I'm thinking maybe the souls of the dead just fought an epic battle overhead!'

'That, or Queen Tiye came to give us a helping hand in how to find her!'

He stared at me with eyes turning violet. 'You think she's here too, don't you?'

'Yes,' I said, realising for the first time that it was true. 'And I have an idea where to look. You said something when we were with Skylar at the back of the temple the other day. The day she told us the queen was here.'

He looked back at me in open enquiry, not following.

'When she asked where the doorway was – I'm sure she said something about it leading to another high gate on the outer perimeter wall that encircles the temple. And you said she was right. That there was once a mirror of the Eastern High Gate, so presumably a Western High Gate, at the opposite end of the enclosure.'

Adam was nodding slowly, eyes bright. 'Yes! It may once have formed part of the royal harem, or possibly been a tradespeople's' entrance. That's right!'

'If memory serves, you said it had fallen into ruin and no attempt had been made to re-construct it. Well, it seems to me, it might be a good place to look! Maybe the queen was planning on leading Skylar through the doorway and out the other side!

His expression blazed with possibility as he grabbed my hand. 'Merry; you are a wonder! Let's go!'

It was weird re-tracing our steps out of and then around the back of the temple. The sun shone fiercely, drying the puddles to damp patches that dried up altogether as we walked. The evidence of the sandstorm was in the drifts piling against the outer walls and foundation stones, but a light wind would soon blow them away.

This time, our interest was in the mostly-mudbrick, thick boundary wall enclosing the temple; the impregnable security barrier Ramses III had doubtless built to protect himself from rebellion in the time before the harem conspiracy was even thought of. Unpopular, despotic and self-indulgent, he had not been a benevolent ruler of his people. It didn't need the history books to record the workers' strikes that plagued his final years. The impenetrable perimeter wall told its own story. Atop the eroded mudbrick, it was still possible to see ruined structures that might once have served as sentry points, or maybe grain stores to keep the king well fed while his populace went hungry.

As we reached the back of this enclosure, I could see that Adam was correct: there had once been a more substantial structure built here. Gone now, I tried to imagine the twin of the fortress-like *migdol*-style gateway we had entered through on that first morning, where poor Skylar Harrison had the first of what I was now thinking of as her visitations from the queen.

As we approached, it was to see smoke rising from the tumbled ruins.

'What's that?' I asked in alarm. 'Fire?'

Adam strode closer. 'I'm thinking that's where that thunderbolt we heard struck. The stonework might have shifted. Please be careful, Merry.'

Moving to join him and looking at the spot, the same lightning strike seemed to explode inside my brain. 'Damn right the stonework has shifted!' I yelled, making no attempt to mask my excitement. 'Tiye wants us to find her!' I didn't care that I sounded like a crazy woman. As Adam had already pointed out, none of our recent experiences with Skylar Harrison made any sort of sense. I'd stopped looking for a logical explanation, decided simply to run with it.

He caught my exhilaration and let out a loud whoop. 'Bloody hell, Merry! This is *madness*!' But I could see he was as fired up as I was, which, given the smoke still drifting up from the ancient ruins, was possibly not the best analogy.

Moving gingerly, we picked our way across the freshly tumbled, uneven stones littered with mudbricks towards the place the thunderbolt had hit. It seemed to have demolished what might once have been a section of wall.

I let out a yelp and Adam grabbed me as the ground I was standing on gave way. Steady again, we stood stock still, holding onto each other and looked around.

'Yes!' he spoke in a thrilling whisper, lest to raise his voice might set off an avalanche of sand, stone and mudbrick. 'There! Look!' He pointed. 'It's blown a hole in the ruins. I might just be able to crawl through!'

'Adam, no!' I said in alarm, looking at the smoking gash in the ancient edifice. 'It's too dangerous. The stone is too unstable. What if it falls in on you?'

He looked at me searchingly for a long moment. 'We've come this far on the strength of mystic paranormality.' He seemed quite pleased with this, and smiled as he went on, growing in confidence. 'I'm thinking if the queen wants to be found and is using all the supernatural energy at her disposal to ensure it, then it is hardly in her best interests to allow a bloody great chunk of masonry to land on my head.'

'And if she's not?' I questioned, suddenly losing my nerve. 'What if this is all just a fantastical farce that Skylar has dreamed up, and that freak storm just now was exactly that – a freak storm?'

He grinned at me, undaunted. 'You don't believe that any more than I do. There are stranger things in heaven and earth, Merry...! Just because we can't explain them, it doesn't mean they're not real.'

'You're enjoying this!' I accused.

'Hell, yes!' he laughed aloud. 'Aren't you?'

I thought about it. 'I suppose so.'

'C'mon, Merry; where's your spirit of adventure?'

'I just don't want you getting hurt.'

'Then come with me,' he invited, eyes firing signals. 'Let's crawl through that hole together. It will be quite like old times!'

He had me now, and he knew it. Releasing his grip on my shoulders, he took my hand instead and cautiously reached out one foot to test the ground in front of us. The stones and mudbricks held, and we edged forwards towards the hole. I tried to visualise this as the building it must once have been, the imposing, fortress-like gateway with rooms above and on either side of the entrance. It was hard to envision, and I gave up, just concentrated on reaching that smoking hole without tripping and falling flat on my face.

'Ok, let me go first to check it's safe,' he said. He pulled his mobile phone from his pocket, switched on its torch, let go of my hand and dropped to his knees.

I guessed it must once have been some sort of cellar, a small, dark, subterranean, windowless space, perhaps used for storage, with the Western Gateway built on top of it. I watched Adam squeeze through the space, once presumably the entrance the henchmen of Ramses IV bricked up to entomb the queen inside. Then listened to him scuffling about a bit. After a moment, I heard him let out a long, low whistle.

'Ok, Merry; come and join me. But I won't promise you'll like what you see.'

For some reason, hearing this, I felt my blood run cold. I hesitated. But at the same time, I couldn't *not* go in. Crouching, I edged forward, then got down on my hands and knees, which was easier; uncaring of the dust that caked my trousers, and crawled forward.

As I straightened, eyes adjusting to darkness after the bright sunshine outside, I saw what Adam was pointing his torchlight at. My lungs seemed to flatten and my stomach drop.

I had never seen a perfectly preserved human skeleton before. Not in real life anyway. Certainly not such a small one, of a woman whose story I knew, with whom my sympathies lay so strongly. Of course, if I'd thought about it, I would have known this was what to expect. No nicely linen-wrapped mummy, and not the dust I'd quipped about earlier either. In the arid Egyptian climate, I was all too aware that human flesh would desiccate. But bones, well, bones just dried out and stayed relatively intact. Still, my overwhelming reaction seeing the skeleton on the floor was shock, and perhaps a touch of revulsion, a horrible shivery, creepy feeling that had my heart hammering against my ribcage loud enough I thought Adam must surely hear it.

I couldn't honestly say what I had thought we would find. Perhaps hadn't allowed myself to think about it. With all that talk of ghosts, I wonder if I had somehow expected to enter this place to be greeted by an apparition of the ancient queen, a Disney-style hologram, who could tell us her story. But looking at her sad remains, I felt a hopeless melancholy sweep over me.

Adam too was silent and pensive, pressed close alongside me in the confined space.

I reached for his hand. 'Of all our discoveries, I have to say this not my favourite, not by a long chalk.'

'Nor mine,' he squeezed my fingers. 'But she wanted us to find her.'

'I wonder why,' I mused, speaking softly out of respect and reverence for the ancient queen, and perhaps the creepy feeling of being so close to death. 'Surely her fate now will be to be moved to a museum display case. It's not exactly a decent burial or the "rest-in-peace" she might have hoped for.'

'But it brings her back,' he said. 'Not to life, exactly. But gives her back her name and her story.'

'I s'pose so.'

'He glanced sideways at me and smiled in the light reflected from his phone's built-in torch. 'What did you want, Merry? Gold? Didn't we find enough of that in the alabaster box? I'm sure it can be displayed with her so she can be reunited with her possessions.'

'It's not that,' I attempted to explain. 'I just didn't expect to feel so –' I groped for the right word but could only come up with, '– flat.

As if there should be something more – more than just these pathetically sad remains. Perhaps we should go, Adam.' I started to turn away. 'Skylar said this place reeks of death and she was right.'

I felt the stillness take hold of him. 'Wait a minute,' he breathed on a note of discovery, holding me back. 'What is *that*?'

'What?' I glanced at him to see where he was looking, hearing the thread of excitement in his voice.

He pointed the beam of torchlight at the sad little skeleton's hands. 'What is she clutching hold of, Merry?'

I didn't dare reach down and touch her to find out. So, Adam had to. He lifted the object with painstaking care from between the bones, using a tissue pulled from his pocket to protect whatever it was.

'It's a ring!' I exclaimed, feeling my sense of desolation lift. 'Wow! Considering Ramses IV took everything else from her, I wonder how she managed to keep it?'

'But look!' he said, studying it in the torchlight. 'It's been worn away on the top. Whatever stone or inscription it may once have had inset or stamped on it has been scraped off...'

I stared, mystified.

'...As if this has been used...' As he spoke, he started flashing the torch beam this way and that in the cramped space.

'The walls!' I exclaimed as the light caught on deep scratch marks where chunks of the once-plastered surface remained intact. 'She's used it to write on the walls!'

Chapter 21

There was no way we could leave after that.

'Ohmygod, Adam! Can you make out any of what it says?' I stepped cautiously aside in the confined interior to give him as much room as possible, while still leaving as much space as I could between myself and the queen's skeleton. I told myself this was out of respect for her mortal remains. But the simple fact was, it creeped me out to look at her still lying where the life had ebbed slowly out of her around thirty centuries ago.

Adam passed me the queen's ring while he held his torch up to the ancient scratchings, squinting at the plaster as he tried to decipher what she had written. Watching him, I gave the doomed queen top marks for bravery, her determination to use her time to the best possible effect. Almost as if she had prophesied that one day she would be found, determined to tell her story. Her eroded ring sat heavy in my hand resting on the tissue. A curiously personal item, it felt somehow shocking to know that the last living flesh it touched had been hers, that it had remained clutched in her hands after the last breath left her body, during the however-many months or years it had taken the soft tissues of her corpse to slowly dry out and disappear, and onward through the millennia, while her exposed bones presumably fossilised to preserve her in the skeletal state we found her in now. It was an unimaginable passage of time. I tried to wrap my brain around the three thousand years she had lain here in this dead-aired, stifling, cramped tomb-dungeon. Chills took hold of me again and I shivered despite the cloying air.

'It's not very clear,' Adam grunted, pulling me back into the present.

'I imagine she was scratching away in the dark,' I observed, surprised to hear my voice emerge quite normal sounding. Crouching, I put Tiye's ring carefully on the ground alongside her. It somehow wasn't right that I should stand here holding it. I slipped the tissue into my pocket.

'Have you got your phone, Merry?'

'You need another torch?'

'I'm thinking if you shine yours at the plaster, I can take some photos of it on mine. It might be easier to work it out on a screen and in better light.'

We fitted the action to the words and spent several focused minutes working to capture as much as we could. Truthfully, I was glad of something to do. Then Adam eased himself past me and over to the hole we'd entered through. He crouched in a shaft of daylight and concentrated on the pictures, expanding the images with his thumb and forefinger, turning his phone this way and that, and frowning at the screen.

'Anything?' I asked after a while.

He looked up at me. 'That bit over there...' he shone his phone-torch at a section of plaster on the wall opposite the queen, '...definitely references Queen Tyti. The word meaning "sister" is repeated, and her name is marked there too.'

'She used her last hours on earth to write about her *sister*?' I said in surprise.

He stared back at me, equally stupefied. 'It would seem so.'

I frowned. 'I know Hori's testament said that Ramses enjoyed playing the sisters off against each other, positively pitted them one against the other, but that seems a bit strange, doesn't it?' I wished I could translate the ancient text so I could join him in trying to decipher the queen's last writings.

Adam shrugged and peered at his screen again, flipping through the images with his thumb. 'And there's some stuff here about Prince Ramses,' he said at last, '...which I suppose stands to reason, since he was Tyti's son. But I'm not really making sense of it. I think I'm going to need to enlist Ted's help again.'

For no reason I could explain to myself, some instinct made me bend forward and pick up the ring, forgetting to use the tissue. I looked down at the worn gold band resting heavy in my palm. 'There must be something else you can make out,' I urged him. 'Anything.'

He expanded the image he was looking at and narrowed his eyes. 'It's possible these symbols here might be translated as "betrayal",' he hazarded.

And then the strangest thing happened. The ring I was holding seemed to grow hot. I felt the most remarkable surge of energy. My vision spiralled inwards, rather as if I was looking at Adam down an inverted telescopic lens. He became a pinprick at the faraway end of a long dark tunnel inside my head. A thunderous roaring filled my ears. I knew I was shaking violently, could hear my own teeth chattering. Voices were clamouring inside my head. I had a moment of piercing clarity. And then everything went black.

The next thing I knew, I opened my eyes to find myself staring up at the sky. I was propped in Adam's lap, sprawled on the dusty ground outside near the enclosure wall, with his arms around me.

'Oh, thank God! he exclaimed, seeing my eyes flutter open. 'Please, Merry, drink some water.' He held his bottle to my lips.

I took a few sips and sat up, swiping at the dust.

'Are you ok?' he asked searchingly, peering anxiously into my face.

'Yes, I think so,' I nodded, feeling a bit as if I was settling back into myself after some kind of weird out-of-body experience.

'My God, Merry! You gave me the fright of my life! One minute you were standing there asking me if there was anything else I could make out, the next you started asphyxiating. I looked up, to see you with this weird, transfixed almost *enraptured* expression on your face. You looked as if you were staring at someone, or something behind me. I even looked over my shoulder to see if there was anyone there! And then you shouted something completely unintelligible – I don't know what language you were speaking, but it wasn't English. The next moment, you collapsed to the floor in a dead faint!' He reached forward and put one hand on each of my shoulders, peering intently into my eyes. 'What the hell happened?'

'I have no idea what happened,' I said truthfully. 'All I can tell you is I know what happened.'

'Merry, darling; you're not making any sense.' He looked doubly worried now. 'Did you hit your head? Should I call for an ambulance?'

'No, no; nothing like that.' I reassured him. 'What I mean is, I know what happened *back then*...'

I saw in his clearing expression that he grasped my meaning. He stared at me in shock. 'You had a psychic vision? Like Skylar Harrison's?'

'I have no idea what I had,' I admitted, knowing I would never be able to put it properly into words. 'It wasn't as clear as a vision. I can't claim that I specifically *saw* anything. I just had this moment of the most blinding clarity, like a shaft of light opening up inside me. And I just, well, I just *knew*.'

His gaze didn't shift from my face. I watched a nerve pulse in his jawline as he stared at me.

'Adam, I'm saying I know how the harem conspiracy was discovered and foiled.'

'Go on,' he invited me to elucidate, still looking as if he might prefer to call for an ambulance. If it's possible for a man to look simultaneously relieved, appalled and anxious Adam managed it.

I didn't let it put me off. Found I needed to put the assortment of insights I had in my head into words, hear myself say them aloud. So, I fixed my gaze on him and began. 'Tyti used some of her women to spy on Tiye. Their rivalry was real. The two sisters hated each other. Despite all Tiye's precautions, Tyti's spies got wind of the plot and carried it back to their queen. Tyti, of course, told her son Ramses.' I shuddered at what I was about to say. 'Hori told us Prince Ramses had a brutal streak. He captured one of Tiye's women and tortured the truth out of her, then killed her and made it look like an accident, so Tiye would never suspect there had been a betrayal. Then, over months, he cunningly infiltrated the conspiracy, planting one of his henchmen on the inside to gain the trust of the conspirators and report back to him. So, he knew exactly what was planned for the attack during the Beautiful Feast of the Valley. Not only did he let it go ahead, but he also secretly supplied the weapons through his double agent.'

Part-way into this speech, Adam's hands dropped from my shoulders. He was gaping at me open-mouthed.

'But that's not all,' I went on. 'Hori seemed to suggest in his transcript that Prince Ramses took himself well out of harm's way on the night of the planned attack on the king.'

Adam nodded.

'That's not true. The prince was there. He laid the trap so that as the conspirators arrived at the Eastern High Gate, they were ambushed by his own men, rounded up and tied up with gags in their mouths. It was Prince Ramses' men, not the conspirators, who surrounded the king when he came to take his pleasure in the harem quarters that night. The man wielding the knife that slit the pharaoh's throat was Prince Ramses himself! Hori was the one with the axe that severed the king's toe!'

'Hori?' Adam's eyes snapped. 'He wasn't bound and gagged with the others?'

'No. It had been agreed the conspirators would all wear hoods with cut-away eye holes, just in case. Prince Ramses had his men do the same, so Hori was none the wiser until the assassination was done. Then he whipped off his hood, Prince Ramses did the same, and Hori realised he and the conspirators had been played as pawns in a trap set by the prince to kill his father so he could seize the throne for himself.'

'Then I don't understand why Hori was silent on the murder in his transcript,' he looked at me in confusion. 'I mean, I know the Egyptian writings never call a spade a spade, but...'

'That was the bargain he made,' I explained, cutting him off. 'It's why he was let go when the other judges were mutilated – he knew the truth about who murdered Ramses III, and, of course, he had the dead king's blood on his own hands too. Prince Ramses planned it that way. Hori begged for the lives of Tiye and

Nebenkharu, promising never to reveal what actually happened as his part of the bargain.'

'But the prince betrayed him,' Adam argued. 'He put them both to death anyway.'

'Well, yes,' I admitted. 'Which, to Hori, was as if he had signed their death sentences himself. The astonishing part is that Prince Ramses let Hori live. But he seemed to take a malicious pleasure in knowing he had played both ends to the middle.'

'But how did Tiye come to learn of all of this?' Adam asked. 'Always presuming this is the story she scratched onto the walls in her living tomb,'

'Prince Ramses bragged of it to her, while they were bricking her up. He wanted her to die knowing she had been outfoxed. He told her Hori betrayed her to death.'

Adam slumped back in the dust and favoured me with a long, loaded look. 'Well, I'd like to say your fiction-loving brain has gone into overdrive. But I guess I'm staring down the possibility that my wife is telepathic!'

I thought about that for a moment, wondering if I was that or maybe a loony tune, and the men in white coats ought by rights to be coming to fetch me. There was something deeply uncomfortable about what had just occurred. Yet, at the same time, it left me curiously calm. Somehow, I didn't think it would ever happen again. And I had the strongest sense the same would hold true for Skylar Harrison. I shrugged at him. 'Call it a hunch.'

'Well, I suppose we can test it. If Ted can make more sense than I could of the writing Tiye scratched onto the walls as she died, then I guess we'll know for sure whether everything you've said stands up to scrutiny.'

'It will,' I said with perfect confidence. Feeling suddenly light and giddy, I stood up and swiped clouds of dust from my trousers. 'I guess we should get Feisal Ismail over here,' I remarked as Adam got up too.

'What the hell do we tell him about how we came to find her remains?'

'I'm not sure either I or Skylar will want to admit to the truth,' I acknowledged, glancing over at the hole where the ancient queen's remains – and her story – lay ready to be reclaimed.

He took my hand and we turned to look at each other. Our words overlapped as we spoke together. 'We could say we were acting on a hunch?'

As I think I had expected, our scooters were pretty much as we had left them in the Medinet Habu car park, showing little-to-no sign of sand or water damage; certainly nothing beyond what you might expect from a normal downpour in an arid, dusty climate. And the guards in the security kiosk waved us off readily enough, with a few jokes about the English and rain, but giving no indication that they had experienced anything overly extreme while we had been on site.

'Did we imagine it?' I asked uncertainly.

'Both of us?' he queried.

I shrugged, wondering what would have happened if we'd taken the chance of running on to the guard post during the storm. Well, we would never know now. 'There's a lot about today that I'd like to keep strictly between you and me, if it's all the same to you. I'm having a hard job getting to grips with it myself. Let alone attempt to explain it to anyone else!'

He draped an arm across my shoulders. 'I promise I won't be queuing up to tell anyone about our inexplicable encounters with the paranormal.'

'Pact?'

'Pact!'

'Are the photos you took still on your 'phone? Or have they mysteriously disappeared?'

He took his phone from his pocket. 'All present and correct. The ones I took of the walls – although I'm not sure we should admit to Feisal we've been inside – and the ones I took outside, showing the hole.'

I nodded, pleased to know there was some concrete evidence of what we had discovered. Adam had stopped short of taking pictures of the queen's skeleton. It seemed irreverent, disrespectful, and was unnecessary if she was to be handed into the Ministry's care. He'd put her ring back between the bones of her hands and cleared away the footprints we'd left in the dust. I was confident we could invent a plausible reason for our visit to Medinet Habu today and convince Feisal to come and investigate the hole we'd spotted in the ruins at the back of the temple enclosure.

Ahmed was onboard and cock-a-hoop when we got back to the *Queen Ahmes*. 'Such dramatics, my friends!' he cried out from the upper deck as we approached along the jetty. 'You must come so I can tell you all that you have missed!'

'Where is everyone else?' Adam called back.

'The famous ones, they are in the lounge-bar.' he informed us. 'They have much to talk about!'

The Hollywooders were indeed ensconced inside having a private powwow as we made our way through the dahabeeyah. We excused ourselves for interrupting them and left them to it, climbing to join Ahmed on deck in the shade of the canvas awning. Rabiah brought us peppermint tea and a plate of her own recipe chocolate chip cookies. Sinking into the comfort of our padded armchairs, which had quite clearly taken not the slightest beating from any freak weather conditions, we looked at Ahmed expectantly.

He brought out his mobile phone with a flourish and propped it in the deepest part of the shade, wedging it up against the teapot with a coaster so we could all see the screen. 'Merry and Adam, I have taked a video of the whole press conference. I wanted to keep for myself a souvenir of these amazing times. It means I can show to you what transp – er – what happened.' His eyes were bright and snapping, like big shiny brown buttons. I felt sure his barely suppressed excitement was to blame for his inability to bring the right word to mind. For an excitable character such as Ahmed, it was quite something to see him this animated. Reaching out, he pressed the "play" button. Adam and I leaned forward to watch.

The press conference, held in the same room at the Luxor Museum where Feisal Ismail had hosted the private viewing last night, was well attended. A whiff of Hollywood glamour attached to a significant historical find proved an intoxicating, irresistible lure both to national and international media agencies. They had mobilised quickly.

The configuration of the room had changed; the round tables draped with linen topped with flower arrangements replaced with banks of seating facing a raised dais set with a single long table draped in cloth, with several chairs lined behind it, a big presentation screen above. The precious antiquities in their darkened protective cabinets were on display on either side, ready for the moment the lights would be switched on. Each was encircled by a red-velvet-roped barrier, so no-one could step too close. Feisal had set the stage to perfection for his big reveal.

After the assorted men and women of the Press were fully assembled, cameras, recording systems and notebooks at the ready, Director Ismail led the Hollywooders into the room to take their seats on the raised dais. Drew Trainer and Mackenzie King book-ended the row of seats behind the cloth-draped table, with Talia Nolan and Natasha Redwood seated next to the director, and Skylar Harrison and Lori Scott alongside the leading man. I wondered whether keeping two Hollywood beauties separating our two would-be Helens was deliberate. I was unsure whether to be surprised to see Talia Nolan in attendance. I guess since she'd been included, at Feisal's request, in last night's reception, it perhaps would have taken more explaining to exclude her today. She looked stunning in an all-white jumpsuit cinched in at the waist with another of her trademark gold belts, an armful of gold bangles jangling on her wrist and enormous golden hooped earrings in her ears. Anybody else might have struggled to pull it off. Not Talia Nolan. She looked every inch the rich and famous movie star. Where last night Skylar Harrison outshone the rest, there was no doubting today which of the beauties all eyes were irresistibly drawn to.

Feisal, wearing one of his trademark crisply cut suits, stood in front of a laptop set up on a lectern erected on the left-hand side of the long table at which the movie contingent settled themselves. The stage lights came up illuminating Feisal and the Hollywooders but keeping the artefacts darkened. Camera shutters clicked and whirred before an expectant hush fell over the room.

'Ladies and gentlemen of the Press,' Feisal began, speaking into a small microphone on the lectern. 'The toast of Hollywood has come to Luxor to dramatise an episode from our magnificent ancient history. But sometimes it happens that real life is every bit as sensational as the blockbuster films we love to watch in movie theatres.' He proceeded to give a speech very similar to the one he'd made last night. This time when he paused, it was to play a video recording on the big presentation screen showing the moment of discovery. This had been cobbled together from the mobile phone recordings of the crew who, witnessing the find, had the presence of mind to whip out their mobile phones to record it for posterity. For Talia Nolan and Skylar Harrison's sake, I could only be grateful they hadn't thought to do so a few moments earlier.

'As you can see,' Feisal spoke into the mic, 'The heavy wheels of the trailer trucks set up for use by the actors disturbed the ground on the forecourt to reveal an alabaster box buried under the hard-packed ground.'

It was explanation enough. No one need ever know about the melodrama that had preceded it.

Alongside me, Ahmed swelled with pride as the video recording shifted to show Adam opening the box under Habiba's supervision. 'I filmed that!' he boasted.

On our police pal's camera screen now, Feisal went on with the conference. 'Luckily, the film crew had an Egyptologist on site, who was able to call in our local representative from the Ministry of Tourism and Antiquities, as you can see, to ensure the box was investigated in a properly controlled manner. It meant we could start to hazard a guess at the provenance of the items before bringing them back here to the museum to be properly conserved and studied. You see them here now...' he indicated the objects in their protective display cases, to the collective gasps of his assembled audience as the cabinet lights came on, illuminating these treasures in all their dazzling glory. No doubt about it: there was a touch of the Hollywood about our Ministry director. Move over, Indiana Jones, I thought with a smile. 'The objects themselves are suggestive,' he went on. 'But it is the papyrus – that most treasured of ancient discoveries – that tells us the story of this miraculous find and fills in the blanks on the three-thousand-year-old murder-mystery we have come to know as The Harem Conspiracy.'

It was a suitably engaging introduction, luring the audience in with footage of the moments of both discovery and opening. I spared a thought for Howard Carter. He could never have imagined it.

'Shortly, I will hand over to our Hollywood guests, as I am sure they will want to tell you how it felt to be on site for such an important discovery, and, naturally, will answer your questions. But, before I do; sit back, my friends. Let me tell you the story that emerges from a dark, sinister chapter of Egypt's history, a tale of collusion and violence, of incest and betrayal, of brutality and vengeance; all captured in the remarkable eyewitness account you see displayed here before you.'

He managed to condense it into the essential storyboard version, just enough to fill newspaper columns and online media clips. The full detail could be saved for the books and documentaries that would doubtless follow.

Forget books and documentaries! After the Hollywooders had each said a few words – banal and predictable ones if you ask me about how "awesome" it was to be there at the moment of discovery (Honestly! This lot needed someone to write a script for them!) – the first question asked by a media hack from the audience was the obvious one, addressed to Mackenzie King. 'Are you tempted to switch movies and tell this story instead?'

The director smiled and inclined his head. 'I would be lying if I said the thought had not occurred to me,' he drawled.

'And who would you cast as Queen Tiye?'

Mackenzie King studied his fingernails, hands splayed on the tabletop in front of him. 'Well, I guess I would need to audition for the role. That's the usual way of casting for a movie.'

'Miss Nolan,' attention turned to the screen siren. 'Would you want to throw your hat in the ring for the part? After all, you famously turned down Helen of Troy.'

Watching Ahmed's small mobile phone screen propped on the table in front of us, I could still easily see the frisson of discomfort this sent through the actors seated alongside her on the podium. Perhaps taking her cue from the director, she took her time about answering, appearing to measure her words. 'I would need to see the script,' she said, at last. 'And I guess it would depend on who was calling the shots.'

'May we know ma'am, why are you here in Egypt? We understood Skylar Harrison had been selected for the role after you pulled out.'

Instead of responding directly, Talia Nolan, Oscar-winning actor and twenty-first century movie icon did something utterly astonishing. She reached out and took one of Mackenzie King's hands in hers, interlacing her fingers with his on the tabletop.

The sound of camera shutters clicking was deafening even through Ahmed's mobile phone recording. Flashlights popped. Adam and I gasped.

Up on the dais, Mackenzie King turned his head to look at her. Between them, they seemed to come to a joint decision. 'As this appears to be a day for world exclusives, here's another one for you,' Talia announced. 'The reason I came to Egypt, and the reason I am still here now are two different things.'

Ohmygoodness, I thought as the nature of Mackenzie King's "offer" hit me between the eyes. I supposed I should have seen it coming but hadn't. Natasha Redwood had said they'd once been involved romantically but, given the whole hotel bathroom lock-in scenario, I'd thought anything of that nature impossible. But what was all that stuff about her consulting her agent?

Seated alongside her, I saw the heads of the other actors snap sideways to look at her. Drew Trainer was forced to lean forward so he could see her around his three female co-stars.

Talia Nolan knew the floor was hers and took it. 'There is perhaps something you should know,' she said, looking around at the gathered assemblage of media men and women. 'Hollywood may seem very glamorous to all of you. In fact, it is not so different from the pharaonic Egypt we have all heard about here today. When too much power sits in the hands of certain men, it can create a coterie of partially enfranchised women, often forced to make their own luck, to change their fate, doing things they would rather not do to get a break. I was one such of these women.'

Realising I was holding my breath watching Ahmed's phone screen, I let it out slowly.

'Victor Bernstein may have been thrown in jail in America awaiting trial,' she went on. 'But somehow through his network of likeminded sleazoid pimps, he was still managing to call the shots. I stood down from this movie in the wake of the #Me-Too Movement because I was among Victor Bernstein's first victims. I hate to say it, but it's possible I owe my Academy Award to him.'

The silence in the museum's makeshift press room was palpable, seemed to have an energy of its own. I could sense the electrifying atmosphere. Not hard to imagine headlines across the globe as her avid audience scrambled to beat each other to the presses.

'I pulled out of the movie and turned down the role of Helen because I wasn't brave enough, back then, to say "Me Too".' She hung her head a moment, then looked up with a sweeping glance that somehow managed to make eye contact with everyone in the room. 'I am saying it now.'

I glanced sideways at Adam with a sudden frown. 'So, what has this whole thing been about since she turned up on set?'

It was almost as if she'd heard me, for all that Ahmed's recording was of a session held earlier in the day. Or maybe she had just been gathering her thoughts, determining how to continue with her confession.

'I realised I had made a mistake,' she admitted. 'Especially when I heard that Mac King had come on board as director. There's a saying that a penguin is a bird, but not all birds are penguins. It fits Mac down to the ground. By shunning the movie, I turned my back on the wrong player. Sexual harassment and sexual assault against women by scores of powerful men in America, in Hollywood in particular, will only stop if we take back power and work with those men who are as shamed by association as we are by the things we have done to get to where we are today. And that means speaking out. I see that now. Not cowering away lest we be judged.'

'Here here!' Lori Scott spoke up loudly.

Talia Nolan glanced sideways at her and nodded to acknowledge this support. 'I admit, I came out here to Egypt, determined to seize back the role by fair means of foul.' She laughed bitterly. 'I am a woman. I can use sexual allure if I need to, right? Does that make me as bad as the men who exploit it?' She didn't wait for a response, instead answered her own question. 'Yes, perhaps. But there is an old axiom that all is fair in love and war. And I did love Mac once...'

She appeared mentally to drift off for a moment, as across the hushed room microphones and cameras recorded her every word, look and gesture. I took my hat off to her. Known for fiercely guarding her private life, when she decided to fling the doors open, she went all out. When her pause had drawn out long enough to be suitably dramatic, she pulled herself back from her reverie. 'But then, last night, I heard the story associated with the objects in this room; heard the harem conspiracy against King Ramses III; understood how similar the king's harem of ancient Egypt was with the misogynistic practices allowed to perpetuate in Hollywood: an abuse of women by certain men in power. And, listening to that story, I was taught a valuable lesson about what happens when rivalry gets out of hand, especially between women who should by rights support each other. Queen Tiye was a tragic figure in many ways, but she was also a street fighter. She attempted to take control, over-reached herself, was betrayed, and paid the ultimate price. I realised I was going the same way: that if I let this jealous need to come out on top consume me, if I trampled Skylar underfoot in the stampede, I was no better than the men I despise.'

She sent an apologetic glance down the table at Skylar Harrison, staring back at her in open astonishment. Then turned her head sideways and addressed her next words directly to Mackenzie King, for all that she was still talking for the benefit of her transfixed audience. 'So, I called Mac up late last night and told him I relinquish Helen and accept his generous offer. I will become Executive Producer on this movie! And I vow to do a better job of it than Victor Bernstein would have done!'

'Wow!' I breathed. 'I didn't see that one coming!' I looked at their co-joined hands on the cloth-covered podium-top. 'So, what's *that* all about?'

Talia Nolan's gaze swept the assembled press corps again. 'And, when Mac told me that he regretted his failure to out Victor years ago and would join me in giving evidence against him, I asked him to marry me!'

The noise that greeted this revelation was not the expected one of camera snaps, gasps, nor even shouts of congratulations, or indeed any other sentiments from the audience or the flabbergasted Hollywooders seated, slack-jawed, alongside her on the podium.

'What was that?' I asked Ahmed in shock, watching as his screen went black and an enormous crack resonated out of his phone, sounding a bit like a gunshot.

'That, my friends, was a thunderstorm directly overhead! It crashed and banged over the museum for about ten minutes. Never have I heard such anger in the sky. The lights were out for the whole time, so I stopped the video recording. When the thunder it was over, Director Ismail, he pulled the conference to an ending. I think he was not very happy about the way Talia Nolan she stealed the show!'

'And where is Feisal now?' Adam asked.

'Ah!' Ahmed looked at us and his eyes snapped some more. 'Yes, that is a very strange thing I have to tell to you. 'When the lights they came back on, and the journalists they had gone, Skylar Harrison, she turned to Director Ismail. She asked him if there was such a thing as a Western High Gate at the Medinet Habu temple.'

Hearing this, I reached blindly for Adam's hand.

'The Director, he asked her why she should ask such a question as this. Skylar Harrison, she said she had something called a "hunch". I think that was the word that she used.' Ahmed frowned and shrugged. 'Anyway, she telled to him to take a camera and go there to look and see. She said that there might be something there for him to find.'

Adam glanced sideways at me. We shared a long, loaded look.

'Director Ismail and my Habiba, they go to Medinet Habu now. I telled to them that I would bring back the Hollywood people to here, collect both of you and take the two of you back to there.'

Adam let out a whoop. 'God, don't you just love a hunch?'

Epilogue

I'm a sucker for a happy ending.

Ramses IV exacted a terrible revenge on his aunt, Queen Tiye, for conspiring to wrest the succession from him. But she had a victory of sorts in the end. Her skeletal remains, even now, were being conserved to go on display among her treasures in the new Museum of Egyptian Civilisation being built in Cairo. That she would be alongside the preserved mummies of her husband and nephew was an irony not lost on me. But Pentaweret was there too, his identity restored to him as Prince Nebenkharu, which might give her comfort. For Tiye and her son to have their names spoken was to grant them eternal afterlife: a happy ending by anyone's reckoning

So, too, had things among the Hollywooders sorted themselves out. They remained onboard with us for a further six weeks and I got my wish to see a blockbuster movie in the making.

Mackenzie King stuck with Plan A, filming his epic tale of Helen of Troy in Egypt at the court of Ramses the Great, although he ordered a major script revision to downplay any suggestion of rivalry between the three queens, making them instead pillars of strength of who stood behind the great pharaoh, contributing each in her own way to his glorious rule. The message of the movie became that behind every great man is a great woman. Or, in this case, three great women!

But Mackenzie King allowed himself a Plan B too, engaging a scriptwriter to draft him a screenplay of The Harem Conspiracy. In this, his three warring queens could tear each other's throats out with aplomb; rivalry, jealousy and intrigue written into every line! What surprised me very much was his decision that it wasn't just the historical story he wanted to bring to the big screen. He and Talia Nolan engaged Skylar Harrison in a private tête-à-tête, and she agreed to have her experiences dramatised for the film. So, it would be a time-slip movie, one of reincarnation and time travel; Skylar's character a twenty-first century transmigration of the ancient queen, whose visions land her slap bang back in the middle of the action. See? That's how Hollywood re-imagines things.

'It's not so strange,' Adam remarked. 'Let's be honest, Mackenzie King has a deft touch when it comes to portraying all things metaphysical. Just look what he did with *The Princess and the Pea*! He had us all believing the princess could feel the damned thing through a hundred mattresses! I'm only surprised he was so sceptical of what Skylar was going through in the first place.'

The fact that Mackenzie King wanted a character in the movie to play a version of himself was perhaps his way of apologising for this transgression.

A changed man since he and Talia Nolan had, in effect come out about their shame at not speaking out sooner about Victor Bernstein, I was glad to find my secret crush had not been misplaced after all.

And I could only be glad for Adam that his pin-up of choice was a much warmer individual now she'd dispensed with the melodrama.

So, all things considered, it was a perfectly satisfactory outcome to the sort of adventure I had once thought I could live quite happily without.

The End

Author's Note

One of the many strange things about the assassination of Ramses III was the long-held belief among historians that he had somehow survived the murderous attempt on his life. This was based on the opening preamble to the Turin Judicial Papyrus, asserting that it was Ramses III himself who initiated the trial of the conspirators. The text details how he set up a commission of twelve judges to try the cases, and states that the judgements and penalties are their responsibility, without reference back to him. These texts certainly seem to imply that he was alive to set the judicial wheels in motion.

By the end of the trials though, it is made clear that the king is dead. He is referred to as the Great God and King's Father in one of the documents, clear evidence that he is now deceased.

For a long time, scholars took this to be evidence that he had survived the conspiracy, although dying soon afterward.

Equally strange was how early examinations of the pharaoh's mummy missed the deep gash in his neck under the linen wrappings. Scholars theorised that the assassination attempt recorded in the papyri had been by way of poison, perhaps snakebite. The large wound in his neck was revealed by CT scans taken by Zahi Hawass and his team in 2012. These scans also showed his severed toe. The severely slit throat would have killed the pharaoh instantaneously.

The most obvious explanation for the strange preamble to the records of the trial and conviction of the criminals is that it was a way of legitimising the process, and perhaps providing an explanation for why Ramses III wasn't personally presiding over the proceedings as might be expected.

But if his successor Ramses IV was an unpopular choice, and if the jurors were perhaps sympathetic to the conspirators' cause, it's tempting to speculate that the new pharaoh felt the need to call upon all the majestic authority of his dead father in setting the wheels in motion.

That Ramses III left all the labels blank on the processions of princes and princesses carved into the walls of his magnificent temple at Medinet Habu is inexplicable and mysterious. Egyptologists have had a devil of a time trying to work out his family relationships. For many years his queens were completely unknown: Tiye mentioned only in the context of the Turin Judicial Papyrus, and Tyti, despite having a tomb in the Valley of the Queens, only finally identified as a consort of Ramses III through a fragment of papyri and the labels within her son's tomb.

Only Iset Ta-Hemdjert, likely to have been a foreign bride, is definitely shown on a contemporary monument, and then only once.

This failure to acknowledge his wives and offspring for posterity is mystifying. It represents a departure from his imitation of Ramses the Great in almost everything else. Coupled with the pharaoh's assassination, it hints at intrigue and possibly rivalry within the royal house.

That Ramses III was the last great warrior pharaoh is undoubted. His success in holding back the collapse of Egypt's great empire, while others around the Mediterranean crumbled is undisputed. But the economic malaise suggested by at least three Deir el-Medina strikes towards the end of his reign hints perhaps at a broader dissatisfaction with his kingship. A dispute over the succession may have served simply to reinforce that he was no longer fit to rule and precipitated the violent action to remove him.

With so much textual and monumental knowledge about the reign of Ramses III – The Great Harris Papyrus (now in the British Museum), the Turin Judicial Papyrus recording the fate of the conspirators who led the coup d'état, the monuments he left behind and not forgetting the preserved mummies of Ramses III, Ramses IV and "the screaming mummy" – it is perhaps strange that historians are not able to give a more complete account. It is almost impossible to state with any confidence which of Ramses III's many sons were born to which queen.

As always it is the gaps in what we know that create the opportunity to weave a story. I have attempted to piece together the evidence in a way that seems to me to make sense and provides motives for the actions of the principal characters.

As ever, until such a time as more evidence is unearthed (and, let's face it, discoveries are being made in Egypt all the time), a story is all it can remain. Fiction can fill in the blanks.

To date, the fate of Tiye and the women of the harem remains unknown. Nothing is known about Tiye's identity. She is most usually described as a minor queen of the harem. But this has never rung true to me. How could a junior ranking queen with no apparent influence incite an insurrection that was certainly successful in killing the pharaoh, and could very well have succeeded in over-turning the succession? Powerful men rallied to her cause. So, I have imagined a role and status for her within the royal family of the early 20th Dynasty that I think fits the known facts. Ramses III is known to have married and borne children with one full sister; why not two?

Similarly, the true characters of Ramses III and his son Ramses IV are lost in the mists of time. It does seem clear that Ramses IV was the intended heir (despite the lack of label texts on his father's monuments) although only after older brothers died. Still, he clearly had the most to lose in any attempt to circumvent the line of succession; and the most to gain through the early demise of his father if the succession could be secured.

What is known about the unfortunate Prince Pentaweret is exactly as described by Adam in chapter 13. The "screaming mummy" was indeed found in the TT320 royal cache, wrapped in a goat skin. The DNA sequencing makes it clear this individual was related to Ramses III and clearly suffered an ignominious death and burial. I have imagined an identity for him. Knowing that Ramses III named his sons after those of Ramses the Great, I looked to see if there was a name missing, and spotted Nebenkharu. This is of course a conjecture of my own devising.

As for Hori, all we know about him is that he was a royal standard bearer, one of the original judges caught "making beer hall" (which we assume means drinking and carousing) with women of the harem and the convicted army general during the trial. While the others suffered the indignity of mutilation, the texts tell us he was let go with a severe reprimand. Around this mystifying fact, I have built my story.

As for the paranormal aspect of this story, all I will say is this: while for many, it may be a leap too far, there are enough reports of unexplainable happenings and apparent clairvoyance from apparently rational individuals across all walks of life to make me feel ok about using this device for my fictional story.

And finally, when I started the research for this novel, the #Me-Too Movement had been all over the Press. I felt I could not bring Hollywood to Luxor without making some reference to such a landmark shift. As I started to write, I found I could draw certain parallels to link my ancient and modern stories.

I hope you have enjoyed my conjectures. Those of you interested in the New Kingdom of ancient Egypt, may wish to check out the chronology on the next page.

Please do leave me a comment on my website www.fionadeal.com. I also read and very much appreciate all reviews on Amazon.

Fiona Deal
May 2021.

Chronology of New Kingdom Pharaohs

Several of my readers have asked me to include a chronology of the pharaohs of the 18th and 19th Dynasties and their links to my books, so here goes …

Pharaoh	Comment	Approximate Dates
\multicolumn{3}{c}{**18th Dynasty**}	
Ahmose	Expelled the Hyksos, hated foreign invaders of Egypt, who'd presided over a time of chaos and conflict. United Egypt	1557 – 1541 BC
Amenhotep I	Son of Ahmose. Little is known about him.	1541 – 1520 BC
Thutmosis I	A warrior who expanded Egypt's territories. Married to Queen Ahmes. Parents to Thutmosis II and Hatshepsut. First pharaoh to have a tomb in the Valley of the Kings	1520 – 1492 BC
Thutmosis II	Married to his half-sister Hatshepsut. They had one daughter, Neferure. He also had a son by a royal concubine (Thutmosis III)	1492 – 1479 BC
Hatshepsut	Declared herself pharaoh after the death of her brother-husband Thutmosis II. Ruled jointly with her infant nephew-stepson Thutmosis III. *Carter's Conundrums* *Hatshepsut's Hideaway*	1479 – 1458 BC
Thutmosis III	Warrior pharaoh famous for his expansion of territories into Levant and Nubia. Under his rule the Egyptian Empire was at its greatest extent. Late in his reign he obliterated Hatshepsut's name from temples and monuments. Some posit Thutmosis III as King David of the Bible. *Hatshepsut's Hideaway* *Farouk's Fancies*	1458 – 1425 BC

Amenhotep II	Son of Thutmosis III. Ruled at the height of Egypt's power.	1425 – 1400 BC
Thutmosis IV	Son of Amenhotep II. Famous for his "Dream Stele" at the foot of the Sphinx. May have been the Pharaoh in the Bible story of Joseph and the Coat of Many Colours – the interpreter of dreams. *Farouk's Fancies*	1400 – 1390 BC
Amenhotep III – The Magnificent	Father of Akhenaten and grandfather of Tutankhamun. Ruled at the height of Egypt's Empire period. A great builder, who had a long and peaceful reign. Some posit Amenhotep III as King Solomon of the Bible. *Farouk's Fancies*	1390 – 1352 BC
Amenhotep IV / Akhenaten	The second son of Amenhotep III. Founder of the Amarna Period in which he changed the state religion from the polytheistic worship of animal-headed gods and goddesses to the monotheistic worship of the sun disc, the Aten. He built a new capital city, Akhet-Aten. He changed his name to Akhenaten to reflect his religious belief. Married to Nefertiti. Had 6 daughters. Some posit Akhenaten as Biblical Moses. Some believe he was Tutankhamun's father, although debate rages about this identification. *Tutankhamun's Triumph* *Akhenaten's Alibi* *Seti's Secret*	1352 – 1336 BC
Smenkhkare	Shadowy figure about whom very little is known. May have had a co-regency with Akhenaten who may have been his father or brother. Some believe he was another son of Amenhotep III. May have been Tutankhamun's father. *Tutankhamun's Triumph*	1336 – 1332 BC
Tutankhamun	Thought to have come to the throne as a boy of 8 or 9 and died at 18 or 19 – hence the term "the boy king". Howard Carter famously discovered his intact tomb in 1922. He reverted to the old polytheistic religion of	1332 – 1324 BC

	ancient Egypt and changed his name from Tunankh-Aten to Tutankh-Amun. Debate rages about whether he was the son of Akhenaten or Smenkhkare. *Carter's Conundrums* *Tutankhamun's Triumph*	
Ay	Grand Vizier to Tutankhamun and an important official in the reigns of Akhenaten and Smenkhkare. Possibly the brother of Queen Tiye, wife of Amenhotep III, and possibly father of Nefertiti, Akhenaten's Great Royal Wife. Succeeded Tutankhamun due to the boy king's lack of an heir, possibly enforcing his claim to the throne by marrying his granddaughter and Tutankhamun's widow, Ankhesenamun. Some posit Ay was son of Biblical Joseph. *Tutankhamun's Triumph* *Farouk's Fancies* *Akhenaten's Alibi*	1324 – 1320 BC
Horemheb	Born a commoner. Was a Military General during the Amarna Period. Seized the throne on Ay's death, possibly enforcing his claim by marrying Ay's younger daughter Mutnodjmet. Obliterated images of the Amarna pharaohs and vandalised and destroyed monuments associated with them. Some posit he was the Biblical Pharaoh of the Oppression. *Tutankhamun's Triumph* *Akhenaten's Alibi* *Seti's Secret*	1320 – 1292 BC
19th Dynasty		
Ramses I	Of non-royal birth. Served alongside Horemheb in the army. Succeeded Horemheb due to H's lack of an heir. Some posit he was the Biblical Pharaoh of the Exodus. *Seti's Secret*	1292 – 1290 BC
Seti I	Son of Ramses I. Regained much of the territory lost under Akhenaten. *Seti's Secret*	1290 – 1279 BC

Ramses II The Great	Ruled for upwards of 60 years, coming to the throne at 25 and dying in his 90s. A prolific builder who usurped many previous temples and monuments. He is credited for finishing the hypostyle hall at Karnak and for building the Great Temple of Abu Simbel. He also built a new capital city, Pi-Ramesse in the Nile Delta. He continued expanding Egypt's territories until he hit a stalemate with the Hittite Empire, at the Battle of Kadesh in 1275 BC, after which the famous Egyptian-Hittite Peace Treaty was signed. His Great Royal Wife was Nefertari. He had a huge harem and was said to have fathered over 100 children. *Belzoni's Bequest* *Nefertari's Narrative* *Ramses' Riches*	1279 – 1213 BC
Merenptah	13th son of Ramses II, as the elder sons all pre-deceased their father.	1213 – 1203 BC
After Merenptah the 19th Dynasty entered a confused period, only lasting approximately 12 further years, and with 3-4 rulers. It appears to have been characterised by civil war, possibly because Ramses II lived so long and had so many children born of different wives, many of them or their descendants perhaps staking a claim to the throne.		
End of 19th Dynasty		
Seti II	Believed to be Merenptah's son, Seti II ruled during a period of dynastic intrigue. It seems that during his reign a rival king, Amenmesse, seized the throne, possibly ruling for 2-4 years. Most historians see this as an interruption to Seti's reign and believe Seti was subsequently restored.	1203 - 1196 BC
Amenmesse	Possibly a half-brother of Seti II, he appears to have seized the throne, possibly by force. The cartouches in Seti II's tomb were deliberately erased then repainted.	?
Siptah	Came to the throne as a child after the death of Seti II but his parentage is unknown. Scholars debate whether his father may have been any of the three preceding kings, including Merenptah.	1196 – 1190 BC

Tausert	Last known and female pharaoh of the 19th Dynasty. It is thought her independent rule lasted no more than a couple of years, but she assumed Siptah's years into her own reign. She is known to have executed her Chancellor, although many credit him with helping her to power. Her reign ended in civil war.	1190 – 1188 BC
20th Dynasty		
Setnakht	Seized the throne through civil war. His identity is unknown, but many posit that his wife Tiye-Merenese may have been Merenptah's daughter. It is also suggested Setnakht may have been descended from Ramses the Great, possibly from one of the elder sons who predeceased their long-lived father. As such, and if married to his fully royal cousin, he may have considered himself to have a superior claim to the throne. *Ramses' Revenge*	1188 – 1186 BC
Ramses III	The last great warrior pharaoh. He fought wars against foreign invaders and kept Egypt strong while mighty ancient empires were falling. In the latter years of his reign are records of the first recorded labour strikes in history. After a long reign of over 30 years, he was murdered as a result of a harem conspiracy led by one of his wives. *Ramses' Revenge*	1186 – 1155 BC
Ramses IV	Came to the throne after his father was murdered. He had the conspirators arrested and executed. He was likely a man in his forties when he became king. Despite big plans he only ruled for approx' 6 years. His mother was Tyti and it's possible he married his sister or half-sister Tentopet. *Ramses' Revenge*	1155 – 1149 BC

Ramses IV was succeeded by his son, who ruled for maybe 4 years. He died young without an heir and was succeeded by his uncle, another son of Ramses III (and Iset Ta-Hemdjert), the second prince to bear the name Amen-hir-kopeshef, who became Ramses VI. He was succeeded after reigning for around 8 years by his son, who seems to have ruled for around 7 years as Ramses VII. One of the last surviving sons of Ramses III, Seth-hir-kopeshef, then came to the throne, ruling as Ramses VIII possibly for as little as one year. His successor, who ruled as Ramses IX had one of the longer reigns of the dynasty of around 13 years. There is no evidence to indicate the relationship between the final kings of the 20th Dynasty, Ramses IX, X and XI. What seems clear is that the once mighty New Kingdom was crumbling under a succession of weak rulers who – despite adopting the name of their illustrious forebear, Ramses the Great (and even Ramses III) had no way of emulating their power or glory. Egypt's mighty Empire period was over and never re-gained its majesty. Law and order were breaking down and it wouldn't be long before enterprising priests hit on the idea of hiding the remains of Egypt's glorious past rulers in caches that wouldn't be discovered for millennia.

About the Author

Fiona Deal fell in love with Egypt as a teenager, and has travelled extensively up and down the Nile, spending time in both Cairo and Luxor in particular. She lives in Kent, England with her two Burmese cats. Her professional life has been spent in human resources and organisational development for various companies. Writing is her passion. Other books in the series following Meredith Pink's adventures in Egypt are available, with more planned. You can find out more about Fiona, the books and her love of Egypt by checking out her website and following her blog at www.fionadeal.com

Other books by this author

Please visit Amazon to discover other books by Fiona Deal. The author reads and appreciates all reviews.

Meredith Pink's Adventures in Egypt

Carter's Conundrums – Book 1
Tutankhamun's Triumph – Book 2
Hatshepsut's Hideaway – Book 3
Farouk's Fancies – Book 4
Akhenaten's Alibi – Book 5
Seti's Secret – Book 6
Belzoni's Bequest – Book 7
Nefertari's Narrative – Book 8
Ramses' Riches – Book 9
Ramses' Revenge – Book 10

Also available: Shades of Gray, a romantic family saga, written under the name Fiona Wilson.

Connect with me

Thank you for reading my book. Here are my social media coordinates:

Subscribe to my blog: http://www.fionadeal.com
Visit my website: http://www.fionadeal.com
Friend me on Facebook: http://facebook.com/fjdeal
Follow me on Twitter: http://twitter.com/dealfiona

Printed in Great Britain
by Amazon